PERDITION

The Templar Thriller Series

BOOK III

By

PJ Humphreys

PERDITION

THE TEMPLAR THRILLER SERIES

Book III in the series
2nd edition issued 2022
ISBN 978-1-9163167-3-7

Compiled by:
Rod Craig: 05.08.2021
Jackie Harding: 16.12.2022 / 20.02.2023

ALSO BY PJ HUMPHREYS

THE '*TEMPLAR THRILLER*' SERIES:

BOOK I: ARK

BOOK II: PROPHECY

BOOK III: PERDITION

BOOK IV: PARADOX

STAY IN TOUCH:

Website:	https://thetemplarthrillers.com
Instagram:	PJ Humphreys Books
Instagram:	pj_humphreys_books_
Facebook:	The Templar Thriller Series
Email:	info@thetemplarthrillers.com
YouTube:	PJ Humphreys

Where can I get PJ Humphreys' books from?

Amazon: PJ Humphreys Books

Also available to order at selected Bookshops

ACKNOWLEDGEMENTS

Joanne, for her unwavering support and steadying hand through the entire journey of 'Perdition' and the 'Templar Thriller' series of books. For her ability to unblock the blockage when I am stuck and staring at empty pages — screen.

Christine, for reading the draft manuscript and highlighting my grammar errors; and for being an ardent supporter of the 'Templar Thriller' series.

The Author Lucinda E Clark, for her much-appreciated support (You will find Lucinda's own work at https://www.lucindaeclarke.com)

Rod Craig, for his patience and attention to detail in formatting the first edition of 'Perdition'.

Jackie and Kevin Harding, for their invaluable diligence in editing the manuscripts to make sure I make as few mistakes as possible and for their creative input on the cover design.

ABOUT THE AUTHOR

PJ Humphreys is the author behind the Templar Thriller Series of books. He has consistently denied any direct involvement with the Templars or the Illuminati, but undoubtedly there is a close association somewhere.

His novels are described as exciting, passionate and informed. Like his characters in the book, PJ has spent his life travelling the world and now splits his time between several continents in order to continue his research and writing, and, as he puts it, his search for answers and meaning.

While PJ's skill in writing was honed at an early age, it was interrupted by a career in the British military and then, international education. But he re-engaged with writing and began creating the now popular and much-loved Templar Thriller Series of books.

PJ currently lives in Spain and Kent with his wife Joanne, his two adored dogs and Sam the cat.

Perdition

'A state of eternal punishment and damnation into which a sinful and unrepentant person passes after death.'

Chapter 1

John

'... she went forth, and said unto her mother, what shall I ask? And she said, the head of John the Baptist' (Mark 6:24).

He stood motionless. His eyes closed, arms outstretched, palms upwards and his head ever so slightly tilted back. It was a still, warm day. He breathed deep into his nostrils and inhaled the smell of the river and the warm Middle Eastern air. The air was full of the smell of goats, sheep, campfires and cooking spices that had woven their rich aromas into the light winds.

The river stretched out before him; it was the *Nahr Al Sharieat* – the river Jordan. It flowed from the sides of Mount Hermon, between Syria and Lebanon and into the Sea of Galilee. The river was the only sound he allowed into his head. The hectic sounds of tribal nomads camped by the water, their livestock, their children with their playful chatter were filtered out by his meditative praying; it was the highest form of prayer.

He could feel the river's motion through the ground where he stood. Its waters raced and swirled and in other parts where it was shallower, it meandered steadily along, guided by the riverbanks. The place where he stood was on the Jordanian side of the river, a place called *Al-Maghtas*. It was already well known. Many had visited that place but over the next two-thousand years, many more would come. They would come to the place where he had stood.

The warm, light breeze rushed through the rich riverbank vegetation and whistled lazily as it threaded its way through the reeds, causing them to tip and sway in gentle harmony with each other.

The sun was going down but he could still feel its warmth on his face. He wanted to stay there, on that spot, deep in his communion with God. He wanted to linger in the peace and tranquillity he felt in that place, that place by the river, but his homeland was not full of peace and tranquillity, and he knew that much was about to change.

A black-crowned night heron flew overhead and screeched out at a turkey vulture sitting menacingly in a tall lemon tree. Closer by, a man's voice called out, "Take food with us, *Yochanan Ben ZacharYah*." They knew the man praying wouldn't answer, not whilst he was praying. No one knew his last name, his given birth name, and if they once did they had long forgotten it. They just called him John and for his last name, they used what he did, Baptist, they called him John the Baptist.

He was born to elderly parents, Zachariah and Elizabeth, in the Herodian Kingdom of Judea. His parents had prayed to God to bless them with a child and He obliged. The child grew and so did his grace and his desire to do good. John became a priest of the order of *Abija*. After living an ascetic life in the desert, he started to minister on the banks of the river Jordan. Some called him a holy man, others a quack, a fake, a fraud. By the time John was in his late twenties, he already had a following of disciples; now people called him The Prophet.

He ministered to those who wanted to ensure the salvation of their souls when Judgement Day came, the End of Days. That day when the Great Tribulation would befall mankind. However, he preached that those who followed Christ and God's word and who practised His commandments, would survive. In the End of Days Christ would return, all believers would then meet the Lord in the air: The Rapture. The bodies of dead believers would be resurrected, and all believers, living and dead, would be glorified. The rest would face the Great Tribulation, that time accounted for in Revelation. Revelation 6, 8, 9 and 16 gave glimpses into the horrors and living hell for all those who could not be saved. John preached the imminence of God's final judgement and he baptised those who repented in self-preparation for the End of Days.

Before, people had started to call him the Messiah but John was clear to them, he was not the Messiah: '*I baptise with water those who repent of their sins and turn to God. But someone is coming soon who is greater than I am, so much greater that I'm not worthy even to be his slave and carry his sandals,*' (Matthew 3:11).

On the banks of that river, on that day, John's thoughts turned to the first time he'd met the man they called Jesus, the man he knew as the real Messiah, the man who was prophesied to come in the *Old Testament*; the man he himself prophesied would come.

He was thinking about the moment when he baptised Jesus Christ in the water of the river that now swirled in front of him, in the very spot he now stood, *Al-Maghtas* – baptism. John the Baptist – *Yochanan Ben ZacharYah*, stood thinking about the man who would try to bring about salvation on Earth. John had fulfilled the Biblical prophecy by recognising Jesus as the promised Saviour. John had baptised people with water in repentance for the forgiveness of sin. He preached, however, that a saviour would come and he would not baptise people in water as he did but with the Holy Spirit as Jesus now did.

John stood motionless. His eyes still closed, his hands still outstretched, palms upwards. He breathed deep into his nostrils again and inhaled the smells he knew so well, the smells he loved so much; they were the smells of home.

He opened his eyes and smiled; he thanked God for the life He had given him. For allowing him to do His work. For allowing him to be one of many that had told of the coming of Jesus Christ, the Messiah, His son. He thanked God that he was the one that had baptised Jesus.

He turned towards the setting sun. He knew, like the sun, his time on Earth had almost come to an end; his light was beginning to fade. Now he smiled again because he knew that others would come after him, to carry on the work of saving souls. He knew that men, women and children would come. They would be dressed in white, with white stoles around their necks, and they would baptise and give

3

thanks to the Lord for sending His son. He knew they would come, a thousand, two thousand years later, they would still be coming, coming to that place.

John's homeland was ruled by King Herod Antipas. He had been appointed by Rome as the tetrarch, the ruler, of Galilee, in northern Palestine. The king liked his life. He liked his lavish life. He considered himself a good king, a just king. He did not want the same reputation that his father had had. His father was King Herod the Great, the man who had tried to kill every new-born child in his search for the baby they were calling the new Messiah: his father was the architect of the 'Massacre of Innocents'.

The king had a good life and when his half-brother and wife divorced, the king was delighted. He had always secretly desired his half-brother's wife. He quickly scooped her up for himself and promptly married her. It didn't matter that she was considered by many as foul and vengeful, considered trouble and manipulative; he desired her. He showered her with gifts and his attention. His courtiers, although they would not say, didn't care for the new queen. They said she was spiteful, an ambitious person, but they would only say this in whispers. Her name was Herodias. However, the king was not concerned with the wagging tongues, or about those that privately questioned the morality of his actions. Some even went so far as to class his actions as incest. He was the tetrarch; a few wagging tongues and a handful of disobedient locals bore no matter to him. He enjoyed living the life of a newlywed and for the most part, his realm ran smoothly, which allowed him a lot of time to spend in the company of his new wife. But, the trouble that had been fermenting in the outlying towns and villages, because of his marriage to her, started to come to his attention with increasing frequency.

There was a man, some said a wanderer, a nomad, others that he was from 'that' place. He was a local, a man whose voice was already sought out by crowds. He was a man people took note of. This man preached the repentance of sins. He preached the existence of a God, different to those of the Romans. He preached his God was the one true God. He preached about the coming of the Tribulation for sinners and the Rapture for those who repented. He had prophesied the coming of the Messiah, the same Messiah that the king's father had tried to kill in infancy.

Curious, the king went to hear this man speak, this wanderer, this preacher. He liked the man; he seemed virtuous, kind and sincere. The king lived his life in splendour and unchecked. The man lived a pauper's life. There was no reason for the two men to cross paths. Then the man made the king's business, his business. The man, who people called John or the Baptiser, began to openly preach that the king's marriage to his brother's ex-wife was wrong; he preached it was a transgression of Mosaic Law. He preached it to his ever-growing followers. He used it as an example of wrong, illicit desire, depravity, weakness and immorality.

It didn't take long for the queen to find out what the man was saying at his gatherings about her husband, and about her. She was furious at the public slander of her name and the attack on her standing by a common vagrant, who placed people in the waters of the river Jordan and proclaimed them clean of their sins. She wanted the troublemaker dead. She made her feelings known to her husband and demanded his death. However, the king struggled with his wife's request to have the man slain for his impertinence, his disrespect of a royal and his impudence. It set a precedent, she told her husband; it would encourage others. However, the king, whilst still liking John, was also very wary of the growing numbers of followers John had. The king did not want an uprising. He didn't want to follow in his father's footsteps. He didn't want a displeased wife.

The king knew the power of the people, the restlessness of the crowd. They called John a prophet, a Seer, a teacher. And so, he gave the order for John to be arrested and put into jail, whilst he pondered how to deal with the problem without fanning the flames of an insurrection. He also came under increasing pressure from his wife, who claimed her virtue had been questioned by a commoner.

For his birthday, the king decided he would throw a great banquet for all the important people in the area and for his most trusted generals. The banquet was held at the palace-fortress of Machaerus, near the Dead Sea. It had been built by his father, King Herod the Great. It was a splendid occasion for all those who attended and the king was pleased with the pageantry and the lavish feast for his guests. It was a great success and opulence, luxury and abundance wove together like the diamonds, gold and silk worn by most of the guests.

His wife's daughter, Salome, the king's stepdaughter, was young, pretty and vivacious. She wanted to please her new stepfather on the celebration of his birthday and so she danced for him in front of all of his guests. It was an entrancing display. When she'd finished, there was rapturous applause. The king was so enthralled by her that he told the child, before all of his guests, "Ask me for anything you want, and I'll give it to you," to which the crowd cheered. The king gave his oath in front of everyone that she could have whatever she wanted. "Even," he announced raising his arms in a great show, "half of my kingdom if you so want it, my child." Excited, the child ran off to seek out her mother and asked her what she should ask for.

The queen did not hesitate; she saw her chance. "Tell our king to bring you the head of John the Baptist." Her daughter abided her wishes.

The king had given his oath in front of everyone. He was trapped. How could he go back on his word? How could he refuse now? The crowd started to chant for the king to give the girl her wish. And so it was done and after a short while the head of John the Baptist was brought into the banquet on a silver platter. The crowd cheered and the queen sat in total satisfaction that the troublesome commoner would trouble her, or her good name, no more. But the queen was not done with John just yet. She ordered his head to be buried separately from his body and it was all to be done in secret so his followers would not know where John was buried. The king's resentful wife had John's head buried near her palace. However, his disciples found out where it was and they were able to retrieve it.

Much later, one dark night, a servant who knew where Herodias had buried John's head, took it and reburied it on the Mount of Olives, on one of Herod's estates and there it rested and only a small number of people knew where it was. However, it wouldn't stay there; the head of John the Baptist would be moved several times over the years and then it would disappear. And so, over centuries, the location of the head of John the Baptist became one of the world's greatest human mysteries and finding it and possessing it became an obsession for some, and for others, a duty.

Date: 22nd December 2012
Place: Jordan

Daniel stood on the riverbank next to his grandfather. It was a hot day. One of them had travelled on a false passport from Bagdad, Iraq and the other on a genuine passport from Dubai. The two had never actually met face-to-face before. They had only spoken to each other twice, both times on the telephone, once when Daniel was four and again when he was six years old.

His grandfather had nine children, all born in Iraq. However, like Daniel's father, they had all left. The old man hadn't seen any of his nine children since and he had only been able to speak to them on snatched calls every two or three years because of the restrictions placed on him. He could escape, be smuggled out, the same way he was able to make the trip to Jordan, but he would not leave Iraq. There were too many poor and needy that would be left behind; he would not forsake them. And, his children could not risk going back to Iraq, as being his children would certainly ensure major restrictions were placed on them, and maybe they would even be banned from leaving.

In his own county of Iraq, Daniel's grandfather was forbidden from possessing any form of digital or electronic communication devices. He was not allowed a passport; he was not allowed to travel. He had been classed as a terrorist by the old regime, as a radical and activist by the Allied Forces that had occupied Iraq from 2003 until 2011, and as a rebel and a troublemaker by the new, fractured regime. He was none of those things. He was a holy man. He belonged to one of the oldest religions in the Middle East, some say the oldest.

The old man and the young man stood side by side on the banks of the river, the river Jordan, at the place *Al-Maghtas*, the place where John the Baptist had preached to his followers and where he had baptised those who repented their sins.

Daniel's grandfather was a Mandaean, a member of the ancient, Middle Eastern religious sect independent of Judaism, Christianity and Islam. They were said to be the true followers of John the Baptist. When the Portuguese arrived in Iraq in the 17th century, they called them 'Christians of St John.' Now in 2012, very few Mandaeans remained. Having been persecuted across the Middle East, especially in their traditional bases of Iraq and Iran, they were near to extinction. The Iraq war did not treat them well and many fled as refugees. Daniel's grandfather stayed behind to help the infirm who could not travel, those who could not get out. He sacrificed his life with his children to look after the sick and the needy and he'd been doing so ever since.

"We have waited patiently for two-thousand years," the old man said to his grandson, without saying what they had waited patiently for. He turned his head away from the river and towards the land and stared off into the distance, past the fertile banks of the river and into the barren and harsh desert. "Our prophet baptised here, he preached here, lived here. Our Prophet was murdered in this land, his head cut off."

"Did they pay, Grandfather, the people who killed him?" Daniel asked, more to make conversation than with a real sense of interest. He did not follow his family's beliefs; he was not religious.

"The old king, King Herod," his grandfather started, "the man who murdered many, many little children when Jesus was born, died in Jericho. He had a very painful death; he screamed with pain for many weeks, they say. He died at sixty-eight years old. His son, who beheaded our prophet at the demand of his wife, died, now what is the word? Ah, yes, exile, he died in exile. The Roman, Caligula killed him. He died but not before playing his part in the crucifixion of the Messiah, with that snake, Pontius Pilatus, who ordered the trial of Jesus and his crucifixion. These were bad lands for our people, for our saviour and for our prophet. Many lie buried in the sands of this land."

The old man turned back towards the river and smiled when he saw a passing reed raft with sleepy fishermen on board.

"*As-salamu alaykum* – peace be upon you," one of the fishermen called. He raised his hand in gesture, palm facing outwards, his words almost drifting off on the light breeze as soon as they left his mouth.

"*Alaykumu s-salam* – unto you peace," Daniel's grandfather called back. He also raised his hand, palm facing outwards. He nudged his grandson, "*akhlaq* – manners, your manners for our brothers?"

"G'day," Daniel called and then gave a half-hearted wave.

"Gurr-day, Gurr-day," his grandfather rasped. "What, you have no Arabic?" His grandfather's English was slightly tainted by a number of free-spirited rolling r's but it was still very understandable. "What kind of education have they given you over there? You have no Arabic, Ismail?"

"I never learnt Arabic, Grandfather. I was born in Australia. I am an Aussie, not an Arab. I don't know anything about Arabs. I'm sorry but I'm from a different world to this. This is not my world. My name is Daniel, not Ismail. My mother changed my name when I was six, when she left my dad and married her fancy man. My name has been Daniel Hightower for twenty-four years. That's who I am."

"You name is Ismail Ismail. It will always be Ismail Ismail in the eyes of God," his grandfather said. "This is the name you were given. This is the name your father baptised you with. Ismail is your first name and Ismail is your family name. That is who you are. Ismail Ismail. 'Hightower!' What name is this for a Mandaean?"

"Grandfather, I'm not a Mandaean. I'm sorry but I'm not."

Daniel's grandfather's name was Jamal. The name meant handsome, but Jamal was seventy-six years old and wore a look on his face that read hardship and poverty. If he'd once been handsome, it was a long time ago. His furrowed, lined, tan-leathered face sported a white beard and deep, rich brown eyes peering out from below large, bushy white eyebrows. His face had a kind look but it also showed the repression and hardship he had suffered.

9

The old man watched the fishermen as they moved further away and drifted meanderingly along the river, pushed and rocked gently by the tempo of its current. He looked upriver to see where the screeches were coming from. In a part of the river where it was calm and slightly set back in a shallow D shape, a group of semi-clad young Arab boys were swimming and splashing in play and great enjoyment. The old man laughed.

"The Christians turned baptism into a sacrament but we Mandaeans use it to celebrate our weddings, our funerals, and many celebrations. Our river ceremonies purify our body and soul; they hold and bind us, though we are few now. And those boys, look how they love its waters."

Daniel saw the boys upriver and wished he was with them. He was hot and he was sticky and took no joy being out in the midday sun – and being called Ismail by his grandfather irked him. He didn't want to offend his grandfather but he had no intention turning Arab on this trip.

Daniel had received a call from his father that morning. He was in Dubai and looking for work in construction. He found it hard to get work back in Australia because of his past. He'd only been in Dubai for three days and was searching the jobs pages of the English newspaper when his mobile phone rang. His father told him that his grandfather needed his help. There was a ticket waiting at the reception of his cheap hotel, and he had seventy minutes to catch his plane. He was told that the ticket was for Jordan, where his grandfather would be waiting for him. Despite his best efforts to get out of it, Daniel caved in early on in the call, and agreed. His father had stood up for him during his dark days. He had never once turned his back on his son or walked away from him.

Daniel caught his plane, making the trip to Jordan for his father. He loved his father. His mother had long since disappeared and left no forwarding address.

At the age of six, his mother and father had divorced. His father and his mother had never got on. His father had been a refugee, arriving with nothing and had struggled in those early years to find work. His mother was third generation Polish. She was strong minded and hard in nature. Originally from Alice Springs, she had sought a better life further south where it was cooler and there were better prospects. She'd moved to Geelong, Victoria's second largest city after Melbourne. She stayed with relatives and there she met Daniel's father, who had been attending night school to become a bookkeeper. She thought he would make something of himself and have money, but she got fed up waiting. Daniel's parents divorced and his mother was soon living with another man, a man called Ted Hightower. Ted was a truck driver who liked women, beer and his mates. They moved to the other side of Melbourne and Daniel only got to see his father twice a year. His mother married Ted Hightower in less than a year and changed his name to Daniel Hightower. She forbad him to ever tell anyone he was half Arab. She called his father a dirty desert Abbo.

By the time Daniel was ten, his stepfather, Ted Hightower, after a string of affairs ran off with another woman. His mother spent less time at home from then on, and more time in bars, so Daniel pretty much had to fend for himself.

At fifteen years old, Daniel's best friend, Paddy O'Brien, was horrifically murdered by a street gang. He was stabbed multiple times and died in the street in a pool of blood. There was no reason for the attack and his assailants were never caught. Daniel and Paddy had been the best of friends, doing everything together; they had been inseparable. Daniel should have been with Paddy that day but he'd stayed at home to help his mother who had been badly beaten by a drunk in a neighbouring bar.

Daniel found out who the gang were and joined the rival gang. Not long after, he got his revenge. The police became frequent visitors to his house over the years, always looking for Daniel for one crime or another.

By the time he was eighteen years old, the gang had grown and were now into serious crime. Daniel – Danny Hightower – was well known to the authorities. His mother had been gone a year by then. Later, he heard she had remarried at least twice more but he wasn't sure; he didn't care. Others said she had been strangled whilst working as a barmaid in an outback mining town up north.

When he was twenty years old he was caught by the authorities breaking into an auto parts storage unit and trying to make off with most of the contents of the unit. He was charged on five counts: three counts of theft, which included two priors, one count of possession and distribution of stolen goods and one count of being a member of a banned organisation — he was identified as the gang's number two. He went to jail for nine years. When he got out, he moved in with his father, which had been two months before travelling to Dubai. He couldn't find work because of his record but heard that there was work in the Gulf. He could never repay his father. He was ashamed of the trouble he had caused him, the grief he had brought into his life. He could never repay him, but this, he figured, going to Jordan, might be a start.

His grandfather closed his eyes and recited a passage of the sacred book, the *Ginza*. He could still speak the Aramaic language, most of which had only survived in liturgy.

The old man's mobile phone rang. He took it out of his pocket and fumbled with its keys.

"Damn, how old is that thing?" Daniel asked, "It's the size of a house brick."

"My friend Hassan let me borrow it. He bought it in 1995." Jamal then eased away from his grandson. He held his hand over the mouthpiece of the phone and his mouth, so that his voice was mumbled.

Daniel could not hear what was being said but he did hear his birth name a few times, and he caught the name Payne St Clair, which meant nothing to him. The call was long. It sounded important but he left his grandfather to it and walked off a hundred yards or so. The boys upriver had gone now. He heard the *Dhuhr*, the midday call to prayer, and figured they had gone to pray with their fathers in the mosques, as he had prayed with his father, when he was a young boy, before his mother took him away.

12

A small scorpion, a baby, almost translucent, scampered past Daniel's foot. It was not fast enough and Daniel crunched it under his trainers. His grandfather was back by his side, looking down at the dead scorpion and shaking his head.

"I am conflicted my grandson. Mandaeans believe it is a sin to cause pain to any living being, even animals. We do not bear weapons, we do not spill another's blood, even in self-defence."

"Not to be rude, Grandfather," Daniel began, "but I have no such conflict. I have learnt that if something looks like it can harm you, and it's heading your way, it normally means it's going to harm you."

"Perfect," his grandfather said. "We will need that. God is great for He made sure you were close by when our need came. Did your father tell you why I need your help?"

"My father just told me that you had asked for me and that the family had all pooled their money to buy my ticket to get here and for a hotel room for a couple of nights. That's all I know. My father said you would tell me more when I got here."

Jamal wore the traditional white Middle Eastern clothes, including a turban. Daniel wore western clothes. Daniel stood out on the riverbank in his bright shorts, T-shirt and old trainers. He looked like a tourist. He was a stocky thirty-year-old. He had long brown hair, parted in the centre. He normally had a three-day old beard. Only his tattoos gave any indication of his past.

"We wear white, our *Rasteh*," his grandfather started, looking down at his dress, "because it's pure. White represents faith, white represents the cleansing."

"I know, Grandfather," Daniel replied, "my father told me. He also told me about his journey out of Iraq, that it had been really harsh and he'd faced many difficulties and nearly died many times along the way. He told me many did die. I asked him how many Mandaean were left in this world and he said about sixty-thousand but most of them lived abroad as migrant settlers. He said there are only about three-thousand or so Mandaean left in their homeland."

Jamal nodded, sadly, he was one of the remaining few. His wife had died many years ago and he now lived alone in an ever-shrinking

13

community on the plains of Iraq. His life was a difficult life; it had always been like that but his faith was strong and his belief unshakeable. His mobile phone rang again. "Ah, it's for you," he said without even answering it.

"Me? No one knows—"

"It's my friend in America, a Mandaean priest called Joseph. He wants to speak to you now. Here, my grandson, take the brick." He smiled and gave Daniel the phone.

"Hello," Daniel said tentatively.

"Thank you for agreeing to help us my son," the voice at the other end of the phone began.

"Help you, sorry, what—" Daniel started to say.

"It is of extreme importance to us, to me, to your grandfather and to our whole community."

Daniel didn't understand. He thought he had missed something, a whole pile of something.

"We have been waiting for it for two-thousand years," the voice at the other end of the phone continued. "We are so excited. Many people have claimed to have had it, have the skull of our beloved prophet, John the Baptist, St John. Do you know about a reliquary, Ismail?" Daniel wasn't given time to say 'no.' "Christians place small pieces of a saint's bone, hair, or pieces from clothes they wore, into a reliquary, a small box, inside a church's altar. It is a common Catholic practice. This gave rise to many rumours and claims about the location of the prophet's head." The caller's accent was American and his tone serious but excited.

"People say that the skull is kept in the church of San Silvestro, in Rome, Italy. Others say it is in Damascus, Syria, at the famous Umayyad Mosque. So too, they say, the 13th century cathedral in Amiens, France was purposely built to hold the head of John the Baptist. And, the saint's skull is said to have been found by Duke Wilhelm V of Bavaria and now resides in the Residenz Museum in Munich, Germany. Many people have tried to find it. The circum-stances of his execution; the separation of his head from his body by a spiteful, over privileged and malicious queen for being the washer of sins, for his life as a prophet who foretold the coming of Christ. All that made the prophet one of history's most important holy men. The resting place of our revered prophet, the pious redeemer has eluded us all for two-thousand years.

"We, his followers, have never lost faith that we would find it. We are indebted to you Ismail for agreeing to go get it for us."

What! was the only thought in Daniel's head, quickly followed by *these guys are fucking crazy*.

"You must come to America today," the voice at the other end of the archaic phone continued. "We have a new passport for you so you can get in. They are not keen on letting felons in."

The man at the other end of the phone, a man called Joseph, a professor of law at Atlanta State University, proceeded to tell Daniel that his grandfather had his flight tickets to Newark airport and a new passport. Someone would meet him when he arrived. Then he told him to have a pleasant flight and said that he was excited, so very excited he was coming.

Daniel shook his head. "Wait, what, why am going to the Unit—" The phone went dead.

His grandfather took the phone from Daniel. He struggled to get it back into his pocket as he spoke. "Why? To get the head of John the Baptist for us." The phone was finally squeezed into his pocket. "Your plane leaves in two hours."

Daniel just stood there. "This is bloody crazy. What are you talking about?"

His grandfather took a chain and pendant from around his neck and placed it over Daniel's head. "*Darfash*," he said, "it will keep you safe; it has kept me safe."

"Why are you asking me to do this, Grandfather? I have no idea what I'm doing. This is nuts."

"We thought, my grandson, you would find it for us. We now know where it had been hidden but it was stolen from that place, so you need to find the thief, and get it back. That's all. We thought that you would be able to handle trouble and you would be

15

good at sneaking around." The old man smiled, thinking his explanation was a good explanation.

"Sneaking around? What in Christ …" he stopped himself, "… what in bugger's sake do you mean? Sneak around? Sneak around what? Where? Why sneaking around?"

His grandfather started to walk towards a line of taxis that were lined up a few hundred yards away, waiting for tourists to finish taking pictures with their cameras and video cameras.

"Joseph will tell you everything when you get there. Now, you need to get into one of these taxis and go straight to the airport. You don't have much time."

"You're not coming, Grandfather?"

"Who me? No, no, not me. It is far too dangerous for me and I'm not a good sneaker. But when you are finished, promise me you will come back to see me."

"Where will you be Grandfather?" Daniel asked.

"Oh, I will be right here my grandson. I will be right here by the river."

"We can meet at a hotel where it will be more comfortable, Grandfather. There is no need to meet here."

"But how can I baptise you my grandson, if we are at a hotel and not here by *his* river?"

Chapter 2

The Lawyer and the Relic Hunter

Date: 15th November 2012, 2 a.m.
Place: A secure warehousing facility at Heald Green, on the outskirts of Manchester, England

It was November and it was a frosty, dark and drizzly autumnal night. The majority of people were warmly ensconced in their homes, mostly asleep and only a few late-night party stragglers and wandering tom cats were still out. It was a lousy night for anyone or anything to be outside, which made it a good night for a burglary, a good night for this burglary.

She was sheltering from the drizzling rain, watching, listening, waiting. She was squinting her eyes to make it easier to see through the drizzle and into the night. The buildings' exterior lights were on and the area was well lit. The rain danced in flurries through the beams as the wind caught it and orchestrated its descent.

She was just seven miles away from Manchester city centre. She could almost smell the city from where she was, almost feel its vibe, which she missed so much. She sucked in the cold night air again and then let it go. It bellowed like a puff of white smoke into the frosty night and then disappeared into the wind driven rain.

She was seventeen miles away from where she had grown up but she had no desire to go back. She'd once told a therapist that her life there had been complicated. She was now twenty-one years old and was still affected by it.

She shook the drizzle from her waterproof clothing, breathed in the Manchester air again and savoured the moment. Then, she let it go once more and refocused on the crime she was about to commit. *Game face on*, she thought to herself.

This was her fourth job for him. She wondered how many more she would have to do before she was free of him, free of his hold and his threats. He hadn't said. She hadn't asked. Perhaps she should have but she had been in no position to bargain, no position to set demands. The jobs were her dues, her debt, because they were his restitution. They brought her the guarantee he offered, the fickle, precarious guarantee.

She was starting to worry that she was beginning to like what she was doing. The contradiction of hating what she was doing, with loving what she was doing, messed with her head. She hated it; she loved it. She knew crime but had never considered herself a criminal, not in this way. She'd been close up and personal to other peoples' crimes, but they were never hers. She shook the drizzle from her waterproof clothing again. *Game face,* she repeated inside her head, *time to go to work. Focus my girl.*

She stamped her feet. Her thermals kept her body warm but she had made the mistake of not putting on winter socks. She would not make that mistake again. Her thin climbing shoes offered no protection from the cold. She needed to keep her feet warm, keep the circulation going; she would need them to be sensitive when she went up top, or she would fall to her death.

She flicked the rain from the end of her nose and looked around. Sixteen industrial warehouse units stood side by side in a row, each a large unit, all with blue roller shutter doors. Each had a number emblazoned on the front in large, white numbers. Behind that block of sixteen, she knew there was another row of sixteen with yet more roller shutter doors and more numbers, all cardinal numbers, no letters. And behind them, yet more. The gated industrial park had nearly three hundred units on site. It was a large but inconspicuous place. It looked like every other industrial park on the outskirts of every other major city.

The roller shutter door was set back by a foot from the face of the building. She moved out of its protection from the rain and looked up to the roof, squinting. It looked high from her ground position. She took hold of the six-inch cast-iron drainpipe and placed her left foot on the first metal wall-fixing bracket. The cast-iron drainpipe was wet but her black climbing shoes and neoprene, waterproof gloves held her firmly. She was nimble and agile. She was trained. She was strong for her frame. She climbed up the drainpipe with relative ease, one foot, one hand at a time. No mistakes. No falls. She controlled her breathing: slow and steady. She made it without a hitch.

At the top she pulled herself over the white, thick tongue and groove facia board and the cast-iron guttering attached to it. It was tricky because there were no natural hand-holds to grab onto on the roof. So, she had to haul herself over the guttering by swinging her right leg onto the roof first and then her right arm, which left her lying lateral to the ground below. Then she had to roll forward half a rotation, against the pitch of the roof, to clear the eave.

She lay on her side, her body facing the apex of the roof of unit number 9. Climbing onto this unit's roof gave her the best cover because it was the unit furthest away from any CCTV cameras. There were two cameras and alarm boxes per row of units. One of the CCTV cameras was just two units down from where she needed to be, unit number 13.

She lay still at the top for a while, breathing slowly and listening. She checked her watch, the dimly lit, green digital display just visible – she'd turned the dial face light down low before she'd left. She squinted at the face. She was on time. There were many moving parts to the plan, his plan. Accurate timing bound each part of them together. If she got the timing wrong, the plan would unravel and she knew she would be screwed.

She had a short distance to go to get to the roof of unit number 13. She moved into a crouched position and readied herself. She counted, "One, two …" Now her heart was beating faster. It always did at this point. She felt it pound. She knew it was excitement and adrenalin and not trepidation, nervousness or even fear. She was not scared. She knew scared would make her sloppy and lose focus. It would put her in harm's way. She knew fear would get her caught, or at this height, dead. The sensation she felt was the same sensation she had felt on each of the jobs she had carried out for him.

Her eyes closed and she slowed her breathing down. "Three." Her tall, nymph-like figure ran across the metal corrugated roofs of units 9, 10, 11 and 12 and on towards the large skylight of unit 13. She made sure she stood on the tops of the galvanised sheets' fixing bolts. The slightly raised bolt heads and washers, gave her black climbing shoes just enough hold on the wet and slippery metal – now she needed the sensitivity in her feet to feel the small one-inch round bolt heads.

She was at least thirty feet off the ground but the height didn't bother her, she barely noticed it. Dressed in black, with a black ski mask, she was virtually invisible to anyone looking up at the roofs. It was late, around 2 a.m. there would be no reason for anyone to be out and if they were, she would give them no reason to look up. She crept quietly; she made no sound.

She already knew the two security guards would not make another round until about 4 a.m. They wouldn't change their routine; they hadn't done so in a week the time 'he' had been watching the industrial park and putting his plan into place. For now, at least, she knew they would be safely tucked away in their Portakabin, heater, kettle and TV on. The compound had lots of CCTV coverage, but she knew the security guards would not be paying attention. *He*, the man, the man who liked to refer to himself as her handler, and referred to her as the relic hunter, his relic hunter, had planned the day and time of the burglary to coincide with a late-night TV channel covering a major US poker tournament in Las Vegas: 'Late-Night Poker US.' The coverage tonight was of the final table, eight contestants with a buy-in of two hundred thousand dollars and a 1st place cash prize of one million dollars. The tournament started at 6 p.m. local time, 2 a.m. UK time, just as the security guards finished their security check, just as she made it to the base of unit number 9 and had eased back into the shadow of its doorway. The programme was due to finish at 8 p.m. local time, 4 a.m. UK time. Her handler had carried out a detailed search on each of the security men. One came back flagged; he had a bad gambling habit and he had been to Las Vegas twice. His weakness was poker. He would be watching the tournament and his buddy would join him.

She made it to the skylight of unit number 13. She started to prise the skylight open with a twelve-inch pry bar, which she'd taken from the black backpack she was carrying. She paused and looked around; it was all quiet. She looked for her accomplice across at the street that bordered the fenced perimeter of the industrial park, but she couldn't see him. He was somewhere in the shadows, parked in their getaway car waiting for her call.

She eased the skylight up very slowly, just enough to slide a false contact strip into the alarm contacts on the window and the frame. The security up top was basic. Contact was made; it was a secure connection. She raised the skylight, just enough so she would be able to slide her body through. She wedged the pry bar against the skylight and its frame to hold it open. She found the skylight relatively light, considering it was three feet by five feet, with half-inch tempered, wire reinforced glass. She tied her knotted climbing rope to the roof light's four metal back-stays. She paused. She looked around for any sign of movement again. It was quiet and still. She lowered herself down the nylon climbing rope. Once through the skylight, she paused again, reached up, removed the pry bar and lowered the skylight back down.

Her accomplice was told that the plan was not for him to enter by the skylight. He would enter by the unit's side door. She entered via the skylight because it meant she did not trip the more complicated door alarms. This would give her lots of time inside the unit to look for the right container. Then, once she'd blown the door with C4, she would have time to search for and locate their mark. They calculated that the small amount of C4 would not trigger any of the alarms and no one would be about to identify the dull sound as explosives. Once she had found their mark, she would signal him and meet him at the door. He would scale the outer fence, as she had done and make his way straight to the unit. She would slip the locks and the door would open.

At this point, the alarms would trigger because they did not have the door alarm codes. Inserting contact strips would not work on the doors, as they did on the skylights because the door alarms needed a digital code and were more sophisticated. He was told that he would have to verify the item as the piece they wanted, at which point they would both leave. Whilst breaching the door would set off the alarms, they would have plenty of time to make good their escape and would be long gone before the police arrived. He was told the police would not get there for at least ten minutes. The security guards would not approach the scene; their MO was to call the police in the event of a break-in. They were a visual deterrent on site only. That was the plan he was told and the plan he believed.

She placed one hand over the other, legs at a right angle in front of her, she slowly lowered herself into the blackness of the unit. It was colder inside than outside. Effortlessly she made it to the floor. Her years in gymnastics at county level, and finally a year as part of the British gymnastic team, gave her the skill and dexterity she needed.

The intel she was given, by the man that liked to call himself her handler, was that she would find three metal, medium sized shipping containers inside the unit. Each would have an air purifying system and a bio heating control panel on the outside. The temperature inside was always kept at 21 degrees Celsius to protect their cargo. She was also told that the containers were due to be transported to the docks late on the 16th, which was the next day, so she had one chance to find their mark.

She started looking for the markings on the containers. He'd briefed her that two of the three containers would be marked. One container would have the letter P and one the letter R. The letters were painted at the base of the containers' doors, invisible to the naked eye, but visible with infrared night vision glasses. The third container had no markings.

"Make sure you get the forger, your accomplice, into the container marked with the letter R. You have to be in the one marked P." It was important; he'd made her repeat it six times.

She pulled down her infrared goggles and found the two

containers that had the lettering. She noted the one she would need to enter and the one she would need to get the forger to go into. They had planned how they intended to do that: first the ruse and then, the bait and switch.

Time for the ruse, she thought, *act one, scene one.* She placed a small amount of C4 on the doors of each of the two containers she had identified.

And action, "Shit," she cursed loudly. The curse echoed in the vastness of the cold warehouse unit. "Shit," she said again, making sure he'd heard her. Her earpiece crackled, as she knew it would. He'd seemed extremely nervous on the drive up to Manchester but he needed the money. She figured he would have worked himself up into a mild panic just sitting in the car, in the shadows. He would make mistakes in his decision-making.

"What? Are you in?" The man's voice was edgy and had a slight London accent.

"Yes, I'm in," she replied. "How's it looking out there?"

"Nothing. Nobody about," the man said. "All quiet. What was the 'shit' for?"

"The containers all look the same; no damn differences. They don't have serial numbers on them. I was expecting a serial number." The ruse had begun. They actually all had serial numbers on them, on a small plate at the back. She knew he wouldn't look; there would be no time and not enough light, and anyway, why would he? She'd told him there were none.

"What do you mean, no serial numbers?"

"I was told there would be serial numbers on the containers. I was given the serial number of the container with our mark inside, but there's nothing. I've checked them three times now. I don't know what's going on. I would need to blow the doors of all three to make sure we get what we've come for."

"Blow them, then," the voice in her earpiece rasped back with incredulity at her dithering. "I've spent the best part of three months of my life preparing for this job. I'm not walking away now. Blow all the fucking doors!"

"I don't have enough to blow all three," she replied, trying to sound as disappointed as possible, now in full ruse.

"Shit."

"Yup, that's what I said."

"How many can you blow?" he asked.

Not too enthusiastic, she thought to herself. "Two, I guess but—"

"No buts. Blow two," he interrupted.

"Look," she said, "I know what's at stake here. We turn up with anything less than what we've been contracted to get, we'll both end up dead and floating in some scummy Mancunian canal and I have no intention of ending up in any scummy canal, let alone a Mancunian one."

"Just blow two for Christ's sake and let's get on with it! It's our only play, right?"

And now for the bait and switch, she said to herself. "I won't have time to search both containers for the painting on my own."

"Then I'll come in. I'm on my way. Get them ready."

She smiled: *Bad decision-making. Baited, bait taken and now switched.* "Okay," she said into her coms piece. "How will you get in?" She knew already what he would say. There were only two ways in for him and one required him to be thirty feet off the ground on a wet, metal, pitched roof.

"I'll ram the car into the roller shutter door. The car will take it; it's German. I'm not going on that fucking roof and we won't get in through the doors because of the locks."

"Fine. It will set off the alarms, but we know the guards won't come running. So, I figure we'll have about ten minutes to get in, search the containers and get what we want. Because there are two of us, I think we should have time." Given that the police response units would drive at an average of eighty miles per hour on all but empty roads at that time in the morning, she knew that the most they would have would be between four and six minutes at most before they arrived. What her accomplice failed to remember was that they were just seven miles from the outskirts of Manchester city centre. He was an art forger, a good one who could recreate most of the masters and it would take a trained eye to spot the difference, but he was not a thief, nor was he a local familiar with just how easily the police could get there.

Again, her earpiece crackled. "I agree, ten minutes is long enough for us to find it and for me to verify it. I'm the expert. I need to be in there. You have no idea how precious and rare this painting is; you have no idea how valuable master pieces are."

She couldn't help herself. He'd irked her. "Really?" Her sarcasm laced the word curtly. "I did my research for this job. The *Mona Lisa* was stolen in 1911 by three Italian handymen in the Louvre in Paris. It took the authorities twenty-eight months to find it and get it back. That painting is worth around nine hundred million dollars today. Van Gogh's *Congregation Leaving the Reformed Church in Nuenen*, stolen in 2002, is worth around five to six million dollars. How I'm doing?" He didn't answer. "Look, I'm blowing the container doors in one minute. I suggest you crash through the side gate, the one I scaled earlier, at exactly the same time the C4 goes off. So, it will be on my signal, agreed?"

The man agreed. "I'm ready, let's just get on with it." He hit the start button of their getaway car, a 2010, black three litre BMW with false plates that her handler had got for them. The engine purred into life.

"On my signal then," she said looking at her watch, "In twenty, nineteen, eighteen … three, two one." The C4 blew. The locks on the opening-bolts to each of the two container doors blew and both doors flew open.

Barely had the word 'one' left her lips when there was a crash outside and then a screech of brakes. He drove the BMW through the wired, galvanised side gate. The thin, rusting chain and cheap lock offered no resistance. Moments later there was another screech of brakes, and then another crash. He ploughed the BMW into the blue roller shutter door of unit 13. The door buckled with the impact but stayed in position.

As soon as he hit the door, the young woman threw her night goggles into her backpack and retrieved one of the two torches she carried. Then, she went straight for the container with the letter P on it.

The front end of the black BMW was all smashed in. The brakes screeched again as it reversed and was then driven headlong into the door once again, but now at a much faster speed. This time the right-hand side of the door gave way; it was now buckled and ripped out of its channelled framework, with a section hanging off. There was enough room for him to squeeze through. The units' alarms were screeching out. Piercing. The flashing, red, rotating lights, atop of the alarm boxes, positioned on each corner of the unadorned, banal looking row of units, were lighting up the exterior of the buildings. Dogs on the nearby housing estate were barking loudly. The tom cats started their eerie cries. As the seconds passed, so did the cacophony.

She appeared from one of the containers and barked at him above the din of the alarms. "Check that container," she pointed to the nearby container as she threw him the second torch from her backpack. "I got this container covered."

He was so pumped-up; he didn't stop to think why she had brought two torches. He ran inside the container and was faced with a treasure trove of fine art and jewellery, plus over twenty packing boxes. He knew he couldn't keep the painting for himself, a 16th century Magellan, of the fourteen stations of the crucifixion, but he could keep whatever else he could carry. He found the painting almost straight away. He looked at his watch and calculated he had about five or six minutes. Nobody had said anything about not taking other stuff. There were packing boxes everywhere. On a small table at the back was an attaché case; it was closed but unlocked. He opened it and inside found five Patek Philippe watches and three Rolex Daytonas. He picked up one of the Rolexes. "Paul Newman's Rolex Daytona sold for eighteen million", he said to himself out loud, as if to give himself encouragement for what he was about to do, "and the Patek Philippe watches will go for more." He started looking in the packing boxes whilst stuffing his pockets with watches. He wondered what else he could carry.

She checked her watch, they had been in there three minutes since the alarms had been triggered; it felt like three seconds. Finally, she found what she was looking for, a small, plastic shopping bag stuffed at the back behind some sealed packing boxes, just like her handler had said it would be. She looked inside the bag. There was a cigarette packet. The most expensive item in all of the three containers was lying inside a cigarette packet, inside a used shopping bag. She quickly put the plastic bag into her black backpack and left the container. She checked her watch one more time.

"It's not in this one," she called out to the man in the other container. "I'll keep watch outside. You have enough time to search that one. We can't leave without it. Let's hope it's there, so search well. Don't miss anything! Don't cause me to float in a scummy canal tonight!"

He heard her but he was too overwhelmed by his good fortune of being faced with an abundance of highly valuable objects to respond to her. He had no idea how long he had been in there but to him it was seconds. He didn't know what to touch first, what he should take. He was giddy with expectation and thoughts of how his life was about to change. His greed removed his logic.

She was outside when she heard the police sirens join the building alarms to ensure no one would sleep and the dogs would remain barking all night. The blue flashing lights of the police cars started to fill the industrial estate with a psychedelic staccato effect, joining the red rotating alarm lights.

The man left inside the container didn't hear the police. The units' alarms drowned out their sirens and their arrival. He wouldn't

27

hear her warn him, because she didn't; that wasn't the plan. The plan was that he was the patsy, her scapegoat, who would never know what had happened; he would believe a completely different story.

The first he knew of the arrival of the police was when they flicked the fuse box switch of the thirty or so argon industrial ceiling lights. The place lit up like a football pitch. The light exploded into the container; it hurt his eyes after the torch light. Then he heard the shouts of the police as they made their way into the warehouse unit by the same entrance he had used, via the buckled and twisted roller shutter door. A police dog led the way and six police officers followed, with batons and tasers at the ready.

"This is the police," they started to shout at the top of their voices to frighten and confuse, as police do when they enter a building to apprehend someone.

"We have police dogs in the building. Lie on the ground and put your hands behind your head, NOW!"

Two policemen entered the container but five seconds after, the police dog bit into his right arm.

Her handler had planned that the forger would be the fall guy. The forger would naturally believe that she had barely made it out in time, and he was just unlucky and got caught. He would not tell the police about her because he didn't grass. However, he would have, if he had known that it had been a set-up. He was the set-up. So, he would just tell the police that he was after the 16th century Magellan of the fourteen stations of the crucifixion, which of course would be there, probably in his hands at the point of arrest. They would run a check on him and it would quickly come back that he was a serial forger and had spent several stints at the pleasure of Her Majesty. They would assume that he was up to his old tricks again and his intention had been to steal the painting and then make a number of copies and sell them on to unsuspecting collectors. Finding other stolen items in his pockets would just underscore his criminal and felonious nature. He would not be able to tell them how he knew the painting was there, because he didn't actually know. Even she didn't know; only the man who had planned the robbery did.

Of course, the forger didn't know that the plan was not to steal the painting, despite it being a rare and valuable piece. The plan all along was to steal the item hidden inside the plastic shopping bag and cigarette packet. They wanted the police to focus their attention on the painting and on the forger, so that the young woman could make good her getaway with the item and not leave any loose ends. The forger didn't realise how lucky he was. There were only two endings for him; one was to be trapped and caught, ending up in prison again, and the other would have involved a Mancunian canal.

By the time the shouting started inside the warehouse unit, she had already run across the internal service road and scaled the perimeter metal fence with ease. She was now five hundred yards away. Her adrenaline still pumping, she was on a high; exhilarated. She had successfully completed yet another job. This one was high stakes because it was the first one that involved another party. Another person that was integral to the plan, not the robbery, but the getaway – she had no concern for the forger; his fate was not her concern.

Anything could have gone wrong. There were so many moving parts to the job. She felt a sense of satisfaction. She was pleased with herself. What the item was that she'd stolen didn't matter to her. It could have been the biggest prize of all time or scrap. She didn't know what it was. She didn't care. What mattered to her was the fact she, and she alone, had executed the plan and walked away with their mark. She found herself smiling. Her annoyance at herself for enjoying her criminality was swamped by her sense of daring and accomplishment.

Walking briskly, she removed her black jacket, quickly turning it inside out to reveal a blue jacket. She'd turned the black backpack inside out, it was now red. She threw her gloves and ski mask into a storm drain, along with her night goggles, pry bar and torch. She took the mobile phone from her pocket; it was a burner he had given her. She did a quick 360-degree scan; there was nothing, no people, no traffic, no police, just neighbourhood dogs barking but becoming more distant with every step she took. She pressed the speed dial and called her handler.

*

Timothy Crowthorp's mobile phone rang. The man who liked to call himself her handler hit the green answer button on the touch screen display and listened as she spoke. He smiled when she told him that she had the item in her possession. He smiled again when she said the forger was now in the hands of the police. The plan had worked, his plan. He told her that he would pick her up in fifteen minutes at the pre-arranged meeting point, a McDonald's drive-through.

Timothy Crowthorp, the ex-QC who had worked for Salah El-Din four years ago, hung up. He placed his mobile phone back into the centre console of the Jaguar car and plugged it into a charger cable.

He'd left his engine running for the last hour. It was cold out but warm inside. He caught sight of himself in his rear-view mirror. He couldn't help feel smug: *from prison to freedom,* he thought as he looked at himself. *From losing everything to now having almost everything.* He cracked a grin; he allowed himself a moment of self-congratulation.

 He eased the car forward from out of the side road he'd been parked up in for the last hour. He'd parked the car slightly back from the junction with the main road. The side road hedgerow gave him extra cover.

He checked his lights were on, seat belt on, interior light now off, main beam off; he wanted no reason for the police to stop him. He accelerated slightly, but not too much. Just enough. The dark green Jaguar hit sixty miles per hour on the dual carriageway. There was no traffic on the road other than an occasional lorry on its way to making or returning from its delivery. He set the cruise control to on and headed for the McDonald's drive-through.

The two men had watched the young woman and the forger carry out the robbery. They knew every step the woman would take; they were fully aware of the plan. Their instructions, as always, were explicit: if the young woman failed, she and her accomplice were to be killed. Then, they were to find Crowthorp and firstly bind him and then slit his mouth from each corner to his ear lobes. Then, they were to slice off each of his ears and finally, gouge out each eye. They were to leave him like that and let him bleed out, slowly. *See no more, hear no more, tell no more!*

Chapter 3

Sancti Furem – Holy Thief

The Templars protected the weak and defended the good and honest people against those who were bad. Criminals, murderers, thieves, tyrants, opportunists – there was a long list of evil people and organisations they had fought over the centuries. Where there was serious crime against a religious order, crime involving its revered icons, objects of worship and historical importance, the Templars would help.

The Templars knew that to millions, the Roman Catholic Church represented a way of life, a credo, doctrine, ideology, a belief that gave them comfort, guidance and a sense of belonging: a purpose. But to others, the artefacts of the Roman Catholic Church were a way to make quick money. No other part of the Roman Catholic Church presented that temptation, with its architectural charisma, magnetism and enticing allure of its riches, more than the Vatican itself, the seat and the See of the Roman Catholic Church.

Artefacts were stolen, including religious icons, statues, crucifixes, paintings, priceless ceremonial jewellery and even stained-glass windows. The perpetrators walked away with large, sometimes vast sums of money for their illegal toil and risk. Following the trail was often almost impossible for the police, but sometimes possible for the secret Order of the Knights Templar, because they worked in total secrecy and anonymity.

Sometimes the criminals actually stole the church's money

directly and bypassed the need to steal an artefact and the risk of selling it on. The theft of money was notably from banks associated with the Vatican, or the Vatican bank itself, called the Institute for Works of Religion (IOR). The IOR, a privately held financial institution, was based inside Vatican City. Its role was to safeguard and also administer money and assets meant for works of religion or charity. Fiscal crime had gained pace as the years went by and advancing technology offered a certain type of criminal a digital key to an abundant and well stocked Aladdin's cave.

The ex-FBI agent, Courtney Rose, had upgraded and installed an advanced, robust and protected electronic superhighway of servers across the Templar network, which made tracing and tracking digital crime easier. However, in the past, like the police, the Templars had often come up against the Church's wall of silence and secrecy, which thwarted their efforts to help. The Vatican thrived on secrecy. Nearly all crimes against the Vatican in the 20th and 21st centuries were not reported outside the inner circles and higher echelons of the smallest independent state on Earth – measuring just a fifth of a square mile. It was closed, private and self-governing.

The Vatican, brimming with valuables at every turn, was a magnet for criminals, from those who liked to work alone, to small and large organised gangs. But it was not just the valuables on public display that brought in the criminal factions. The real value in the Vatican normally lay deep underground. The most valuable, the most sacred artefacts that were not on display, attracted the worst type of criminality and presented the most consternation for the Church authorities because of the sophistication and expertise of the thieves they attracted. These robberies were nearly always carried out for an anonymous collector. Men, women, investment syndicates, corporations with seemingly unlimited funds, would place their order and a criminal or criminal gang would be contacted and offered the job of obtaining an artefact for them. The buyers, operating clandestinely, almost always worked through a series of agents, whom they rarely met, making tracing them impossible. Even if the police managed to apprehend the criminals who had stolen an item, the criminals rarely knew who their buyers were. It was a highly lucrative but dangerous game.

St Clair knew there was a long list of unscrupulous buyers wanting the unobtainable, the irreplaceable, those historical artefacts and relics they were not meant to have. Whilst they had never been invited into it, the Templars knew that the Vatican library, which held over a million books, was one of the world's oldest libraries. It was where scholars worked with limited access, so as to limit any one person's ability to steal the valuable, very valuable and the priceless. It held a collection of – and not on display for public consumption – ancient books, parchments, scrolls, essays and treaties, kept safe in secure, underground rooms, including the Vatican Secret Archive, the central repository containing official papal paperwork from the Holy See over the centuries. Hidden away in more secret vaults deep underground, with their own engineered atmosphere, impenetrable walls, ceilings and floors, sealed doors, combination locks, alarms, cameras and sensors and guarded day and night by well-trained, armed guards, were the most revered religious artefacts: the priceless pieces that formed the foundation stones of much of the world's history. These vaults contained just some of the Church's most secret assets: religious, historical, intellectual, and relating to art, science, mathematics and philosophy.

Many had estimated that, along with their other assets and those artefacts that could be valued, as many were so rare, or so unique that they were practically beyond valuation, the Vatican's wealth was near to eighteen billion US dollars. Of this wealth, their Italian stockholdings were worth over one and a half billion US dollars: that was fifteen per cent of the total value of the shares on the Italian stock market.

Great amounts of money attracted well-trained, well-equipped criminals. Great amounts of money also tempted those within the inner circle of the Vatican walls. In 1981, the Vatican bank was the main shareholder of Banco Ambrosiano. Friar Paul Marcinkus was head of the Institute for Religious Works. He was charged as an accessory in the three and a half billion US dollar collapse of Banco Ambrosiano.

The Ambrosiano was accused of laundering drug money for the Sicilian Mafia.

The Templars always knew that they only got to hear of very few instances of 'inside' crime; the world outside got to hear even less. The Vatican, notoriously guarded and secretive, kept their dirty laundry well and truly hidden. But even the ultra-cautious Church, with its vast and complex inner workings, driven by the powerful cardinals, the government of the Church, could not, at times, solve certain problems from within. Seeking outside help was not to every cardinal's liking. In fact, many of them were fervently and rigorously opposed to it. However, the criminality that was outpacing law enforcement, was also outpacing the Vatican. The Catholic hierarchy, who were resolutely steeped in tradition and cannon law, were not steeped in criminal practices.

Date: 17th November 2012, two days after the theft in Manchester
Place: Vatican City

The pious and highly conservative ecclesiastical body of Catholic cardinals, who managed the affairs of the global Catholic religion and the complex affairs of the Vatican City and the Vatican state in Rome, thought long and hard on the day of the 17th. They never made hasty decisions and now was not going to be the exception, regardless of the crime. What had been stolen was of major importance and significance to their Church. It was an object that had been revered in lore, law, legend and history. However, none of the cardinals could see what lay directly in front of their eyes: that the theft in Manchester had been an inside job! They were too busy reeling from the theft. Arguments about what to do about it had plunged them into temporary myopia. The item was stolen on the 15[th,] just two days ago. They had sent their investigator the very next day, on the 16th, to confirm it had been taken. They had been told by their chief of police that if they were to stand any chance of getting it back, they would have to decide on their course of action now. Their chief of police had also told them that he could not handle this crime alone with the resources he had.

He gave them an option.

Reaching out to the ultra-secret group they had turned to on five other occasions in the past twenty years, as the chief of police had suggested, was a deeply serious matter. Reaching out to anyone outside of the church was always deeply serious. The seat of the Catholic Church was never quick to air their problems to the outside world, and never quick to request help from outsiders. They knew that in doing so, inevitably, they would have to open their doors somewhat wider than they liked. They only turned to outside help in the direst circumstances. This action was a last resort and one that required much debate, some argument and much lobbying. But for a small group within the College of Cardinals, it meant clandestine meetings, scheming and insidious politicking – the beating heart of the inner workings of very conservative men with parochial, selfish, ambitious agendas. An *éminence grise* behind every door, outside every window, lingering in the opulent, lavish and ornate halls and corridors of the Vatican buildings, to espouse their views, with their red robes frenetically flowing – the red signifying the blood of Christ, – the frenetic movement signifying much haste and intent. They would hurriedly move from person-to-person to pass on their concerns and enforce their thinking on the matter, walking purposely in every corridor that led to the Pontiff. They wanted their way and would fight hard to get it. They did not want outsiders. They knew if they could get the Pope involved, they would indeed get their way. His decision would be final because he could not make a wrong decision! The declaration of 'papal infallibility' was the ultimate 'free pass,' for him and in this case, for them.

Much like most cloistered, secret organisations, the Catholic Church straddled the juxtaposition of having to be very much in public view with their desire for absolute privacy. They needed the public because they added to the number of worshippers in an age of declining numbers and because of the offertory – congregational donations during services. The average committed Catholic donated around seven pounds per week, an immense amount of money when multiplied by the number of church-goers. And finally, they needed the testate donations received from the faithful, who had passed on into the Kingdom of Heaven, which also amounted to huge sums.

It was a dilemma that their Eminences, the immediate layer of power that lay just below his Holiness the Pope, struggled with. There were those who rejected all outside help, believing that it would always end in the erosion of the Holy See's privacy – the jurisdiction of the Bishop of Rome, the Pope. And there were those who actively welcomed outside help and in doing so, were labelled as 'progressives' 'reformists' and 'liberals.' In the end, however, it was decided by secret ballot, that this time, they really did need help, despite all the arguing, bullying and gaslighting by an influential band of ultra-conservative cardinals. And so, the order was given to make contact with the outsiders.

Date: 18th November 2012, three days after the theft in Manchester

The outside organisation they decided to approach had proven themselves to be extremely helpful to the Holy See on five past occasions. They worked fast and seemingly unhampered by the bureaucracy of the Italian law enforcement agencies, or the debilitating procedures and processes of international agencies like Interpol. In addition, the organisation had demonstrated a deep sensitivity to the less public side of the Vatican.

Whilst the more conservative, conventional and traditional cardinals conceded to the results of the vote, they insisted and got their way, that Cardinal Cristoforo Paradiso would be the Vatican's liaison person with the outside organisation. Many of the younger cardinals – younger meant being under seventy but generally over fifty years old – sighed with some despair at the compromise they had to make, fretting that not having help from the outside might be better than having Cardinal Paradiso in charge of proceedings. However, the deed was done and the younger cardinals shook their heads and added a new prayer to their morning ritual prayer: 'Lord help the outsiders,' joined their 'Apostleship' of prayer.

The young cardinals knew that Cardinal Paradiso would thwart the outsiders at every step. He was the last person they would have chosen – although none of them would have said that directly to the infamous Cristoforo Paradiso! They knew that the only hope the outsiders had would be in the form of the man in charge of the *Corpo della Gendarmeria dello Stato della Città del Vaticano* – the Vatican City State Gendarmerie Corps: the Vatican police. The chief of police, a man called Dámaso Nef, was leading the investigation and it was Nef who had requested outside help after the theft had been confirmed by the man he had sent to Manchester, on the 16th. Over the years, and unbeknown to the cardinals, he had maintained a back channel with the ultra-secret organisation he was about to contact.

The Vatican City State Gendarmerie Corps, founded in 1816, always had a small number of employees; their current number was less than a hundred and fifty staff. They were stretched thin and not only did they not possess the manpower, they did not have the expertise for this kind of crime. The Gendarmerie formed part of the security forces of the Vatican City and the extraterritorial properties of the Holy See. They were responsible for security, border control, traffic, public order and criminal investigations – a to-do list that never ended.

Dámaso Nef stood out for two reasons: he was tall and distinguished looking – not haggard and somewhat tired looking like a lot of the police he worked with. His father was a Spanish Catholic, so Nef carried his father's Spanish surname as his first name. The second reason he stood out was he was a man of candour. He didn't play the political games that often stymied and obstructed progress within the Vatican, unless he couldn't help it.

Nef kept himself fit and took care of his appearance. He was a nice man, married with a young daughter. He sported a well-trimmed beard and moustache; he was slightly thinning on the top. He wore a broad cheery grin when he laughed, which was often and especially when he was with his family and he and his wife, Elena, were playing with their daughter, Uma. He played golf on the weekends; he was a good golfer with a handicap of five. He never drank alcohol. He was an intelligent man; he was liked by his staff and respected by most cardinals. Nef was able to adeptly traverse the complex politicking that had leeched into the inner power struggles and the hidden trap doors characterised by rivalries and factionalism in the Vatican.

Place: Police Headquarters, Vatican City

Dámaso Nef entered his office. It had two large metal windows and pale cream walls that had been recently painted: the smell of fresh paint still hung around and his office windows were cracked open slightly to ease the pungent smell. His desk was awash with papers and files, but they were all stacked in neat piles. He disliked untidiness, which he thought unprofessional and a sign of laziness.

There were twenty-three files on his desk: ten were cases for him to look at, all new and urgent to review. Thirteen were ongoing investigations. The one on the top of the pile was a closed file. It was an A4, manila folder, which was sealed and marked: '*Privato, solo all'ettenzione del capo della polizia* – Private, for the attention of Chief of Police Only.' Underneath the title of the file was printed in red: '*L'anello del re* – The king's ring.' He had been briefed so he knew its contents.

He closed the blinds to stop the glare of the sun on his computer screen. He had a hundred and three emails waiting for him in his inbox. He searched for the one he wanted. It had just come in, so he found it relatively easily. The email was a formal confirmation from the prefect that he could contact the outsiders. Cardinal Paradiso was cc'd in the email, along with several others from numerous departments within the curia, the administrative institutions of the Holy See and the body that all affairs of the Catholic Church dealt with. There were representatives in the email from the secretariats, congregations, pontifical councils, pontifical commissions, tribunals and many more. He wanted to make sure he had the approval in writing before he reached out; he'd been caught out before and suffered the wrath of some of the cardinals. Now, there it was on his screen. He saved the email but only after making two hard copies. One copy would go into the file that lay on his desk, the file marked '*L'anello del re*' and the extra copy he would take home. It would be put with a number of other documents he kept hidden in his attic: insurance in case he was ever used as a pawn or scapegoat by some of the more manipulative and insidious cardinals.

His black coffee was waiting on his desk, its aroma temporarily masking the smell of paint. There was a small digestive biscuit on the saucer; he smiled at the gesture by his secretary. She would always give him a biscuit anytime she thought he was stressed and his blood sugar might be low. Dámaso Nef didn't have a blood sugar problem but he was always stressed; he was appreciative of his secretary's thoughtfulness though.

He closed his office door. Nef considered his options. He would not use the landline. There was no proof, but he knew the likelihood was that someone would be listening. In the institution he served, he knew that there was always paranoia about being left out of the loop and omitted from decisions. Someone's eyes and ears were always watching, listening, snooping and spying. The cardinals' administrators, priests loyal to their eminences, were always eager to please their masters.

Nef ate the biscuit and searched for the number on his mobile's speed dial. He pressed 'call' and waited. He knew the drill. He would first speak to a lady who he had never met and would never likely meet. He knew his call would be recorded and it would be traced. He knew she would be exceptionally pleasant and engaging. She would hold a brief conversation with him but all the time she would be busy confirming his location. He didn't know that she was in a secret location in Islington. He had never heard of Islington, but he knew she was British, so assumed that she was somewhere in Great Britain. He could have traced the call himself but suspected that they had all calls cloaked and so he would be wasting his time. His past experiences of them were that they were far more technologically advanced than his own force and far more tactical and covert than any other organisation he had come into contact with. He heard the ring tone.

*

40

Date: 18th November 2012
Place: Remote castle, Scotland

St Clair was in the reception room with Jonathan and Dominique, and, as always in the winter, there was a log fire burning in the stone hearth, as there were log fires burning in most rooms in the castle. The fire hissed as the flames licked the fresh wood. The three Templars were talking about the cottage where Jonathan and Dominique lived. St Clair was always worried that they were too far from the castle and he could not protect them. They wouldn't let him put any Knights with them or even near them. Even Zakariah, Dominique's father, couldn't persuade them to accept more precautions and use the increased protection offered. They were adamant that employing the old Templar trick of hiding in plain sight, was their best chance of having some semblance of a normal married life. But St Clair was worried for them and wanted to try again to persuade them to rethink their security arrangements. All Knights were on increased alert, all operations reduced to only those most vital, yet still there were many of them around the world. St Clair knew that they had beaten the hornets' nest of the Abaddons, loudly and bloodily in Romania. They had left their calling card, their mark on the dead bodies, a small, bloody red cross on the foreheads of Zivko's men. So, he fretted about the young couple's vulnerability, but he would not issue them with an order to move. That decision was theirs to make, so they stayed put and he fretted.

Jonathan and Dominique were sitting in the two wingback armchairs that were positioned in front of the fire. St Clair was sitting in a yew and walnut smokers bow chair that creaked with age every time he shifted position, and smelt of the bee's wax, which had been used to clean the deep grained wood. Jonathan had managed to get St Clair off the subject of them moving, but he knew it would raise its head again. He was regaling them with stories of his first meeting with St Clair and his first meeting with Dominique. The mood was humorous and none of them could believe it had been four years ago.

Off to one side of the room, on a large wooden table stood an assortment of pots brimming with golden honey. The walls of the room were almost bare, but for a few old pictures, which were too small to make out unless you stood really close to them. The wattle and daub ceiling, a later addition to the room in the 1930s, an attempt to retain the heat, was yellow in patches from the smoke of countless log fires over the decades. The floor was made of light-coloured flagstones, about four inches thick and partly covered by a large, blue ornate rug that took away the coldness of the stone. The three doors that led off to other parts of the castle remained shut.

St Clair eased himself out of the yew and walnut smokers bow chair, which creaked all the way until his frame left it. He made his way to a small maple drinks cabinet that stood against the back wall. It held over thirty different, assorted whisky bottles. He started to pour drinks for them but then the telephone on the drinks table rang. St Clair answered it. He held the cordless phone under his chin so he could continue to pour out their drinks, but then stopped. The call, that had come into the castle routed via a secret location in Islington, was from the Controller. She told him that she had the Vatican's chief of police on the line, Signor Dámaso Nef. This would be the sixth time since the Templars had first been introduced to the Vatican by a high-ranking Interpol official, that they had been asked for their help. The high-ranking Interpol official had originally suggested them and vouched for them, as a group of extremely highly-principled professionals with security clearances with the FBI, Interpol, and Omega 1 and Omega 1S clearance with MI5 and MI6. He had also told the Vatican that this group normally only involved themselves in crimes against religion and its people, and that meant against any of the mainstream religions. They were unprejudiced when it came to their help. Whilst there were no formal or structured lines of communication between them, Dámaso Nef and Payne St Clair, the Templars' Grand Master, had always kept the back channels open. The Controller told St Clair that she had run the checks and confirmed it was Nef.

"Did he say what he wanted?" St Clair asked the Controller.

"He didn't and I didn't ask. He sounded a little flustered so I thought I had better put him directly through to you."

"Thanks Tiff. By the way, how are things in Islington?"

"Okay, but we will need the refit and upgrade soon. I can almost hear the mainframes groaning with the increased coms traffic we've been having."

St Clair smiled. "I know. I have spoken to Courtney and she and Bertram have a plan. It looks like the team will be installing the new upgrades in the New Year. Hang on in there, Tiff."

The Controller in Islington thanked him and put the call through.

"*Ciao amico mio come stai?*" Nef's voice was friendly but a little edgy.

"*Tutto bene*, Dámaso, thank you. How are you?" St Clair asked.

"I am good, St Clair." Nef's English was perfect. "Maybe I am a little older and a little wider around the waist since we last spoke, but I'm good."

"And your family? How is your daughter, Uma?"

"Ah, very well, very well indeed, *grazie mille*." He paused as if the next sentence was important, which of course it was. "The cardinals have given their permission for me to request your help again my friend."

"If it is possible, of course we will try."

"*Bene.*"

"Why don't you start at the beginning?"

"You have time now?"

"For you, always my friend, but do you mind if I put you on speaker. I am with colleagues." Nef agreed and St Clair pushed the speaker button.

"Can you hear me okay?" Nef asked.

"We can hear you just fine," St Clair told him.

"*Bene.* I will start then." The room in the castle went quiet as Nef spoke and only the hissing wood broke its silence. "One of the church's most precious and important items, from its signet ring collection, was stolen three days ago on the 15th, from Manchester, England. It was part of a consignment of Vatican assets being

43

transported in three shipping containers. The assets were going to different countries around the world. The cardinals do this for security reasons but also to make sure they are available to be seen by their flock in as many countries as possible."

"If your security is good, it seems sensible and reasonable," St Clair said. "I have seen your security measures up close from our dealings in the past. I am surprised that the thieves were able to track it to the UK and steal it."

"And now you start to see why we need your help, but it gets a little bit more complicated than that. For many years, the signet ring was held in a safe in the basement of a normal, simple looking building, one of hundreds, if not thousands, of properties that the Church owns. It is something we do. We keep certain items in the last place someone would expect to find them because they are often safer there than the places everyone would expect to find them, including the criminals.

"All the properties that we use for this have alarms and CCTV cameras of course. Some weeks ago, one of the operators in the CCTV control room monitoring a number of the properties, became suspicious of a person hanging around. This is not a building that people normally take any interest in. Nothing special about it. Nothing with history. The CCTV cameras picked out the man who looked like, we think, a Japanese tourist. Each time, he stood across the street from the building and each time, he took pictures, staying for fifteen minutes, and then he left. This was his routine three times in three days."

"You said that this property held the stolen signet ring, right?" St Clair asked him.

"*Si,* it was in that building. So, I followed protocol. I informed a number of cardinals of a possible problem at the property and told them that I had posted one of my men in the street that day. The Japanese man came again, just like before but this time it was different. He was there for only a few minutes. He took a call on his mobile phone and then he left, hurriedly. He did not come back again. It almost seemed like he knew we were there. The cardinals on the security committee decide that the signet ring would be placed in one of the containers that were going to

Manchester first. Then each container was being transported to different destinations around the world.

"Some of the assets in the containers were purchased by the Church as investments, some were historical or religious pieces. All were precious to the Church and most very, very valuable. The item that was stolen, the signet ring, is all of those: religious, historic and priceless. And, here's the added complication: it was the only thing that they took during the robbery in Manchester."

"You sent someone to check the containers?" St Clair asked. "And the police checked the customs manifest?"

"The real manifest was not something the local transport people had. Because of what had happened outside the building, we decided not to include the item on the customs manifest. In fact, it was placed inside a cigarette packet, inside a plastic bag and left on the floor of the container."

"Smart," St Clair said. "It's the last place someone would look. But, someone did!"

Nef went on to tell St Clair that the local police had caught the thief red-handed, that he had been caught in one of the three containers when they arrived. Nef said that the police told him that the man was known to the police. He was a forger and was after the 16th century Magellan painting of the fourteen stations of the crucifixion. He had a pocket full of valuable watches and the painting he was also in the act of stealing. He confessed to the police that he was going to make copies of the painting and sell them on, eventually selling the original to the highest bidder. He told them that he was alone.

St Clair laughed. "Seems our work is already done, then?"

"*Non cosi in fretta* – not so fast," Nef replied. "The British police did not know what else was missing, remember: they had a different manifest. I think the forger is a, how do you say, a *falsa pista?*"

"A red herring," Dominique called out. She spoke perfect Italian; she'd lived in Italy for many years and her mother was Italian.

"Yes. I think he is a red fish." Nef raised his voice to answer the person in the background. "The only thing stolen was the only item not on the manifest."

There was a pause in the conversation and then St Clair asked the obvious question: "Who did the signet ring belong to?"

Nef knew that, of course, he had to tell the man on the other end of the telephone, but despite taking precautions, he was troubled in case the conversation was overheard. He took a sip of his coffee and checked his door was still closed. His eyes darted to the windows; no one was lingering outside the windows. Still, he didn't want to come right out and say it.

"The *digitus secundus,* the Jupiter finger on the hand. The arch line under the Jupiter finger," he said, almost whispering his sentence. "You know of this?"

"I know of this; it is called Jupiter's ring," St Clair said.

"Yes, yes, *l'anello del re.*" Nef looked at the file in front of him, the one marked '*Privato, solo all'ettenzione del capo della polizia* – Private, for the attention of the chief of police only,' underneath, the title of the file: '*L'anello del re.*' "You know what I mean by this '*l'anello del re,*' St Clair? You know my meaning now?"

St Clair's realisation of what the chief of police actually meant just dawned on him and his face gave it away. "I know what you mean," St Clair confirmed.

Dominique didn't. She looked at Jonathan. She figured this was Vatican business so, as an ex-priest, he would know what it meant. Jonathan shrugged his shoulders to communicate that he had no idea what it meant.

St Clair sipped his whisky, slowly; everything was now slipping into place. What Nef had just told him made finding the signet ring almost impossible. However, even if St Clair wanted to help, he knew now he couldn't. They had started talking about a robbery. He now knew that it was far more than that. He knew that Nef had bigger problems to come, and so did they. It was the last thing he wanted, another set of troubles, but he sensed they were heading his way.

"You and I have known each other a long time, Dámaso. I think you already know my answer and you know why I cannot help you."

This time Jonathan looked at Dominique. It was her turn to shrug her shoulders.

"*Merda* – shit!" Nef exclaimed.

"*Merda*?" Jonathan mouthed to Dominique. "What *merda*?" His hand went for the coins in his pocket, his tell-tale sign that he was nervous, but she had taken to hiding all their loose change.

"You think it is a job from inside the Vatican?" Nef asked him.

The fire hissed and somewhere off voices could be heard as a group of Knights were walking along one of the many corridors in the castle. St Clair already knew that if it was an inside job, then helping the chief of police would be virtually impossible. He'd had experience of the cardinals politicking before. The experience and frustration he had faced from a section of the cardinals had almost cost the lives of some of the Templars.

St Clair sipped at his whisky. Then he spoke.

"You have two very big problems, my friend. Firstly, there are only three kinds of people who steal religious objects of this magnitude and can pull off a job of this complexity. There are those who steal for money. These are just criminals. Sophisticated they may be, resourceful and clever, yes, but criminals all the same. They sell to collectors, individuals, groups or syndicates: people who will pay large sums of money to get their hands on the impossible. The problem here is, if the piece has gone to one of these, you will spend years trying to find it because the piece will be hidden away in some secret location just for their own private viewing. Next, there are those who steal because they have a grievance against the Vatican, or Catholics or God. This theft is normally motivated by politics or religious differences, often grievances that can go back a few thousand years. These are much easier to solve because the perpetrators often broadcast their crime, although getting an item back can cause wars. And then we have the third kind, a blend of the other two. They collect only the revered, the most unobtainable religious artefacts and also, but sometimes because of it, they have a grievance against the church. There are only three people I know like this, three people who would dare to do something on this scale. One is rotting in a

Russian cell and I think she is still there. The second has not been seen or heard of for over a year and rumours are that he is dead. And the third is a man, who, if he does have your signet ring, and I suspect he does, you my friend would be better off forgetting about."

Nef started to say something. St Clair knew he was about to say something along the lines of 'I cannot forget about it, it's my job—' St Clair saved him the trouble.

"If it is him, and if he even suspects you know about him, if he even gets one hint that you are on to him, he will be gone. He will disappear and I can assure you, you will never catch him. We have first-hand experience of trying to find him. But, before you ever got close enough, he would kill you and he will kill your entire family. That, my dear friend is your first problem. Your second problem, you already know, and it's the reason I cannot help you. This is clearly an inside job, and I cannot help you to find your traitor. As outsiders, we could never have the access we would need to even begin to unravel this treachery. My guess is that someone with a high security clearance or a very senior clergyman is your traitor. Dámaso, I am not a betting man, but if I was—"

"You would say that it had to be a senior clergyman, a cardinal," Nef said.

"I just go on the facts. The call to the Japanese man casing the building: it had to be someone warning him that day. And, the fact that he even knew the signet ring was in that place. How did he know? Who knew? The containers in Manchester – whoever stole the signet ring from there, how did they know the containers were there? Knowing exactly where to find the signet ring, the least likely place it should have been, in a plastic bag on the ground. The elaborate red herring so the police would think they had caught their man. It gave the real thieves time to escape. I think you have an insider all right and a powerful one at that."

"You think it's our *Sancti Furem?*"

"Holy Thief," Dominique whispered, translating for Jonathan.

Outside Nef's office, there was a commotion and someone was knocking on his office door.

"I have to go. Thank you, my friend," he said. "You are telling me to find *Sancti Furem*. This is our only hope of retrieving the Church's possession. I will try, but we have been looking for him for a long time. I will let you know how it goes." Nef was about to say his goodbyes, when St Clair interrupted him.

"Dámaso, send me the stills from the CCTV pictures of the fake tourist outside the building. We'll take a look at them and see if we can help you match him on our database. With your permission, we will ask a couple of agencies to also take a look, but we will not mention where this came from."

"That would be helpful," Nef said. "Oh, I nearly forgot, Falvio, the officer I sent to Manchester to check what had been stolen, he reported that the local police were following up on a report that two men had been seen, how do you say, *in giro*?"

"Hanging about," Dominique called out.

"The lady has good Italian," Nef said.

Jonathan looked at his wife with pride.

"Her mother was Italian; she is fluent," St Clair told Nef.

"*Molto bene, Signora.* The local Manchester police said that the two had been seen hanging about not far from the crime scene. They are checking the petrol stations, local hotels and shops in the area in case they used any of these places. If they come up with anything, I will send that to you also."

St Clair and Nef finished their call. St Clair finished pouring the drinks, then sat back down in his smokers bow chair – it creaked with his arrival.

"It's the *l'anello del re*?" Dominique asked St Clair. "It's the *l'anello del re* that has you spooked. Nef talked about the arch line under the *digitus secundus*," she turned to Jonathan. "*Digitus secundus*, it's Latin, it means second digit."

"Precisely," St Clair confirmed. "The index finger, but the *digitus secundus* is also known as Jupiter finger in palmistry. The Jupiter ring is a curved line just under the base of that finger."

"But, Jupiter is not a king," Dominique said. "Nef said *l'anello del re,* which translates as 'the king's ring'."

"Remember, he whispered those words to me, Dominique, and then asked me if I knew what he meant by *l'anello del re*. Jupiter ring is one name for that line at the base of the index finger; the other name it is given is Solomon's ring. He was trying to tell me that the signet ring of King Solomon had been stolen. And he did it that way because he knew not many people would be familiar with palmistry. If it was Solomon's ring, it has his seal carved within its face.

"I told him he had two problems, in fact there are three, although the third is not his problem; it will more likely be ours over the coming weeks. I think the ring was stolen for a specific reason and I don't mean just for its historical importance and value. I mean something far more nefarious, something dark, something very dark. If you know the ring's history, you will know what I mean."

They all finished their drinks in silence.

Payne St Clair's Higher Council of the Templar Order was down two Council members. The Nine Worthies were now just six Worthies and counting himself made seven. André Sabath could no longer participate on the Council. St Clair's strong right-hand Knight, his best friend, was terminally ill and lying paralysed in a hospital bed in Lebanon and they all knew, including André, that he had little time left. The other Worthy, Norman Smith, a member of the Higher Council and also their Sergeant at Arms for many years, had retired after a lifetime of service. St Clair knew he would need a full Council in the coming weeks because they had re-engaged with the Abaddons in Romania and if his hunch about the ring was right, more trouble was heading their way. He would call the other six together to discuss the appointment of two new Worthies and, to tell them about the ring.

Payne St Clair could feel the low menacing hum of it coming; the foreboding was barely perceptible, but it was there, like the faint sound of a far-off drum. The rhythm slowly grew, ever heading towards them. And the rhythm had a name, and its name was **Abaddon.** But now there was a new menace coming out of the shadows and he knew its name; its name was Salah El-Din and he was about to make his move.

Chapter 4

The Lawyer and the Devil

Timothy Crowthorp's Crown Court trial, in October 2008, lasted just four short days. Many had expected a case like that to last a lot longer; they usually did, at least twice as long, if not more. The case made the news; it made the national news because he was a lawyer and a QC. The newspapers had a field day with the story and it was reported that a number of his ex-girlfriends – albeit who had all been paid escorts – made five thousand pounds each for their stories. However, those who had information of a more salacious nature, were paid even more. Unable to counteract those stories because he was confined to police custody and all his assets were seized, so he had no money anyway, the stories ran and ran. However, he'd figured the best way to stay alive now was to remain in police custody and to keep as quiet as possible. He knew a certain person wanted his life. He was disadvantaged, alone, broke, but being protected for free. On some days, the irony of it pleased him; on others he was too depressed to care.

There was never any doubt what the outcome of the trial would be. The evidence against Crowthorp was more than watertight and extremely admissible considering he had made a full confession on the tapes sent to the police, and when formally charged by police, he again confessed. Many were surprised, if not a little confused, by his eagerness to confess, which added immeasurable value to his prosecution's case, but no one other than him knew that if he had any chance of living, it would be hidden away behind tall walls and wire fences. Despite this, he knew that the man who was his boss, a pathological and violent man with innumerable resources, would take his life sooner or later.

The presiding judge sent Crowthorp to prison for seven years but not before lecturing the hurriedly disbarred QC. In his closing remarks, the judge called Crowthorp, "… a scourge on the profession of law, a man that fashioned his life on a canvas of greed, enticed by the seduction of money and the exuberance of power." He said he found no evidence, not even a hint, of best intention in the disgraced QC's actions. He told him that his obvious enmity to those around him was clear and that he had shamed the legal profession, the law and the people's trust in lawyers – although the press had a field day with the judge's last statement: people's trust in lawyers!

Post-trial, some said that the lawyer defending Crowthorp gave the case less than his best and didn't seem too sad about the outcome.

The trial of the estate boss, who Templars had left for the authorities at Birmingham, New Street train station in 2008, had taken place just one week before Crowthorp's. Crowthorp's testimony helped with his conviction but the prosecution had a fairly cast-iron case anyway. The estate boss was tried and despite his substitute lawyer's attempts – his normal lawyer was incarcerated in a prison cell not too far away – he was sent away to serve a fifteen-year sentence for the possession of narcotics, distribution and intent to distribute, and a charge from a previous case that had been pending, plus an additional three years for the drug money he was carrying at Birmingham, New Street train station.

At the same time, indictments, charges, trials and sentences were taking place against a number of people in the US and the UK. People from Scotland Yard, the FBI and the DEA were all being tried in what was known in the newspapers as the 'UNITY Trials.' Guilty verdicts were handed to every defendant and many were sent away for a long time.

*

At first, Crowthorp really struggled in prison. He was a small man, five foot five, with a balding head. He was thin and stooped when he walked. An only child, he found social pleasantries difficult and he had a disagreeable habit of smacking his lips every time he spoke. He was unmarried and had no family – so no one came to see him – but he'd had a series of girlfriends before going inside, all much younger than his fifty-six years. The fact that they were only interested in his money never bothered him. He was a realist, who liked to have young, pretty women on his arm. Some of the inmates nicknamed him Louis Dega, after the small, frail bookkeeper who was in prison with Papillon.

Crowthorp had worked for the ruthless criminal, Salah El-Din, for many years. He had been paid well to keep the estate bosses out of prison. The estate bosses distributed and sold Salah El-Din's drugs to the poor and to the wealthy alike – as long as they could pay there was no discrimination. Those drugs came from Colombia where Salah El-Din worked side by side with the cartel. However, all of that came crashing down once the Templars had interrogated Crowthorp and were finally able to see what and who made UNITY, Salah El-Din's criminal organisation. Crowthorp's revelations, Interpol, Morgan Clay being planted inside the criminal's UK headquarters, John Wolf, the Indian finding Stranks, André Sabath and his Knights in Cairo, the Knights who fought Salah El-Din's men in Cumbria and many, many, more played their part in the criminal's downfall but the trigger point was Crowthorp.

The ex-lawyer had been an outcast within the legal fraternity on the outside. Other lawyers disliked him and he disliked them. He provoked lengthy debate amongst the clerks of the court. They based their lives on traditionally accepted values and legal applications; he based his purely on how much money he could make. They saw him for what he was, a crooked lawyer. He had, it was whispered, turned native, become a crook like the mysterious client he represented. Back then, before his demise in 2008, his life was good, but one late night the Templars tracked him down to his flat in Canterbury, Kent, in southern England. They had knocked on his door and stupidly, he'd removed the security chain and opened the door to them.

Payne St Clair, the Order's Grand Master, had administered sodium thiopental straight into Crowthorp's main vein in his left arm. It took fifteen minutes to work. Dominique had set up a video camera. Once the truth drug had begun to work, the questions began.

"Where is Salah El-Din?" the Templars asked.

"I spoke to him last night, at his Knightsbridge offices." Crowthorp gave the Templars the address and the address where Stranks could be found. The questions went on and on and gradually it dawned on Crowthorp what was happening. He figured out what they had injected him with. He knew he was doomed, everything he knew would come spilling out of his mouth. Salah El-Din would kill him for his treachery. Crowthorp knew this was exactly how the narcissistic, egocentric, criminal would see it: treachery. His life was over. For two hours, he told St Clair, Dominique and the ex-priest, Jonathan Rose, the answer to every question they asked.

The Templars sent the video tape of Crowthorp being questioned to the police – anonymously. Timothy Crowthorp went to prison in 2008 and had spent every day of his sentence looking over his shoulder for his boss's retribution in the form of another inmate with a steel shank in his hand, but it never came. However, the wait itself had almost killed him and there were days when he wished it would just happen and it would all be over. Timothy Crowthorp slept poorly that first year in prison.

However, in time, the ex-QC started to make a name for himself. He started reviewing the case files of other inmates: he studied their cases, wrote their appeal papers and briefed their Briefs. This afforded him some protection from the inside. However, he knew that no matter how much he curried favour with other inmates, when his ex-boss wanted him dead, he would die, and painfully.

Soon he began to enjoy light duties and the first choice of goods from the inmates who ran the illegal commissary. All in all, despite the fact that he had a death sentence hanging over his head, and he was incarcerated, he considered himself lucky – in comparison to a dank, shallow grave, and his mutilated body lying stripped of its skin. He'd read about the ex-newspaper reporter in America, John Dukes. About his decomposing body, stripped of all its flesh. Two starving cats had eaten part of his face. The landlady reported she'd heard screaming but had ignored it because she often heard him screaming. The message that had been left on Dukes's wall by his executioners read: *Nathaniel, so it is again*. Nathaniel, also known as Saint Bartholomew, was a disciple of John the Baptist. He suffered martyrdom in Armenia when he was skinned alive.

*

As 2012 dawned, Crowthorp began to think less and less about the fate that awaited him; it had been nearly four years. Whilst it was always on his mind, he was able to put it to the back of his mind and get through his days without that sick, churning feeling in the pit of his stomach 24/7 that had engulfed him during his first year in prison. Then a chance meeting changed the game completely.

A young inmate was signed into the medical bay for close observation: he'd been there a number of days. He'd been lucky; the prison doctor had given him painkillers a week before because he'd been badly brutalised by the other inmates, which was a regular occurrence. He was bloodied, bruised, with a cracked rib and a fractured collar bone when he was carried into the medical bay by two prison guards. The painkillers had an adverse effect on him and he was rushed to hospital; there they diagnosed him with Stevens-Johnson syndrome, a condition caused by an adverse reaction to certain medication, in his case, the painkillers. He'd started with plain flu symptoms, but it quickly manifested itself as a red rash and blisters on his skin; also, his mucous membranes, the lining to the canals leading to his respiratory system, were under attack. He was in a bad way. He was lucky though; the doctors at the hospital quickly diagnosed it. Now he was back in prison, in the medical bay, the affected skin finally dying and peeling off.

Crowthorp was sent to the medical bay for treatment. He had slipped on a newly mopped floor and twisted his ankle. It was just him

55

and the young inmate in the medical bay and when the doctor had finished applying a stretch bandage to Crowthorp's ankle, he left to make his rounds with one of the prison guards.

The young inmate was chatty. He realised that Crowthorp was not like the others and this put him at ease straightway. He found the older man educated, and he seemed to have no desire to rape him, unlike half of D wing. The young inmate introduced himself as Michael, but Crowthorp already knew he was the disgraced Catholic priest other inmates had talked about. Michael had had a hard incarceration so far. He wasn't strong or muscular, he didn't have friends in there, and he was not affiliated with any gang inside, so he had no protection. He was alone, easy prey for the imprisoned, pent-up, sadistic bullies who plagued him daily. Despite this, Crowthorp found him engaging and scholarly. It was the first conversation Crowthorp had had since being sent to prison that didn't involve a discussion about sex, cigarettes, innocence, sex and cigarettes!

The two men talked for nearly two hours. The normal guardedness was now gone as the two men, without ill intent to the other, sat and chatted like normal people. As Crowthorp got to know more about Michael, and Michael began to know more about Crowthorp, they both began to realise that they might be able to benefit each other, that each had the ability to change the other's situation. By the time the doctor was back, they'd agreed on their plan.

Later that day, after being signed off sick and released by the doctor to go back to genpop, and armed with two aspirins and a fresh stretch bandage, Timothy Crowthorp hobbled back to his cell. He sat alone on his bed; his cell mate was working in the laundry and would not be back for three hours. He pondered his options. Up until a few hours ago, he'd had no options. It was the same routine every day, seven days a week, fifty-two weeks a year. However, there was a chance, a really slim chance, if he played his cards right. He shook the thought from his mind; *one step at a time*, he thought. He knew what he needed to do with the information Michael had shared with him but Crowthorp was scared. What if his old boss had forgotten about him, or lost track of which prison he was in, or was just too busy with whatever illegal enterprises he was involved in now to think about him, if he now made the call and his plan didn't work, then he doubted he would see out the end of the week. He could, he considered, do nothing with the new information. He could keep his head down and go on the way he had been going but he knew it was never going to be good enough for him. If there was a possible way out, he wanted to take it. He wanted his old life back. He wanted the power over others again, instead of the way it was now: everyone had power over him. He wanted the money and his lifestyle back.

"But are you willing to gamble with your life?" he muttered to himself. He sighed and stared at the barren cell he called home. He listened to the bangs and the crashes, to the shouts, the slamming of metal doors, rattling keys, scraping of chair legs. He listened to the muffled voices of too many people in too small a space. The sound of prison was depressing, it was alien, suffocating, but he'd noticed, as the years had passed, despite hating it, it had become acceptably familiar. He knew he was becoming institutionalised. He decided to make the phone call.

He sent word he was calling in a debt from one of the criminals he had helped with his complicated case. The contraband mobile phone, smuggled into the prison a week earlier, was sent to his cell.

Timothy Crowthorp was a clever man. In the court room he had been a master tactician, orator, storyteller and closer. Now he needed all of those skills and every ounce of his cunning. He needed to deliver an outstanding, convincing closing argument, with more persuasion and attraction than he had ever done before. This time, it was not his client's life that was on the line, it was his. Crowthorp had an ace card to play; he knew his boss's weaknesses.

He sat on his metal framed bed and made the call. He was nervous. He was calling all the old numbers, all the old 2008 numbers in the hope that not all of them had been seized by the authorities that had dismantled UNITY; he hoped that one of them still worked. He listened to the ring tone of the fifth number he'd called; it clicked and someone answered.

*

Salah El-Din

Salah El-Din had spent the time between 2008 and 2012, rebuilding a drug network of supply and distribution, which spanned halfway around the world, with himself as the middleman, the deal maker. He'd made new friends, powerful and violent friends; he'd also rekindled old cartel friends in South America. And he did all of this largely hidden away from the world.

However, the ruthless criminal could never entirely leave his most driving passion, more important to him than money and power: his yearning, need and fixation with acquiring precious, venerated objects for his collection. For him and him alone. His particular penchant was for religious relics and artefacts, mainly Christian, Muslim and Jewish. He was obsessed by them: possessing them dominated his life. They were his children and he would die for them. They engulfed and controlled his life and they always had.

He knew each piece in his collection intimately, every twist, cut, scratch, colour and stroke because he had craved them, needed them. He tracked them down and then he stole them, often with terminal consequences for the owners. Then he hid those stunningly, beautiful, historical works of great importance away in secret vaults and secret rooms: they were his and for his eyes only. His desire to own them equalled his need to take them from their owners; it was a drug and his addiction's edict. They had no right to them. They did not appreciate them as he would. They belonged to him.

He despised the weak and took advantage of them; he despised the strong and destroyed them. He had always got what he wanted. He had maimed, tortured, disfigured, imprisoned, blackmailed, intimidated, persecuted and slaughtered for the things he most craved.

However, there was one very specific religious object he desired more than any other, the very thing he could never have, the thing that he'd sacrificed his entire criminal empire for, the thing he had always believed existed, although millions of people didn't. His relentless, savage pursuit of it drove his behaviour: a psychological canvas against which his crazed and evil life was fashioned. He craved the Ark of the Covenant.

He had never given up in the belief that the Knights Templar had not totally perished at the hands of the king of France in 1307 and, along with things they had taken out of the Holy Land, a number of them had escaped from France and survived. But not only survived, he was convinced they thrived. Whilst the memory of the Templars had slowly faded and centuries later they were all but forgotten. However, he was one who had always believed that they were still out there, in the shadows. He believed they had the Ark of the Covenant, the one thing he coveted most. And, Cumbria four years ago had confirmed it for him.

From his humble beginnings as a small-time crook, Salah El-Din had grown into one of the most influential underworld criminals in London, Washington and Cairo, where he mostly operated. In those cities, he had systematically set about removing his rivals to take over their operations. And, with his wealth increasing, he paid off judges, politicians and senior-ranking law enforcement officers; in 2008, at his zenith, he was one of the most powerful figures in organised crime.

There was evidence that when he was still a very young boy, he had been involved in the death of a young Christian Arab. Beaten and stabbed repeatedly, the boy's body was found at the bottom of a well in the local village. Because of this and his worsening behaviour, he was made to pray alone every day and was not allowed out of the house. He was whipped every day and given only rice and water as penance for the shame he had brought on the family name. But villagers recollected that the boy grew worse. Many, in recalling him, said, "He was possessed with a wicked Jinn, a demon;" they all admitted that they had been scared of him.

His father, a religious zealot, was known to beat his six off-springs harshly and regularly, and Salah El-Din more so. His father had mysteriously died; they said it was a slow and painful death.

Salah El-Din lost millions when his criminal empire collapsed in 2008; he lost many of his treasured objects as they were taken in raids across his properties. However, since 2008, Salah El-

Din had been stock piling new cash reserves, and he was rebuilding his private collection. Slowly his hidden treasure of stolen, rare, religious artefacts was starting to grow again. It was impressive even in its reduced state, but no one ever saw them except for him. He never sold anything from his collection. He never acquired anything for his collection that he thought he might one day sell. To him that would be pointless and prove that the object held no real meaning to him. What he acquired he wanted. What he wanted he stole. He rarely paid. The act of taking it from another gave him almost as much pleasure.

He had lived well in his buildings in Cairo and Washington but he loved staying at 890-923 Knightsbridge Court Crescent, London, his main UK property. It was there that he felt safest; it was there he kept most of his valuable collection. The Middle Eastern looking man, in his mid-fifties, tall with silver hair, sharp features and piercing black eyes, could occasionally be seen there but never for long. The irony of having felt safest there with what happened to him there, was not lost on him.

During the years between 2008 and 2012, Salah El-Din had slowly rebuilt his criminal activities. However, this time he allowed no digital records, no computers, no records. All of the latest digital protections had been installed at his Knightsbridge Court property. His depraved IT magician, Stranks, saw to that. Lasered patchwork beams protected the offices and corridors at night, re-usable paper so none ever left the building and if it did, it was weighed against a running tally. Chipped name badges tracked every employee and every visitor, so security knew where everyone was at any time. No unplanned meetings with other colleagues were allowed – no corners to whisper in. Stranks had set up multiple IP addresses for him, in multiple countries; Stranks configured complex stack servers in Knightsbridge, so that his dealings could not be tracked or linked. He had a virtual superhighway of data flowing to keep his illicit empire alive. It was Knightsbridge where he was infiltrated. It was Knightsbridge where his secrets were stolen, and it was Knightsbridge where he lost the majority of his collection. Despite his technological ring of steel, designed, installed and maintained by Stranks, it had not saved him. In the end, his downfall was the technology and his lawyer, Timothy Crowthorp.

Now he made sure that he had nothing that would entrap him. No technology. He had no one close, no Stranks, no one other than paid protectors who were excessively loyal. He made sure they knew nothing. He only gave his orders at the last minute and he rotated the bodyguards on a regular basis so there was no pattern to his activities or theirs.

His skill at staying below the radar had enhanced since 2008; he became a harder target for the authorities to catch. Despite the ensuing years, they had not been able to locate him or find any trace of him. Many of the people who had originally worked on 'Operation Roulette Wheel,' had moved on. Some had left and a few had died. His case docket had been joined by many more. He was still a wanted man, one of Interpol's and the FBI's most wanted, but so were many thousands of others.

Salah El-Din had forsaken the UK, USA and Egypt and had spent most of his time between Spain and Salalah, in the south of the Sultanate of Oman and Asia. Opium consumption was big in Asia and he still had many contacts in Colombia – the ICC had not managed to close down all the cartel's operations, and they were up and running again within six weeks. Asia was a perfect bounce back location for him. He had established supply contacts across Central America and Mexico and for the past few years, Afghanistan. His new Asian partners liked the Arab; he delivered what he said he would and he understood their business.

Salah El-Din was soon back on his feet. And the old demon of greed, his barbaric nature and, of course, his craving, lust and infatuation with the Ark of the Covenant, and therefore that meant the Templars, was stronger than ever.

*

Place: Spain

Salah El-Din was at his *casa de campo* – house in the countryside. He had bought it through an offshore company, so no paper trail. The seven-bedroom house in the Spanish region of Valencia on the *Costa Blanca* – White Coast, was his new haven. His appearance and skin tone made him look like a local, and because of his olive skin, he was often mistaken for a Spaniard.

There he could relax a little. He was not known and he made sure he portrayed the lifestyle of a private businessman with a Spanish retreat. He kept two bodyguards with him at the house, and three other bodyguards were housed in a small rented house just next door. In the old days he had had just two bodyguards: after their death by the Templars, he decided to double that number. However, all his bodyguards were Asians, and when they told him that the figure four is sometimes pronounced '*shi*', which means death, he sent for a fifth bodyguard from his friends across the water. They were all trained assassins; all had exceptional fighting skills, but were thugs, killers and extortionists all the same. They were all Japanese Yakuza.

The day was hot. Salah El-Din was listening to his glorious Wagner, air conditioning on full, fans spinning frantically. His shutters were down to keep out the sun and he sat alone in his den, just off the master bedroom. His two bodyguards were busy maintaining the house and their boss's lifestyle.

A phone in a canvas holdall he kept underneath the bed buzzed. It was the only phone he had kept from 2008. He'd received just two calls on it in four years. All the other phones in the holdall were burners – he got through eight per month. The phone buzzed again. Only five people had that number, who were mostly in Salalah. He answered the phone.

Timothy Crowthorp moved uneasily on his prison cell bed. The mattress was thin and lumpy; he'd never got used to it and he never would. His stomach churned. Then there was the click of the call being answered. A pause, then he heard the voice. It was the voice he had not heard since 2008, four years ago. The voice he thought he would never hear again. He steeled himself. He needed all his wits about him now; he didn't need the alarmed, anxious dread he was feeling.

"Yes." The cold voice at the other end of the phone seemed to hang there. His voice was harsh, icy and without emotion. It was him; it was Salah El-Din.

Crowthorp had not spoken to Salah El-Din since his capture and internment. He had seven numbers memorised, which he'd used to contact his boss in the old days. This was the fifth he'd tried: it worked.

"It's me," Crowthorp managed to muster. "Please don't hang up, not until you have heard what I've got to say." The silence seemed to hang there like the moments before the hangman releases the trap door lever and the crowd gasps.

"You're not dead then, Lawyer?" The silence finally broken; the scorn connecting the words was tacit. "I'd almost forgotten about you. You are still alive and I am reminded I need to kill you. HMP Bristol, isn't it? D wing?" His voice clipped, curt and woven with impassiveness. Every vowel, noun, adjective and verb was pronounced with menace, just as Crowthorp remembered it.

Crowthorp shivered. "I just need you to listen to me for thirty seconds. That's all I ask. You do what you have to do after that."

There was a pause, then Crowthorp heard, "Thirty, twenty-nine, twenty-eight—"

"There is a priest here in prison," he started hurriedly. "He's serving a five-year stretch and has done three years of it so far. His name is Father Michael. The Church stripped him of his priesthood, of course, but the inmates still call him Father Michael."

"Twenty-five, twenty-four—" the menacing voice at the other end of the phone counted with purpose.

"He's not had a good time of it in prison. Inmates are contradictory by nature; they commit criminal acts, but pray to God every night to help them, and look after their mothers. So, any person of the cloth who has defiled their vows is always in for a hard time. Currently he belongs to a rather nasty thug in here that runs most of D wing. Father Michael runs errands for him, prays for his mother's health and reluctantly comforts him when the lights go out. Occasional he gets passed around; he gets brutalised on a regular basis."

"Nineteen, Eighteen—"

63

He knew he was giving details that the man at the end of the phone didn't want, nor had the patience for. "Michael told me that he used to work in the Vatican, for over ten years, before his incarceration." Crowthorp thought he heard a beat change in Salah El-Din's breathing at the mention of the Vatican. "His criminal career ended abruptly when he was caught passing through customs at Heathrow airport with a ruby and diamond encrusted bracelet that had been stolen from Catholic Church offices in Abuja, Nigeria. Father Michael had just landed from Abuja. Airport police, Vatican police and Scotland Yard, all believed he was not the planner of the heist, but merely a willing lacky. Whoever else may have been involved, Michael never did reveal. I did a little digging. I reached out to some of my ex-informants who knew about the robbery back then and they told me that many believed it had to be a total inside job."

"Twelve, eleven—"

Jesus, Crowthorp thought, *this has to work.* "So, one day when I was in the Medical bay, we started talking and Michael told me a lot of things; he said he would tell me a lot more if I could help him. I told him I could help him, maybe get some time knocked off his sentence and get him full protection whilst he's in jail." Crowthorp paused. There was no jury for him to stand in front of, to look deep into their eyes and show them he was a compassionate lawyer who just wanted justice done. But he didn't need to see a jury; he knew Salah El-Din was hooked by the next words that came out of his mouth.

"I know this story, Lawyer" Salah El-Din said, no longer counting. "There have been a number of thefts of Catholic assets where the authorities have thought it was an inside job. There are rumours of such a person inside the Vatican. I have tried to find this person myself, Crowthorp. I am not convinced he exists. What eviden—"

"*Sancti Furem,*" Crowthorp said, cutting him off, as if dealing the winning piece of evidence at a trial. He was mindful he had just been referred to as Crowthorp again, and not 'Lawyer.'

"*Sancti Furem,* the Holy Thief," Salah El-Din said.

"Michael told me that behind closed doors it is what the Vatican police call him: *Sancti Furem* – the Holy Thief." Crowthorp paused. He waited to hear the counting. There was none. *Got you*, he thought, *I got you*. "Michael says he knows who he is. For protection and my help with his case, he will tell me, tell us. I told him what I wanted. He will make the introductions. I want to give this to you."

Salah El-Din now controlled his breathing. He was aware it was getting heavy. "How does he know this man?" he asked.

"He was his consort. This man had been Michael's priest when he was growing up, before the man rose to dizzy heights within the church and headed for the Vatican. He had Michael perform oral sex on him, when Michael was just ten years old. On Michael's twelfth birthday, the man took him to bed and had sex with him. And then he regularly had sex with him after that. Michael told me he loved the man. I guess Stockholm syndrome. Eventually, Michael became a priest and it didn't take long for the man to arrange a job for him at the Vatican, so they would be close, so Michael would be obliging again".

"Priests!" Salah El-Din's voice rose. "I hate priests. And you believe this fool?"

"Yes, I believe him. He has no reason to lie because he knows he gets no help until he has made the introduction and I have confirmed we have the *Sancti Furem*."

The silence wasn't long. Salah El-Din was already structuring the steps in his mind of what would need to be done to verify the story, and then to maximise the contact, to the full.

"This means you get access to Vatican treasu—"

"Shhh," Salah El-Din interrupted. And then he said, "Welcome back, Timothy."

Crowthorp breathed a massive sigh of relief. He'd gone from dead, to Lawyer, to Crowthorp, to Timothy and all within ten minutes. *The defence rests my Lord*, he thought and then smiled.

He attended his second parole hearing not long after that call and this time parole was granted. His ex-boss, now his boss again, had done what he did best. He had manipulated, frightened, blackmailed and threatened people to get what he wanted: Crowthorp out of jail and back on his payroll.

*

Date: Later that year

It was November 2012 and Crowthorp and the young woman had stolen a number of valuable items for Salah El-Din – although the woman never knew who Crowthorp's boss was, or indeed that he had a boss. However, the Manchester job was their fourth job, and it was the first working with information supplied via Michael, who was now also out on parole, from the '*Sancti Furem* – the Holy Thief.'

Crowthorp planned all their jobs. Once he was given their mark, he was the initiator, the person who called the shots before and during the robberies. He was never too close to the scene of the crime, but always close enough to pick up the young woman at the end of the job. His boss would tell him what to steal and Crowthorp planned the how.

The young woman was the perpetrator, the person who went in, the person who carried out the crime. She had the gymnastic skills that made her a good thief, a cat burglar. She had speed, was never afraid, always focused, always professional. She was agile and could get to, into, across, up or down most places where others would struggle.

The young women didn't want to steal for Crowthorp, but she had no choice in the matter. He'd started to look for her before he left prison. He'd managed to hide away some of his money from the courts who had imposed draconian – in his view – civil forfeiture in his sentence and had seized all of his assets, including his bank accounts. However, his illicit stash was safe and practically untraceable – he'd learnt a trick or two from his old boss.

He had employed a number of specialists, ex-police who had leaned too much towards the criminal side and got kicked off the force. One of them located her; she was studying at a UK university. After he got out of prison and had got his life back on track, Crowthorp went to see her. He made her a Godfather offer, the kind you can't refuse, the kind that would be terminal if you did refuse. She started to steal for him.

It was all going well for the crooked lawyer, Timothy Crowthorp, and he now considered himself safe. However, he did not realise just how unsafe he actually was. He was always watched. Every job that they did, there were always the watchers close by: he never knew. Crowthorp had made the mistake of thinking he was back in a position of trust with his boss. He never was; no one ever was. Salah El-Din's evil, narcissistic and murderous tendencies had only grown stronger since Crowthorp had been in prison. Having his criminal empire, UNITY, dismantled by numerous law enforcement agencies in 2008 had left him more dangerous than ever before.

*

Salah El-Din

Salah El-Din was nearly back to where he had been before his downfall, following the battle with the Templars in Cumbria.

What drove him had not changed in all those years. His fixation never faltered: to seize the Ark and kill the Templars, all of them. One action needed the other action for his perfect storm. They were symbiotic: they were his life. However, this time he would not fail. This time he would have his prize and he would have their deaths.

He knew that back in 2008, he had made the mistakes and not the Templars. They had not made any mistakes. In the ensuing four years he had played those events over and over in his mind because he had failed. He had lost the battle and lost the Ark and barely escaped with his life.

He could still see the Cumbrian farmhouse in his mind's eye. It was the 16th August 2008 and he'd spent months preparing to kill the Templars and take the Ark. His ship's captain, Murry, had the anthrax on board and was sailing straight for Israel. Getting the anthrax was no mean feat, but worth it because the Templars agreed the trade: the Ark for the lives of the Jews, just as he had guessed they would.

He had the Templars arrive at the farmhouse in Cumbria, his location for the trade. He had one of his snipers hidden near the hedgerow and a small group of armed mercenaries hidden in the coppice at the back of the farmhouse along with two more snipers. He had felt safe. He had felt powerful. He'd wanted to be there, to see it for himself, to see the Ark. It was a risk, but he couldn't help himself:

he could not entrust the trade to anyone else, his hubris clouding his natural instinct to never allow himself to be caught out in the open or be seen.

They had arrived early. He could still feel the tension that had gripped him. He was about to get what he had strived for all his life; it would put all of his other prized artefacts into the shadows.

He remembered being in front of them, talking to them but knowing something was wrong. He couldn't put his finger on it but he felt it. Now, thinking about it, they were too confident for people who were about to give away the greatest religious artefact mankind had ever known.

Then the Templar revealed to him what was happening, what chaos and destruction they were wreaking across his organisation as he stood on a farm track. He remembered giving the signal to his bodyguard, his sniper and the armed men waiting in the coppice. The bullets started hailing down and all hell broke loose. He could still see the mayhem in his mind, hear the tumult; he could sometimes still smell the gunpowder.

He remembered seeing a woman open the door of the white van and fall; she'd been hit. Then he saw the priest from Washington, Rose, hit in the upper body and it looked bad. His men from the coppice were advancing.

He had dived at the man with the white hair and white beard. He didn't give him a chance to go for his gun. They both hit the ground hard, but Salah El-Din was winded. The white-haired man took out a small four-inch blade from an ankle sheath. He had tried to block the thrust, but he was still winded and much of his strength had been sapped. He had felt the steel slide into his side and the pain hitting him.

The noise had been deafening and he knew help was not coming: his mercenaries were pinned down. It was then he started to look around for the closest spider hole. He had six built, six holes dug in the ground, about four feet deep and just wide enough for a man to crouch down in. The top, a trap door, was made of strong wood, unyielding if anyone walked over it and covered with surrounding foliage. He'd learnt the trick from a Japanese contact who had called them octopus pots. He'd told him that the Japanese had used them in the Philippines and Iwo Jima.

He remembered lying on the ground and feeling his blood soaking into his shirt and sticking to him. Then his break came. Someone called that the priest was dead. The man with the white hair and white beard shouted, "Get him to the Ark, quickly!"

He saw his opportunity. The nearest spider hole was just twelve feet away. He started to crawl. The group of Templars were by the priest, their eyes firmly fixed on the priest, and as for the Templars behind him, his mercenaries were in a ferocious firefight with them.

He slid the trap door open and slipped inside, feet first. From a small crack in the wooden door, he could see the Templars kneeling. The priest's body was placed on top of a box, an alloy box. They all seemed to be waiting for something. The priest looked dead. Then the box disappeared, but the priest remained in suspension.

He remembered the pale blue smoke, small at first. Then he had heard a strange rumbling noise; it was like faraway thunder. Then a shimmer. A square shape began to form. He wiped the sweat and the dirt from his eyes. The shape was gold, then silver, then lots of colours all fusing into one another. And then he was mesmerised because there, not but fifty yards away was the Ark of the Covenant. He had believed it for so long, but now it was in front of him. The four gold rings and the two gold cherubim facing each other. The Ark hovered above the ground; he saw the brilliant white light radiating from its core. Then he saw the priest rise and all his faith in the Ark and all the power it would give him, lay in front of his eyes.

He'd stayed in the spider hole for fourteen hours, until he thought it was safe. He was tired, wounded and weak. The two men he had messaged pulled up on the track and flashed their lights three times. He slid the trap door lid back and painfully and slowly crawled out of his hole. In the car journey to the private airfield and a waiting plane, he treated his wounds from the medical supplies the men had brought.

With every passing day since, he had slowly put his revenge plan together. He would have his Ark and he would have their deaths.

*

It was now 2012 and he was ready to move against the Templars again, but this time, he had no intention of making the same mistakes. He realised that four years ago he had underestimated them; thought them institutionalised, locked in their own world, like the religious devotees and religious leaders he despised so much. He thought them cut off from the outside world. However, what he had learnt four years ago was that they were far from cut off; they hid in plain sight, they were very much organised, equipped and highly skilled and trained. He would need the help of an army to defeat them and he knew exactly who he needed to convince to help him do so, a man he had never met, but a man who had an army. He needed a way to get his attention.

He had spent the last four years planning just how he would get his revenge; four years planning how he would get the two things he wanted most, needed most: the extermination of the Templars and their ward, the Ark of the Covenant.

After the lawyer had obtained the ring for him on the 15th November, he'd retrieved it from the drop-off point he had arranged with Crowthorp. Crowthorp didn't know who was picking it up. He had just assumed it would not be his boss in person, but it was.

Salah El-Din then travelled directly to Wales on the same day. He didn't want to go; he didn't want to be back in the UK. He had not been back since 2008. However, he'd eventually found the old woman living in Wales and he needed her help, but she was a dangerous lady and he needed to be cautious around her. He travelled as a Spanish businessman. Both Spain and the UK were part of the European Union, so it was easy for him to get in.

He'd driven to her isolated cottage deep in the Welsh hills. It was a bleak, rainy day. The wind was ferocious and grey skies announced it was not about to change soon.

Her cottage was old, dilapidated and run down. The cottage was surrounded by bed after bed of herbs. A fire pit lay close by and in the ash were animal bones. Nothing else was around for miles.

He'd gone to see the old lady, the Hag, with a proposition. He figured, for the ring, she would help. She did. That day she left for the North West of England. The first bishop died between the 15th November and the 21st December; another two bishops in the UK were found poisoned. One part of his plan was now in play.

He then sent the lawyer and his thief to New Jersey, for one last job, although the thief and Crowthorp didn't know it was to be their last job!

Salah El-Din was extra vigilant now that his dual plan was in play and the first part was going to be the hardest: he needed *him*. He needed the man he had never met, the man with the army. He needed to convince *him* that he could help them rid the world of the Templars. The problem was that this man and *his* army also wanted Salah El-Din dead.

They had stumbled across *him* in Salalah when he had had the phones tapped of Saeed Al Bateat a young Yemeni intelligence officer. The *man* also had men tailing Al Bateat and was also tapping his phones. They both tracked Al Bateat and then they both tried to track each other. The difference was that *he'd* slipped the net and was back in his ring of steel in Salalah. However, *he* also found out that one of the men tracking Al Bateat lived in the Yemen. He found out where he lived. *He* knew he would need that information one day soon.

He'd also found out that a group of Templars had arrived in Abu Dhabi. *He* himself had left a trap for them at their hotel, where a hotel manager recognised two of them from the ID photofits *he'd* faxed to all of the main hotels in Abu Dhabi. *He'd* guessed they intended to meet up with Al Bateat in Abu Dhabi and they were obviously planning to kill him. However, the other group got there first. They killed some of the Templars; *he'd* heard a lot of them died. And, in the end, Al Bateat and his family were burnt alive but neither the Templars, nor the other group, managed to get him, but it was close, too close for comfort.

The man he needed to approach and his army were zealots and fanatics. They were not people you could bargain with. However, he believed that they wanted the Templars dead more than his own death. He would gamble on that fact. Plus, he now offered them gifts: dead bishops, three of them and the fourth, the most important one about to happen. Through his actions, he was hoping to convince them that he could be useful. He would show them he was useful. He planned to reach out to them, to the Abaddon *Alqatala,* the Abaddon assassins, just as soon as he had killed the final bishop on the 25th December. He had a man in Salalah who would take word to them via one of their own men in the Yemen. But behind their backs, he would also reach out to the Templars.

His plan for the Templars was already in play. Steal some-thing so precious, so historically important, of such magnitude that the Templars would have no choice other than to investigate and try and get it back and when they did, his men would be waiting for them in New Jersey. They would abduct one of them, maybe more and that would be his security blanket.

He would contact the Templars and suggest a pact, a partnership. He would offer to get the artefact back for them and, he would offer his help in trapping the Abaddons. His security would be the abduction of a Templar, he would tell them that he would release the Templar just as soon as the Abaddons were gone. But of course, he would never release a Templar. Besides, if his plan worked, there would be no one to release them to!

None of this would have been possible but for a stroke of luck back in September. That stroke of luck was the genesis of his plan. That one piece of luck allowed his plan to be activated because it took away one big problem that he had: he'd had no idea where the Templars were. That changed. All his old estate bosses, those not in prison, had photofits of people he wanted found and amongst them, were Jonathan and Dominique.

In September, one of the estate soldiers had seen a Facebook posting his cousin had made. He liked the post and was about to scroll on when he looked more closely at the photograph. His auntie had taken a selfie of herself and her friend she was staying with for a weekend break in Scotland, a lady called Elaine Wall. They were out on a nearby beach walking Elaine's dogs, Dusty and Nell, and the auntie had taken a selfie. And there, as clear as day in the background were two of the people his boss wanted, Jonathan and Dominique Rose.

Salah El-Din was told and then knew that all he had to do was have the beach watched and sooner or later, the priest or the woman Templar would probably turn up. He would reach out to them with the offer. They would take his message back to the Templar in charge. Then he would sit back and watch his double, double cross work, as his two enemies destroy each other.

*

Place: New Jersey

Crowthorp watched from across the street. The church was just on the edge of the town, so quiet but with enough buildings, roads and alleyways around it for them to head for, should they need to run. His rental car was parked two blocks away. They could make the dash in just a few minutes, should there be a need to.

The relic hunter made her way into the church, unchallenged. She entered the church via the vestibule door and ignored the fact that the alarms were all on. She'd been told it was taken care of. The alarm was linked directly to the private residence of the bishop. The bishop, who would have heard the alarm go off in his quarters and called the police, was lying dead, his face purple, his tongue hanging out and swollen. Again, the Hag had done her job and was already leaving the country on route to kill her fifth bishop, the important one: she was on her way to Rome.

The relic hunter switched on her flashlight; she'd been told it was safe to do so. She was unaware of the dead bishop and the Hag.

The church smelt musty and had a sickly, sweet smell, the smell of burnt incense. She hadn't been in a church since the age of three, when she had attended her cousin's christening: there had never been another need to go again. She didn't come from that kind of life.

The relic hunter found the artefact in the reliquary, hidden

73

within the alter. The lawyer had planned it well with the information he had received from the *Sancti Furem* – the Holy Thief, via Father Michael. She took the artefact quickly, wrapped it in bubble wrap, placed it inside her flowery backpack and left the church by the same door.

He crossed the road to meet her and then the lawyer and the relic hunter walked back to the parked car. No rush, just two people out together. He'd made her take his arm, just for effect.

His boss had told him he needed to stay in New Jersey with his accomplice after the job was done. He told him they should assist the men he was sending there in any way they could. He didn't say who the men were, or indeed what they would be doing there.

Crowthorp didn't like it; he was suspicious. His boss texted a mobile number and told him to call it when they had the item from the church and had got back to their motel. Something just felt off about this job, something was different, but he couldn't put his finger on it. He started to think about insurances, how he could give himself a route out, just in case.

He was beginning to get a sense that his boss's plan was that he and the young woman would never leave New Jersey. He didn't tell her anything. She didn't figure in this; he owed her nothing. She was indebted to him. If it came down to it, he wouldn't save her.

Chapter 5

A Busy Day

It had been eight months since the Templars carried out the extraction mission in Romania. André Sabath was in hospital, in intensive care and he was close to death. The torture and the medical procedures he'd suffered at the hands of the Abaddon leader, Zivko Gowst, caused irreparable damage to his organs.

As soon as the Templars had got him back to safety, they moved him into a private hospital in Lebanon, so that he would be near to his family, and they near him. The hospital had some great doctors and surgeons but Sabath had arrived gravely ill. After exhaustive tests, the doctors told his family that his condition was terminal. There wasn't anything they could do for him other than make him as comfortable as possible and try to ease the pain he was in. They didn't know how long he had left to live but they said he would be lucky to see October. But Sabath was a fighter. October came and went, then November came and went and André Sabath was still alive. He was a man of strong resolve and faith. He astounded the doctors with his fighting spirit.

Sabath knew he was dying but despite his condition, he'd managed to brief St Clair and the others about the failed operation in Abu Dhabi and their ambush.

Whilst he still could, Sabath wrote letters to the families of every Knight who had died and told them of the bravery of their loved ones. He told the Templars Zivko Gowst's name and described him. This also confirmed Morgan Clay's (the Templar's ghost man), suspicion that Zivko Gowst, the man they called the Ghost, had funded the Abaddons and had been doing so since 1955, and that it was he who was the link to the Panama offshore companies. Now at last they had a description of the man who led their enemy, the enemy the Templars had been fighting since the crusades.

All the new intel, the debriefing by André Sabath and what they found in Zivko's camp after the extraction battle, was a major breakthrough for the Templars, but it had all come at a heavy cost. They'd lost five combat Knights. They had also lost Nickolin Klymachak, the man they fondly called the Russian. In total, Romania had cost the Templars six lives and four wounded, which included Luther Jones, who led the Alpha extraction team. Whilst none of the wounds were life-threating to the survivors, it took months for some of them to heal before they could return to duty. They also lost eight of their Lebanese Knights, who had flown down to Abu Dhabi to support Sabath. With a total of fourteen dead, although they had killed twenty hostiles in Romania, the Templars had taken their heaviest loss in nearly fifty years.

Four months after Romania, André Sabath started to lose feeling in his limbs and his movement slowly ceased altogether. By November he was completely paralysed and needed a ventilator to breathe and twenty-four-hour clinical care. He was fitted with a computer that detected the movement of his eye lids: it was the only movement he had left and the only way he could communicate with the outside world.

By December, the Templars were still reeling from their losses in Romania and Abu Dhabi and from the inevitable death of André Sabath, one of their most celebrated Knights, one of the Nine Worthies, and a member of the Higher Council of the Order of the Knights Templar.

Some of the Knights who had taken part in the rescue mission had taken leave in the days that followed, the younger Knights mainly, those who had faced combat for the first time. They needed time to process what had happened. In those months before Christmas, the castle felt empty, despite the fact that the Headquarters of the Knights Templar was always full of people: a malaise hung over the Order as they waited for their friend, Brother and Knight to die.

Billy Jack, the Templar's new Sergeant at Arms, took to his duties with relish. He was back doing what he loved, what he felt he was born to do, what defined him. He was back soldiering. Billy Jack was responsible for combat Knights, those Knights who were mission 'active.' He was responsible for their training, for their weaponry, their munitions and for their support and auxiliary equipment. The Order had a number of Templar satellite stations around the world. These were the on-the-ground eyes and ears of the Templars, with a small band of men and women at each one, hidden in plain sight, running electronic surveillance and data capture operations. And, if there was a mission in their area, they would act as the command and relief station. Billy Jack was responsible for ensuring the satellite stations were fully equipped and protected, and the 'active' Knights were armed. He supported senior Knights with their ongoing missions around the world with tactical planning and support functions. There were always ongoing missions for him to support.

Billy Jack didn't know André Sabath; he'd not met him before seeing him in the encampment of Zivko Gowst's makeshift hospital in Romania. He felt sadness for the man he'd helped save but there was nothing he could do to help Sabath now. So, Billy Jack spent a lot of his time with the younger Knights who had experienced combat for the first time. Billy Jack had suffered severely from PTSD due to his own combat experiences, so he knew what some of them were experiencing. He made it his concern to help the young Knights. He made sure that they were okay and that when they were called into battle again, they would be stronger because of the Romanian experience.

Luther Jones, also ex-SAS like Billy Jack, helped him with the younger Knights. Luther had seen combat over many years and because of the many battles he had been in, Luther was seen by a lot of Knights as the ultimate Knight. He was fearless. He was smart in a combat situation, a planner, strategist and fighter. He was a skilled warrior who everyone liked and many hoped he would join the Council one day.

The daring deeds of the extraction team soon spread throughout the Order and it wasn't long before a new name was being talked about, Cameron Jack: the Lionheart. Word of his bravery and skills soon spread following his audacious flight across the camp in Romania and his fight with Zivko's main lieutenant, Bo Bo Hak, which bought time for the Knights trapped inside the makeshift hospital to get out.

As for Cameron Jack, he spent most of his time after Romania taking on his new role as Master of the Blade and that meant training Knights in the use of the Katana sword. He had been a pupil of two of the finest swordsmen in the world: they had been his Senseis. Then he became the teacher: he became the Sensei and now he was training Templar Knights. He devoted much of his time to making sure the Knights had the right skills to be able to defend themselves by using the sword effectively in offence positions and as a formidable defence weapon.

They all knew the story. The Katana sword, used by the Samurai in feudal Japan, was first introduced to the Templars by Father Durand, a Cathar holy man. Father Durand was trained by a Japanese Shinto monk. The monk, whose name was Kiyoshi, meaning soundless, had been a Samurai warrior in Japan before a dispute with his feudal master. He trained Father Durand every day, six hours a day for three years, to become a master with the blade. When the Cathars joined with the Templars during their own persecution and annihilation in France, the Cathars taught their skills to the Templars. From then on, every Knight Templar was meticulously trained in the use of the Katana sword. Whilst the Templars were now like any modern army, and carried handguns, rifles, machineguns and a whole range of other small artillery, the Katana sword remained their weapon of choice. It was silent and it was lethal in the right hands.

Cameron, many said, looked a little bit like Orlando Bloom but with blond hair. He was of mixed race, with high cheekbones and pale blue eyes, almost turquoise, which gave him a steely warrior look. He was about five feet eleven inches tall, medium build and with a warm and genuine smile. He embodied the values of martial arts, honour and courtesy; he lacked hubris and bravado. He was calm with a respectful manner – but his manner could also have a cold edge to it. The man with a first from Queens, London, did not draw attention to himself; however, those who knew the fighter, knew that inside that exterior a Samurai lurked, a master swordsman, a warrior.

He spent time with St Clair and Jonathan Rose on some of their weekly visits to the Ark. When he had first seen the Ark, it had shocked him but it also left him feeling safe, although he didn't know why. The fact that the religious icon was real blew his mind, as it did with everyone who saw it for the first time – and then every time after that. The Ark and the Order gave Cameron a sense of belonging and purpose, as it did with them all.

He liked those visits to see the Ark, especially when his grandfather also went along. Walking by the light of the burning torches they carried and also by the light of the wall-mounted burning torches, it gave the route a special atmosphere – Templars were strong on traditions. St Clair would lead the way – he'd walked that way a thousand times and more. The cool air from a vertical ventilation shaft kept the temperature cool down there, but it also played games with the flames of their torches with projected shadows dancing across the walls. The tunnels, expertly excavated and formed, had the most exquisite vaulted stone arches: barrel, domed, ribbed and pitched vaults supported the ceiling. In perfect symmetry, the stonemasonry looked like subterranean art, the proportions and balance, stout and strong, yet integral and beautiful.

Like Jonathan, Cameron's favourite part, other than being in the presence of the Ark itself, was a stretch of about five-hundred yards. Along the walls were small niches and, in every niche, an urn, ten inches high, black in colour, a rounded body but with a narrow neck. Each had a lid on it. And on each black urn was the Templar red cross. They were the ashes of nearly every Knight that had fallen in combat. Centuries of proud and valiant men and women who had served their God and their Order, with total commitment and grace. St Clair always whispered a prayer as he passed that place – Jonathan had started doing the same and now Cameron and Billy Jack also took on the habit.

Two miles in, the tunnel would suddenly turn sharp left at a 45-degree angle: this meant the end of their journey. Without hand-held torches, it looked like a dead end. However, as they approached and the light from their flames hit the rock, a door could be seen nestled in an alcove. A seven-digit code opened the reinforced, tungsten door to reveal a small, perfectly rounded room with the same exquisite stonework in the form of a cupola domed stone ceiling and inside, the Ark of the Covenant was kept in a dull, silver alloy box.

Romania had shown Cameron that the Templars had enemies, bad enemies and he would need to be fully committed to them if he wanted to help.

In the months since Romania, he had formed a bond with Jonathan and liked the ex-priest from Washington DC. They were of similar natures, not showy, but quiet, pleasant to be with but with a strong conviction to others. They spent many hours together when Cameron was not training Knights, talking and just hanging out together. They could often be found outside the castle walls, in one of the glens, walking along soft, fertile grass and heather, discussing the Templars, self-defence techniques and, of course, the Ark of the Covenant. Cameron had many questions and felt at ease discussing them with Jonathan more than any other.

On one of their walks, Cameron asked Jonathan why the Templars had painted a small red cross on the foreheads of the dead criminals in Romania, after the extraction battle.

"So, the devil will know who to take," Jonathan had told Cameron.

"You mean like the mass slaughter of Cathars in France?" Cameron asked.

"I don't know, Cameron, you're the history guy. Tell me what happened."

"*Caedite eos. Novit enim Dominus qui sunt eius,*" Cameron began. "Kill them, for the Lord knows those that are his own. In the

12th century, the city of Béziers, in southern France was once a stronghold of Catharism; Cathars were also called Albigensians. The Catholic Church had denounced them as heretics. This acted as the trigger for their eventual genocide. It's called the Albigensian Crusade. Béziers was the site of the first major military action against the Cathars: The Massacre at Béziers.

"The slaughter of the citizens of Béziers took place on the 22nd July 1209, after Pope Innocent the third had declared the crusade to eliminate Catharism in Languedoc. The army, arriving at Béziers, were very aware that it was not just Cathars who lived in the city. There were many Catholics living there. Not knowing how to identify the heretics from the Catholics, the commander famously turned to his troops and said these immortal words: '*Caedite eos. Novit enim Dominus qui sunt eius* – Kill them all. For the Lord knows those that are his own.' Today, this is most commonly recounted as 'burn them, burn them all, for God will know his own.'

"Men, women and children perished; they were slaughtered in cold blood on the streets of their city as it burnt. God did not know His own. It was the first time that France saw genocide against their own and on their own soil on such a scale. However, what it did do was to drive some of the Knights returning from the crusades in the Middle East, to become Cathars."

"Then they shared their secrets," Jonathan interrupted. "The Templars revealed they had the Ark and the Cathars that they had the prophecies."

"And those prophecies talked about us!" Cameron exclaimed. "You know what I still can't get my head around? That they got and then tested my DNA, and it matched with *Richard Coeur de Lion*, Richard the Lionheart. That's crazy, right? Oh, and now St Clair keeps calling me Lion or the Lionheart all the time so everyone is doing the same. It's embarrassing!"

Jonathan laughed. "You think that's bad?" he said putting his arm around Cameron's shoulder. "I don't think you know this but the first time I came to the castle, and St Clair insisted I stay overnight, they took my toothbrush and had my DNA tested. And, it was

Dominique who took it when I'd gone to breakfast the following morning; who marries a toothbrush stealer?"

Now they both laughed.

"But, it gets worse," Jonathan continued. "My DNA link was to the daughter of the Maid of Orléans, to Joan of Arc. So, I know St Clair calls you the Lionheart, he has names for nearly all of us, but just think how lucky I am to be *the Priest*. If he hadn't given me that name, he could have easily called me *Joan*, or worse still, *the Maid*. And just you wait till you hear St Clair's new name for Bertram. It's hilarious."

On those walks and during the time they spent together, Cameron learnt a lot from Jonathan. He was fascinated by the prophecies that had led St Clair and the Templars to Jonathan, the Seer and to himself. The whole thing seemed crazy to him. One minute he was giving talks and lectures about the use of the sword in warfare in history and the next, he had joined an Order he often identified as mercenaries and murderous adventurers.

Jonathan enjoyed his times with Cameron too and the two men became firm friends. And, the fact that it was Cameron who had saved Dominique's life, during her fight with Bo Bo Hak, made his affection for the quiet Ninja, as he called him, more special.

*

The British police in Manchester had a fairly cast-iron case involving the two shipping containers that had been broken into using explosives, on the industrial park on the 15th November. The thief had been caught red-handed. Nothing was stolen. The case was all but closed. The only outstanding issue concerned reports by three members of the public. Two of them were returning late from a party and one was a shift worker on his way to a bakery unit. They all reported that they had seen two men hanging about near to the scene of the crime. It was late, they all said, around 2 a.m. It was cold and raining, not the kind of weather you would expect to find people loitering, unless they were up to no good. The Manchester police assigned a young detective to follow up the reports. It was his first case. He had no support – why should he? It was an open and shut case. Through good police work and a lot of shoe-leather hours, the young detective was able to determine that there were indeed two men there. Plus, he found evidence that they may have been at the scene earlier that day also. Whilst their trail had gone cold and they were long gone, the young detective was able to find them on two sections of footage, one from a CCTV camera at a petrol station, and the second from a security camera at a garden centre close to the industrial estate.

Over a month later, the stills of the men from the CCTV footage were emailed over to Dámaso Nef, the chief of police at the Vatican City. Nef sent them directly to an email address he used for communications with the secret organisation he had asked to help.

Date: 22nd December 2012
Place: Remote castle, Scotland

It was early morning, 22nd December, when St Clair received the photographs from Nef.

St Clair sent messages for a number of Knights to come together for a meeting at 1 p.m. He sent the photos from Nef to each one of them in advance via email and they got them on their smart phones. They were all still trying to get used to the phones Bertram had invented called Lips In Synchronised Animation, LISA, which locked onto their eyes and used biometric retinal scans to switch the phones on and off. The phones actually only had three buttons: press red for emergency, I'm in trouble; green for I'm okay, I can't answer the phone but all is well; and the black one set off the phone-bomb. Bertram had told them, "The phone is intuitive and predictive, so it learns how you use your phone; the more you use it, the more it gets to know your style and will begin to give you short cuts that should be fun and save you time."

It was turning out to be a busy day for St Clair. Some people were arriving at the castle that day; other people would be arriving between the 24th and the 25th. Some members of the Higher Council were on their way because there was to be a vote on the two vacant positions on the Council. The vote would take place on the night of the

25th. It was a big issue: places on the Council rarely came up. The selection process was intense and exacting. A Knight could not put themselves forward, or propose another Knight. Only the Council could propose and only they could select and vote. The process was done in secret with deep tradition, the way the Templars did everything.

Payne St Clair, as the Grand Master, had already sent his suggestions to the other Council members a few weeks back, although it pained him greatly to consider the replacement for his friend, André Sabath. André was still alive but only days away from death and St Clair had to address the vacancy. He needed a full complement of Worthies now that the ring had been stolen, because he was convinced that there could only be one reason why.

The Council could make their own suggestions, but with a cadre of just three-thousand Knights, they knew every Knight and were pretty much aware of each person's strengths. The Order was a Brotherhood; it was also a Sisterhood. It was a family of valiant fighting Knights, men and women, who worked and lived for a common cause and with the same morals, values and beliefs. They worked as one, fought as one and they did it all in anonymity.

St Clair had called Dominique, Jonathan, Bertram, Luther Jones, Zakariah, Cameron, Courtney and Billy Jack to the meeting. The Indian, John Wolf, would be linking in via a video conference call from Kentucky, in the US.

However, Cameron Jack had called St Clair within five minutes of receiving his email that morning and opening the attachments. They spoke for about ten minutes and then Cameron Jack left and drove straight to the airport.

Jonathan Rose and Bertram Hubert Klymachak De'Ath – who had maintained his name change since the death of his friend the Russian – were chatting because they had arrived early for St Clair's meeting.

"Forty-one, twelve," Bertram answered when Jonathan asked if he'd been there long.

"Oh," said Jonathan; it was all he would risk. He had, as most of them had, learnt that if Bertram said anything they didn't understand, they would ask Courtney, who was his boss, to explain it to them. Bertram's explanations were notoriously more complex than the thing that caused the confusion in the first place. So, Jonathan left the 'forty-one, twelve' well alone.

Jonathan really liked Bertram; he made him smile. He loved the fact that Bertram was on the spectrum of eccentricity, and at the same time, was an obvious genius. Bertram sat opposite him with his white teeth flashing out from his deep brown skin and his curly, unkempt hair flopping about as he enthusiastically spoke about garage music and hip hop. He kept pushing his black square glasses back up his nose from where they kept slipping as he became more animated, the more excited he became.

"My new favourite is not hip hop or garage, though," he said, as if revealing a national secret. "I have discovered Alice in Chains, *yer, they come to snuff the rooster*." Bertram started to sing. As usual, he was dressed in a green tartan, tweed cloth suit, with waistcoat, a fob and brown shoes, scuffed. An Oxford graduate who had a 'first' in Computer Science, he specialised in nanotechnology, artificial intelligence, blockchain, advanced electronics and gaming.

"Heavy," Jonathan said, "about Vietnam."

Bertram stopped singing. "I love that you know that. And, I might add, I love how you and Mrs Dominique, your significant other, found each other in a sally." Bertram had a very peculiar way with the order of words and their usage."

"A what, Bertram?" Jonathan asked.

"A sally, Mr Rose Jonathan."

"Bertram, you know you can just call me Jonathan, just Jonathan is fine?"

"I will Mr Rose Jonathan," Bertram said.

Jonathan thought he might change the subject from roosters and sallies and find out more about the slightly odd Knight who, despite being twenty-five years old, looked twelve!

"Bertram, do you have a significant other, maybe someone you met at sally?" Jonathan asked, having no clue what 'sally' was.

"Ah, Mr Rose Jonathan, yes," Bertram said, lowering his voice and his head. He sighed a deep and mournful sigh. "Miss Madison Davenport." However, he seemed to perk up a bit when he said her name. "In the mornings, when she did finally wake up, because she wouldn't get up until the streets had aired, oh no, not her, she'd be off quicker than a dirty shirt. I'd be stood there, like Johnny on the spot, but she'd be off."

"Wow, Bertram. Is she in Scotland?"

"Oh, no Mr Rose Jonathan, no, no, no. She's dead."

"Dead?"

"Gone. She was killed in a road traffic accident."

Jonathan was about to offer his condolences.

"She was my life. She would sit like a queen and move with grace and style." He laughed at a memory. "She suffered from dysania and liked me to tickle her columella nasi after we'd eaten."

"Did she now?" Jonathan said, taken aback. He fidgeted uncomfortably, not wanting to press any further for fear of what Bertram might say. "I wonder what time St Clair and the others will get here?" he said, trying to change the subject.

"Ah," giggled Bertram, "James B. Yesh, Mish, Moneypenny. He does, doesn't he, he looks like James Bond?" He started humming the theme tune.

Payne St Clair walked into the room and Bertram quickly looked at his phone – giggling.

Courtney sat beside Jonathan. "Pssst," he whispered to his sister, "you never told me that Bertram had a girlfriend who died in a road traffic accident. I was so shocked."

"He didn't," Courtney whispered back.

"He did; he just told me. Her name was Madison Davenport."

Dominique sat down on the other side of Jonathan. "That was his cat," Dominique said.

"A cat!" Jonathan exclaimed. "Who names a cat Madison Davenport?"

"Bertram," Courtney and Dominique said in unison.

"But," Jonathan lowered his voice a bit more, as if he was about to reveal a dark secret, "he said that she suffered from dysania and liked him to tickle her columella nasi after they'd eaten." He turned to his sister. "There! You're the clever one in the family; what do you make of that?"

Courtney laughed. "Dysania is what they call it when you struggle to get out of bed in the mornings, a bit like you, if I recall?" Dominique nodded. "And, a columella nasi is the bit between the nostrils. The cat liked its nose rubbed."

"You were right, Jonathan," his wife said, "Courtney is the smart one in the family." Both girls laughed and high-fived.

But Jonathan thought for a moment or two. "And a sally? Apparently, we met at sally or a sally, I'm not quite sure?"

"It's a sortie, or skirmish," they both answered.

"Which is indeed how we did meet, my sweet," Dominique said.

"I'm going to have to do more reading," Jonathan sighed.

They were all there now. The meeting room had two large wall-mounted screens. The pictures that Nef had sent over, the ones he had obtained from his own CCTV operation room and the ones from the Manchester constabulary, were on one screen and on the other, the beaming face of the Indian, John Wolf, appeared. He had a huge mug of coffee in his hands, steam still rising from it.

"Hi Wolf," St Clair greeted him. "What time is it there now?"

"Just after seven," Wolf said.

"Well thank you for getting up early. I know you are an early riser anyway, but good to see you. I don't know if you can see everyone, but in the room with me we have Luther, Zakariah, the Girl, the Priest, Courtney, our Sergeant at Arms, Billy Jack and Cerebral."

Bertram gushed with pride at his new name.

"The Lionheart has left for the airport," St Clair announced to everyone. "I will explain why in a moment but first, some background. Back in November," he continued, "the chief of police at the Vatican, Dámaso Nef, contacted me. They'd had a robbery, not in Rome but here in the UK, in Manchester. Nef doesn't normally get involved if it's outside Italy, but because the asset stolen had not been handed over to their new custodians, Nef was still technically responsible.

"The Catholic Church was transporting a number of assets to different Church held properties around the world. All of the assets being transported were in three mid-sized containers. They were being held in a warehouse unit in Manchester, on an industrial estate, until their ships were due to sail. They were only there for a few days. Very few people knew they were there. The containers held a lot of valuable cargo. The police caught the thief red-handed, or so they thought. They also believed that nothing had been stolen. But it was all a smoke and mirrors job. We believe the thief was placed in the job as the patsy, but didn't know it. The real thief or thieves, got away with the most valuable thing in the containers, the thing that was not on the customs manifest. So, the police didn't know it had been stolen."

The meeting waited patiently for him to answer the obvious question: what? Dominique and Jonathan already knew because they had been in the room when Nef had called St Clair. In fact, St Clair had asked Jonathan after the call with Nef to research the ring and to get as much information as possible. Nef had also sent over what the Vatican knew about it, or at least what they were prepared to share. St Clair didn't trust the cardinals a hundred per cent; their politicking made them somewhat duplicitous at times. St Clair asked Jonathan to brief the group.

"The only item that was stolen was the signet ring of King Solomon. There are two facts about this theft that you should bear in mind. One, whoever took it knew exactly where it was. Not only that it was in Manchester, on which industrial estate, the unit number and which container it was in; they also knew the ring was inside a cigarette packet, inside a used, plastic shopping bag on the floor, hidden in plain sight."

"*Sancti Furem* – Holy Thief," Luther said, "I remember the stories from the last job."

"It's not proven," St Clair said, "but, it seems pretty obvious now that it was an inside job and that's why I had to tell Nef we could not help. If it is an inside job, then we have no chance of tracking down the ring or the person that gave away its location. We would spend years trying to find the *Sancti Furem* inside the Vatican. However, I really don't think that matters right now and it's not the point of this meeting."

"Then what is?" Courtney asked.

"I think the ring was stolen for a specific reason and I don't mean for its historical importance and value. I mean something far more nefarious, something dark, something very dark given the ring we are talking about. There were lots of things in those containers that amounted to a fortune. So, no, I really don't think this was any ordinary robbery."

St Clair indicated for Jonathan to continue. All eyes turned to the ex-priest.

"The story goes that the ring was engraved by God and given to Solomon. The ring was forged from iron and brass and those metals were used to seal in commands to both good and evil spirits. In one metal were the commandments to evil genies, or demons, and in the other, those to good genies. Because the name of God was engraved on the ring, and because of the symbol on the face of the ring, it is said that Solomon could control demons.

"The legend of a magic ring is all over our history books. They talk of the incantations that Solomon devised to use with the ring to summon good genies and exorcise bad genies. Of course, we guess that it would therefore work the other way round: they could summon bad genies and exorcise good genies. This offers us our first clue as to the reason why it might have been taken.

"On its face, the ring has a six-pointed star. Six-pointed stars have been used as a talisman since the time of Solomon, some say because of Solomon. Others say because of Solomon's father, King David, the man who united Israel and Judah. And of course, the man who also carried the Ark of the Covenant long after he slew Goliath. The six-pointed star is in synagogues and on the flag of Israel. It's a fairly common symbol, but with the right combination of ritualistic elements … we guess the ring's not been taken to do good."

The consternation on Billy Jack's face was visible. St Clair saw it.

"Billy, I don't blame you, if you're asking yourself if he is really talking about a magic ring? We expect everything to be in a physical form, because that's what we see. We struggle with things we can't see. But demons and spirits are just as real as God. If you believe in God, then you must believe in demons and spirits. And Billy, if you are still unsure, remember that about thirty feet below us is the self-levitating, invisible, until it doesn't want to be, Ark of the Covenant and the Ten Commandments given to Moses by God. And, if you need a last nudge, our American friend here was dead and then the Ark brought him back to life."

Billy Jack nodded. "Got it, thanks."

"Hey St Clair," the Indian called, "if you told Nef that we don't want to get involved, why are we getting involved?"

"Because we need to find out if my hunch is right, Wolf, and to do that we need to find out about the ring. We need to understand it more because if it was stolen because of what it can do, then I believe I know who stole it."

They all looked at St Clair waiting for a name to come out of his mouth. St Clair sipped his coffee. Then he eased back in his chair.

"St Clair?" Wolf asked.

"Salah El-Din."

It went very quiet. No one spoke. They had been chasing the violent, murdering criminal for four years, ever since he had managed to escape their net in Cumbria. They had hoped that they could track him down after a young Yemeni intelligence officer, Saeed Al Bateat contacted them with a definite sighting. The man who thought he was the reincarnation of Saladin, had been seen in Salalah, in southern Oman. But the young officer was careless and got himself killed, along with his family. The Templars' hopes of getting Salah El-Din vanished with the death of Al Bateat. Their last connection with the criminal was when he sent assassins to kill Zakariah, Jonathan and Dominique at their hotel on Yas Island, in Abu Dhabi four months ago.

It was Wolf who broke the silence. "So, what's next? What do you need us to do?" he asked.

"We need to attack this on two fronts," St Clair stood up and started pacing the floor. He checked his watch. He knew two of his Knights had planes to catch and two had a train to catch. They just didn't know it yet! "We need to find out about the ring. I think that will confirm that Salah El-Din stole it and what he wants with it. So …" he paused a little, not deliberately, but he knew what was coming. He cleared his throat. "We … we need to go and see Aldrich."

There were startled looks on the faces of Zakariah, Luther, Dominique and John Wolf. Their reaction was palpable and the others picked up on it immediately.

"I have two train tickets to Cambridge. I need two Knights to go and see him," St Clair announced.

Zakariah, Luther and Dominique almost sat on their hands for fear of moving them and it being mistaken for lifting them up to volunteer. Wolf quickly switched the video camera off so there would be no mistake. The others saw their reaction and didn't budge for fear of whatever they were afraid of.

"Of course," St Clair started. Those that knew him best, knew he had already made up his mind. He just wanted them to think it was their own idea. "Of course, we need someone with a fairly good knowledge of religion, someone who already knows a little about the ring …"

Jonathan felt their stares on him. He looked for help from Dominique but she was sitting firmly on her hands and looking down. "I guess," Jonathan began, seeking out the change in his pocket, "I could go, maybe. Perhaps?"

"Splendid idea. I think we can all agree with you, Jonathan." St Clair pounced straight away before Jonathan could take it back.

"You can't send him on his own!" Zakariah made the mistake of coming to Jonathan's rescue, just like St Clair knew he would. Jonathan was his son-in-law after all.

"Thank you, Zakariah, good idea and thank you for suggesting it. That's settled then, the Priest and Zakariah will go and see Aldrich." St Clair gave a train ticket to both Jonathan and Zakariah. "Afraid you need to leave now; your train leaves in ninety minutes. There's a car waiting out front."

Wolf put his video camera back on and had a smile and a look of relief on his face, as did, Luther and Dominique.

Jonathan and Zakariah picked up the train tickets and reluctantly began to gather their things to leave the meeting. Neither noticed that each train ticket had a name on it, their names.

"Who is Aldrich?" Jonathan asked Zakariah as they were walking out of the meeting room.

"Aldrich Manwin Tucker, a Professor of Supernatural, Occultism and history of Satanic Medieval Renaissance at Cambridge University, a bit of a specialist in black magic."

"I didn't know you could do a degree in magic. Is he a Templar?"

"No, but he kind of thinks he is, so don't tell him any different. We don't want him going all nuts on us. He's quite bonkers. And whatever you do, don't mention a sword."

"He's not bonkers," St Clair called after them.

"He eats flies," Zakariah called back. "You and I saw him eat flies."

"He doesn't eat flies, they were raisins," St Clair offered.

"Raisins don't have wings."

The rest of the meeting had taken a twenty-minute break and they were all now back in the meeting room: Dominique, Luther, Bertram, Courtney, John Wolf, Billy Jack and Payne St Clair who was again standing and intermittently pacing.

"Yesterday evening, the Catholic Church suffered their second loss. It was one of their most treasured relics: one of their top five. I spoke to Nef this morning. He called me just after seven our time. He told me what had been stolen but he also said there had been a spate of deaths by poisoning, and yesterday a fourth bishop was poisoned. The first death was on the 16th November. Coincidence or not, it was the day after the ring was stolen. The last death was yesterday, the 21st December, the day the second artefact was stolen.

"Nef is not on the case. The Vatican will not allow him to lead the investigation because it happened in the US, so their folks in the US are handling it. Thirty minutes after that call, I got a call from Father Angelo Fugero. He's the Vatican representative in New Jersey. He would not tell me over the phone what was stolen. He said he would tell me what once I got there, but Nef had already informed me.

"Wolf, Dominique, Father Fugero will be your contact once you get there. Wolf, we have you going out of Logan at 4 p.m. your time today, if that's okay?"

Wolf nodded in agreement.

"Dominique, you are booked on the overnight to Newark. I'm sorry it will mean missing Christmas with Jonathan but we'll look after him for you and I will explain everything to him when he gets back from Cambridge tomorrow or on the 24th if Aldrich detains them."

"No problem," she said, "I'll be packed and ready to go. Wolf, I'll see you at Newark."

Wolf nodded.

"What do you need me to do?" Luther asked.

"Nothing, Luther. But I do need you to be here on the 25th, around 6 p.m. Did you have anything planned?"

"Just going to visit the graves, so I will be here way before six," Luther told him.

"Good. Thank you, Luther. Also, plan to be back down south on the 26th. You'll have work to do and I want you to take Billy Jack with you." St Clair didn't elaborate and Luther Jones didn't ask. He had no need. As always, he knew that when his Grand Master needed him to know, he would tell him.

Billy Jack nodded, "Good with me."

"Good. So, let me tell you how I think this is panning out. The Council and I think the ring was stolen because of the legends that surround it. Clearly someone believes it has some sort of talisman power. We think that someone is Salah El-Din. If we are right, it means he is working with the *Sancti Furem* – the Holy Thief. If that's true, then he practically has the key to the Vatican treasure. However, we are guessing it's not what he wants right now because he's made no attempt to take anything else from Rome. The ring seems to be the key. So, if we can find out more about the ring, and that's now down to the Priest and Zakariah with Aldrich, then I am hoping we will have a clearer picture as to Salah El-Din's plan.

"Wolf and Dominique will see what they can find out about the robbery in New Jersey and the murder there of the bishop. Obviously, they are all linked: the death of the bishops, the ring and what was stolen in New Jersey.

"We have an extra problem though that only came to light this morning and it was the Lionheart who picked it up. Look at the photographs Nef sent over."

They all turned towards the screens.

"The ones on the left are the ones his own people got off their CCTV. The ones on the right are the ones the Manchester police sent Nef. Let me zoom in." St Clair used the remote and the picture on the wall screen grew bigger. Then he honed into one point, the neck of one of the men in the pictures.

"We know the man who was watching the house where the ring was being kept in Rome, who fled rather quickly, is also one of the two men on the right. The two men on the right were seen the night the ring was stolen, in Manchester." St Clair zoomed into the face of one of the men. "There," he said.

They could all see it now. The man's collar was open and they could just see the edge of a tattoo.

"I'm not getting it. What is it?" Billy Jack asked.

"Your grandson has seen that colour ink and that pattern before. There was just enough for him to identify it. It's Yakuza."

"Shi—" Billy Jack managed to stop himself; he was still getting used to clean language.

"Indeed," said St Clair, smiling. The Lionheart has gone to Kyushu in Japan to consult with Tanjkna Sugata-san, his old Sensei.

As you know, he's retired and now lives off grid, so the only way to contact him, is to go and see him.

"Okay, now the part you all want to ask me about. What was stolen in New Jersey?" St Clair did not pause for effect. What he was about to tell them would have effect enough. "It seems, Knights, that all this time, the Roman Catholic Church had the skull of John the Baptist. They had it and they had hidden it in a small church in New Jersey."

The room was almost silent before St Clair revealed what had been stolen. Now it was deafeningly silent and they each absorbed what St Clair had just told them.

"Damn," Luther exclaimed. "Do you think Jamal knows?"

"I called him straight away, Luther. I could not keep this information from our old friend, not after all of the years they have been searching."

"How did he take the news?"

"He took his false passport and headed for Jordan. Said he was going to arrange to meet someone there and they would be going to New Jersey on their behalf and he asked me to tell our team to look out for him." St Clair looked at Bertram and Billy Jack. "Jamal is a good friend of the Templars and he has helped us many, many times. He is a Mandaean holy man. The Mandaeans have been searching for John the Baptist's head for over two-thousand years."

"So," Billy Jack started, "this Salah El-Din – and I've been briefed on him – we think he has the ring for something, he's murdered several bishops for something and he stole the skull of John the Baptist for something, which I still can't get my head around. Presumably he did it with the help of this *Sancti Furem,* this thief inside the Vatican."

St Clair nodded.

"What do you want me to do?"

"Go with Luther on the 26th and, in the meantime, make sure our Knights are ready, and pray," St Clair said.

"Consider it done," Billy Jack said.

"And me, Mr St Clair?" Bertram asked. "What do you want me to do? Mr St Clair number two and Mr Rose Jonathan have gone to Cambridge. Mr Indian Wolf and Mrs Dominique will be in New Jersey.

Mr younger Jack has gone to Japan and Mr older Jack is going to get things ready for a fight."

St Clair stood up and started to pack his papers away. Other people were doing the same. The meeting was over.

"Drones," St Clair said to Bertram. "You were telling me about your idea for drones the other day. I want you to tell me more about it. Come and see me tomorrow, any time, and take me through your ideas. I want you to build us some drones."

"Stealth sky-eyes, Mr St Clair and I will be with you at thirty eleven." Bertram was now walking out through the door.

"Good!" St Clair looked at Courtney for translation.

She whispered, "He means 11:30 a.m. He says that the minutes are the most important things so they should come first. The seconds are too short to worry about and the hour is just the end result of the minutes."

St Clair shook his head and smiled. "Okay," he called after Bertram, "thirty eleven it is. I'll see you then, Cerebral."

Chapter 6

The Devil You Put Behind You

Date: 23rd December 2012
Place: Japan

Cameron's BA flight landed on time. The screech of the tyres and reverse thrust of the engines announced their arrival. The flight was full. Tokyo was a popular destination for business people and tourists alike. He'd managed some sleep during the flight but it was restless. The fact that he had come to see his old Sensei held mixed emotions. He had not seen him for years and because he lived almost off grid, and did not use any technology, it was difficult to stay in touch.

His carry-on bag was light; he'd planned to stay two nights at the most. The pictures Nef had sent through worried him a lot and he was eager to ask his Sensei about them. If he confirmed what Cameron already suspected, Cameron knew he would need to get back as quickly as possible. He knew his Sensei would be able to tell him one way or another.

He reached into the overhead locker and retrieved his bag. The doors of the plane were opened and a long line of passengers started to make their way along the two aisles towards them. As always on a flight to Japan, as the majority of passengers were Japanese, the queue was orderly and polite. However, he got the same stares he normally got when he was there, the same stares he got every time he went to Japan. Whilst it was not rare to see a *gaijin* – outsider, anymore, it was still rare to see a black person, *kuro gaijin* – a black outsider. The fact that Cameron was of mixed race seemed to add to their inquisitiveness. This, coupled with the fact that he looked a little like Orlando Bloom, added to the younger generation's fascination of him and he often heard them whisper to their parents, *mite*, Legolas – look, Legolas.

Cameron was gripped by a sense of excitement and a feeling of coming home as he quickly made his way through customs. His use of Japanese was always helpful. Most visitors had a few words only, an awkward *Kon'nichiwa* – hello or an *Arigatōgozaimashita* – thank you, and that was it. Most tourists just spoke in their own native tongues, but more loudly when trying to be understood. Cameron had taken an interest in the language because of his martial arts. He needed to learn commands for fighting, words that described a fighter's outfit, words for scoring, for moves, attacks and defences. As he had been a frequent visitor to Japan, he quickly picked up the language because unlike learning it in a classroom, he was immersed in the language; he knew that if he did not understand it in a fighting bout, he would be at a major disadvantage. Now he could get around Japan without too much trouble.

Japan suited Cameron because of his nature. Even at an early age, there was something about his character that people noticed. He wasn't shy or aloof, but he wasn't one to shout about things, to draw attention to himself; like the Japanese, he was a little reserved. He was well mannered, like the Japanese. However, early on his school-teachers could see that he was developing a steely determination. He was a popular boy. He got good grades and rarely got into any trouble. The values displayed in martial arts, along with the discipline required, the honour, the courtesy, the lack of hubris and bravado, fitted Cameron's calm, respectful manner. But his manner also had a no-nonsense determination to it when he had a sword in his hand.

Even in some of the dojos in Tokyo, they had heard of the foreigner who had trained with the famous Hinata Satō, who had been a renowned Kendo teacher, a master swordsman and a grandmaster. And then, when Satō retired, the foreigner had trained with Tanjkna

Sugata, another famous swordsman. They knew that the foreigner had gone on to become a competitive fighter in his own right and won countless competitions across Europe: a swordsman of stealth, with great natural and explosive power but also a great tactician. What they didn't know was that the foreigner had served as an officer in the British Intelligence Corpse and then spent five years in the SAS.

When he first arrived in Japan, all those years ago, Cameron had fallen in love with it: the Japanese people, the sights, the smells, the sounds, the food, the culture and the architecture, and the sheer politeness of the people. He found them nice natured, accommodating and respectful. However, as his visits increased, so did his understanding and his awareness that not all things were polite and accommodating in Japan. He realised early on that Japan, like every other country, had bad people, but he was spared interacting with them, interacting with the Yakuza, the Japanese mafia, who were ruthless extortionists, drug traffickers and murderous gangsters.

Outside Narita airport, Cameron hailed a taxi. He had to catch a second flight to reach his final destination, but first he wanted to visit the old dojo. He took almost the same route he had taken many times with his grandfather, when he was a teenager. The taxi headed for Chiyoda City, then, across three rivers, almost side by side and in to Katsushika. The taxi driver knew where it was: most people in Tokyo did. The taxi driver pulled up outside the old dojo but kept the engine running; it was cold out. The old dojo was now empty and in a bad state of disrepair. It didn't look like anyone had been in there for years.

Cameron got out of the taxi for a few minutes to take a look around and to feel the presence of the old place again. He couldn't help smiling at the memory of his grandfather, when they had met Hinata Satō for the first time.

"He looks like Mr Miyagi from the Karate Kid film," his grandfather had said about Hinata Satō.

Cameron had told his grandfather to shush, in case he was heard.

"But he does," his grandfather had insisted. "Wipe on, wipe off, wipe on …"

Cameron saw the image in his mind of Hinata Satō, white hair, receding on the top, revealing a shiny forehead. He had a white goatee and strangely, his eyebrows were black. He was small and whispery in stature. He didn't look like a swordsman: he looked more like a bank clerk or Mr Miyagi, but he was a 10th Dan grandmaster; he was eighty-three years old!

Cameron put his hands in his pockets; it was cold out and he wanted the warmth of the taxi's heater again. He was sad to see the once thriving and famous dojo, now reduced to a vandalised slum. Once the dojo reverberated with the cries of 'kiai,' as student after student thrust blows at their opponents. The noise inside the dojo was always loud and intoxicating. Now it was silent and dead. Cameron turned his back on the place he once called his second home and got back in the taxi.

The taxi headed back to the airport so that Cameron could catch his internal flight. Tokyo was a mixture of ultramodern and traditional, with its skyscrapers and shrines and temples living side by side in cultural, modernism and history, all nestled up close and personal: the Meiji Shinto Shrine, with its towering gate and surrounding woods, the Imperial palace and countless other attractions and monuments standing side by side with neon-lit skyscrapers and plasma TV screens mirroring Times Square. He knew he was about to leave all this behind. Kyushu, his final destination, was smaller; it was less hectic and frenetic, more rural and scenic, and moved at a much slower pace than its country's capital.

Cameron could have taken the *Shinkansen* – bullet train, but that would have taken over five hours to get there. It was his preferred mode of transport because it would have taken him through some of Japan's most stunning and picturesque countryside, but he decided to take the plane instead. The flight would take just under two hours and he did not know how long he would need once there; there was no guarantee that his old Sensei would even be there.

Date: 23rd December 2012

Place: Kyushu, Japan

By the time Cameron arrived in Kyushu, he was pretty worn out. He'd left Scotland on the morning of the 22nd, just after speaking with St Clair. It was now late afternoon on the 23rd. He hadn't slept that well on the overnight flight from the UK and the internal flight from Tokyo had been full. He'd been squashed for an hour and a half between two feuding sisters and was glad to grab his bag when it landed and leave the plane. With no customs to check through, he was quickly out of the airport and standing in the taxi rank. He only had to wait a few minutes for a ride.

He took a taxi from the airport. They drove for about an hour. It was very cold out, around 5 degrees Celsius but warm inside the vehicle. The scenery of Kyushu's hinterland, speeding by outside the passenger window was exquisite, as he always found most of Japan, once he left the metropolis behind.

He'd pre-booked a room at a local hotel about twenty minutes from where he hoped he would find Tanjkna Sugata. The room was cosy and warm and he was thankful for that. He took a hot shower, dried himself with a towel that had been hanging over a heated towel rack and then had an early dinner: sushi, tofu and tonkatsu, pork chops coated in *panko* bread crumbs and deep fried until they were golden brown. He ate and just drank sparkling water. At around 6 p.m., he asked the hotel receptionist to call him a taxi. He gave her the address where he wanted to go and asked her to make sure the taxi picked him up after about two hours.

Cameron read on the back of the tourist map that Kyushu in the southwest, was the third largest island in Japan, and a subtropical paradise, known for active volcanoes, natural hot springs and a famous 8th century Shinto shrine. He knew that he would not have time to enjoy either the natural or historical beauty of the island. He was on a mission and he worried that time was not on his side. The taxi driver knew exactly where to go and he knew the man Cameron was looking for.

The drive out into the countryside took about twenty minutes.

101

The further out they drove, the more dispersed the domestic buildings became until they were infrequent. A house here, a farm building there. The lush green vegetation spread out over the island like a velvet cloth. Stunning mountain volcanoes were looming in the distance, standing over the countryside in a constant reminder that what nature gives, nature can also take away, and in a most ferocious and deadly manner.

The old taxi struggled as they began to climb up higher into the hills. It was still light but dusk would soon be upon them, it was winter, so daylight was at its shortest. Cameron was hopeful they would get there before dusk came. He got his wish. The taxi driver crunched the gears as he ground to a halt just before a wooden *torii*. The *torii*, a traditional Japanese gate made of two bowed upward pointing wooden beams and two, slightly splayed posts, was, the taxi driver said, the start of the man's property; his house was about a half a mile walk along a track. Cameron paid the taxi driver and then fastened up his thick, quilted coat – he had gone prepared.

It was quiet now that the old taxi had disappeared over the next hill and descended down into the adjacent valley. Not far off, someone was playing a *shakuhachi*, a Japanese bamboo flute, used by Zen Buddhists in meditation and for spiritual focus, known as *suizen*. Cameron caught its melodious notes. He knew who the player was; he'd heard him play many times. The haunting music drifted into the night, meandering through the valley. It was the only sound. It was eerie.

The house was small but the decking around the outside gave it a larger look. Off to the right was another building; Cameron already knew what it was from the Japanese characters painted vertically on the side. It was the man's dojo.

The door screen opened and a silver haired man, in casual Japanese dress, stood in the doorway with his hands on his hips in that proud, oak-like stance of his.

Cameron had first met him all those years ago when he was just sixteen. Tanjkna Sugata was the old master's best student and second in charge at the dojo: he was the *deshi*. Back then, Tanjkna was a man in his mid-forties and nature-wise, he was very much in the mould of his master. However, he was taller and stockier than his master. His black hair was always swept back and he always wore it in a bun on the top of his head – a *chonmage*, the traditional Japanese top knot. Now he was sixty and the black hair was gone, but it was still swept back and in a top knot. Both the old master, Hinata Satō and Tanjkna Sugata, his successor, had been the Templar's Master of the Blade. Now the new Master of the Blade stood in front of his old Sensei.

Cameron bowed and greeted the man with great respect. "It's been too long, Sensei."

"Cameron-san, we are not Sensei and student anymore," Tanjkna said, his words in that very Japanese staccato, clipped manner. He spoke in English despite knowing that Cameron could hold a fairly good conversation in Japanese. However, Cameron was the guest so Tanjkna considered it good manners to speak to him in his own tongue where he could. "We are brothers, we are Templars. *Ubi positus est, ut omnis* – where one stands, so stand us all." He then let out a rueful sigh. "It has been too long Cameron-san, but you look well. Now, come, I have been expecting you."

This surprised Cameron because the old man hadn't been notified he was coming. "Tanjkna-san, how did you know I—"

"My niece, she works at the hotel; you asked where I lived. You asked her for a taxi to here."

"But, you don't have a telephone?"

"The blessing of village jungle drums." And with that Tanjkna burst out laughing. "Now, please," he stepped to one side and gestured for Cameron to go inside the house.

Cameron took off his boots. Just inside were a pair of *uwabaki* – indoor slippers. He put them on.

Inside it was warm, and there were no chairs, like a lot of Japanese rooms. Tanjkna always sat on the floor, on small cushions. A small low-lying table held some rice cakes and the fermented rice drink, *sake*. A cast-iron wood burner stood to the side of the room, with a stack of chopped logs next to it and the fire burning brightly inside. The walls were bare but for a few pictures of Tanjkna and his old

103

Sensei, Hinata Satō. On a cherry blossom bureau, held on an elaborately carved stand, were Tanjkna's two swords, his Katana sword and the smaller sword, his Wakizashi sword. There was no one else in the house, so Cameron determined that he had still not married, but he knew it would be too impolite to ask.

The two men sat and talked for almost an hour about the old days and about their old Sensei, Hinata Satō. They talked about the dojo and Tanjkna confirmed that he knew the dojo had fallen into ruin. Both men were sad that the place that had shaped them as men, for Tanjkna had first gone there when he was seventeen, no longer existed as they knew it. The men reminiscing couldn't have had more different backgrounds. One of them, an English boy of mixed race, had lost both of his parents in a tragic car accident, and the other, a young criminal on the run, had been taken in by a stern old teacher of Kendo.

However, soon the reminiscing stopped and the conversation finally got onto Templar business. Whilst Tanjkna had retired, he still received written briefings that were posted to the hotel where Cameron was staying, and where he now knew Tanjkna's niece worked. Tanjkna had received the Romanian extraction report. He was desperately saddened by the loss of the Knights in Abu Dhabi and in Romania. He asked Cameron for a status update on André Sabath's condition. He had already been told that Sabath would not make it, but he just wanted to hear it from Cameron. Cameron confirmed it.

Tanjkna asked Cameron to take him through the extraction mission step by step. He frowned a lot, tutted at some of the decisions and shook his head at the loss of the Russian, who he knew very well. He was horrified at the death of Tarik Tahir, the Knight that Zivko Gowst had tortured and whose back he had cut open, pulling his rib cage and lungs out, spreadeagled. He was also horrified by what the Templars had found when they went back into the camp after all of Zivko's paid mercenaries had died. However, he made Cameron take him through the fight he had had with Bo Bo Hak in great detail. He wanted to know how his *deshi* had done. Cameron could see in his eyes that the old warrior wished he could have been there. His face shone with pride – although Cameron needed to look closely because he wasn't a man to give much away – as Cameron relayed the fight sequences: the attacks, counters and his defensive moves.

"Mmm, Satō-san and I taught you well."

"If you'd taught me poorly, someone else would be sitting here right now and not me, and they would be telling you how badly I had died and you had wasted your time teaching me, and you would have agreed with them."

Tanjkna smiled.

Cameron checked his watch. He was waning: jet lag and thousands of miles travelling were now taking their toll on him. Tanjkna noticed it.

"Your bed is made up, Cameron-san."

"No, no, no. I will not impose on you. I have a good bed at the hotel and you can have your privacy."

"Too late; your taxi driver is my second cousin. He will not be coming back as you instructed. So, you are stuck here with me for tonight."

Cameron knew his old Sensei. He would not take no for an answer and Cameron would not disrespect him by turning down his offer of hospitality. He lowered his head and bowed slightly.

"But, before we sleep, you have not come all this way to eat my rice cakes and keep your old Sensei company. So, Brother Knight, tell me how I might help you?"

Cameron took out the envelope that contained copies of the photos Nef had sent over from Italy: the ones Nef had got from his own CCTV and the ones the Manchester detective had sent through to Nef. Before he'd left the castle for the airport, Cameron had had them enlarged. Tanjkna saw it straight away, as Cameron had done as soon as he had seen them a day earlier.

"You need to tell me everything," Tanjkna's voice lowered. "This is not good, Cameron-san. You know what these are?"

Cameron nodded affirmatively.

Before Cameron had left for the airport, St Clair had fully briefed him on everything he would tell the others later that day about the ring. That was now nearly twenty-four hours ago. Cameron briefed Tanjkna with exactly the same information. When he'd finished, Cameron rested the photos on the low-lying table and spread them out. The tattoo of one of the men in the photographs was clearly visible. The end of the dragon's tail, in that distinctive twist, was plain to see. The colour green, specially mixed and only used for them, was staring back at the two Templars. The distinctive markings and that colour of ink were only used by one group in Japan: Yakuza.

In one of the pictures, one of the men's left hand could be seen in the photographs, with a quarter of his little finger missing. In a ritual known as *yubsitsume*, Yakuza are made to chop off the first quarter of their little fingers to show remorse for an offence they have committed against their own gang. The self-mutilation continues for those who have to atone for more offences, as more parts of fingers are removed; it is a form of apology. Cutting off fingers and being tattooed is a way that gang members show they are committed to the Yakuza life.

However, Cameron had heard that there was one Yakuza gang, the *Nagal tsume* – long claw, named because of their reach and their vengeful hand against any that crossed it – that required their members to chop off the first quarter of their little finger as an initiation. They were notorious for their strict codes of conduct and organised nature. Notorious for their absolute dedication. Cameron had seen a number of Yakuza styled tattoos before, but he had only seen one man with that dragon design and that colour green before. It was on the neck and shoulders of the man sitting beside him, Tanjkna Sugata.

Date: 24th December 2012

It was 4 a.m. and Cameron had slept remarkably well. The pleasant aroma of jasmine from burning incense helped ease his wandering mind as he slept. The *sake* had also played its part.

He did not know what time it was but he was vaguely aware that someone was in his room; he could not be sure it wasn't a dream. That feeling lasted for just milliseconds and then his combat instincts kicked in. He sprang out of bed and took up a wide defensive stance, waiting for the attack, but it didn't come. His sight moved from bleary to clarity.

Tanjkna bowed. "Cameron-san, we must go, we have to get to Tokyo. Your bag is here from the hotel and the taxi is waiting to take us to the airport. He is outside." Tanjkna was dressed in a *hakama*, a pleated male skirt and *hori,* a long-sleeved, block top, pulled together and held by his *obi* belt.

"You are formally dressed, Tanjkna-san." Cameron was surprised by what he was wearing because Japanese only normally wore their formal dress for ceremonies and at martial arts contests.

"Hurry, Cameron-san, the plane will not wait for us."

Tanjkna did not speak on the way to the airport. Cameron did not ask where they were going or why; he knew his old Sensei well enough not to. Those who had only known Tanjkna briefly would not pick up on the nuances of his body language and the subtle difference in his poise, but Cameron did. He knew Tanjkna was now more serious, more concentrated; he just didn't know why his old Sensei seemed so focused.

They arrived at the airport on time.

The taxi driver, Tanjkna's second cousin, seemed to know what was troubling Tanjkna. As Cameron grabbed the two carry-on bags, the taxi driver and Tanjkna stood in front of each other outside the revolving doors of the Departure Hall. They bowed in respect, but the taxi driver seemed to hold the stance longer, as though he did not want to let it go, did not want to let Tanjkna go. Then Tanjkna nodded to him, and it seemed to Cameron that he was saying, "It's okay." Finally, the taxi driver raised himself and for a second, he seemed to go to hug Tanjkna. Tanjkna uttered a word Cameron did not know, but took for a colloquial word. The taxi driver smiled, bowed slightly one more time, turned to Cameron and bowed to him. Then he got back into his taxi and left.

Tanjkna did not speak on the plane. Again, Cameron did not ask where they were going or why. Tokyo held a thousand memories but he knew it had its two faces: the good and the not so good. He couldn't help feeling they were heading into the latter.

After landing, they made their way through the airport quickly. Time was of the essence but Cameron didn't know why; he just kept pace with Tanjkna as he moved through the crowds with a purpose. They caught a taxi at the arrival's taxi rank. Cameron put the carry-on bags into the boot. Tanjkna had got into the back of the taxi and told the driver where they were going. Then Cameron got in beside Tanjkna. They pulled out of the airport and hit the busy expressway.

They had been travelling for less than fifteen minutes but Cameron already knew where they were heading. He'd travelled that route many times with his grandfather; he had travelled that route just the day before. The taxi was headed for Chiyoda City; it would then cross three rivers to get into Katsushika. They were going to the old dojo.

"You never asked me about it," Tanjkna saw Cameron looking at his Yakuza tattoo; it was showing slightly.

Cameron had read a lot about the Yakuza. He was fascinated because they had originated from 17th century Samurai warriors. He understood that some of their ritualistic, strict codes prohibited them from committing any act that went against *Ninkyodo* – chivalry. Their original purpose was to impose and serve their own form of justice. Cameron had spent enough time in Japan to know it was not a hypocritical ethos. To the Yakuza, it was a way of life: honour, chivalry and criminality, entwined, side by side and, for its members, it was an absolute lifestyle, even a religion.

Cameron eased back in his seat. "It was not my place Tanjkna-san." He bowed his head slightly to reinforce the respect he meant by that.

"You have my permission now. Please," Tanjkna said.

"You were Yakuza?" Cameron asked.

"Almost, yes, Cameron-san. As you can see." He looked at the driver, who was focused on the road in front of them. Tanjkna pulled back his collar a little. "I have the tattoo of the *Nagal tsume* – long claw. But as you see," he held up his hands, "I still have all my fingers." He smiled a little. "The men in your photographs are *Nagal tsume*. We need to find out what they were doing in Rome and what they were doing in Manchester, England."

"And you know who to ask?"

"*Hai* – yes." For a second, Tanjkna forgot and spoke in Japanese.

"And that's where we are going right now?"

Tanjkna nodded. "We are going to see Soto; he is *oyabun*. He is one of the bosses."

"You said, almost, that you were almost Yakuza, almost *Nagal tsume?*"

"My Sensei, our Sensei, Hinata Satō-san, saved me. My *yubsitsume,* my initiation of cutting off part of my finger was just weeks away. I had proven myself keeping out trouble-makers in some of our illicit gambling dens and had been on a number of house robberies. I was given permission to have the tattoo. In Japan, tattoos are normally a sign of a gangster; very few non-Yakuza have tattoos.

"One day I was walking past Hinata Satō-san's dojo and I went inside. I felt like I had gone home but I had never been in there before; it was most strange. Hinata Satō-san asked me if I wanted to learn and I said yes. He knew I was Yakuza because I did not hide my tattoo. Most would have not welcomed me, but he did. I could not stop going there. I could not stop thinking about it: the discipline, the fighting, the skills, the honour, the beauty of it. It's what I had always looked for, a home. I'd had no home before Hinata Satō-san.

"With the *Nagal tsume,* I was now in trouble because I stopped turning up. I went to the dojo instead and trained. I told them that I was not going to have the *yubsitsume.* I was not going back."

They had left the expressway some ten minutes back and were now in the Katsushika district; they were just a few minutes away from their destination, the dojo.

"Hinata Satō-san went to see them, the *Nagal tsume*. He was a man very respected and well known. He had helped the people of Katsushika. He was a famous sword fighter, a 10th dan. He asked them not to kill me; they had already made the decision to kill me by then. He argued with them for a long time and he put my case to them. Finally, they agreed to let me go, but I could never go back or meet with any of the *Nagal tsume* again. Also, they demanded a finger as penance, for my shame. I was not there; I was not allowed to go but they demanded a finger there and then. Hinata Satō-san offered his hand, but another brushed it away and laid his hand on the table and he sliced off his finger for me, for my shame. I never went back after that. So, you see, I was, but almost."

The taxi pulled up outside the dojo. There were two black sedans parked outside. Tanjkna paid the taxi driver, who pulled away faster than normal. He had already sensed who the sedans belonged to.

Cameron and Tanjkna stood outside the old dojo on the pavement and looked up, sad to see its demise.

"Who owns it now?" Cameron asked looking at the graffiti on the walls, the smashed windows and hole-riddled roof, now home to a number of wild pigeons.

"The Yakuza boss of Katsushika district, Cameron-san."

"And who are we meeting?"

"We are meeting the Yakuza boss of Katsushika district, Cameron-san."

"And who sacrificed their finger for you and took on your shame?"

"The Yakuza boss of Katsushika district, Cameron-san, but all those years ago, he was not the boss. He was just another eighteen-year-old street boy, hungry and with no future."

"Anything else I should know before we go in?"

"Yes. The Yakuza boss of Katsushika district is my brother."

"Well, this is going to be interesting," Cameron said.

Chapter 7

The Witch Hunter

Date: 22nd December 2012
Place: Cambridge

Their train journey south from Scotland to Cambridgeshire was uneventful; they found it long and tiring though. St Clair had arranged train tickets for them because he knew that despite stopping at many stations along the way, the train journey would be quicker for Zakariah and Jonathan, than travelling by road. Drivers were already experiencing long delays on the motorways, and the A and B roads were starting to see a number of accidents due to the snowy conditions. It was three days before Christmas and it seemed like everyone had somewhere else to be, other than where they were.

After the first hour into their journey, they had already read the couple of newspapers and magazines that they had purchased from the station kiosk, just before boarding the train. Neither had music to listen to because they had left fairly quickly and only had time to pack an overnight bag in case they needed to stay in Cambridge more than a day. Their mobile phones didn't have music on them, but they did have a bomb with a blast arc of fifteen feet. Jonathan didn't use his phone much and when he did, his heart raced and he made sure his thumbs were as far away from the black button as possible!

The hypnotic sound of the train wheels hurtling along the tracks added to their feeling of tiredness and the rhythm gently rocked most passengers to sleep after an hour or so. Jonathan didn't want to sleep.

He knew if he did, he would have trouble sleeping that night. Besides, he was always on edge when on a mission, even one as seemingly safe as this one: meeting a professor at Cambridge University. However, deep down he knew it wouldn't be safe. Missions never were with the Templars; they always had a habit of turning into life or death situations. He knew that if not this trip, it would be the next stage of the mission, or the stage after that, when danger and death would enter into the fray.

Jonathan tried to pass the time by pressing Zakariah for information about the man they were travelling to Cambridge to meet, Aldrich Manwin Tucker. However, Zakariah seemed to be reluctant to say too much. Jonathan didn't realise that Zakariah was worried that if he said anything, Jonathan would jump off the train at the next station, head back to the castle and leave him to face Aldrich Manwin Tucker alone. Jonathan pressed him about the fly eating comment. Zakariah just shrugged his shoulders and said, "Check his teeth for wings," which didn't help steady Jonathan's nerves.

The journey passed without incident and without any more details for Jonathan. He wished Dominique was there with him, but she too was travelling, although he didn't know that at the time. Eventually, they settled into the drowsy state that everyone else in the carriages was feeling and the hours passed by, along with the countryside, towns and cities outside their carriage window.

By the time Jonathan and Zakariah's train pulled into Cambridge train station, it was already 5 p.m. and too late to go and see Aldrich. They decided they would find a place to stay and visit him the next morning.

They found a quaint, 18th century four-star hotel on Glisson Road, near to the university cricket club and just a short walk to where they needed to be the following morning. There were plenty of rooms available in the city because it was just three days before Christmas. On their short walk to the hotel, Jonathan kept thinking about the last time he had been in a hotel room with Zakariah. Back then, they had had to jump out of the balcony doors into a swimming pool, two floors below, with people shooting at them from the floor they had just jumped from.

"You okay?" Zakariah asked him as they walked along. Jonathan had gone quiet. Zakariah's breath was visible in the frosty night air.

"Fine," Jonathan announced.

"Good. You know what I was just thinking about?"

Jonathan shook his head and waited.

"I was just thinking about the last time we were in a hotel room together ..."

The Controller in Islington had called Aldrich earlier that day and advised him to expect the two Knights. After checking in, Zakariah left a voice message for Aldrich on his answerphone to say they would be there by 9 a.m. the following morning. Zakariah was pleased Aldrich did not pick up, but he knew that he was fairly safe. Aldrich rarely picked up the telephone when it rang. Zakariah then telephoned the Controller in Islington to confirm they had arrived and what their plans were. She would log their position and let St Clair know.

It was a bitterly cold evening but after freshening up a little, they decided to walk around the city to get some air and clear their heads. They were glad of the exercise after the six and a half hour train journey from Scotland.

It was a beautiful starlit December night. The sounds and the hustle and bustle of the city followed them as they walked. People were talking, laughing, walking, running, drinking, singing, eating and just generally enjoying their night out, their sounds reverberating off one building and onto another. The smells that lingered in the air were rich with Indian, Chinese, local cuisine bar food and kebab shops. Everything was lit up with a great show of multi-coloured, Christmas decoration lights. Christmas music piped out of various venues: Slade and *Merry Christmas*, Band Aid and *Do They Know it's Christmas?* and the Pogues and Kirsty MacColl with *Fairy Tale of New York* all seemed to be on a continuous loop. The music and lights laced the atmosphere with a sense of happiness and optimism.

Zakariah had been to Cambridge a number of times: the last time he was there was also to see Aldrich and he was with St Clair that time. However, that was a number of years ago, before he'd left the Templars and tried to find a new life for himself in a desperate attempt to distance himself from the things that kept reminding him about the loss of his wife and the brutal way she had died. He blamed himself for not being there to protect her when it happened because he had stayed an extra day on a mission he had led. He could have left on time but didn't, and this drove his persecution of himself for years.

He was pleased he was in Cambridge with Jonathan. He liked spending time with his son-in-law. He found him great company to be with and he was really pleased that his daughter, Dominique, had found someone like him. He had always thought his daughter would die an old spinster because she had never shown any interest in men; then the ex-priest came along and captured her heart.

Zakariah liked the city. He liked it for its history, for its architecture and how it, like many other university cities, was transformed because of the influence of the student population, into a young, vibrant place: the symbiotic nature of the old and the new working in perfect harmony.

In contrast, Jonathan had never been to Cambridge before, but he too liked university cities because he found that they all possessed a vibrant nature, generated by their multi-cultural, young enquiring minds, albeit as temporary residents only. Back home in his city, Washington DC, students from Howard, Georgetown and George Washington universities mingled with locals, tourists and law makers from the Capitol, creating a cornucopia of temporary and permanent metropolitans that he loved to be among.

Lots of people were out late-night shopping, dining, drinking or just enjoying the festive spectacle that the council of Cambridge had put on for students, visitors and residents alike. Whilst most students had already left for the holidays, a number of students had stayed on: those cramming in last minute work to catch up, those who had decided that Cambridge offered more fun than a large turkey dinner with bickering relatives back home.

Zakariah and Jonathan found a small bistro called Max's. At a table for two and in front of a large window that looked out onto the busy pedestrian walkway, they ate ribs and drank a beer each, chatted and watched the world go by. For a short while, they forgot why they were there, the ring, Salah El-Din, the Abaddons, the missions they had been on and the missions that were happening in different parts of the world as they ate. They talked about films, books but mostly sport: they were both keen sports fans. Zakariah promised to take Jonathan to a football game and Jonathan promised to take Zakariah to watch the Washington Redskins, his home team, when they were both in America next.

Jonathan really liked Zakariah. Zakariah's missions with Luther Jones were almost legendary in the Order. Jonathan always found him to be polite, graceful in his manners and mannerisms. He had a soft well-educated accent, just detectable in his speech. When Jonathan's sister, Courtney, had first met Zakariah in Washington DC, he'd smoked: he no longer did.

The two men sat chatting as the rest of their night passed pleasantly.

Date: 23rd December 2012, 9 a.m.
Place: University of Cambridge, Medieval Studies: Department of Supernatural, Occultism and History of Satanic Medieval Renaissance

It had taken them around thirty minutes to find the office. Jonathan and Zakariah now stood outside the door of office number 31A, of the faculty building: Professor Aldrich Manwin Tucker's office. Every door they passed along the winding corridors had glass in the top part, so you could see into the offices. There was no glass in this door, which only added to their apprehension. The drab corridors surprised Jonathan; he expected them to be more decorated, perhaps more ornate, given where they were, but they weren't.

Other than the cleaner who had directed them, no one else seemed to be around. They both stood waiting for the other to move. They both felt claustrophobic, Zakariah because he had been there

115

before and knew what was coming and Jonathan because he hadn't been there before and didn't know what was coming but was worried what it would be.

"You knock!" Zakariah whispered to Jonathan, as they stood there unsure.

"Knock, me, knock? Do I look like a knocker? You're more of a knocker than me," Jonathan suggested, with the change in his pocket making a racket as he played with it nervously. "You know, this is how I felt when I first went to the castle and had to decide to ring that bell or run, and look how that turned out. I was killed in Cumbria. So, you knock."

In the end though, the decision was taken out of their hands.

"What!" a stern voice roared through the door. It was sharp and haughty, like an ex-public-school boy, who had become a parody of an ex-public-school boy in adulthood, mixed with an ageing colonel, who expected his officer's batman and his childhood nanny to be at his beck and call.

"He heard you," Zakariah whispered. "He heard those damn coins rattling in your pocket. We're in for it now."

The door opened, not just opened but flew open like it had been set off with an explosive device. *That's why there's no glass in his door,* Jonathan thought, as his heart jumped.

"Ah! They sent the thief then, did they?" the man who had flung open the door said looking at Zakariah. "So, they let you back in did they, Thief? Well don't even think about stealing any of my papers. You keep your slippery hands in your pockets at all times, my boy. I'll be watching you. I told St Clair to ban you and not to let you back in. Fallen Knight, fallen arse. They should hide the bloody silverware now you're back!" His high and mighty demeanour was imposing, intimidating and almost as explosive as the door. Aldrich saw Jonathan standing behind Zakariah. "Ah, the *mortuus sacerdos* – the dead priest! St Clair sent a thief and a corpse to come and see me."

Jonathan strained to see his teeth, but it was difficult standing behind Zakariah.

"I hope you've brought my sword. I bet you've both got

116

swords; everyone has a bloody sword, but I don't have a sword. Why don't I have a bloody sword? He told me I would be getting a bloody sword."

Jonathan stepped out from behind Zakariah, opened his mouth and went to speak. He was just about to say yes, he had a sword, in fact they all had swords, but Zakariah gave him a startled look when he realised Jonathan was about to give the game away. Jonathan closed his mouth again.

Then, just as quickly as Aldrich had got onto the subject of swords, he got off it again. "Tea?" he said, as sweetly as an old grandmother and beckoned them into his office.

Zakariah and Jonathan entered meekly. Zakariah put his hands in his pockets. Jonathan also had one of his hands in his pocket, rattling his change nervously.

Aldrich's office was large, old and had obviously not been part of any repairs or refurbishment project for quite some time. It smelt musty and it smelt of pipe tobacco. Yellow stained coving and two huge ceiling roses blended nicely with the yellowing, plain walls. The ceiling was about eight feet high, Edwardianesque in height and decor. There was one window; it didn't look as if it had been opened for some time, so the pipe smoke had nowhere to go other than to seep into the walls and ceiling. The window had sixteen small square glass panes and on two of them hung sticky fly paper. Jonathan couldn't take his eyes off the sticky fly paper. It was too far away for him to see if there were places with only wings left behind and their bodies gone.

Inside the room, it was immediately obvious that it was a haven for dogeared papers, aged and yellowing files of different descriptions, books and magazines of more multiple descriptions and an assortment of folders marked, *Test Papers for marking* and dated three months ago. The place was full of written stuff in various formats, sizes, ages and condition. The literary tomes, digests and works wrestled for space on the overflowing floor-to-ceiling shelving, affixed to every wall. His dark oak furniture, with green leather inlay, had seen better days. His desk was piled high with papers; his green, padded swivel chair had his indent impressed on its seat. There were two whiteboards full of dates, arrows joining one set of scribbled text with an assortment of unrecognisable diagrams, and another arrow or two heading towards speech bubbles with rambling notions and ideas.

In the corner, next to one of the boards, two fly fishing rods leaned against a coat stand, surrounded by three angler's baskets, large green waders and a small table with an assortment of reels and plastic boxes on it and with small drawers spilling over with different coloured and shaped fly hooks. Hanging on the coat stand were an old, weather beaten Barbour waxed coat and a hat that had obviously been run over at some stage by a very large truck.

The office of Aldrich Manwin Tucker precisely matched his eccentric, self-aggrandising, larger than life, life. He looked about a hundred years old but was in fact only seventy-two years old, although he had forged a birth certificate when he'd first joined the faculty and so had been working well past his retirement age. He had also put down his nationality as German, which was odd because he spoke no German, but he did speak with a Welsh accent. Nobody had thought to check when he'd joined the faculty and now it was too late; besides, no one in HR would volunteer to ask him.

Whilst Zakariah and Jonathan found somewhere to sit, Aldrich busied himself making tea from a dented metal kettle, which was placed on top of a small, blue primus camping stove. Jonathan noticed he'd put five heaped spoons of loose tea into a cracked, china tea pot with 'Property of British Rail' written on it. Then he strained the tea through a tea-stained strainer, all which Jonathan had never seen before. They were both handed their tea in china cups and saucers, not matching, and also somewhat stained. He asked them if they wanted milk or sugar and they both declined. Jonathan sipped his tea and nearly spat it out; it was the consistency of treacle. Zakariah didn't taste his tea, he'd been there before!

Aldrich slurped away at his tea. "Hobnob?" he bellowed, holding up half a packet of biscuits. He bellowed all the time as if they were thirty feet away and not six feet.

As he spoke, Jonathan was again straining to look at his teeth; he was looking for fly wings but now the Hobnob crumbs made it difficult to tell.

"No Hobnobs? Good! More for me then." He gave a haughty laugh.

Aldrich wore a brown corduroy suit that looked like it would have been better on a much larger man, a checked shirt and a tie that looked like it had been crocheted. His brown brogues were scuffed and had not seen polish for quite a while. He wasn't a big man; he stood five feet nine and weighed around ten and a half stone. He was partly bald with only his hair on the sides and the back of his head surviving; white, but uncombed, it sprouted off in several directions. There was a half-hearted attempt by him to occasionally brush it with his hand over the top of his head. He was missing two bottom front teeth, and a number of teeth in the right side of his mouth, top and bottom, had worn where he obviously held his pipe, which he now lit. Great heaps of smoke came out of his mouth and blanketed everything within four feet of him.

"I am assuming that neither one of you has my sword then?" he bellowed from behind another nimbus forming cloud. "No portmanteau, I see?"

"It's a big luggage bag, I think," Zakariah whispered to Jonathan whilst trying not to move his lips as he spoke.

They both looked sheepish, as if they had forgotten to bring the tickets to a world-famous concert to someone standing outside the concert hall waiting for them. Zakariah took the plunge. "No sword I'm afraid, Aldrich. St Clair never mentioned bringing a sword, but we will be sure to tel—"

"Then, Thief, if you have not brought my sword, state your and the Corpse's business, and let's get on with it! Time is time, and time is time again. Again."

Jonathan looked at Zakariah and he saw that Zakariah had no idea what it meant either. "Solomon's ring has been stolen," Jonathan said. He thought he would try and get the conversation going. The change in Aldrich's demeanour was instantaneous.

"*The* ring?" he asked, taking the pipe out of his mouth for the first time since he'd lit it and emphasising *the*. He placed the pipe in a pipe rack with a number of others, surrounded by pipe ash. "Do you know for sure that it is *the* ring?"

"The Vatican had it, and they have confirmed that yes, it is *the* ring, Solomon's signet ring," Jonathan answered.

"What else, what else, Corpse? quickly now!" Aldrich sat back in his swivel chair, intrigue and excitement written all over his face.

"It was stolen from a warehouse unit in Manchester on the 15th November. Whoever stole it, knew exactly where it was."

"Ah, *Sancti Furem* – the Holy Thief shows himself again," Aldrich thundered. "Damn that fellow!"

"You think it's a *he* then?" Zakariah asked.

"Catholic Church is not over brimming with females in positions of power, positions where they would know about these things, so yes. I think it's a safe bet it is a *he*. What else Corpse?" He turned back to face Jonathan. "Hurry."

Jonathan could tell that there were two Aldrich's, the crazy one and the richly talented, investigative learned professor, but both wrapped up in the sharp, acidic tongued, bellowing eccentric. "St Clair believes that the ring was stolen for a specific purpose, not for its historical importance, or its value, but, he believes, for something far more nefarious, something dark, something very dark given the ring we are talking about and what has been written about it."

Aldrich wiped Hobnob crumbs from his jacket and shirt. "It was one of the seven seals of Solomon; it was his signet ring," Aldrich said, now searching for a dusty book from one of the shelves. He found what he was looking for. He turned the pages and revealed a painting of the ring of Solomon. On the face of the ring was a star. "There has been much disagreement and argument over whether that star is a five-pointed star, a pentagram or a six-pointed star, a hexagram."

"I read it was a six-pointed star, like the Star of David, King David, his father," Jonathan said. "I read it was engraved by God, forged from iron and brass. Inside it had sealed commands to both good and evil spirits. Because the name of God was also engraved in the ring, people said that Solomon could control demons. And, in the wrong hands, the ring would call up bad genies and exorcise good genies. This is why St Clair thinks it was stolen."

Aldrich lit his pipe again. "It actually has five points, not six. It is a pentagram and not by accident. It protects against evil spirits. Many Templar graves have the pentagram on their tombstones. There are those who believe that the Order started to use the five-pointed star only after they found what they found in Jerusalem and only after they left the Holy Land.

"But," Aldrich leaned forward, his pipe still in his mouth, "if you wear the ring upside down, and you have the two points pointing upwards, instead of downwards, this is the symbol of evil; this sign attracts sinister forces. It reverses things, it reverses the order of things. If you know how to use it and have the right incantations, it is a dangerous amulet. When turned upside down it becomes the hieroglyphic of black magic, the dark arts."

And there we have it, thought Jonathan; *it didn't take long for the bad stuff to start. Now we're going to have dark arts. That's not going to end well*. His hand was back in his pocket, coins rattling.

"Damn it, Corpse!" Aldrich exploded, "This is bloody exciting, so, bugger me Brigadier, lets press on! The ring, many have tried to find it because of the wisdom it is supposed to bestow upon its wearer: 1 Kings, 10:24 *'And all the Earth sought to Solomon, to hear his wisdom, which God had put in his heart.'* However, many have sought it for the wealth it is purported to bring. Whilst Solomon was famous for his wisdom, said to have been a gift from God, he was also as famous for his staggering wealth and his mines, King Solomon's mines." Aldrich reached for a large, black Bible on his desk. "In the Bible," he turned the pages. "yes, here, it talks about the gold that Solomon had. He received six hundred and sixty-six talents. His gold cache would be around twenty-five tons of gold for each year of his forty-year reign. But remember, nowhere in the Kingdom of the Israelites can that kind of gold be found. 1 Kings, 10:23 '*So King Solomon exceeded all the kings of the Earth for riches and for wisdom.*'"

Aldrich turned in his chair and crossed his legs. He looked thoughtful. "I concur with St Clair," he finally announced. "The ring was not stolen because of wisdom or wealth; the ring was stolen because of the potential power it has. Remember the legend says that Solomon was able to learn the names of the demons that plagued his kingdom and discovered how they persecuted humans because of the ring. He even put them to work, including Asmodeus, King of Demons. He commanded them to help with the construction of his temple, the temple that housed the Ark of the Covenant. However, I think we know that it was not taken for good; it was taken for its Solomonic magic and its ability to tap into darker things. Yes, I do concur with St Clair."

"So, how is it being used and why?" Zakariah asked, "To use it you need to know the incantations, or know someone who does?"

Aldrich took a quick glance to check that Zakariah still had his hands in his pockets. "Think of it like voodoo. You need an amulet, you need certain words, incantations and you need access to your victims."

"Since the ring was stolen, three bishops have been murdered," Zakariah told him. "And we received a message late last night from St Clair. A fourth bishop has just been murdered, this one in New Jersey, in the States. He said he would brief us when we get back because there's more to the story. Something was stolen but he didn't say what. He said he would also brief you later. As for how they all died, they wer—"

"Poisoned," Aldrich interrupted, "they were all poisoned, right?"

Zakariah and Jonathan both nodded.

Aldrich went silent, puffing on his pipe and doing his bit towards global warming. He was deep in thought, so they decided not to interrupt him. Jonathan was staring at the fly papers behind Aldrich but still could not see if there were wings with no flies on them. His attention turned back to the desk. He hadn't noticed it before but there was a riding crop on his desk. He nudged Zakariah and indicated towards the desk.

"What?" Zakariah asked.

"There," Jonathan whispered, looking towards Aldrich's desk.

"What?" Zakariah asked again.

"There! He has a riding crop on his desk. Look! Why does he have a riding crop on his desk? Who keeps a riding crop on their desk?"

"You've listened to too many confessions as a priest, Jonathan. He's quite the accomplished horseman. He once rode naked through Nottingham chasing a witch."

"And you could have told me this last night?"

"Would you have slept?"

"No."

"Would you have come?"

"No."

Aldrich came out of his thoughts. "Tell me," Aldrich asked, "who does St Clair think took the ring?"

"Salah El-Din," Zakariah replied.

Aldrich thought for a moment longer. "Then it makes sense. He has found someone with the knowledge of the ring and knowledge of the incantations. Now, what else?" Aldrich stood up and started wiping off everything on one of the whiteboards. He started scribbling. "Bugger me, Brigadier." Aldrich continued to write and ask questions. Aldrich's second white board got wiped and he started on that one with his notes. They were both soon full. He'd refilled his pipe four times; he now refilled it again.

"Could this be the Ghost, Zivko Gowst, behind all thes—"

"No, no, no, no, Corpse. Zivko and the Abaddons are not behind the ring but bloody riveting stuff, ay?"

They had been in Aldrich's office for over five hours. The old cast-iron radiators kept them warm, although Aldrich's attempt at his own cloud formation was taking its toll on their throats and lungs. Now the white boards resembled a mixture of an early

Picasso and a good day at a Montessori nursey with a group of five-year-olds.

Aldrich was standing back from his two white boards, his expression pained. He looked at them hard. He tilted his head one way, then he tilted his head the other way. He paced. He crouched, bent and leaned both forward, then backward. He sat, then stood, then sat and stood some more. He swore a lot and smoked just as much. Then finally, after an age, he announced, "We have a problem."

Zakariah and Jonathan waited to hear; it was not readily evident to them from Aldrich's whiteboard notes. However, in the middle of each board, in red and circled, all the comments, arrows, lines and dotted lines led to the word 'Hag.'

"If Salah El-Din has the ring then he has a Hag. And it could only be a Hag from the old Order; they would know the incantations, that is if any of them were left."

"Hag?" Jonathan asked.

"Hag my dear Corpse. I guess the closest would be crone or witch. Think of Salem on your side of the pond. But, this is a very old witch." Aldrich's expression now grew serious. "Someone with knowledge of this ring knew they needed a Hag. And, they knew that the Hag that would know the incantations could only come from one of the old Orders, the *Cailleach* or *Gwrach Marwolaeth*. The *Cailleachs* are all dead now, the last of them in 1902. At one time you would find them in Scotland, Ireland and the Isle of Man. So, this has to be the Order of *Gwrach Marwolaeth*."

"What does *Gwrach Marwolaeth* mean?" Jonathan asked, ten seconds before he'd wished he hadn't.

"*Gwrach Marwolaeth* means witch of death."

Jonathan's hand reached for the change in his pocket.

"The Order of *Gwrach Marwolaeth* were from Wales but we killed the last of them a long time ago, or so I thought up until just now."

More smoke followed. He sat on the edge of his desk and picked up the riding crop. Zakariah felt Jonathan's elbow dig his side.

"But you know," Aldrich said thoughtfully, "there was a

rumour at the time that there was a sister, but we could never verify it and in all these years there has never been a sighting of her. Not a word. *Nada.*"

"You are a witch hunter?" Jonathan asked.

"I was a *Gwrach* hunter, yes."

"And that's how you met St Clair?"

"Not directly, but yes."

Jonathan wanted to know more about how dangerous the *Gwrach Marwolaeth* were, so he mistakenly asked.

"Experts with poisons, Corpse; in fact, it was their trade mark. Hard to detect in autopsies. They need a vehicle to get to their victims though. An amulet, a doll like in voodoo and then they have their *sillafu*, their spell. It's really an ancient form of hypnosis and it was very, very effective. If they had you within eyesight and earshot, then you were pretty much sunk. The only thing that saved victims was if the Hag was detected before she got close enough to you to work her hypnotic *sillafu*. But if she had the ring …" He trailed off and then caught his thread again.

"One of their favourite *sillafus* was recreating the phenomenon known as sleep paralysis. It is when a person feels the presence of a supernatural being which immobilises them. They describe it like having someone sit on your chest. The *Gwrach* Hags were cursed killers and this *sillafu* was a crippling condition, a frightening one. Often the victims were in a paralysed state for months and some died."

Aldrich pulled an old, dusty, leather-bound book from one of the over-spilling shelves. He pushed a pile of dogeared papers away and made a space for it on his desk. The others gathered round as he looked through the pages for what he wanted. He stopped at a picture.

"This is the old Order of *Gwrach Marwolaeth*," he said looking at the old sepia photograph of a small, wizened old woman, chained by manacles to her hands and feet, her eyes wild, her mouth foaming. There were five men around her. "See how they all have ear protectors on so they could not hear her spewing her ancient words. This one killed nine people before she was caught. She was put to death in secret; the authorities never made her existence public."

He turned to another page. The picture in front of them was of a man. He was obviously dead and lying on a blood-soaked bed. "Another of their *sillafus*. This is where they plant an extreme thought in their victim's mind. This is one of the nastier ones, body integrity dysphoria. Through powers of suggestion, they are able to make someone believe that they must amputate a limb or other body part. The condition, which exists in some without having a vindictive Hag whispering in your ear, is caused by a mismatch between someone's mental picture of their body image and their actual physical self. Simply, part of the brain that deals with body image is screwed up. It all comes from here," he pointed to a picture of the brain, "the sensorimotor limb area. The Hags intone hypnotic chants of the *sillafus* and people take to cutting parts of their bodies off."

The caption underneath the picture said that the man died of blood loss; he had removed his left arm and was halfway through amputating his right leg.

"For us to find the *Gwrach* Hag, and find her we must unless you want more dead bishops, we must look to Wales, for that's where they came from, their base. They would travel far and wide, but they would always return to their base.

"The Hag would have needed to get close to the bishops to administer her poison. Normally, a Hag will pour a few droplets into her victim's mouth, but, she needs to get close enough to do that. I think she is using the ring to amplify her incantations. If her victim enters into her trance, they will let her in, open all doors, unlock all locks, disable and disarm all alarms." Aldrich started boiling his kettle again. Above the open flamed primus, was a sign, 'No Smoking' and by the side of that a fire alarm, and above that, a water sprinkler. He turned to Zakariah and Jonathan and held up the kettle. They both refused, saying no three times, just in case he didn't hear the first two nos. He sat back down at his desk and dipped six Hobnobs into his tea cup – there wasn't much tea left in the cup after that.

"Did St Clair say why he thinks Salah El-Din wants the bishop's dead?"

"He didn't say. All he said was that we need to find out about the ring. I think he knew you would have a good idea who could use its powers, but as to why Salah El-Din is doing this, he doesn't know."

"Mmm. Okay. Let's see if we can figure this out. Right. Time to focus. Hobnobs away then." He put the biscuits into a drawer. "There are two things that we need to be mindful of. Firstly, he is not likely to kill bishops under instruction from another. In fact, I suggest we can strike that reason off our list. For himself, he has killed bishops and clergy in the past, right?'

"Yes," Jonathan said, remembering his ordeal at the small church on Zakynthos.

"Indeed, but four and in a short space of time raises doubts over whether it's for himself. There is no obvious gain for him to kill bishops. He does things for gain. Whilst he may despise the clergy, and clearly he always has, he would not kill without gain. And anyway, if I am right and I will come to this in a minute, there is no reason to kill."

"Then he did it for another," Jonathan started, "but—"

"But willingly, Corpse. He killed them willingly for another."

"Why?"

"Perhaps to win favour. Perhaps to attract another's attention. Perhaps it is a trade: a quid pro quo." Aldrich thought about it. "My bet would be he is doing this as a quid pro quo and he's showing his strength, and showing someone his willingness to trade."

"And you don't think the bishops died because he was stealing from them, from the Vatican?" Zakariah asked.

Aldrich glanced down at Zakariah's hands. They were still firmly in his trouser pockets. "If he's stealing Vatican property, he can do that without killing or potentially leaving additional evidence for law enforcement. He has an insider because he would not have known about the ring and the ring's whereabouts without help, he would not have known about the *Gwrach Marwolaeth*, and that they would possess the incantations to use the ring. On both counts, he has had inside help all along."

"From within the Vatican?" Jonathan said.

"Indeed, Corpse. *Sancti Furem* – the Holy Thief is more complicit than it first seemed. Salah El-Din is probably the only person we know who could have got to the Holy Thief."

"So, we need to find Salah El-Din and the Holy Thief?"

"You do, Corpse."

"And you, Aldrich. What are your plans now?" Zakariah asked him.

"Why, to find the Hag of course. Exodus 22:18, '*Thou shall not suffer a witch to live.*' But you, Knights, you be careful out there! 1 Peter, 5:8 '*Sober-minded; be watchful. Your adversary the devil prowls around like a roaring lion, seeking someone to devour.*' You watch yourselves with Salah El-Din!"

Jonathan smiled, "Ah, but we have our own lion; we have a Lionheart."

They said their goodbyes. Jonathan and Zakariah were staying one more night because they had missed the last train back to Scotland. They would catch the first one in the morning, on Christmas Eve.

They asked Aldrich if he needed anything.

"Yes," he roared from behind his cloud formation. "Three things. One, tell Proctor I will need to speak to him about Wales. Two, ask St Clair to find out if there is anything that links the dead bishops, other than that they are bishops and, of course, that they are dead. Number three, tell St Clair I will need Luther."

"We will," Zakariah assured him. "Is there anything else?"

"Yes, Thief," Aldrich barked back. "There is. You can tell Luther to bring my bloody sword. Now bugger off and keep your hands in your pockets on the way out. We have cameras you know!"

Chapter 8

Brick, New Jersey

Dominique was booked on the overnight flight to Newark. It was uneventful. There were no reports to read, no intel given by the Vatican. She ate a light meal on the plane and tried to watch a movie, but she got bored with the size of the small screen and so she switched off her light, covered herself with a blanket and slept.

Date: 23rd December 2012
Place: The town of Brick, Ocean County, New Jersey

She arrived fresh into Newark International airport on the morning of the 23rd December. She was happy to be back in the US; she liked the US and liked Americans – one American ex-priest in particular. She cleared customs fairly quickly. Her passport, containing the name Julie Meadows, didn't raise any red flags and the usual stern-faced border control staff smiled as he stamped her passport and waved her through. The baggage hall was mayhem; everyone was trying to get somewhere else for the holidays and delayed flights, tired children, overworked baggage handlers all added to the lack of Christmas spirit and good cheer. She found her bag and made her way out of the baggage hall.

She picked up a rental car from Avis, which had been pre-booked for her. After checking for dents and scratches, with the help of a chatty Raymond, the Avis man with the clip board and a check list attached to it, she typed in the address of her hotel into the satnav.

She was sad to be missing Christmas with Jonathan. She knew he had gone to see Aldrich with her father. She had never met Aldrich but had heard all the stories and winced at the thought of her poor husband meeting the Welsh eccentric. She knew her father, Zakariah, would look after him though, and make sure that he came to no harm. He was now well-trained, or as well-trained an ex-priest with an aversion to training could be, so she took some comfort in that.

She cleared her head and focused on the mission in hand. She was eager to get started, to meet up with the Indian, John Wolf. It had been months since she'd seen Wolf, other than in numerous video calls. She liked Wolf, and together they made quite the practical jokers. The current long running one they had instigated, with the help of Courtney, Jonathan's sister, was telling Bertram that the Controller in Islington was named Daisy Picking.

Dominique pulled out of the rental carpark and headed for the Garden State Highway; it would be about a fifty-minute drive to Brick in Ocean County, depending on traffic. She was in luck; traffic was light.

After a fairly pleasant fifty-minute drive, Dominique pulled the car into the front of the hotel and popped the boot. She tossed the keys to the valet, smiled, gave him ten dollars and went inside, followed by a bell boy carrying her bag. Once inside, she took the bag from him and tipped him the same. He went away pleased.

It was quiet inside the 'Metro on the Inn' hotel. Piped music wove its way through the building, unobtrusive at first, but slightly irritating if you listened for too long. The thirty-minute melody was on a loop and it played twenty-four hours a day.

Dominique was glad to be inside in the warmth, regardless of the entertainment.

"Yes, Ma'am, how can I help y'all today?"

"Checking in please." She handed the receptionist her passport and confirmation email.

"Why yes Ma'am; I'll have y'all checked in in no time at all," the receptionist said. Her name badge announced her name was Sally-

May Bernstein and her lilt announced she was not a New Jerseyan but from the south, the Deep South.

Dominique looked around. She saw the Indian sitting in front of a log burning fire: cowboy boots, denim jeans and a checked shirt. He'd flown out of Logan, so he'd been there a while. A half-drunk mug of coffee sat in front of him. The receptionist noticed Dominique looking.

"Ain't he just the hottie? I gave him my number y'know. I know I shouldn't but have you seen how firm his butt is?" She chuckled girlishly. "Y'know, I reckon he's Indian. He's first nation and I ain't never been with no Indian before. You know what they say about first nation men?" She winked. Then she handed Dominique her room card. "That's room number twenty-six. Now, y'all have a lovely stay with us here at the Metro on the Inn, and if y'all need anything, y'all just come and ask Sally-May Bernstein, y'hear."

Dominique walked towards the elevator. Wolf followed her some paces back. They didn't speak to each other in the lift; the CCTV camera was on. They got out of the elevator on the first floor. Ever since Abu Dhabi, Jonathan had made her promise to always try and book rooms on the first floor of hotels, just in case she needed to make yet another quick exit.

There were no CCTV cameras in the corridor, so they walked side by side but Wolf noticed that she kept looking at his back.

"Is there something wrong back there?" he asked.

"Nar; just something Sally-May said."

"Who is Sally-May?"

"The girl at reception."

"Ah!"

They got to Dominique's room. Wolf was already checked in. He'd already been in Dominique's room, after checking the register whilst Sally-May was very kindly getting him two envelopes he didn't need from the stationery cupboard in the back.

On her bed was a small holdall.

"See you've been in my room already. You remembered what Bertram said about our phones?"

"Verbatim. He said they have a device that will allow you to unlock digital locks. For example, hotel rooms that use a touch contact key configuration or most cars that use electronic fobs, or doors that use digit sequences. Clever lad our Bertram. By the way, the bag is curtesy of Bill Meeks."

She knew what was in it. She favoured a Heckler Koch.40 and a pump-action 12-gauge shotgun, designed for smaller shooters. It had a seven-shot magazine and a specially modified handgrip stock. Also in the bag was a shoulder rig. She checked the weapons, expertly.

The room was a standard, bland room but it was comfortable and most of all, the hotel was fairly empty, with just a few visitors visiting their families in Brick for the holidays. This meant they did not have lots of people to watch, or to worry about.

Once she'd finished checking her weapons, she took out her mobile phone and mouthed to the phone's screen: 'Call Islington and switch to loudspeaker.' They heard the Controller's voice. Dominique updated the Controller on their plan. The Controller logged their location into the computer, and the rest of their proposed locations for that day. Then she checked the locators, the tracking devices built into the credit cards Bertram had invented. The polymagnetite multilayer skins, compressed together with nano circuitry imbedded within the centre skin layers, had a built-in nano chip tracker. This meant the Templars could be found almost anywhere. After Romania, every Templar was issued with a card. They now kept the card with them at all times. Each card transmitted by bouncing its signal off any nearby satellite, and as there were thousands of satellites in the sky, this gave them extensive range and coverage. Its battery life was around three months; however, it would constantly recharge through either body warmth or solar energy from the sun. If it was exposed to either of these, it would transmit without pause indefinitely. St Clair never wanted another situation where a Knight went missing and they failed to find them. They were lucky to have found them in Romania. He wanted to ensure everyone was findable in the future, wherever possible.

The Controller told Dominique that their signals were working. Then Dominique wished her a happy holiday because she knew she was away over Christmas, at least for a few days. The Controller was always away at Christmas for a few days and she always visited the same place. She wished Dominique a safe mission and then she hung up.

Next, Dominique followed the same procedure with her mobile phone, but she called Bill Meeks. St Clair had called Bill the day before Dominique left Scotland and briefed him on their mission. St Clair asked Bill to do some digging to see what he could find out about the theft, and if there was anything else out of the ordinary. He knew Meeks could not do much to help them because it was out of his area; he was based in Washington.

Meeks answered the phone; he was working from home. He told Dominique that the theft of the saint's skull had not been reported, only the murder of the bishop. He told her the local PD were all over the murder because they were taking heat from the diocese to arrest someone and quickly. He also told her that there was some chatter about a few extra criminal types in and around Brick. He was still checking it out, but he warned her to be careful and he would circle back with them as soon as he had more news. Dominique thanked him and hung up.

Next, she called St Clair and they had a brief conversation. She told him that Wolf was arranging their meeting with Father Angelo Fugero, the Vatican representative, the man who had telephoned St Clair the day before, on the 22nd.

St Clair reminded her that Fugero would not say what had been stolen, but Nef had called him just before Fugero, so they were already one step ahead of the Vatican. He reminded her that they needed to be several steps ahead because they clearly had a traitor in their midst. She asked him how Jonathan had got on with Aldrich. He told her that they had got into Cambridge too late to go and see him. They were going to

133

see him at 9 a.m. UK time, so they would still be with him.

"Poor Jonathan," she said.

"He stood up to Salah El-Din. I'm sure he can deal with Ald—" He thought about it. "Well, maybe not." They both laughed and St Clair told her not to worry, Jonathan was with her father; Zakariah would look after him.

"I know," she said.

Dominique had been given the role as 'Guardian of the Seer' – which she loved, and teased Jonathan mercilessly about, because he was the Seer and she kept telling him he had to do exactly as she said, always. There was a time when she could not wait to leave on her next mission. She loved the adventure and the excitement, even the danger. She was independent and strong-willed. She was pretty, intelligent, a 7th Dan in Karate. She was made for adventure. However, now, every time she went away anywhere without Jonathan, she missed him and couldn't wait to get back. She missed his wit, his laughter, their Thursday evenings making toasted ravioli and drinking Dolcetto red wine in front of the fire and talking about their dreams and aspirations, or watching old black and white movies together. She missed her dogs.

Later that morning, St Clair sent Dominique and John Wolf a message to say that Jonathan and Zakariah had sent a quick update, and Aldrich believed he had identified the poisoner. Aldrich had said he doubted if the police would identify the poison, but to check, just in case.

Whilst Dominique freshened up, Wolf waited in the hotel reception. He called Father Angelo Fugero on his mobile phone. Father Angelo Fugero was expecting the call, he had received a call earlier advising him that a man would contact him sometime that day. The priest didn't know, but the call came from an unlisted and untraceable number in Islington, England. Wolf told him they were on their way and asked the priest to meet them at the church. The priest said he was already there and would meet them at the front of the church, on the sidewalk. Wolf told him that they would like to see the police's preliminary crime report and the toxicology report, if he had them. Father Fugero confirmed he had the toxicology report and that he would bring it with him, but there were no other reports so far. He was still waiting for the police's preliminary crime report, because they were still investigating the crime scene at the bishop's house.

Wolf hung up. He was standing in front of the burning log fire, flicking through one of the table-top magazines.

Sally-May watched him intensely from her reception desk. The tall, lean man with solid broad shoulders looked a proud man. He had shoulder length jet-black hair, parted in the centre, chiselled and weathered features with deep tanned skin. She noticed a sparkle in his eyes, when he'd checked in, and knew he had a sense of humour. What she didn't see was that they were also the eyes of a hunter, the eyes of a man who could survive on the ranges, the eyes of a man that embodied the old wild west. When he had checked in, his rich, gravel voice had got her at 'Wilfred Dupont,' an alias Wolf used a lot.

Sally-May took a call that came in on the six-line switch board. She wasn't concentrating. She looked at Wolf again. *What's not to like*, she thought. *And no wedding ring. Mama will adore him.*

Through the mirror directly in front of him, Wolf could see Sally-May staring at him. He thought he saw her wink.

Dominique saved him. She walked through the reception area and heads turned. Her long black, leather coat flowed in pursuit of her purposeful walk. It hid her shoulder rig and the gun inside it; it also housed her small shotgun, hidden in an inside pocket of the coat. Her black hoodie – hood up – black boots, and black trousers finished off the picture. It read: mean, tough, do not mess with! Wolf, like nearly all the Templars, also wore the same style coat, because they hid their weapons well, especially their favoured weapon, the Katana sword of the Samurai, which they could conceal in a back-body webbing that held their lightweight titanium *saya* – scabbard and sword. However, Wolf was just packing a six round Beretta M9 semi-automatic handgun and, of course, his first weapon of choice, a fourteen-inch bone-handled knife holstered in its sheath by his side; both weapons were hidden by his coat.

Dominique noticed the attention Wolf was getting from Sally-May and whilst it made her smile, they didn't need the additional attention. *Time to put a stop to this, permanently*, she thought. As they'd had time to check out the hotel and make sure it was safe, she would now risk them being seen together.

She went over to the reception desk. "Any messages for me?" she asked and gave her room number.

"No Ma'am," Sally-May said, never taking her eyes off John Wolf. "I think he's Comanche you know," Sally-May said, almost drooling her words.

"Really?" Dominique replied. Then she turned to Wolf and dashed Sally-May's hopes in just nine words. "Come on Geronimo, time to choose the engagement ring." They left together hand in hand, desperately trying to hide their smiles.

"Geronimo, really! Cheeseekau would have been more accurate," he whispered.

"Who's ever heard of Cheeseekau?" she whispered back.

"Oh, I guess the entire Shawnee nation, that's who."

"Good point," she replied.

"Okay then, Mary Poppins, let's go." The Indian said loudly. He started whistling 'Just a spoon full of sugar' on their way to the valet station outside.

Father Angelo Fugero was an archdeacon, he made a point of telling them at least three times. They'd pulled up just behind his car, which was parked directly outside the church. He was standing on the sidewalk waiting for them, a little cold and a little impatient. Behind the church was the house where the bishop had lived. Its front door was taped with blue and white barrier tape with 'CRIME SCENE DO NOT ENTER' printed across it. There was one policeman standing outside, guarding the crime scene until it was cleared and the house was released back to the diocese. There had been no witnesses to the murder and so the police only had the forensic evidence inside the house to go on. The problem was, they hadn't come up with anything so far. It was a high visibility case and the news networks were all over it. The commissioner wanted answers, but so far, they had none to give.

In seniority, Fugero was directly below the bishop, and he made a point of telling them that, as he shook their hands, Wolf's first. Wolf noticed this. He told them they could go into the church but not into the bishop's house; that was still a crime scene. He always spoke directly to Wolf. Wolf noticed this, too.

Fugero was a man in his late fifties, a bland looking man; if anything, he had the look of a man who'd spent all his life in administration, a bureaucrat with grey hair and an ashen complexion, medium build, height; medium everything. He handed Wolf the toxicology report inside a manila envelope. Wolf didn't take it. He smiled, and then pointed towards Dominique.

"She's in charge," he said. Wolf wanted to make a point. Fugero nodded, but Wolf could tell that he was rattled. He could tell he was one of those men who really didn't believe in equality, but in the dominance of his all but patriarchal society he lived in. Fugero sighed a little and gave the document to Dominique but she didn't take it.

"Oh, you can give that to my man. He will keep it for me." She winked at Wolf as she turned towards the church. "Now, lead on! One has much to do on one's agenda today."

Somewhat indignant, Father Fugero took them into the church via the side door, which he announced was called the priest's door. He wanted to make the point that they were privileged by him allowing them to enter that way. They walked through the chancel, the area used by the church's clergy and choir. The church smelt of church, a little musty with heavy traces of incense from numerous Masses over the years. It was a well-kept church, clean and neat, a church you would never enter and think, *there is something of great significance here*, but the Templars knew that was the point, which made it more plausible that the thieves had had inside help.

The priest stopped at the altar, the scene of the robbery. It

137

looked like any other stone altar. Inside a secret door was a steel safe. Father Fugero punched in the six-digit code. Inside the safe was a bronze reliquary box. He took the reliquary box out of the safe and opened it. It was empty.

"The skull of the saint had been here since 1932," he said, "until it was stolen, two days ago, on the 21st. Their Eminences in Rome decided all those years ago that the skull of John the Baptist should rest here, in this box, in not so plain sight. Here for safe keeping. It is a tragic thing, a dastardly thing that has happened. We have lost the saint and our bishop. This is the devil's work." He didn't take his two visitors for religious people; he took them for outside, private investigators the Vatican had employed to try to get the skull back. An Indian and a woman. He would not have made that decision: an Indian and a woman.

"The veneration of relics of the saints comes from the early years of the Church in Rome," he started to lecture them. "It started when the Christians met in secret, in the catacombs where they kept the tombs of our martyrs. It's where Mass was said in secret. But, make not the mistake and think that the Christian's veneration and reverence was worship of the saints; it was not. It was a reminder that God worked through them, and through their deaths.

"When Christians did not have to hide any more, we kept the practice of keeping a reminder of a saint. We kept a relic of them. A physical reminder: sometimes hair or bone, sometimes a piece of cloth from their clothes or a small piece of an instrument of torture that was used on them. So, you see, when we celebrate Mass, we celebrate it with all the saints and angels in heaven. Our bishops consecrate our church altars. They and what they contain are the essence of our worship. Now, ours is gone." The priest sat down, his head lowered; he truly was affected over the theft and the death of his bishop.

Dominique took the toxicology report out of the envelope. It was an initial summary. It said that they'd extracted the toxins but could not fully identify their composition. The report said they had analysed the bishop's blood, his urine, oral fluid and hair for toxins. Inside the envelope were also reports marked 'Medical,' 'Clinical,'

'Forensic,' and 'Laboratory.' They were all marked, 'Initial Summaries.' They were 'initial' because it was still early days in the process and more work would be done to identify exactly what poison had killed him. However, Dominique and John Wolf knew initial summaries were generally right.

"They're inconclusive," the priest said.

"He was murdered," Dominique replied. "Poisoned. No sign of a struggle, yet he was conscious when the toxins entered his blood stream. The toxins are pretty complex. He suffered. We know a lot, Father."

"So, what are you saying?" he asked her.

"We should leave the finding of his murderer to the local PD, although I suspect the murderer is long gone, and my colleague and I should focus on trying to get the skull back."

Wolf nodded in agreement.

"I want to be kept informed of every move, then. It is imperative that the Church is kept informed, Miss ..." He thought for a moment or two. "I didn't get your names."

"We didn't give them," Wolf said.

"Oh, you can call me Poppins," Dominique said with a wry smile.

"How will I contact you, Poppins?" the priest asked.

"We'll contact you. Now, thank you for the reports and the tour." She turned to Wolf. "Come along please, spit, spot, best foot forward."

Wolf and Dominique left the church in fits of laughter. Their plan was to head back to the hotel and call St Clair if he was still up and bring him up to date with what they had found out and seen. Outside the light was beginning to dim; it was still afternoon, late afternoon, but the winter nights had long since set in.

Wolf started the engine and turned the car's heater up to maximum. "Did you see him, at our six?" He asked Dominique without looking at her, but glancing in his rear-view mirror at a man standing some way off.

"Yes, I saw him. He definitely had eyes on us. What do you think?" she replied.

"I guess we could circle back around and see if he's still here, or take off and see if we can lose him. There are several cars back there. I'm betting one of them is his. Or, we could take it slow so he can follow us back to the hotel. We would be more in control there, because we know its layout. Or, I guess I could just walk up to him and ask him what's so interesting about us."

"I like option three, the going back to the hotel, only because they have food and a hot bath and a bed. And, you're right, it's our turf. Besides, he's not a professional. I saw him on the way in. Let's give him some help and see what he does with it."

Wolf put the car into drive and slowly pulled away. He checked the rear-view mirror. "Yep, he's heading for his car. Dang it, that's interesting; it's a rental like ours. That means he's most likely from out of town, out of state, or from out of the country."

"Dinner for three then," Dominique said, removing the gun from its holster and making sure there was a round in the chamber.

The young woman had watched Dominique and Wolf arrive. She watched them meet a priest. She saw them go into the church. She also watched the other man. That man had arrived late the day before and then hung around. He was there again. He stuck out because he was watching the church from the sidewalk, not hidden. He'd paced up and down, trying to keep warm, stamping his feet and wrapping his arms around his body every time he stopped, but he never left the sidewalk. She was not a professional, but she knew that was an idiotic place to watch from. He'd looked out of place. She nicknamed him 'Flapper' because of the way he kept flapping his arms about to keep warm. When the two people left the church, she couldn't make out their features because they were too far away and one of them, the smaller of the two, had a hoodie on. She also suspected they too had spotted Flapper on the sidewalk – it wasn't that difficult. She watched Flapper get into his rental car and follow the two people who had met with the priest.

Like Flapper, she was also cold. She was also pissed off that she was the one who had to stand out in the cold each day; despite the increasing number of pieces of clothing she put on daily before leaving the flea-ridden motel they were staying in, she got cold thirty minutes after arriving and stayed cold until she left, a little after 6 p.m. when he picked her up.

She didn't like being there, hidden behind railings and a desperate-looking row of bushes. Her sole job was to note any visitors to the church or the bishop's house, get their car registrations and relay their descriptions to the man who left her there every day. Other than Flapper, this was the first time that new people had come. Flapper had not met with the priest nor had he gone into the church; they had. She knew this was significant.

She fretted daily. Everything about them still being in the US was wrong and she knew he thought it too; she could see it on his face. For the first time, she saw he was worried but he didn't say. He wouldn't say. She had stolen the package from the church, as she had been told to. They had been given the address of the church, given the precise location of the package and the combination number for the safe she found inside the altar. She'd taken the package and looked at it because of its odd shape. It was the first time she had looked at what she'd been asked to steal. It looked and felt like a human skull, inside its purple, large velvet pouch. When she took it out, she discovered that that's exactly what it was and she wondered why anyone would want to steal a skull from a church in New Jersey and then have people wait around to see who turned up. It made no sense to her, other than it was wrong. Something was off and she knew she was smack in the middle of it.

He, the man who took her there every day to keep watch, the ex-lawyer, Timothy Crowthorp, wasn't that far away, about five miles away in the flea-ridden motel. Not that he would have been any use to her if there was trouble. She had resolved way back that if trouble came knocking, she would leave him behind to occupy whoever was after her. She was thankful it was not today. It was even too cold to run.

The alarm on her digital watch went off; it was 6 p.m. She

141

waited for him, impatiently. She was cold and hungry. She thought about her options. She wanted to get out of there, out of New Jersey and America, but if Crowthorp was still alive, it wasn't an option. She couldn't kill him; she wasn't a killer. She was trapped.

It was the 23rd December; they had arrived in America on the 19th December and she had stolen the skull on the 21st December. She had now been in America for five days and there was no sign of them leaving anytime soon. She had been watching the church for two days now.

She wanted to be away from Crowthorp. She despised him, right down to the fact he kept a skull locked in a minibar.

She was becoming more and more convinced that he was in the same mess as she was: it was not his decision to be there, and he had no say about when he could leave. She had never met the person Crowthorp worked for but was now convinced he worked for someone. He had never said anything about a someone, and she knew he would not. He rarely told her anything, only what she needed to know to steal the items he told her to steal. At first, she had thought it was his ego, his sense of master and servant; him referring to himself as her handler had made her think that. However, now she was not so sure.

She didn't like the position she had become entrapped in but couldn't see a way out. Manchester had been the last job. Now Manchester and the rainy weather of the North of England seemed far more accommodating than the snow of New Jersey and this terrible feeling she could not get rid of, the terrible feeling that she was completely screwed.

The car pulled up. She appeared from out behind the railings she had been standing behind for hours. She looked cold as she got into the car.

"Flapper was there again; second day now," she said directing every air vent to blow hot air onto her feet, face and hands. "But, two more people came today. They met with the priest. Went into the church. Were in there about an hour. I didn't get a good look at them; they were too far away but they just felt different to Flapper. Flapper also spotted them. He was doing his usual idiotic stuff to stay warm, so I'm sure they saw him. When they left, he jumped in his car and he followed them. He obscured their registration with his car; idiot. I gave you his registration yesterday; did you manage to trace it?"

Crowthorp thought about answering or not. He was told she should know nothing. "I did," he said. He told her because he didn't want her asking a whole load of questions all the way back to their motel; it didn't work.

"Well?" she asked, almost demanding.

He knew she was cold and tired but he had no patience with her. "There is no 'well' for you. You have one job: to keep watch." He turned sharp right and just missed a pedestrian. "For fuck's sake," he rasped.

"What do you mean there is no 'well' for me? I'm stuck here with you. I should know."

Now he was angry. "You should know nothing, you little bitch. You just remember you cost me my old life. You, you did that. I am allowing you to pay off that debt, and it's far better than the alternative my relic hunter, believe me. You are in no position to demand anything."

She was silent all the way back to their flea-ridden accommodation.

As soon as they got back, she went to her room. The room was dank and it smelt. The furniture was cheap and broken. The sheets were old and yellowing. Outside it was cold; inside the heating struggled to cope.

She went straight out onto the balcony, despite it being cold. He always had his patio door slightly cracked open, to let some air in; they both did. The smell in the rooms could get almost putrid if no air was let in. She knew he was making a call because she could hear him through the paper-thin walls. She jumped across onto his balcony. Her footprints were now in the freshly laid snow, but he never went out there so it was fine. She could hear the conversation but only one way. She knew he was pacing because his voice ebbed and flowed. She heard him tell the person on the other end of the phone about another

143

day of Flapper – although he didn't use the name Flapper. He also explained about the two new faces on the scene. Whatever the other person said to him, it was long. Crowthorp said he would wait for them to contact him. Then Crowthorp hung up. She jumped back across the balconies and slipped back into her room; then she had a hot bath.

Every night he did the same thing; he ordered takeaway. He would never let her go out in public, other than the journey to and from the church. After his call, he ordered takeaway again. He chose; he never asked her what she preferred.

He banged on the wall as her cue that the food had arrived. She dried herself and dressed quickly. He would not wait to eat. He would already be eating.

She always found him quiet, unless he was upset. Then he was vitriolic, vicious and cruel. The crooked lawyer, who had kept criminals out of prison for years, had ended up in there himself, for four years. They always ate in his room, never hers. He'd left the room door ajar for her. He seemed particularly quiet. Troubled almost. She knew he was definitely worried and if he was worried, she knew she should be too. They ate in silence. He allowed no alcohol, so all she had was bottled water he'd picked up. Bottled water, silence and a meal that tasted wretched.

The knock at the door startled them.

"Just keep your mouth shut," was all he said to her, before he opened the door. She knew he was expecting the visitor because he didn't check the spyhole in the door to see who it was. He opened the door. An Asian man stood in the doorway. There was no sign above him saying 'a dangerous man.' There didn't need to be. She had been around enough of them and taken enough beatings from such men to know what he was; her radar was going crazy. He looked at her. It was not a good look.

He asked to see it. Crowthorp unlocked the mini bar and took the skull out of its velvet pouch. The man nodded. He then made a call whilst Crowthorp put the skull back. The man spoke in a foreign tongue: Chinese, Japanese or perhaps Vietnamese. She didn't look at him. She knew not to look back at him, not to make eye contact; dangerous men never liked that.

Crowthorp went outside with the man, first giving her a glance. He looked nervous and then he shut the door. She ran to the door and pressed her ear against it. She heard bits of the conversation. The Asian man said the watching was done, others would take over now. She heard the Asian man say they had got the address of the other watcher from the rental car company; she knew it could only be Flapper. They had been following him since yesterday because of her. Now she was sorry she had given Crowthorp the information. The Asian man said that his car was now parked near to the 'Metro on the Inn' hotel, about twelve miles away. They were watching him and now watching the hotel, because they believed that was where the two new people were. Her heart skipped. She heard the Asian man say "Get rid of the girl and do it tonight. No loose ends. I'll be back for you and the package later; we'll get rid of the body."

She felt sick and giddy. She made for his patio door but suddenly stopped. She checked the mini bar. Crowthorp had not re locked it when he put the skull back. She grabbed the skull, opened the patio door, closed it almost shut behind her and jumped from his balcony to hers. She went into her room. She put on as many pieces of clothing as possible, grabbed only what she needed and put the skull into her backpack. She went back outside onto her balcony. To her right, the highway was only about a thousand yards away but she would have to walk across barren land and up and over a small embankment and down onto the highway. The snow looked around a foot deep. There were no tracks in the snow. To her left was the car park, fifty yards away. She looked directly down to the ground. There was about a foot gap against the building where the snow had not settled because of the wind direction. She knew that if she went across the virgin ground, she would leave clear footprints signposting where she'd gone.

She shimmied down the outside rainwater pipe and edged along the thin strip by the building that had no snow. She got to the carpark, which was full of footprints going in all directions. They would not be able to track her. She knew the risk was the Asian man had not come

145

alone and someone was waiting in a car, in the car park. She hoped that if there was another person that they were inside the flea-ridden motel, in the reception area, getting warm. She ran across the car park as quickly as she could without slipping and breaking her neck. She left the car park and moved onto the sidewalk, hugging the hedgerow. Cars sped by her. She turned right at the gas station and then headed straight for the highway with her passport, fifty dollars and the skull of John the Baptist.

Date: Two days later, the 25th December 2012
Place: Brick, Ocean County, New Jersey

She'd been hiding out for two days. The cab she'd caught on the night of the 23rd, when she'd fled from certain death, took her within a mile of the 'Metro on the Inn.' She remembered its name from Crowthorp's conversation with the Asian man and knew that was where Flapper was most likely to be. She needed to see Flapper.

She found another flea-ridden dive and checked in. This one was mainly frequented by prostitutes, drunks and drug addicts. It was not a pleasant place but with only thirty-five dollars left in her pocket after the cab fare, she was short of options. She hadn't eaten for two days but what she had done was find Flapper. He'd been parked just a hundred yards from the 'Metro on the Inn.' She found him on the 24th, the day after her escape. Other than loo breaks, Flapper had not moved from that position. She didn't know if he left the car at night and slept somewhere else because she did not go out at night; it was too dangerous, not from her pursuers, but from the seedy street dwellers.

She needed Flapper because he had seen the two people who had met with the priest. She assumed he had seen their faces. She assumed he was now staking them out. Whoever they were, their arrival seemed to have altered things: the watching came to an end, Flapper was found and tailed and she, she was to meet a grizzly end. She figured the two people had gone to the church because of the bishop's death, or the theft of the skull, or both. Either way, what she had in her possession, combined with what she knew, might just buy her a way out.

It was Christmas Day morning, and the world was happily going about its Yuletide business. Even the seedy street dwellers had gone somewhere else, she suspected to a church or a refuge centre for a Christmas meal. She hurried through a number of alleyways. She stayed off the main streets and sidewalks. Thanks to her, they had Flapper's car registration, which meant they found the rental car company, which meant they had his hotel address and passport details. She also knew they were watching him and because of that, thanks to her, he was as screwed as she was.

She edged along the final twenty yards of the alley, hugging the walls. Above her emanated noises from floors and floors of apartments: Christmas songs, laughter, shouting, arguing, screaming and crying, just like in her own house when she was a child, she thought, but in her house there was a lot more violence.

Flapper was in his car. She picked up three small stones and tossed one at his window. He jumped and quickly turned towards the alley. She waved. It was half-heartedly done but she didn't know what else to do. He looked at her as if she was mad. He turned away and ignored her.

She let out a "Grrr," through gritted teeth, and then tossed the two other stones. He turned his head again and this time hunched his shoulders and raised his palms upwards in a 'what the heck, lady' motion. She waved again. This time he gave her the middle finger. She rummaged about for a larger stone. She found one, thought it too large, but tossed it all the same. It didn't break the glass, but it was pretty close. He wound down the window. He was not happy.

"Fuck, lady, have you gone mad?"

Not an American, she thought. "Come here … you are in danger. I can help you," she called to him.

"You want to try helping yourself first. Go get your fix and you'll feel all better. Now, take off!"

Her next words did the trick. "You have been watching the church in Brick for two days, as well as the bishop's house. You followed two people here, the people who met with the priest at the church. Am I close?" He didn't answer. "Look Mister," her Mancunian accent was now coming out because her stress levels were through the roof. "You are in trouble and I want to help. We can help each other. Please, just give me thirty minutes, that's all."

He rolled up the window. At first, she didn't think he was going to react and she started looking for an even bigger stone – a glass-breaking stone, but then he did. He got out of the car, locked it and ran into the alleyway.

"Okay, lady, you've got my attention."

And you got everyone else's, she thought. "I know a café, ten minutes away but far enough away. It's not safe for us here," she said.

Ten minutes later they were warm and ensconced at a corner table in a trendy café, called 'Pete's.' They both nursed black coffees. The man sitting in front of her was stocky, *around thirty years old*, she thought. He had long brown hair, parted in the centre, not clean shaven and had tattoos that looked like prison tattoos. She had seen a lot of prison tattoos growing up.

"Sorry, Flapper," she started. She thought, *start slow and with an apology,* but she'd been so used to calling him Flapper it just came out.

He stopped sipping his coffee. "Flapper?"

"Sorry, sorry! I didn't know your real n … It was just a nickname I gave … You're right, I—"

"Flapper?"

"Look, it's not a big thin—"

"Flapper?"

"Damn it. Look, you flapped your arms around a lot. I was watching you, I have been since you got to the church. You pounded up and down the sidewalk, sometimes running and then you'd flap your arms around your body."

"It was cold," he protested.

"I know it was bloody cold. I was out there as well but I didn't fl— ! Okay, okay. Let's try and forget the flapping thing. I apologise, Mister?"

"It's not Mister. My name is Daniel, Daniel Hightower."

She was about to say something about the Hightower thing but decided she'd already pushed her luck on the name thing already. "Nice to meet you, Daniel. From your accent, I'm guessing Australian?"

"Yes, I'm an Auss—"

"I'm sorry for spying on you," she blurted. She was so desperate to get it out, to tell someone, anyone, what had been going on, to offload the burden she carried so heavily. She had not been able to tell anyone, especially her family. She couldn't tell them that the life of her eldest brother, a vulnerable drug addict in a Coventry prison, was in her hands and her cooperation in Crowthorp's crimes was her brother's pass to staying alive. Now it was even worse because she was on the run with no way of protecting her family. She was on the run from the man who had told her that her brother could stay alive, as long as she cooperated. But, she'd known the second the Asian man told Crowthorp to kill her, because her usefulness had ended, that her brother would also be killed. She had been so scared for the last two days. She just prayed that Crowthorp was too preoccupied with the Asian and her escape, to think about her brother.

"I am sorry, Daniel, I didn't want to spy on you, but I was forced too. God, I feel so bad and so stupid now that I am sitting in front of you."

"You had better tell me what has been going on," he said, his tone understanding. "And, let's see if we can help each other."

She breathed a silent sigh of relief. "I was watching the church," she began. "I was doing it for this guy, nasty son of a bitch. He made me watch the church and the bishop's house. I have been there every day since the 21st. I was further down the road from where you were, near the corner and at the back of the green railings.

149

"I don't know why I had to watch the place. He never told me. He just said watch it and tell him who went there, that was his instructions. I had to report back to him if I saw anyone other than the priest or the police."

Daniel already had a bunch of questions and she'd only said a few sentences, but he decided he would let her finish.

"I'm afraid reporting back included you, Daniel. I told him about you. I told him what you did and I gave him your car registration number. You used your real passport and hotel address when you rented the car, didn't you?"

"The hotel address yes. My real passport, no."

She felt slight relief. "You are a person of interest to him now. He has your description. They have been watching your every move since the 22nd at the church, your hotel and you being encamped down the road from the hotel of, I presume, the two people who were at the church on the 23rd, who met with the priest?"

"You switched," he said.

"Excuse me?"

"You said him, now it's they."

"I thought it was just him, Crowthorp, but now I know it's not. Two nights ago, we had a visitor, an Asian man. I hadn't seen him before. I had never met anyone Crowthorp knew. I thought the jobs I did were just for him."

Daniel looked, his expression tacitly asking for an explanation about the word 'jobs.'

"Robberies. I commit robberies for him. I get into places where you need to be fleet of foot and agile. I guess I'm more of a cat burglar than a real robber. I was a gymnast, a bloody good one and represented my country. I didn't know I was good at cat burglary, but it seems I am, damn good."

"So, you do jobs for this …?"

"Crowthorp."

"Crowthorp fella. But for the last number of days, you have been watching a church?"

"Yes."

"And then, this Asian guy turns up and …?"

"And they go outside the room and I overhear him tell Crowthorp to get rid of me."

"You ran?"

"Shit, fucking right I ran."

"Understandably. You hid. And then you decided to find me?"

"Yes."

"Why?"

"Because I knew you were not with him, Crowthorp, and you might know where the two people were who met with the priest because you tailed them. I figured that Crowthorp and the others were waiting for someone, someone to turn up. That's why they had me watch the place. It's the only explanation. And I can only assume it was those people who turned up."

"Makes sense," he said.

"Have you made contact with them yet?" she asked him.

"No, but I know where they are."

"I have to tell you that I think they knew you were watching them, Daniel, at the church, and I'm pretty sure they knew you were tailing them."

"I'm pretty sure you're right about that because they all but led me to their hotel and have walked past my car several times since. I get the feeling that I'm not watching them; they are watching me."

A million thoughts ran through her mind. She wanted to run to the airport and leave as quickly as possible, but she knew it would never be over. They would always track her down. She had seen too much and knew too much. She was a liability to them, a loose end that needed dealing with. But, she also needed to get to Crowthorp, to stop him killing her brother. She knew that her brother was completely exposed in prison. One dirty syringe, one empty syringe, just filled with air injected directly into his vein. He had no gang affiliation in there. She was his only hope and she was on the run. Her only hope was Daniel and the two people who had met the priest at the church. If they were not with Crowthorp and the Asian man, it meant they were on the opposite side, and that was the side she needed to be on if she stood any chance of leaving the US alive and saving her ill brother. She needed the two visitors to the church to help her. She had no money and was pretty much out of luck.

"Tell me," Daniel leaned forward and asked, "what hold does this Crowthorp fella have over you?"

"My actions put him in prison for four years; he was a lawyer, then got disbarred and lost everything he had. I gave some people his address and contact details. He worked for a big time criminal and they were able to bring the whole lot crashing down to the ground. When Crowthorp got out of prison early, and I have no idea how he did that, he wanted his revenge and he found me and made me one of those Godfather-type offers, the kind you can't refuse, the kind that would be terminal if you did. He threatened my life and the life of one of my brothers."

"Damn!" Daniel looked at her. She was tall and pretty, jet-black short-cropped hair, greeny-brown eyes and a soft oval face. He didn't know that by the time she had reached seventeen, she had been raped, robbed and beaten, all in the comfort of her own home. She'd lived with her alcoholic mother in a two-bedroom flat on a large concrete housing estate, along with her seven siblings.

"So, that's me, but why are you here, Daniel?" she asked him.

He leaned forward and for the first time she noticed what looked like a gold cross and chain around his neck, but she had never seen a cross like it before; it was a gold cross but with a small gold shawl draped over it.

"I'm here for my grandfather." He saw her looking at his cross. "It's called a *Darfash*. I guess you could say it is the sign of my grandfather's people, of their religion. They are Mandaeans. Mandaeism is a really old religion, a very old religion that reveres the old prophets but especially John the Baptist. You will not have heard of them, I guess, because there are not many of them left these days."

She looked at him.

"No, I am not one. You remember the Gulf war, the war against Saddam Hussein?"

She nodded.

"Well, my grandfather, who lives in Iraq with his people, were called the Marsh Arabs by the press. The dictator, Hussein, used them as target practice. They are also called Christians of John, Christians of Saint John and sometimes, People of the Book. This," he held the gold cross, "is not a cross; it is part of a ritual. When a baptism takes place, the holy man drives a stick into the ground, lashes a cross beam and then drapes his cloth, his stole, like priests wear, over the cross beam."

"And why did your grandfather send you?" she asked him.

"Because of the head of the Baptist, John the Baptist. My grandfather's people have been searching for it for over two thousand years. The head of the prophet was in that church, where the Catholics had hidden it. And then, it was stolen."

She clutched her backpack. "And what does the head look like?"

"Well, I've never seen a two-thousand-year-old head, but I would imagine it looks like an old skull." He smiled.

She kept hold of her bag. *Not now,* she thought, *I might need it as a bargaining tool.* So, she didn't tell him that the head he sought was just a few feet away from him.

"That's me. One minute I was in Dubai looking for work, then my dad called me and told me my grandfather needed me, said he had my ticket waiting for me at the airport, and I was on a plane to Amman, Jordan that very morning. It took just over an hour. I was then in Jordan for less than an hour. Then I was on a flight here."

She looked surprised.

"I know, crazy right? Because of time zones working backwards for me, I got to the US around 2 p.m. that same day. Someone met me at the airport, gave me the address of the church and a bunch of money. I rented a car and, you know the rest."

"No wonder you were cold, an Australian, flying from Dubai to Jordan, and then to a New Jersey winter. You know, I think we should go and see those two people tomorrow," she said. We should go and see them and tell them our stories. What have we got to lose?"

"Our lives," he said.

"I think we are both on the edge of that cliff already. We need to find a way off it. They just might have an answer."

"Where are you from?" he asked her.

"Manchester," she replied.

And, what's your name?"

"My name? My name is Dagmar, Dagmar Grey."

Chapter 9

Christmas Day Part I

Date: 24th December 2012

There was no earlier train because of a number of cancellations as a result of the weather and so they had to hang around all morning in Cambridge. When they got to the station it was packed. It was the last day to travel by train; there were no trains on Christmas day.

The journey back up North was just as tiring as the journey down to Cambridge. However, this time there was a lot more conversation between them. First on the agenda for Jonathan, was to find out if Zakariah had seen any evidence of fly eating. He told Zakariah that he had tried very hard to see if there were wings in Aldrich's teeth, or only wings left on the fly paper, but could not tell. Zakariah told him that he was too busy sitting with his hands in his pockets to notice anything.

It didn't take too long, however, for the conversation to move on to the revelation by Aldrich about Hags and the fact that they seemingly still existed, or at least one of them did. Jonathan wasn't a disbeliever in the dark arts; he was a believer because he believed in the opposite side. He believed in angels; he believed in miracles: he was the recipient of one. He just hadn't expected that he would ever become involved with a witch. He thought they were medieval creatures, with medieval ways and medieval dark forces that had only existed in medieval times. That had now changed.

Zakariah's concerns did not lie with the Hag. He had seen far too many things for him to doubt for a moment that they existed. Over the years, he and the Knights Templar had seen evil in many guises. This was just, yet another, one that would test their resolve and test their faith. Besides, the Hag would be Luther's mission now and his friend was the best person to help Aldrich track her down. Zakariah's concerns lay solely with Salah El-Din and the fact that they did not know what was behind the deaths of the bishops. Clearly, he was active again, which meant they had two enemies in play.

They had fought, and fought hard, against the Abaddons for years and it had cost them dearly: it had cost Zakariah and Dominique dearly. Despite Morgan Clay's extensive efforts to locate them, they were as elusive as ever. Clay's patience, tenacity and robust invest-igative skills in looking into offshore companies had slowly paid off. He had searched in Tortola, the British Virgin Islands, Grand Turk, in the Turks and Caicos Islands, St Kitts and Panama, checking any companies that might have been associated with the name *Al'umu Alhabiba* Inc – Beloved Mother, the name of Zivko Gowst's original offshore company. The money trail in Panama and the Caribbean twisted and turned, appeared, then ended abruptly. From nowhere another trail or link would reveal itself and all their energy would be put into that. They were desperate for progress, and desperate to find the source of the money of their elusive enemy. Supported in Panama, Switzerland and Romania by John Wolf, John Edison and the forensic accounting team they then assembled in Barbados, where John Edison lived, Clay had made progress. Now, seemingly, the Abaddons had gone to ground, but Salah El-Din had resurfaced.

Zakariah had been a Templar long enough to know that a fight was coming, perhaps their biggest fight yet. If both enemies came at them at once, they would be truly tested. He just hoped that they would be ready.

He was glad they were heading back to Scotland where Jonathan would be safe. He was the Seer. He was their only Seer and according to the Cathar prophecies, he was the last Seer. Every time Jonathan left the protection of their Scottish stronghold, they risked exposing him. Zakariah was glad to be getting him back all in one piece.

Date: 24th December; late
Place: Scotland

Jonathan and Zakariah arrived back in Scotland late. It was Christmas Eve; it was dark, and it was cold.

Jonathan went straight to his cottage after they arrived at the train station. He was tired and wanted to be home if Dominique called. He knew she had left on a mission but not what the mission was or where it was. As was their practice, only those directly involved in the mission knew the details. This was done for the safety of those involved; their whereabouts could never be disclosed should a Knight ever fall into enemy hands.

Zakariah drove to the castle. Whilst it was late when he got there, he went in search of his brother. St Clair was still up and alone in one of the meeting rooms. He was reading a stack full of reports; he was happy for the interruption. They spent about an hour together and Zakariah told St Clair everything that had taken place in Cambridge. Some of Aldrich's eccentricities made St Clair smile. Aldrich always made him smile. He gave out a hearty laugh when Zakariah told him what Aldrich had called him, and then another upon hearing Jonathan, the priest, was now the Corpse.

St Clair told Zakariah that Luther would be out part of the next day. He needed to go somewhere, but St Clair promised to speak to Luther when he got back to the castle about going to help Aldrich. He also told him that Luther would be leaving for Hull, either the night of the 25th or early in the morning on the 26th. However, once he'd finished his task in Hull, he would then go to Cambridge and liaise directly with Aldrich. He asked Zakariah to fully brief Luther when he saw him before he left for Hull. Zakariah told him he had already sent Luther a message; they were meeting at breakfast in the morning.

"I will speak to Aldrich before I retire tonight," St Clair told his brother. "He will still be up. He doesn't sleep much. What he's seen and done in the past would keep most people up."

Zakariah asked his brother if anyone had been able to make the link between all four of the bishops.

"I have Courtney, Bertram and part of Courtney's team on it. They have been on it for a few days. I agree with Aldrich; it just might hold the clue. We need to find out what Salah El-Din's motives are for killing the bishops. At the moment though, none of it makes any sense."

Next, St Clair briefed Zakariah about the theft of the saint's skull, the head of John the Baptist, in Brick, New Jersey. He told him that the fourth bishop to die was the bishop who lived in the house attached to the church where the saint's skull had been hidden in the altar. He explained that Wolf and Dominique were there and had already met up with the Vatican representative. Bill Meeks was trying to find out what had happened but not much was known. Meeks would go to New Jersey on the 26th if they had not found anything and would take over from the Girl and the Indian to close off the mission.

"Maybe we will know more when the Indian and the Girl get the toxicology report." St Clair Said.

"Aldrich said the authorities will struggle to isolate the toxins," Zakariah told him.

"Then we will know for sure if the bishop's death in New Jersey is related to the other three, if they also fail to identify the toxins," St Clair said. Then he told Zakariah that he had also called their old friend Jamal, in Iraq, about the saint's head. He told him that he could not and would not keep this information from their old friend, not after their two thousand years of searching.

Zakariah was pleased, really pleased. "What did he say?"

"You know Jamal. He took his false passport and headed for Jordan. Said he was going to arrange to meet someone there and they would be going to New Jersey on their behalf and try to find the saints head."

"Do you know who?" Zakariah asked him.

"He didn't say, so I didn't ask but I've told the Girl and the

Indian to keep an eye out. Oh, and on a lighter note," St Clair chuckled, "I've finally settled on the nickname for Bertram."

"And?" his brother asked.

"Cerebral."

Zakariah laughed. "It's brilliant; it's so Bertram."

"He loves the fact he now has a nickname; I'm told he feels part of the gang now."

"You know he keeps telling people you look like Sean Connery, don't you Payne? He's obsessed with it. He keeps saying 'Mish Moneypenny,' whenever he sees you. His nickname for you is Mister Bond, 'Mishter Bond,' as he pronounces it."

"I know," St Clair said. "He makes me laugh so much but I'm not going to tell him." He chuckled again and shook his head. "I asked him to come to talk to me the other day about the drones he has been working on and when I asked him what he had been doing that morning, he told me he'd taken a short break to sketch gusts."

Zakariah thought about this for a second or two. "What do you mean, sketch g—"

"Gusts, gusts of wind. He was up on the battlements sketching gusts of wind."

"How the heck do you sketch a gust of wind?"

"I have no idea. I didn't ask but he makes me laugh so much, my Brother, and we certainly need some light relief around here of late and our Bertram will do that without even realising it."

It had gone midnight and as they were the only ones still up, besides the Knights on watch outside the castle, they took a small nightcap together. They sat chatting, two brothers enjoying a rare moment alone, a rare moment of peace and sibling company. Their journey together had taken many twists and turns over many years. As young men, they had become Templars together, and through the years they had seen most of the bloodiest missions in recent times. They each carried the scars, physical and mental; they carried the memories, both good and bad. Blood brothers, in a band of brothers, a band of Knights.

*

Date: 25th December, Christmas day 2012
Place: A remote castle in Scotland

It was all happening much faster than St Clair had anticipated. He knew Aldrich would not let him down – he never had – but he desperately needed to know why Salah El-Din was murdering the bishops and why he wanted the saint's head. Luther would help Aldrich and hopefully they would be able to track down the Hag. Maybe they would get her to talk, but he knew that was a long shot. Either way, they needed to terminate her. He would call for her sanction at the Higher Council later that night.

Courtney, part of her team and Bertram, were also on the case, trying to discover the link between the bishops' deaths. St Clair knew from dealing with Salah El-Din that the only way to defeat him was to discover his plan. They had done that in 2008 and they had saved many Jewish families from the anthrax which the criminal captain, Captain Murry, had intended to unleash on Israel. Fighting Salah El-Din was like a chess game; it always had been. He needed to anticipate his moves and be ready for them. He needed to find some answers and quickly.

He was standing in his favourite spot, the castle's battlements, his place to be alone, his place to think when he was troubled, or just to remind himself of how blessed he was. It was bitterly cold; a frosty white blanket of snow had been there for days now and there was no sign of the weather letting up. The castle had been a sanctuary for the Templars for decades. Semi-isolated from civilisation, the castle stood amongst miles of Scottish wilderness.

He took out his phone to call Jonathan. He mouthed Jonathan's name at the screen and the phone made the call. *Clever lad our Bertram*, he thought.

Jonathan answered. "Merry Christmas," he said.

"Merry Christmas to you, too," St Clair replied. "How are you coping without Dominique? I am assuming you got the message from the Controller to say she was out of the country?"

"I did, thanks, and I'm good. I spoke to her late last night, to wish her Merry Christmas."

"Sorry we had to ask her to go but we really did have an emergency," St Clair said. "We got a call from Father Angelo Fugero. He's the Vatican representative in New Jersey. Did Dominique tell you what she was doing there?"

"No," Jonathan replied.

"Well, I think you might need to know now, Jonathan." St Clair paused, he wanted Jonathan's attention. "The Vatican has a secret—"

"The Vatican has many secrets; perhaps too many secrets," Jonathan interrupted.

St Clair smiled, "… but this one is one of those very secret ones."

"How very secret?" Jonathan asked.

"They had the head of John the Baptist, kind of very secret."

"Now that's a very secret, secret. You said had?"

"It was stolen when the fourth bishop was murdered. That's why Dominique and Wolf are there."

"So, the saint's skull was not in the Vatican?"

"No. New Jersey. They decided this one was safer hidden in the small township of Brick, in Ocean County, New Jersey. Brick has a population of around eighty thousand people; the Vatican City has a population of around a thousand. However, and here's the reason they did it and do it with a number of precious objects, whilst the Vatican may only have around a thousand people there, they receive approximately ten million visitors to St Peter's Basilica every year. So, every day, around fifty thousand people visit that place. Around twenty thousand people visit the Sistine Chapel every day in the summer. It is a security nightmare for them, so they decided a long time ago to move some of their most sacred objects to places around the globe, where no

161

one would ever guess to look. They hid them almost in plain sight. The Baptist's head was hidden within the church's stone altar, inside a bronze reliquary, placed inside a steel safe with a digital code key. Plus, the altar has a secret door. Apparently, it has been there since 1932. Until it was stolen on the 21st."

Jonathan recited the passage in the Bible. *"When he broke open the fifth seal, I saw underneath the altar the souls of those who had been slaughtered because of the witness they bore to the word of God.'* Revelations 6:9. Wow, this certainly puts a new twist on things."

"Wow indeed, Jonathan. The head has gone—"

"And you suspect an inside job again, like the ring?"

"I see it no other way. This time it was the head of the saint and the life of a bishop, another one poisoned." St Clair heard Jonathan breathe a sigh. The ex-priest knew it was now starting.

"Okay, I'm going to walk the dogs and then I'm coming in. Give me a few hours." Jonathan hung up.

St Clair was about to make his way back inside. He was now cold and was stamping his feet to get them warm but then the Controller called. Although she was on holiday, she told her replacement that she would take the calls on Christmas Day so she could leave early. She could monitor all the calls from her phone anyway, and there were still two other people in Islington monitoring things. St Clair wished the Controller a Merry Christmas and asked if she had any plans. She didn't tell him that she was travelling and still taking calls. She knew he would have been annoyed because she was working on her holiday. She told him she would visit the graves later – but in fact she'd left eight hours earlier and was nearly there: however, St Clair knew exactly where she was at that point.

The Controller told him that Lillia was on the line. St Clair's heart sank when he heard those words. He'd been expecting the bad news any day; they all were. He guessed he was about to get it.

André Sabath's wife told Payne St Clair that André Sabath had passed away earlier that morning. His Christmas Day just turned into a black day. Whilst he was expecting it, hearing the words hurt. They

162

had been friends for a long time and had shared many missions together. One was responsible for the other joining the Order of the Knights Templar. The loss of a friend, a Worthy, a Brother, was hard to take; he would and could never get used to losing a brother.

Now he needed to put his plan into action. He had held off. He did not want to replace André on the Council until there was no other alternative. Now there was not; his friend had died. The Higher Council was down to just seven people; he knew he needed the Council to be back up to full strength with whatever was coming their way. There had always been nine. The original Templars were nine when they set out from France and nine had always been maintained as the number of Worthies. They were his rock, his advisers, his smart, controlled, experienced and wise group that helped him, the Grand Master, lead the Order, to protect their 'Charge,' the Ark of the Covenant, and to protect those who needed their help. He needed to appoint two new Worthies and he needed to do it that night.

Two of the Council were already at the castle, four would video in and he made the seventh. The Council had already met in secret and had already voted on who would be the new Worthies to sit on the Higher Council. Agreement on the names of the people had been unanimous. They each deserved it; they had each served the Order for years; the other Worthies knew that they would each serve the Council well. The original plan was that he was going to tell the two people that night about their nominations, but their appointment would come a little later. He had held off because of André Sabath, but now he had passed, St Clair and the other Worthies would appoint the two that night.

St Clair spent the next hour in the castle's chapel with the other Knights who had come to pay their respects to a fallen Brother, amongst them: Bertram, Luther, Zakariah, Billy Jack and Morgan Clay, all dressed as 13th century Templars. Then Proctor Hutchinson and John Edison, two of the Nine Worthies entered, followed by twenty other Knights. They were all wearing their ceremonial dress; they had all heard about the passing of their Brother, André Sabath.

Jonathan was walking the dogs on the beach. He would take them with him to the castle, but they deserved to stretch their legs before the journey. It was windy and the sky was full of flurries of snow. Jonathan saw Elaine Wall, their dog-walking, dog-minding friend.

Elaine was retired and lived close by with her retired, American helicopter pilot husband, who she'd met when she took a helicopter ride in San Francisco – he piloted the sightseeing rides under the Golden Gate Bridge.

"Hi Elaine," Jonathan called. "Left him indoors I see?"

"He said it was Christmas Day, so he was taking a day off from walking dogs. I don't mind; it gets me out." She looked around. "No Dominique today?" The four dogs greeted each other like old friends and then headed off to the sea, a hundred yards away, and to a game of chase the wave.

"She has a presentation to deliver," Jonathan told her, "in Qatar, for the Ministry of Education. No Christmas there." He smiled.

"That's a shame. Give her my best and wish her Happy Christmas for me when you speak to her. I am glad I've caught you though. A man was on the beach earlier this morning, when I was down here, and asked me if I knew you. I said yes. He gave me this mobile phone." She pulled a cheap-looking mobile phone from her coat pocket. "He asked me to give it to you. He said it was yours. You'd left it behind somewhere. Can't remember where he said, but he wanted to return it." She gave him the phone.

It wasn't his phone. He hadn't seen it before. Seconds later it started to ring. He looked around the beach line and the rough common land surrounding most of the beachhead. He answered the call. He knew the voice. It had been four years since he had heard it, but it was like yesterday. His heart started pounding. He started rattling the change in his pocket with his free hand and wishing Dominique was there.

"I hear that some of your friends had a rough time in Romania?" the voice at the other end of the phone said.

Jonathan didn't respond. The dogs – Dusty, Nell, Cleo and Simba – started barking and his heart jumped again; he thought they

164

had spotted someone. He turned around but it was only a piece of washed-up seaweed they had obviously convinced themselves needed a warning bark.

"We should make a partnership, Priest, the Templars and I. We have a common enemy, no? We got off to a bad start, you and I, just a natural collision of interests."

Jonathan took out his own phone from his jacket pocket and hit the red button: As Bertram had instructed: "Hit red for emergency … it means can't call, can't speak, come and get me. Help."

"I will call again, Priest. Keep the phone with you." The dogs barked again. This time Dusty had the seaweed in his mouth. "You should teach that dog not to eat that seaweed," Salah El-Din said. Jonathan turned around sharply, searching desperately for the sight of a figure watching them.

Elaine now moved a little closer to him. "Are you okay, Jonathan?" she asked.

"I really don't know, Elaine," Jonathan said, "but we need to get off this beach."

Moments later Zakariah rang on his real phone. "Can you talk?" he asked urgently.

"One second," Jonathan said and moved away from Elaine slightly. "I'm okay," he assured Zakariah, "just a little shaken."

After he'd explained what had happened, Zakariah told him that he was already on his way to the cottage and Billy Jack and Marie-Claude would be with him within fifteen minutes. "Don't go back to the cottage. Go to the nearest pub. Text the address and wait there until the Knights get there. I will go straight to the cottage and check it out. If it's all clear, I will let the Knights know and they can take you there. You need to pack some things when you get there. Then we'll take you to the castle. Do you still have the phone?"

Jonathan told him he did, but he really didn't want to have it. "Don't worry, Jonathan. We'll take it from you as soon as we get to you."

"What about Elaine?" Jonathan asked. "I'm going nowhere until I know she's okay."

"Do you know if any of the pubs are open?"

"Yes, the Clansman, about three miles from here."

"Good. Ask her there for a quick coffee. When the Knights get there, I will ask Billy Jack to make sure she gets home okay. Don't worry. Billy Jack will think of a cover story. For now, I just want you to get out of there and get to a crowded place."

Jonathan desperately wanted to call Dominique, but he was too afraid that his call would be bugged. His common sense told him this would have been pretty much impossible because there was no way Salah El-Din could have known his number, or else he would have called him on that phone and not had to go to the trouble of getting Elaine to pass on a mobile phone to him. Secondly, Bertram had made sure the Knights' phones were state of the art and pretty much tamper proof. And finally, all their calls were first routed through the secret satellite communication centre in Islington. Despite all of this and his common sense, he did not call her.

Billy Jack arrived first. He introduced himself as Jonathan's friend. Then Jonathan's phone vibrated. He showed Elaine the text message. It read: 'Pipe burst at the cottage, on way to get you, Jenny.' Ten minutes later Marie-Claude entered the pub as Jonathan's neighbour, Jenny. They both left and Billy Jack offered to take Elaine home. He told her it looked like heavy snow. At first, she thanked Billy but said she could call her husband to come and collect her and the dogs, but Billy Jack insisted.

"Besides," he told her, "be a shame to drag him out on such a cold day. He's probably halfway through *The Great Escape* by now." She accepted.

Once they'd got to Elaine's house, she asked Billy Jack in for a cup of tea and to meet her husband. Billy Jack accepted and spent thirty minutes there making sure they were safe. When he left, he stayed around for another hour watching the house from the road, to make sure they were safe.

Then Billy Jack went to the house of Jonathan and Dominique's housekeeper, Morag Beverly Clements, and told her that the Roses had

had to go to the Middle East at the last minute and would be away for a number of months, perhaps longer. He said that they had asked him to deliver her wages – Billy had stopped on route and withdrawn the money from a Templar bank account. He told her that the Roses were shutting up the cottage and wanted to thank her very much for all her help and support. He gave her the unpaid wages, plus a full year's salary. She was very happy.

St Clair and Courtney were waiting for Jonathan as Zakariah pulled into the courtyard. Zakariah took the dogs for a walk around the grounds, giving Jonathan time to speak to St Clair.

St Clair was visibly agitated by the events. "We need to get you and Dominique within our perimeter. Will Dominique give up your place?" he asked as they walked inside. Jonathan nodded. "Good. Let's arrange to get the rest of your stuff here today then."

"One of the cottages on the estate is empty," Courtney said. "It's called *Ceó Gleann,* which means Glen Mist. It's fully furnished now and it's two miles from the castle and well within our defended perimeter. I called Billy Jack and he confirmed that all the defence systems there are up to date and linked to the control room here. Plus, there's another out-post cottage just half a mile from this cottage, so you will be completely protected." She hugged her brother. "You're gonna give me a heart attack." She turned to St Clair, "Four more Knights joined Marie-Claude and they made a thorough search and sweep of the cottage and surrounding area. They don't think he knew where Jonathan lived. Billy Jack made sure that Elaine was safe and he is happy there is no threat to her. He also said that Elaine had mentioned that she had seen the guy hanging about for a few days, so it looks like Salah El-Din knew about the beach somehow, but not where they lived. Billy Jack, Marie-Claude and the other Knights are staying out there for a few more hours, just to be sure, but they think he will be long gone by now. Oh, and by the way, your housekeeper is a very happy lady; she just got a windfall."

The Templar estate had thirty cottages; they were their first line of physical defence of the castle. They were run, operated and manned, as fully equipped garrison posts, electronically protected and linked to the control room at the castle. Most of them were heavily armed, fitted with perimeter sensors, sound sensors, night scopes, infrared cameras and a range of small arms. Normally in each, two Templars lived and worked; they were the 'frontline.' Every three months, new Templars came and took their turn at the outposts. Everyone was relieved that the ex-priest was safe and he and the Girl, Dominique, would now be close enough to them to be protected.

Time: Later that day

The castle was in full operation mode. St Clair was in one of the meeting rooms with Billy Jack, Zakariah and Jonathan. They were all sitting down at one end of the long meeting table. Tea and coffee were in much supply; they needed it. Someone had kindly left a plate of mince pies, which were all but gone.

Jonathan replayed the events on the beach again, for the umpteenth time. It was obvious to all of them that Salah El-Din would call again and they all suspected it would be sooner rather than later. They still couldn't figure out how Salah El-Din knew where Jonathan walked his dogs, but they resigned themselves to the fact that they might never know.

Zakariah was asked to recount their meeting with Aldrich. Billy Jack had never met Aldrich but was highly amused by the academic's antics, especially Jonathan's vain attempts to investigate his fly eating habit – or not. It was a few minutes of light relief from a difficult day.

Luther was not at the meeting, but he'd already been told at their meeting on the 22nd that he needed to be in Hull by the 26th, the next day. He had an important task to do there, but as yet he had not been told what it was. Billy Jack was going with him and didn't know either. In addition, Luther now had to get to Cambridge and liaise with Aldrich to search for the Hag.

Cameron was still in Japan. He had left Scotland on the 22nd and they had not heard from him since. It had been three days; no one was worried because Bertram and the team tracked his movements through his phone signal and the concealed tracking device Bertram had planted inside their credit cards. They saw that Cameron had gone from the airport to the location of his old dojo, then to the location known to be the home of Tanjkna Sugata, then back to Tokyo and the dojo again on the 24th. It was the 25th and he was now close to the dojo. They tracked him to a hotel. They checked and both Cameron and Tanjkna Sugata were checked in there.

Dominique and Wolf were in New Jersey and had found nothing but dead ends and were getting frustrated by the lack of progress. The Vatican representative was of no help and the police had come up with nothing. Bill Meeks, the FBI operative in Washington DC and a Knight Templar, was still trying to work all of his channels but was coming up empty handed. Despite this, they all felt New Jersey offered them the best hope of a lead. It was the last murder scene, and it was different because something had been stolen. That had not happened before, a murder and a theft. Until they could figure it out, Wolf and Dominique were asked to stay on in New Jersey. However, if they hadn't picked up any leads by the 27th, they were told to book flights and come home.

St Clair had the Higher Council meeting that evening. He needed to appoint two new Worthies. He desperately needed his Council back to full strength. He also needed to secure the sanction on the Hag.

St Clair's phone rang. He answered it. It was the stand-in for the Controller in Islington. She put the Vatican's chief of police, Dámaso Nef, through to St Clair. The news was not good. In fact, it was really bad. St Clair put the call on speaker phone so that the others could hear it.

"Sorry to interrupt your Christmas Day, my friend. I think we need your help. We have a big problem here in Rome and I need to solve it quickly. It is of the gravest importance."

"Dámaso, my Christmas went out of the window long before it even started. How can I help you?"

"A fifth bishop."

169

"A fifth? That's bad," St Clair said, his mind racing.

"But, this one is *the* bishop." Nef accentuated the word 'the.'

"The Pope?" St Clair exclaimed in surprise. "Now that is really bad."

"Someone tried to poison him. The same as the other four."

"How is His Hol—"

"He's okay, a little shaken, but thank God he is safe."

St Clair's mind was still racing. He knew now that Salah El-Din had just made a major statement to someone: all the deaths were a statement. But to whom and why?

"Are you leading the investigation, Dámaso?" he asked the chief of police.

"I am my friend, but like last time, the liaison person is from the College of Cardinals, Cardinal Cristoforo Paradiso and I have been given strict instructions that he will coordinate everything. We are both to report independently to Cardinal Cristoforo Paradiso, if you agree to help us."

St Clair again detected the reticence and irritation in Nef's voice. "And is that how we will operate, my friend, through a cardinal?" St Clair asked him.

"No, it is not."

"Good," St Clair said. "I will have people there by tomorrow. The point man will be a man called Luther. He will have two others with him. Dámaso, one of the men will seem eccentric. Don't take offence at what he says, he really is good."

"A British eccentric, no, surely not!" Nef laughed. "I suspect you have an idea about who might have carried out the attempted murder of our Pontiff?"

"I do," St Clair confirmed, "and if I am right, it was the same man behind the theft of the church's ring in Manchester. And behind the man on your CCTV in Rome and the men from the Manchester police's pictures. They are all tied into this one man."

"Let me know Mr Luther and his team's flight details and I will make sure they are picked up."

They bade each other Merry Christmas and then *buona note –*

170

good night, and then he hung up.

"Zakariah, can you call Courtney and let her know what just happened. Tell her that Salah El-Din has just made his biggest statement yet. If she and her team can find the links between the bishops, we will find out the who and then we will have his plan. We need his plan if we are to defeat him."

Zakariah made the call.

Billy Jack was confused. "I thought Luther and I were heading for Hull, and then he was off to Cambridge."

"He was, Billy Jack, but I'm betting that the Hag will still be there, in Rome. She will wait until news of the Pope's death is announced. She will not leave until it is announced. Luther will be back around 6 p.m. at the latest tonight. I need him for a few hours, then you can both drive down to Hull tonight, or take the train, or drive down first thing tomorrow. As soon as Luther has finished our business in Hull, I want you to stay on and help the Knights there. Make sure our operations are all up to date with the equipment and supplies. Luther will go to Rome with Aldrich and with you, Jonathan." St Clair turned to Jonathan.

Jonathan was not expecting that. He looked at St Clair.

"The cardinals might be men of God, but they can be a pit of vipers and politics, and politicking is as prevalent as morning prayers. Some of the cardinals will do their best to trip you up, most will not be helpful at all and they will stifle you in bureaucracy. I need someone who has at least some understanding of their psyche. You need to do whatever you can to help Luther push past all of that, if you are to stand any chance over there. And remember, mixed up in all of this is someone in the Vatican who has been helping Salah El-Din, the *Sancti Furem,* the Holy Thief. You need to be really careful over there. Zakariah, please call Aldrich and ask him to catch the same flight as Luther and Jonathan; they're all going to Rome."

Thirty minutes after Zakariah had called Courtney and briefed her on what had happened in Rome, there was a knock at the meeting room door. The door opened; it was Courtney and Bertram. Courtney apologised for interrupting them but said she thought they may have just cracked the link between the bishops. St Clair ushered them in; he was eager to hear. All eyes were on Courtney; she was ex-FBI, trained and very good at her job.

"Salah El-Din's call to Jonathan was a big risk for him; we know that. We know he does not like being out in the open, so it has to be a major part of whatever play he has planned. When we heard about the failed attempt on the Pope's life, we knew that that death was going to be his *pièce de résistance*; it had to be, because it was who it was.

"We've been looking for a link, but we kept looking in the wrong direction. Nothing made any sense. We think we know now what he has been doing. We think he has been sending a message to the Abaddons, to Zivko Gowst."

It started to dawn on them; they too were starting to put bits of the jigsaw together.

"Morgan Clay got us on the right track. The first bishop was a bishop who worked in Croatia. However, he was not a native to Croatia, but we didn't know that at first, so it made seeing a link that much harder. He was actually Serbian. He was actually the nephew of a priest in Serbia who had taught Gowst when Gowst was a boy. We think Salah El-Din's first offering to Gowst was a relative of the priest that reportedly had abused him as a boy. That priest disappeared. He was found many years later. He had died a nasty death and there were rumours about the strange Gowst boy. Morgan thinks that if he could join those dots, with all the information he and Wolf had gathered, then feasibly so could Salah El-Din.

"Priest number two was a priest in Egypt. A bit of a fiery character, it seems. He preached that the problems in today's society in Egypt could be traced back to the errors of their Arab forefathers. He made a speech, which was in all the newspapers. Part of his speech was an attack on the old tribes and their beliefs; he had particularly damming things to say about the Malmuks."

"From whose ranks rose the Abaddons," Zakariah said for Billy Jack's benefit.

But Billy Jack still looked confused. "Forgive me, I'm still playing catch up here."

Zakariah explained. "We have fought them many times and in many different ways Billy Jack, and every time both sides have come away with heavy casualties. They only have three missions in life: one is to destroy the Templars, which they have been trying to do for eight hundred years; the second is to kill God worshippers and finally, get the Ark."

St Clair wanted to tell them his greatest fear about the Abaddons but he couldn't. He just thought it: ... *and if they suspect the truth about the Ark, like I do, if they suspect its real purpose, they will destroy it the second they get their hands on it, because they know that if they don't, it will destroy them, as it is written in the Bible.*

"There were rumours, Billy Jack, about the army called Malmuks," Zakariah continued. "People spoke about pagan rituals. Their barbaric nature was not reserved for Christians alone; they also murdered and pillaged Muslim and Jewish communities. We have Canon law, there is Halakha law – Jewish, Sharia Law – Islamic, and then we have Abaddon law: kill the God worshippers.

"At some time during that period, a splinter group broke away and started to follow Abaddon. They took his name, and it was to him, their new Lord, that their allegiance was sworn. He was their Lord Abaddon, and they were his right arm of punishment, retribution and death."

"So, it would seem," Zakariah said, turning towards Courtney and Bertram, "that our priest number two fell foul of the Abaddons and Salah El-Din killed him for them."

Courtney and Bertram both nodded. Then Bertram told them they had found out that the third priest was the priest of the town in Romania near to where Zivko's camp was. After the Templar's extraction mission, there were numerous bodies left at the camp. The authorities took witness statements, mostly from people who supplied the camp and soon it was being branded as a death camp. The local priest had said that the men who ran the camp were murderers and their leader was obviously mentally ill, a deranged man of limited intelligence. So, another offering of a life from Salah El-Din.

Courtney and Bertram went on to say that the fifth priest, the

173

Pope, would have been his pièce de résistance. If they wanted to kill God worshippers, they could not get much higher in Christian terms than the leader of the Roman Catholic Church. The obvious elephant in the room was priest number four and the head of John the Baptist. Here, they said, they had drawn a blank. There was absolutely no connection between the bishop and the Abaddons and they could find no connection between the Abaddons and Saint John. They knew there had to be a link, but they hadn't figured it out yet.

St Clair was pleased they knew the who; they just didn't know the why. The head of the Baptiser and the call to Jonathan was a major part of whatever play he had; they just didn't know what part. St Clair needed the answer and he knew he was running out of time to get it.

Chapter 10

From Adversity Rise Three Templars

Date: 1965
Place: The Four Feathers public house. The village of Stoockburgh, Scotland. Early morning

The Four Feathers pub in the village of Stoockburgh nestled neatly between the uniform ranks of light, reddish-brown sandstone-built terraced houses. The houses, two and three-bedroom dwellings, were all filled with Scottish families – although that was about to change.

The village was a place where people left their doors unlocked, knew their children playing in the streets would be safe and where village life reflected the values of a tight-knit community. It was also a place where, through a terrible disaster, three future Templars would come together and be forever linked to each other.

The pub was the only public house in the small village. It was the epicentre of the village. It was also the home of eight-year-old Tiffany Jane Clarke and her mother, twenty-four-year-old Ruth Jane Clarke. Ruth was a single mother; she'd had Tiffany when she was just sixteen years old. She had not shirked her duties as a mother, despite being so young and despite her pregnancy being the biggest scandal the village had known. Ruth was a good mother. Her parents were the landlord and landlady of the pub. They employed Ruth as a barmaid and between the three of them, they ran the pub, brought up Tiffany and were pillars of the community.

175

It was said of little Tiffany Jane Clarke, that she was as bright as a button, as sharp as a tack and was always into some playful mischief or other. She was top of her class, read well and was good with numbers. Everybody knew her and everybody liked her.

Tiffany was watching him. She was watching the American, the guest – the only guest. She was watching the man who made her laugh, the man who spoke funny, gave her sweets, told her stories and ruffled her hair. She crouched down behind the three, black, rubbish bins. She was hiding. She was giggling. He couldn't see her, but she could see him through the gap between the bins. It was early morning and she knew she should have been getting ready for school but she wanted to wave goodbye to him, to the American.

Across the pub car park, Harry Gannan stood admiring his motorbike. He was in love with his motorbike. He was an American; the American flag designed bandana he wore on his head was a strong indication of it and when he opened his mouth, his west coast, Californian brogue confirmed it. Harry Gannan was six feet tall. He was also good-looking with long blond hair down to his shoulders. His neck was full of love-bead necklaces; his neck was always full of love-bead necklaces. Harry Gannan was charming. It was 1965 and he epitomised the hippie movement that had engulfed most of the Western world. He was a free spirit. Everyone loved Harry, the American.

He looked at his watch. "Damn," he mumbled, realising he would be late for work. He took out a cloth from his leather saddle bag and wiped the light morning dew from his Harley Davidson. He wouldn't go until he had wiped his bike dry, no matter how late it might make him. The black paintwork glimmered in the morning sunlight. He called his bike Janis Joplin, after the American singer, because he said it sounded like her: it had jet-black paintwork, black leather saddle bags with silver rivets straddling both sides of his seat, sparkling chrome, with a high back sissy bar and ape hanger handlebars, and the American flag airbrushed on both sides of his black fuel tank.

Harry put on his black, sleeveless leather jacket – the words 'PEACE & LOVE' were emblazoned on the back of the jacket. He wore no shirt underneath, just a bare, well-defined chest. It was sunny and warm – the rain had let up for once – and he knew he had hard labour to do. The tattoo on his left upper arm showed an upside down M-16 rifle, its bayonet stuck in the ground, with a soldier's metal helmet on top of the rifle, underneath the legend 'Fallen Brothers.'

Harry got on his bike. He flipped the rest stand up with his foot and steadied himself; it was a heavy bike. He sneaked a look towards the pub's upstairs windows. He caught a glimpse of her, with her head just peering from behind the bland, cream curtains. Ruth was pretty, she was vivacious and totally smitten with Harry, the American with the cute smile. He slowly rolled his bike forwards a few yards and then he pushed his foot down on the kick-start: his foot slipped.

"Bugger, shit, bugger," he cursed. He sneaked a quick glance to see if Ruth had seen him. She had. She was laughing. "Bugger, shit, bugger," Harry said again. He struck the kick-start once more. A throaty roar bellowed out from his Harley as Janice Joplin's engine thundered into life. He checked his mirrors and then turned to smile at Ruth; he winked. Ruth saw him and suddenly disappeared – sideways! Harry gave the bike more throttle and Janice Joplin roared into action and he sped away.

Ruth had been watching their American guest from the window of one of the empty guest bedrooms. The pub had three guest rooms; Harry rented one of them and the other two were currently empty. They had been for a while.

She liked the American; she really *liked* the American. She found him charming, exciting and a little mysterious. He was an oddment, a bit of exotic in the small, parochial Scottish village. Harry loved people, films, hippies, peace, love and rock and roll. Ruth loved people, films, hippies, peace, love and rock and roll. Harry loved motorbikes. Ruth took a new interest in motorbikes.

She'd peered from behind the curtain hoping to catch a glimpse of him leaving.

"Shit," she said out loud; she'd got busted because Harry saw her. She darted back behind the curtain, a little too quickly, because she fell off the bedside table she had been kneeling on as her vantage point and the bedside table lamp fell with her. "Bugger, shit, bugger," she cursed as she and the table lamp hit the floor.

"Are you using bad language our Ruth?" Ruth's mother called from down the landing.

"No Ma," Ruth called back, "you must have misheard." Ruth scrambled back onto the bedside table putting the lamp back into position. She looked from behind the curtain again and saw her eight-year-old daughter appear in her pyjamas from behind the three rubbish bins. She had her red wellingtons on, her mother's Celtic scarf, her grandfather's cap and held a one-armed teddy in her left hand and her grandmother's umbrella in the other.

"Bye Harry, bye Harry," Tiffany called after Harry, excitedly.

Ruth knocked the window to her daughter. "Get in here right now," she called.

"Who are you shouting at now, our Ruth?" Ruth's mother called from down the landing again.

"Ma, our Tiffany is annoying one of the guests."

"Ruth, we've only got one guest, dear. What you mean is she's annoying Harry again?"

"Yes Ma."

"Just like her mother, then?"

"Ma," Ruth complained.

"Never you mind, Ruth. Get a move on now and make up the guest's bedroom. Then you need to get your daughter ready for school. Clock's ticking."

Ruth went into Harry's room. It was unlocked despite him having a key. Inside, his bed was a mess; his clothes were spread across the bed. On the wall he'd hung the American flag. The room light was on. She knew that the light had been on all night: it always was. She sat on the edge of his bed and held one of his T-shirts to her face. She breathed in deeply and smelt his smell. Just then, Tiffany burst into Harry's room. She startled Ruth.

"I know you're my daughter and you're only eight, but if you're not ready for school in the next ten minutes, I will give you away to the old giants on the mountain," Ruth said.

"Ruth, you'll have her wetting the bed again," Ruth's mother called.

"Ma, she wet the bed because half the pub kept giving her drinks. Tiffany," she now whispered, "the giants!"

Tiffany ran off to get dressed.

Place: The Scottish countryside. Early morning

Harry and Janice Joplin were roaring along the narrow and winding country roads, Harry's long blond hair, like Harry, a free spirit as it swirled about behind him in the breeze. Harry knew the roads well. He found Scotland stunningly beautiful in the morning light and the sights, colours and smells reminded him of his home. Ten minutes into his journey, Harry passed a local oddball hermit called Claude.

Claude was leaning against a dry-stone wall staring back up to the mountain. Next to him was a small hand cart with bits of rubbish on it. Claude heard the roar of Janice Joplin and knew instantly it was Harry Gannan. He was the only one with a motorbike that sounded like a motorbike – there were two mopeds in the village. He waved to Harry excitedly and Harry waved back to him.

"Hey, hey, Yank! It's me, Claude," he called in a strong Scottish accent. Then he did a little dance until he saw a stick on the ground. He picked it up and lovingly placed it on his hand cart.

Harry turned the throttle of his bike slightly and Janice Joplin roared some more as she sped off into the distance.

Place: The bedroom of Arthur Pembroke. Early morning

Arthur Pembroke was the local chief inspector. He had been told he was being promoted to the post of superintendent, so he was made part of the selection committee tasked with finding his replacement. His replacement for the post of chief inspector was very quickly given to his current inspector, a popular man called Tony Galbraith. And, Tony Galbraith's replacement had already been found but from outside the county, and in fact from outside the country. The new inspector replacing Tony Galbraith, was a young man from Bangor, Wales: his name was Proctor Hutchinson.

Arthur Pembroke was not happy. He wanted a Scotsman in the job and one from his own county, not an outsider. He did not get his way on the appointment and because of that, everyone who knew Arthur Pembroke, knew that the newcomer from Wales was doomed from the start. Arthur Pembroke was a rude, self-opinionated, stubborn, obstinate, self-righteous, cantankerous, ill-tempered, angry man. He was stern looking, an unapologetic man with no friends.

Arthur Pembroke opened his eyes before his alarm clock went off. He always opened his eyes before the alarm clock went off. He stared at his bedside table. A worn book, a copy of poems by the Scottish bard Robert Burns lay open. The book occupied the space alongside an empty glass-tumbler and an empty bottle of whisky. He groaned: he was badly hungover, again. He raised his aching body and reached for his leg brace. He hated it. His leg brace was a constant reminder that he could never be like other people, do the things other people could do. It was a reminder of all of the abuse he'd suffered from the other children at his Kilmarnock school; it was a reminder that he was disabled. It was the cause of his anger and his contempt for others. He placed the leg brace next to his police uniform.

He dressed in front of the mirror: his uniform was immaculate, his tie tied correctly and his white shirt gleaming with a starched collar and starched cuffs. His shoes, as always, were highly polished. His transformation complete, he breathed deeply again; he checked his right leg in the mirror for the umpteenth time to make sure his leg brace was as hidden as it could be. He'd painted the steel foot section of the brace black, so that it stood out less and blended in more with the colour of his uniform trousers and black shoes.

Outside on the street, he eased himself into the police car and started the engine. He checked his mirrors, indicated and slowly pulled away from his wifeless, childless, soulless home. He heard the roar of the engine before he saw it. The black Harley Davidson sped past him before he had time to react. He knew who it was. He hated the

American. He thought he was lazy and self-assured. He believed he needed taking down a peg or two.

"Bastard American, I'm onto you," he shouted.

It took Arthur Pembroke just ten minutes to drive to the police headquarters. He pulled into the car park and into the parking space reserved for him. He turned off the ignition and then eased out of the car. He looked around the car park to see who was in. Everyone who was meant to be in, seemed to be in. They were thirty minutes early because Arthur Pembroke was always thirty minutes early. They felt they had to be: no one wanted to incur the wrath of Chief Inspector Pembroke, now Superintendent Pembroke. He took his briefcase out of the car and noticed the Harley Davidson on the other side of the car park. Then he saw the American. "Bastard," he grunted out loud.

Harry Gannan was wiping his Harley. He looked up and saw Arthur Pembroke scowling at him; he was shouting something. Harry went round to the other side of the bike and bent down to get out of sight. He stayed there until Ted Davies rolled up in his builder's truck, full of sand, cement, bricks, building equipment and his son, Bobby Davies. Ted liked Harry; he was the same age as his son, Bobby, so they all got along well.

"I thought you were travelling around the world, Harry?" Bobby said, as he jumped out of his father's truck and onto the back of it ready to offload the equipment to Harry. "You've only got as far as bloody Scotland."

"I have my reasons for staying," Harry said, emerging from behind Janice Joplin.

"I bet you do." Bobby said and winked. "I bet you do. Anyway, don't you dare go anywhere, not for the next six months at least or all this bloody labouring work will fall on my shoulders."

*

Place: Bangor, Wales

The kitchen was full of the smell of freshly made toast. Outside the sun was shining and the plants were taking full advantage of a sunny day.

The radio in the kitchen was on. Proctor Hutchinson watched his wife, Maggie, playing with their eight-year-old daughter, Molly Hutchinson. He loved them both in equal measures. He smiled as his wife and daughter giggled away to each other at the breakfast table. Molly, still in her pink pyjamas, had toast and jam in both hands, and on most of her face.

Proctor had grown up in Bangor, Gwynedd, northwest Wales, the oldest city in Wales and one of the smallest cities in the UK. He was a rising star in the regional police force. However, he'd applied for a transfer to Scotland; it was the only way he could ensure promotion any time soon. He had only served in the police force for a few years but had already moved from constable through to sergeant in those few years; the next rank in line for Proctor was inspector. He was an exceptional police officer, highly intelligent and naturally gifted for law enforcement, which ran in his family.

One of his mother's ancestors was General Sir Charles Warren. Warren had been an officer in the British Royal Engineers and was famous for attempting to unravel the mysteries of the Temple Mount, Solomon's Temple in Jerusalem, the birthplace of Christianity. Warren had been banned by the Ottoman authorities from excavating by the Temple Mount, but despite this he was still able to covertly sink vertical shafts down into the ground around the Temple. Eighty-five feet below ground level he found, at the base of the original Temple platforms, Phoenician inscriptions which still remained a mystery to archaeologists. Like another army officer before him, a man called Wilson, back in 1864, Warren had also found signs that the secret Order of the Knights Templar, the crusading warrior monks, had been there before him, but also like Wilson, he too left the Holy Land no more informed about what the Templars had actually been doing there. Warren couldn't know that many decades later, a member of his family would eventually find out the truth that had thwarted him and had thwarted mankind for centuries: what the Knights Templar were doing at Solomon's Temple and what iconic treasure they took out of the Holy Land for protection.

Proctor Hutchinson had big plans. He wanted to make his mark in the police force and then he would seek to transfer to the British intelligence services, where his passion lay. His father and his grandfather on his father's side, had both worked for MI5. During the day he kept his part of Wales safe and at night he studied hard to finish his second degree.

The removal people had been to the Hutchinsons' house the day before and, by the time Proctor and his family arrived in their new house in Scotland, all of the furniture and belongings would be unpacked and placed in each of the rooms according to the layout plan Maggie had given them.

By 8 a.m. the Hutchinsons' had their car loaded with essentials and their personal belongings and armed with an A to Z – large road atlas, they set off on the nine-hour car journey north and to their new home in Scotland.

Time: Nine hours later

Proctor's back was aching and his legs were sore, but they were nearly there. Maggie and Molly were excited. They were about to enter the village boundaries. Proctor looked out of the window and saw an odd character walking up the road, pulling a small hand cart with bits of rubbish on it. The odd character noticed Maggie and Molly in the back of the car and he tipped his old, scruffy hat to them as they passed by.

"Look Mummy," Molly said. In front of them was the village of Stoockburgh, their new home, but Molly wasn't looking at the village. She was looking at two shapes behind the houses and above the village. "What are those, Mummy," she asked.

Maggie looked at Proctor. "It's an open cast quarry," he said. "They produce rocks, aggregate and stone for building. I think they are the waste heaps, the overburden."

"They are big, Mummy."

"They are indeed," Maggie replied thoughtfully. There's tons of the stuff."

It was 5 p.m. by the time they arrived in the village. It was busy with cars and bicycles. People who worked in shops, the local steel works and the quarry were all going home. Maggie was map reading and sharing her commentary: "And that," she said pointing, "will be our local butchers. It must only be a five-minute walk from us. And there, look Molly! The Primary school. That's your new school, darling. Proctor, turn left!" Maggie said hurriedly. Proctor turned left, took the next right and finally they pulled up outside a small, three-bedroom terrace house with a 'SOLD' sign outside it.

They all got out of the car, excitedly. It was a little after 5 p.m. Molly ran off to watch two children down the road playing a game with two sticks and a ball. Proctor was getting their suitcases out of the boot of their car. He heard the sound of a motorbike but he didn't see it come into view because he was halfway in the boot reaching for a small bag at the back. Maggie saw it approaching, a black Harley Davidson. The rider slowed up and wolf-whistled at her. She giggled, smiled back and waved. Harry hooted his horn. Proctor, who still had his head in the boot, jumped with a start at the sound of the horn and hit his head. He stood up, rubbing his head and cursed the rider.

"Oops," Harry called and quickly rode on.

Time: Later that night

Maggie was putting Molly into bed.

"I don't like them Mummy," Molly said, her eyes half closed.

"Don't like what, darling?" Maggie asked her, tucking the blankets in.

Molly pointed to the black shapes on the side of the mountain. Maggie closed the curtains and finished tucking her daughter in. She kissed her on the cheek, left Molly's door ajar and left the landing light on. She went into her bedroom. Proctor was reading a file that detailed everything he needed to know about his new duties and the main outstanding cases – he was reading it for the umpteenth time. Maggie looked out of their bedroom window as she got into bed – they had the same view as Molly's window.

"Everything okay?" Proctor asked her.

"Yes. It's just those things up there," she said looking at the black shapes. "They've spooked Molly a little. I think they've spooked me a little too."

Proctor glanced at the bedside clock; it read 9 p.m. "We must be the only people in bed," he said.

"No, I would think everyone's tucked up in bed by now," Maggie replied. "It's a weeknight and it doesn't look like the kind of village that has a mid-week knees-up. In fact, it doesn't look like the kind of village that has a knees-up at all." Maggie switched off the light and snuggled up to Proctor.

Place: Down the road in the village pub, the Four Feathers

The pub was full. The atmosphere was friendly and jovial; it was filled with 1960s music playing from an old jukebox. Ruth was serving behind the bar with her mother and father. Despite the fact there were three of them, they could barely keep up.

In the corner of the room, Harry Gannan was sitting drinking and playing dominoes with three old men from the village. Harry loved their company; he loved their stories and he loved their wicked sense of humour, and, they loved talking to Harry.

Brewdor, the first old man, tapped his last domino on the table. "I'm knocking, Harry, it's your turn. What you got Yankee Doodle?"

Harry was not paying attention. He was looking at Ruth and she kept stealing glances at him.

"Her father will chop 'IT' off if he catches you getting familiar with young Ruth there," the second old man, McEwen, said.

"With a bloody blunt castration knife and no painkillers," Galbraith, the third old man said. The three old men started laughing. "Especially in that shirt. God's teeth Harry! What have you got on?" Galbraith asked him, staring at Harry's shirt.

"It's flower power, man," Harry replied. "It's the sixties man. Don't you dig it?"

"The only thing Galbraith ever dug," Brewdor, the first old man

185

said, "was his allotment. That's not a shirt, Harry; it's bloody wallpaper, that's what it is, and I'm still knocking." All the old men laughed again.

Harry laughed with them. "You dudes crack me up," he said.

Over at the bar, Ruth's mother was watching her daughter. She saw her keep looking over to Harry. She pulled another pint and inched towards her. She didn't want to make it obvious, but she was worried.

"You know," she began sensitively, "that boy is going to break someone's heart one day: I just hope it's not someone I know." Ruth ignored her mother.

Arthur Pembroke was sitting at the bar. He was alone and nursing another double whisky, on the rocks.

"He's like all the young ones today, no bloody discipline, that one," he said with venom and deep disdain. He took another drink of his whisky.

"I don't know, Arthur," Ruth's mum said pulling another pint for a customer. "He's been boarding with us for the past three months and he's not been a bit of trouble, not one bit." She looked over to where Harry was still playing dominoes with the three old men. Tiffany was on his lap, giggling, as Harry ruffled her hair. "But you know," she said, giving change to another customer, "there is something about him. I just can't put my finger on it."

"I'll tell you what's troubling him. Bloody hard work!" Arthur Pembroke interrupted. "That's what's bloody troubling him. Like all the other lazy buggers his age. Bloody hippies; no bloody backbone. Lazy, that's what they are, bloody lazy. Something needs to be done about him."

"I think you're being a bit hard on him, Arthur."

"I'm being no harder on him than anyone else. Communities run on structure, discipline, hard work and the rule of law," he replied. "He should never have come here. He should have kept on travelling like he said he was doing. Wouldn't surprise me if he has a criminal record, a man like that."

The pub door flew open with a bang. Outside it was raining. It had started to rain around 7 p.m. and had not let up in the last two hours. Dewy and his brother walked into the pub, followed by the wind and rain.

"Evening boys," Ruth said. "The usual?" The brothers nodded. Their faces dirty and wet. "Bad night up at the quarry?" Ruth asked them.

"Getting worse. It's a bloody quagmire up there."

Ruth smiled and then saw Harry going outside. The three old men playing dominoes also watched him go.

"Strange bloke that Harry, McEwen said after Harry had left. He never moans or makes a fuss, never argues. You know I can't say I've ever heard him say a bad word about anyone."

"If I were a betting man," Brewdor said, "which I'm not, I—"

"Oh no, course you're not," Galbraith said.

"I would say that the lad has a past," Brewdor continued.

"What do you mean, a past?" McEwen asked.

"I'm saying I like Harry, I like him a lot and when he's good-and-ready he'll tell us, but there is something troubling that young man. Now," Brewdor said, "McEwen, I believe it's your round, isn't it? Don't be shy now wee man."

Outside the rain had stopped temporarily, the sky had cleared somewhat and the light of the full moon was now shining brightly, along with thousands of stars in the night sky. Ruth lifted a crate of empty beer bottles onto a stack of other crates in the corner of the pub yard. She let out a strained "Bloody hell that's heavy." She took a few deep breaths as she reached for the second crate.

She caught sight of the match striking up. She knew it was Harry because the flame struck low, below waist height, then it moved upwards. She knew Harry always struck his matches on the leg of his Levi jeans.

"Who's there?" she called anyway. Harry moved into the open and into the light of the pub's two yard-lights. "What are you doing hanging around the back here, Harry Gannan. What mischief are you up to?"

"The Pole star," Harry said, with a serious look on his face and looking skyward.

Ruth moved a little closer so she could follow the direction he was looking at. "What Pole star? Ah, you wouldn't know the Pole star from your arse."

Harry drew on his cigarette and let out the smoke from his mouth. It lingered for a second or two. "It's good luck," Harry said, still looking skywards. "Good luck to show someone the Pole star, I mean."

"Bollocks," Ruth whispered. "You must think us Scots are all soft in the head."

"Look," Harry said, this time pointing skywards. Ruth moved to his side. Her eyes followed his finger. He moved his face just inches away from hers. "There," he said.

She turned her head slightly towards him and asked, "Where?"

He seized his moment and kissed her. Then Ruth kissed him back. Then they both kissed each other: a lot.

"I swear, Harry," Ruth said, in between pressing her lips as firmly as she could on Harry's, "if you mess me about ... I have a daughter. It's unfair on me and unfair on our Tiffany to mess us about. I really like you, I mean, I really, really like you, but I have to think of Tif—"

Harry held his finger to Ruth's lips. "Shhh," he said, not letting her finish. "I decided the first time I saw you, that very first day I arrived here, that I would never leave this place without you and Tiffany. You are the reason I've stayed." He kissed her again.

Just then they heard Ruth's mother call out from the back door of the pub and they quickly moved back into the shadows.

"Tiffany, who's our Ruth talking to out there?"

Harry and Ruth looked around and saw Tiffany. She had been crouched down behind the bins.

"Shit," Ruth whispered.

"No one Grandma," Tiffany called back, "Mummy was talking to me."

"Okay, darling. Well come on in now, it's time for bed."

188

Harry walked over to Tiffany. He picked her up in his arms and whispered, "You see that star, Tiffany, that one there, that shiny one?" he pointed to the North Star. "In Scotland, it's called the Pole star but the Apache Indians in America, they call it Ruth's star, after a famous lady who was a sheriff, the only lady sheriff in all of America, ever. She had a shiny badge in the shape of a silver star on her blouse like that one. So, from now on, no matter where you are, you can look up at that star and always think of your mummy."

Three hours later the pub was all closed up and everyone was in bed and fast asleep. Ruth sneaked downstairs, through the kitchen and out to the back of the pub. It was raining again, raining hard but she didn't notice. Harry was outside on his bike waiting for her. He watched her lock the back door of the pub and then she ran across the back yard to where he was waiting under one of the Elm trees for cover. She jumped on the back of the bike and Harry kicked the rest stand up and pushed forward so the bike slowly rolled down the small hill. Then he put it into gear and Janice Joplin suddenly roared into life and they sped away, into the dark and into the rain.

Time: Later

It was 4 a.m. Ruth and Harry had been back for three hours. Ruth was fast asleep. Ruth's father passed Harry's door on the way to the toilet. He saw his bedroom light on. He rapped the door gently and Harry opened the door.

"Sorry Harry. I saw the light on. You okay?

"Yer. I must have dozed off and left it on," Harry said, a little flustered.

"Well, good night then."

"Good night," Harry said as he closed the door. Harry walked over to the window, opened the curtains and opened the box sash window. The streetlamp shone through into his bedroom. He lay down on the floor by the window and fell asleep in the light of the streetlamp.

Ruth's father got back into bed.

"Who were you talking to?" his wife asked him.

"His light was on again. Been on every night for three months."

Date: The next day, 7 a.m.

Proctor Hutchinson had been up early: he had butterflies. This was the first day of his new job and he wanted to make a good impression, so he made sure his uniform was smart, no creases, only in the right places. Maggie and Molly had breakfast with him and then they went outside to wave him off.

Proctor got into his car and checked again that he had everything he needed. He checked for the tenth time that morning. He removed his peaked cap and placed it on the passenger seat. He indicated, waved goodbye to Maggie and Molly and then started to pull out. He heard the roar of Janice Joplin coming his way a second before the black Harley Davidson zoomed past him, with its rider waving to Maggie and Molly. Proctor had to swerve back into the kerb. He tooted his horn.

"Oops," Harry called back.

Proctor's drive to the police station only took him twenty minutes. He found a parking spot and turned off the engine. When he got out of the car, he looked at the police station. There was a man standing at the window. He looked stern. However, he wasn't looking at Proctor, he was looking at the other end of the car park. He was looking at a man lovingly wiping his black Harley Davidson motorbike. *It's you*, Proctor thought when he saw the man with the bike.

*

Once inside the police station, he was shown upstairs where all the offices were. He was asked to sit and wait in a small waiting area, with two wilted, potted plants and an array of old magazines. A number of typists watched him as he was served strong tea. He was nervous.

From the largest of the offices, he heard a man shouting. "They reduce my bloody budgets, they increase the bloody conviction targets and now, they send me a bloody child as my new inspector." The man's voice was bellowing out unapologetically.

Proctor noticed that all the typing had stopped and all the typists were now looking at him. Then he heard a female voice mumble something from within the large office.

"Smart, educated. Aren't I smart and bloody educated?" the rant continued. "Holy Christ, would you look at this: interests, communications within intelligence services. My God, they've sent me a bloody idiot." Again, a mumbled female voice could be heard. "What do you mean a second degree? I haven't got a bloody degree, so what good is a bloody second degree?"

Proctor was painfully aware that all the typists were still looking at him. He smiled, lamely. They smiled back, lamely. Then the office door opened, and in that split second, all the typewriters started up again and the noise of clicking qwerty keys and swiped return bars broke the silence. A middle-aged lady came out of the office, looking frayed and told Proctor to go in.

He rose and as he did so he overheard one of the young typists say, "He doesn't look like he will last more than a week."

Oh God, he thought, *oh God*!

By lunch time, Proctor felt as though he had been there twenty years. He was glad to get out of the offices and out of the way of Arthur Pembroke, who he found to be a bully, abrupt and insensitive to all his staff, especially the women. Proctor sat outside in his car and ate the sandwiches Maggie had lovingly made for him.

Out in the car park, it had finally stopped raining. He noticed the Harley rider was sitting under a tree by his bike, also eating sandwiches; he was alone. Proctor took his sandwiches and flask and walked over to the man. Harry nodded, and then smiled and Proctor knew instantly that regardless of the fact he had nearly caused him to crash and had caused him to bump his head, he was going to like this man.

"Heard your greeting from your boss."

Proctor looked quizzically.

"The window was open and we were on the flat roof fixing the leak. That was harsh, Dude," Harry said.

"Is he always that discourteous and rude to people?" Proctor asked.

"I guess … some … mostly, actually, all people, but I think more so with me. I'm kind of like an abrasion to him. He says I've had life too easy, never done a good day's work. He says I lack backbone."

"So, you're not expecting a Christmas card from him then?" Proctor said, laughing.

"Man, that would be a real surprise if one arrived. It would be pretty far out if you ask me. The name's Harry Gannan, by the way. Harry Gannan from the US of A." He held out his hand.

"Proctor Hutchinson," Proctor said "from W of ALES. I just moved here with my wife, Maggie, and daughter, Molly. She's eight. I think you know my wife. You keep waving to her."

Harry laughed. "Hey man, just being friendly with the natives. Besides, nothing to worry about. I got my own sweetheart and she's all I want. Decided a while back I wanted to see the world. So, I got on my Harley and took off. I did ten states, caught a cargo ship, docked in Ireland, and then caught a ferry to Scotland a week later. Landed here about three months ago and, well, been here ever since, man."

"Ah, the girl?" Proctor said.

"Yup, got me a sweetheart and I ain't intending on going anywhere now, not without her anyway. Hey, Proctor, why don't you and Maggie come round to the Four Feathers on Saturday night. I have board and lodgings there, and Ruth, that's my gal, her parents own the pub. Ruth has a daughter, Tiffany. I guess maybe the same age as your Molly. They can play together."

"That would be great," Proctor said. "We haven't really got to know anybody yet."

"Don't worry, Proctor. I'll introduce you to everyone. You'll love the Scots. I do."

*

Date: Saturday night. 7 p.m. five days later
Place: The Four Feathers pub

It was raining, again. Harry, Ruth, Maggie and Proctor were sitting at a table talking and laughing. Tiffany and Molly were playing together nearby. Proctor asked Ruth about Claude.

"He's a bit of a recluse is old Claude," Ruth said, "but he's harmless. Hasn't been down here in the village since, I think, it was the Queen's Coronation. He has a sister in the next town. She visits him every few weeks. He lives in an old croft way up the mountain."

"Let's not talk about old Claude," Harry said. He seemed a little nervous. He'd been edgy all night. He breathed in deep, cleared his throat, unplugged the juke box and then, he announced: "Everyone, Ruth and I are getting married."

The whole pub went quiet. Ruth's parents stopped serving. Her father had a big smile on his face because he really liked Harry.

Ruth's mother was startled. "What?" she called.

Ruth shook her shoulders. "I didn't know—"

Just then, Harry got down on one knee. He took out a ring from his pocket and he proposed. A loud cheer went up.

"I guess the drinks are on me," Ruth's father said from behind the bar. Another, louder cheer went up.

Arthur Pembroke was at the far end of the bar. "Lazy Yank. Told her about your little secret have you, Yank?" he shouted towards Harry, his words slurred.

"What's he talking about?" Ruth asked Harry.

"I have no idea," Harry said.

The pub door opened and everyone turned to see who it was. The new chief inspector was drenched from the downpour outside. He took off his hat and coat and hung it on the ornate, iron coat stand by the door. He took out an A4 brown envelope from his inside coat pocket to shield it from the rain. Then he went over to the table with the three old men playing dominoes, nodding to Proctor Hutchinson, his inspector, as he passed.

"Watch out boys! It's another lawman," Galbraith said.

193

"Evening Inspector. No, wait, let me see now, it's Chief Inspector now, isn't it?" The other two old men, Brewdor and McEwen, laughed.

"Ma said I'd find you here, Da," the chief inspector said to his father, Galbraith.

"You tell your ma that we will have your da home just as soon as we've won all his money playing dominoes, which won't take us very long," McEwen said.

Galbraith ignored his friend. "You'll take a drink with us son?"

"No thanks, Da. I should be getting back to Brenda and the kids, but I'll get you and the boys one. I just nipped in because I wanted to ask you about the American."

"Harry? He's just propo— Why, what's Harry done?" his father asked him.

"Well, he's actually not done anything, quite the reverse actually, but there was an accusation made via the British Embassy in Washington, to the American authorities, accusing him of being a draft dodger. If he was guilty, that's a five-year stretch over there."

"Not Harry," McEwen said, shocked. "Who made the call?"

"Me." Arthur Pembroke staggered over to them, glass in hand. He stood wavering. "I left a message for you today. Too busy to return my call but not too busy to drink, I see." He rasped at his chief inspector.

The chief inspector's father went to say something, but the chief inspector put his hand on his father's shoulder. "Mr Pembroke, Sir, it's late and I'm off duty. I've just called in to buy my da and the old fellows here a drink."

"It's late; it's bloody late. Who do you think you're bloody talking to. If it wasn't for me, you wouldn't have got that bloody promotion. You're a lazy bastard, like that other lazy bastard over there, the bloody Yank." Arthur Pembroke stared at Harry with hate in his eyes.

"Were you born with your arse just under your nose or has it made its way up there over the years all by itself, Pembroke?" Galbraith said in defence of his son. He stood up. He was fuming.

"Piss off old man before I lock you up for loitering, and the rest of these dead beats."

The chief inspector stepped in front of Arthur Pembroke. "I think it's time you went home, Sir." He went to take Arthur Pembroke's arm, but his boss swung at him, hit him on the side of the head and the chief inspector fell onto the table, knocking his father over in the chaos. Glasses and drinks flew everywhere.

Harry ran over to them and stood in front of Arthur Pembroke, stopping him lashing out at the fallen chief inspector yet again. "Enough," he shouted, his frame towering above Arthur Pembroke. "You will not hit this man again, or I will lay you flat on your back."

"Enough, enough," Arthur Pembroke shouted back, swaying unsteadily on his feet. "You bloody draft dodger. You bloody coward. You ran away from your duty, didn't you, Yank? You're a bloody coward and everyone should know it. I'm going to make sure they lock you up."

The chief inspector got back on his feet. He wiped the blood from his nose. "You bloody pompous bastard. You really want to know if Harry is a draft dodger – is that what you want? That's what all this is about isn't it, your dislike for Harry, because he's young and everyone likes him and you, you're too bitter and cold to see your own stupidity. Do you want to know about him?" He turned to Harry. "He called Special Branch, Harry, and then the British Embassy in Washington, accusing you of being a draft dodger. He reported you."

"It's my civic duty, something you lot wouldn't know the meaning of," Arthur Pembroke barked at them. "If he's a draft dodger, and I know he bloody well is, he should be locked up and he bloody well will be, and all of you." He looked around at the patrons of the pub. "You should bloody well thank me."

Ruth moved to Harry's side and took his arm.

"You conceited idiot," the chief inspector shouted at Arthur

Pembroke. He opened the envelope he had been holding and took the fax out from inside it. "Take a good hard look at Sergeant Harry Gannan, Sir. Twenty-five years old. Medically discharged from the army over a year ago, and awarded the Purple Heart for bravery." The chief inspector read and the pub stayed silent. "It says that Harry and some of his men volunteered to clear enemy tunnels, according to this report that came through on the fax machine today. The tunnels were booby-trapped rabbit warrens, described as small, dark, dank tunnels that the Viet Cong used to move around without being seen. His Platoon was boxed in and they had to clear the tunnels to move forward. Harry and five other men volunteered. Something happened and the tunnels blew up. Harry was the only survivor; it took them two days to get him out because the rest of the platoon was pinned down. Two days buried alive down there. When they finally got him out, he wasn't alone. A Viet Cong family had been hiding in the warren of tunnels. The parents had died from the blast, but two little children hadn't and whilst wounded from the explosion, Harry had kept them alive long enough until they were rescued."

"That's why he keeps the light on," Ruth's father said to his wife behind the bar, "he's petrified of the dark."

"I don't bloody blame him," his wife replied.

Date: Three months later. The day before Harry and Ruth's wedding
Place: The police station

It was raining hard; it had been for nearly two weeks and the ground was muddy with the rainfall. Farmers' fields were awash and crops were at risk. Livestock were brought down from the hills to shelter in cattle sheds and barns. Roads were continually flooded and the emergency services were working around the clock.

The first indication that something was wrong was when two telegraph poles started to lean over; then one by one, twenty more in a line fell over in straight succession. The stone quarry's rail track that ferried the aggregate began to buckle. Halfway up the mountain, Claude was lying down, his ear pressed to the ground. Seconds later he leapt to his feet with a start: he had fear in his eyes. He turned to see a brown wave of waste, overburden and rubble, tons of it heading straight for him. It was like an avalanche. Claude turned towards the village below and started to run, yelling at the same time. "Hey, hey, it's coming. Get out, hey—" Moments later he was gone, engulfed by the brown wave.

Ted Davies, his son Bobby, and Harry were inside the police station with buckets and plastic sheeting trying to stop the ceiling from collapsing from the weight of the water seeping through the asphalt flat roof. It was raining too hard for them to fix the leak with tar, so they were dealing with the water damage as best they could.

Inside the police station, a phone started ringing, then another, then another. Then all the phones started ringing. The whole office stopped working. Proctor picked up the phone on his desk. He didn't say a word. He just listened, dumbfounded: shocked. He put the phone down. Everything had gone quiet and Harry moved next to him. Proctor turned to Harry. "The quarry waste. It's avalanched. It's hit part of the village. They think the pub."

"Oh my God," was all Harry could muster.

Arthur Pembroke came out of his office oblivious to the carnage that had taken place just seven miles away. "What the hell are you standing around for?" he barked at Harry.

"We need the keys to the Land Rover, Sir," Proctor said. "We'll need to take the back road. It's the quickest way but it's under a foot of water, and we need the keys to the stores. We need tools quickly. There's been a terrible accident."

"There's nothing going out of my stores till I've verified this," Arthur Pembroke snapped back at him. He pulled out a set of car keys from his pocket. "And these keys stay with me."

Proctor looked in disbelief.

"Now, get back to work! I will find out for myself what's going on later."

"I'm afraid that's not good enough," Proctor said, and punched Arthur Pembroke square on the chin and took the keys.

Most of the police left the office and drove their cars in the direction of the village. Proctor and Harry took the police Land Rover after filling it with picks, shovels and other equipment.

Time: Thirty minutes later

Proctor had to stop the Land Rover a mile away. The road was blocked with cars abandoned by helpers.

Harry looked and saw the path the brown avalanche had taken. It had crossed the stream and the railway track. On the outskirts of the village, he saw the rooftops of a few houses that were buried in the brown slurry, with smoke still coming out of their chimneys. "Shit … shit, bloody shit!" he said. Then he saw the Four Feathers public house, also buried up to the roof eaves.

The chief inspector was already there, with his father, Galbraith. The chief inspector had set up an Incident Post around his police car. In the distance, a group of army cadets were arriving and so were volunteers from the Salvation Army. The Women's Royal Voluntary Services (WRVS) had already set up a tea tent and were organising blankets for the wet and confused residents. A number of men and women were digging frantically around the buried houses and around the pub. Mess and rubble was strewn everywhere: clothes, books, chairs, broken and splintered telegraph poles, trees and part of Claude's cart. Claude's sister was digging through the brown slurry on her hands and knees, calling out Claude's name.

A human chain had formed to move the rubble away as men and women dug with whatever they could find, most with their bare hands. Proctor asked a young schoolboy, an army cadet corporal, called Luther Jones, if he would take some of his team and get the tools from the police Land Rover. Luther Jones and fifteen other cadets from Leicestershire, who were on a week-long outward-bound camp nearby, had heard what had happened and had run to the village. Luther mustered five of the boys and immediately ran off towards the Landover.

*

Harry was watching a rescue worker who was down a hole, headfirst, only his legs and feet showing. The chief inspector and two other men were hanging on to his legs. The chief inspector called to Harry to help them. Harry started to breathe heavy with panic.

"You don't have to do this, Harry, no one would blame you if ..." Proctor began.

Harry wasn't listening. He started to walk forward.

"Harry, you don't have to do this," Proctor called after him.

"I do, Proctor," Harry called back, "of course I do. Look at it ... it will take every one of us, and a hundred more ... God help them!"

Every so often, a whistle blew and everyone stopped and listened. All in all, thirteen people had been found and rescued from the quarry's waste avalanche. But the Four Feathers pub remained the epicentre of activity. It had been reported that it was full of lunchtime patrons and those preparing for Harry and Ruth's wedding the next day. Twenty people were estimated to be missing. Proctor and Harry desperately looked for Ruth, Molly, Maggie, Tiffany and Ruth's parents. They wondered if they had been found and checked with the ambulance crew. They hadn't seen anyone matching the descriptions, but said it was difficult to tell because everyone coming out of the rubble and brown slurry was almost unrecognisable, and in deep shock.

"Try the chapel mate," a young paramedic said. "That's where they're taking the bod ... try the chapel."

Harry waited outside the chapel. Proctor went inside. Two rescue workers carried a small body inside, and then another body arrived. Then Proctor appeared at the door and shook his head: they were not there.

The chief inspector, dirty and sweating from digging, called over to Proctor and Harry. "Can you give those men a hand over there?" Proctor and Harry started digging with the young corporal, Luther Jones and his cadets. They noticed Bobby, the son of the builder, Ted Davies, sitting on the ground crying, distraught because of the carnage. A WRVS lady gave him hot tea and a blanket and comforted him. Sitting by his side was Galbraith, blackened and totally exhausted and on his lap was Tiffany. Harry and Proctor ran over to Galbraith and Harry took Tiffany in his arms.

"It's okay Baby, I've got you now. I'm never going to let you go." Harry was crying.

"We got her a few minutes ago," Galbraith said. "Apparently, she'd been waiting by the bins for you, Harry, for you to return on your bike. When it all happened, she hid in one of the black bins. The slurry took it half a mile down the road before it stopped. It saved her life. Doc says she'll be okay, no physical injuries." He saw the look on Proctor's face. "I'm sorry son, we haven't found the others yet."

It had been two hours since Harry and Proctor got there. Twenty yards away from them, a man was digging alone. He was working furiously. Whilst others stopped every now and then to catch their breath and drink some water, the man didn't. He did not stop. A WRVS lady told Harry and Proctor that he had been digging for over an hour now non-stop. They looked but could not make him out.

It was still raining. The light was fading a little. Building site lights had been brought in from a nearby building site and rigged up with most of the beams focused on the pub. Men and women were exhausted. Tired, dirty faces looked out across the carnage in total despair. The sound of the earlier whistle became less and less as time moved on.

The man who had been working furiously and been digging non-stop, stopped suddenly. Now Harry and Proctor recognised him. The man knelt down in the slurry and the mud awkwardly; he then lifted up a small limp body. It was the body of a little girl. The man started to cry. He started to walk towards Harry and Proctor, blood running down his leg, his brace digging into his flesh, now lacerated and filthy.

Arthur Pembroke stumbled and the young cadet, Luther Jones, ran over to help him. Tears ran down the man's face. "I'm sorry. I'm so sorry. Please forgive me." The body of Proctor's eight-year-old daughter, Molly, lay limp in Arthur Pembroke's arms. Luther took her, laid her down and wiped the dirt from her little face.

In all, fifteen people died that day, four of them children. Ruth, her parents, Ted Davies the builder, Claude, McEwen, Brewdor, Proctor Hutchinson's wife, Maggie, and his little daughter, Molly, were amongst those who died. The man who would one day become a senior member of the British Intelligence Services, and also join the Order of the Knights Templar and rise to become a member of their Higher Council, lost his entire family on that dreadful day.

Date: Present day: Christmas Day 2012
Place: A small cemetery just outside the small village of Stoockburgh, Scotland

It was snowing, windy and cold. The light was fading. No one else was around as Tiffany stood by their graves. She placed a single red rose on each of their graves: for Ruth, her mother, her grandfather and grandmother. Close by were the graves of Ted Davies the builder, McEwen, Brewdor and Claude. Next to Claude was his sister's grave, who had since passed. Proctor Hutchinson's wife, Maggie, and his little daughter, Molly, were buried just a few yards away and next to their graves was the grave of Arthur Pembroke, who had only passed away two years ago. And, next to Ruth's grave, the grave of Harry Gannan who had died ten years back, finally with his 'gal.'

Tiffany looked at their graves and remembered them. She remembered their faces, each one of them, their smiles, their laughs. She missed them; she missed them all.

She'd seen the headlights of the approaching car for a while. It slowed as it approached the cemetery. Then it stopped. The engine was switched off and two car doors opened and then shut. She heard the footsteps on the gravel behind her. She turned around slowly and saw two men walking towards her. The taller man was wearing a grey Ulster coat and a grey trilby. The stockier man was in a hooded waterproof coat, jeans and cowboy boots. They moved beside her. The man in the Ulster coat wiped the snowflakes from the brim of his trilby hat and then buried his hands into his pockets to seek out warmth.

Tiffany looked up at the now darkening sky and through the

snowy haze, the stars were shining brightly. She pointed, "Do you see that star, the North Star. Harry told me that in America it's called the Ruth Star and wherever I was, I just had to look up and I would see my mum."

Both men smiled. "I miss old Harry," the man in the trilby said.

"When Harry adopted me as his daughter," she said, "he also made Arthur my godparent. Arthur took his duties seriously. You know, he never missed a birthday, a school play, a rounders match. He was always there for me, like both of you. You saved me and you protected me."

Just then Tiffany's mobile phone rang, she searched in her bag to retrieve it. The biometric retinal scan locked onto her eyes for user recognition. She answered the call. She didn't say a word. When the call had finished, she hung up. She looked at the graves one more time and pulled her coat collar up around her neck. "That was St Clair," she said. "The Controller said he doesn't want me to go back to Islington. He wants me to go to the castle."

"We know," Proctor Hutchinson said. "We've come to take you there."

She looked at him inquisitively.

"Seems they've chosen their new Council members, Tiff," Luther Jones said, as he moved by her side and put his arm around her. They have named their two new Worthies."

Now she looked inquisitively at Luther.

"Who?" she asked.

Proctor took off his hat. "I'm looking at them both."

Chapter 11

Christmas Day Part II

Date: 25th December 2012
Place: A remote castle in Scotland

It had been a few hours since St Clair had spoken to Dámaso Nef. He instructed his HQ team to set up conference calls with Dominique, the Indian and Bill Meeks for 5 p.m. UK time. They were contacted and a call time and protocol were put into place through the stand-in Controller in Islington. St Clair had also called into the control room, hidden and safe in underground rooms in the castle. Its multiple computer screens, digital platforms and platform stack systems were whirling away collecting, digesting and sieving through news and law enforcement agency data from around the world. He also checked on the five other missions they were carrying out overseas, all live and all with teams of 'active' Knights.

Before his call with the New Jersey mission team, he ate a little dinner whilst reading status reports. He talked briefly to Morgan Clay on his way to the meeting room about their problem with Salah El-Din and then they spoke about the Abaddons. The Abaddon trail was cold again and St Clair could tell that Clay was frustrated. St Clair told him that his hunch was that they would soon be back in the open again.

"I know Salah El-Din is playing us, Morgan. I just can't figure out what his play is. Aldrich was right. The link between the dead bishops is the key but number four has us stumped for now. I don't

203

think he took the head for the Abaddons and there seems to be no link with the fourth dead bishop. Morgan, can you stay on the line? I have a call with Bill and our Knights in New Jersey. It would be helpful to get your perspective."

Clay agreed and St Clair patched him in.

The large screen on the conference room wall flickered. Dominique, John Wolf and Bill Meeks appeared on the screen. Meeks was in his study at home, and Dominique and Wolf were in one of their hotel rooms. St Clair briefed them on his call with Dámaso Nef, earlier that evening.

"You've had a busy day so far," Wolf said.

"And it isn't over yet," St Clair replied. "What do you have for us?"

Dominique took the lead to brief him; she knew he liked brevity and accuracy in status reports and so she hit the headlines straight away, what little there were.

"Nobody knows anything. Why the bishop was killed, why the head was taken or where the head is now. Our tail is still parked just down the road and spends endless hours in his car watching the hotel. Did you get the photos we managed to get of him when we walked past?"

"I did and it is as I thought, he belongs to Jamal. He is the person Jamal sent out there to look for the saint's head. His name is Daniel Hightower."

"It's a good job we didn't kill him then," Wolf said.

"Indeed. He's Jamal's grandson."

"Dang," Wolf replied, "he needs to get himself a new profession because he's pretty rubbish at sneaking about."

"But," Dominique spoke up, "he's been missing for a while now. First time we've walked past and he's not been sitting in his car. We asked a door man across the street if he'd seen the guy that was always sitting in his car and he said he had gone off with a woman."

"Well, I'm not going to be the one to tell his grandfather that his grandson, who is supposed to be looking for the head of Saint

John, has gone off with a woman. I think you should both book your flights out of there tomorrow."

Wolf asked if they should approach Jamal's grandson.

"I wouldn't; no point making yourselves known to him. The more you stay under the radar, anyone's radar, the better it will be. But remember, stay sharp and be careful! We have no idea what Salah El-Din's next move is or where it will be. Get yourselves back home safely."

"Bill, can you get there to clean up when they've gone?"

"You got it; Dominique, Wolf, I will meet you there for the handover tomorrow. I'll bring a couple of Knights with me," Bill Meeks told them.

Time: Later: 6 p.m.

All the Worthies were in full ceremonial dress, both those that were there at the castle in person and those attending via video link.

As was his ritual, St Clair paused outside the door to the great hall and checked his dress in the tall 17th century French mirror hanging on the stone wall. He adjusted his white surcoat, centralising the distinctive red cross of the Templars. Just as there is distinction in Benedictine and Cistercian orders, the Knights Templar wore white to signify purity, symbolising their abandonment of darkness for light, evil for good. He looked into his own eyes, breathed deeply and then exhaled ruefully. He turned the black iron ring handle and entered the great hall.

Even though the castle had electricity and had done so for many years, the great hall smelt of burning wax. The Higher Council held their meetings by candlelight – a tradition important in Templar life. Tapestries depicting medieval adventures and stoic heroism decorated the tall stone walls in the great hall. History radiated from every direction. Carved into the stone hearth were the words, '*Nil nisi clavis deest, Templum Hierosolyma, clavis ad thesaurum, theca ubi res pretiosa deponitur* – Nothing is wanted but the key, the Temple of Jerusalem, the key to the treasure, a place where a precious thing is concealed.' This was the same Latin inscription that once adorned a precious jewel held by the Royal Arch of Freemasonry many centuries ago.

The Worthies were pious people, dedicated to the Holy vows of righteousness; warrior monks, who worked in the shadows, dedicated to the sacred science of the Qumran – the original Nazarene Church.

Payne St Clair, the Order's Grand Master, took his seat at the head of the table. There were four chairs to his left and four chairs to his right. Proctor Hutchinson and John Edison were present in the room; the other four Worthies were attending via satellite video link. It was deemed far too dangerous for the full Council to travel since Romania. Their ultra-secret network, scattered all over the world, was on a code red.

After the ceremony of welcome was complete, they each took the Eucharist, the embodiment of Christ. Now they sat silently in contemplation for a few minutes. At their head hung the Baussant, the black and white chequered war banner of the Knights Templar.

Finally, St Clair eased himself out of the high-backed Jacobean chair to address them. He stood tall and proud, a man who personified reverence and dignity.

"Brothers, by God's grace we are called again. May our Lord watch over this Council and give us the wisdom we will need." He lowered his head in respect and then began. "My Brothers, as you are all fully briefed, and have been throughout the day, we have three orders of business. Our first order of business is the sanction of the Hag. I have already briefed you on the decision to send Luther, the priest and Aldrich and whilst Aldrich is not a Knight, he is one of our most ardent supporters and probably the only man who has met and killed a Hag, or two. And, as you have already given your approval for this, I now move to the sanction itself."

Despite the sanction team pre-agreeing, passing the actual sanction itself was always left until last. This was their way: the most important issues were always left until last. It was a most grave thing to sanction the termination of another's life. The Order, steeped in tradition and ceremony, now followed with ancient custom. St Clair made his case; then each of the six Worthies would remain seated – two at the long table, the others at their own tables – to signify their approval, or they would leave the table, signifying their disapproval. Every sanction had to be unanimous. St Clair stood motionless. He didn't know if they would approve the sanction. Again, as the Knight proposing the sanction, he did not move now or speak; he left them to their debate. Most of the six had been 'active' in their time. They knew the risks all sanctions held.

No chair was moved and approval finally came in the usual manner. Each of the Worthies made the sign of the cross across their white surcoats and when everyone had done this, in unison they whispered, "By God's grace and by His word, that which was cast in stone, we humbly seek your forgiveness. Amen." Approval had been given and the sanction was on. The sanction team would leave the next day, the 26th, to seek out the Hag in Rome.

"Our second order of business is a change I believe we should make. It has been troubling me for some time. There have always been female Knights in our Order as well as male Knights and we have always used the term 'Brother' as a generic term, a gender free term. However, I have been thinking. I have been thinking that our Knights should be Brother Knights and Sister Knights."

All the Worthies smiled and started tapping their tables to show their overwhelming approval. They were all pleased that St Clair had now made the change. They were pleased that eight hundred years of tradition had just recognised both the changing times and the contribution female Knights had always made to their Order.

Next came the ceremony to induct the two Knights onto the Higher Council and by doing so, re-establish the Templar quorum of nine, the Nine Worthies, as it was when the Order was first formed in 1119 and as it had been for centuries. The selection process had already taken place and proposed names had been put forward. Every Worthy had a vote. There were only two names put forward. The two new Worthies had already been voted on and so the formal vote had been taken; now the induction process would take place.

St Clair nodded to Proctor and Proctor left the room to go and invite the two new Knights into the Higher Council meeting.

Tiffany and Luther were waiting outside. They both looked nervous. Both were in their formal ceremonial dress, including their white surcoats with the distinctive red cross of the Templars in the centre.

Proctor stood in front of them. "So proud of you both," he whispered. Then he told them it was time and led them inside the great hall.

All of the Worthies stood, even those attending by video and they were all clapping. Proctor indicated where they should sit. One sat on the left of their Grand Master and the other on his right.

"Let us pray my Brother and Sister Knights," St Clair announced in his rich voice.

Tiffany cast an eye towards Proctor. He smiled and she smiled back; they'd finally made the change.

They all hung their heads. The light of the candles flickered and danced around the room. As always it was warm and intoxicating in the great hall, mixed with history and valour.

For the next thirty minutes tradition and ceremony took over the nine lives at the meeting and all other issues were put on hold. It was an auspicious, important occasion because of the seriousness of their work, of their existence, of their Holy 'Charge.' The Council helped St Clair guide and steer the Order; it helped him with the difficult decisions and provided the conscience of the most secret Order the world had ever known.

Luther Jones had changed his name a number of times over the years. A number of 'active' Knights had the habit of changing their names, especially those with families. Luther didn't have a family. The British Army had been his family and now the Knights Templar were his family, but he still changed his name every so often because he was one of the most mission 'active' Knights. He was born Luther Jones;

he'd had four different surnames since joining the Order and each time he was issued with new documentation. He was back to his original name again, and he was glad that he was inducted as a Council member using his birth name. And, what made it extra special was he was sitting alongside Tiffany and Proctor, two people he'd known since the age of sixteen.

The Worthies, their glasses now filled with red wine, raised them aloft and those in the room turned towards their Baussant, the black and white chequered war banner of the Knights Templar. St Clair made the toast.

"To our new Brother and Sister on this Council. May they, like us, be guided by a higher purpose and a firmer resolve. For all those we have lost, our absent friends and to our dear departed friend André Sabath. To all our Brothers and Sisters still out there on 'active' missions. For our 'Charge,' its grace, may it one day reveal the enigma of its true purpose.

"Brothers and Sister, by God's grace and by His word, that which was cast in stone, *Ubi positus est, ut omnis* – where one stands, so stand us all."

The induction ceremony was over and the issue of Luther's replacement was raised. Luther was the station commander for the UK Eastern region, based out of Leicestershire. St Clair asked Luther who he wanted to appoint as his replacement.

"I want to promote Tony, Tony Handley," he said. "Tony is a great Templar; he is really well respected, intelligent, knowledgeable, caring and generous. He is a very proud man and always puts others first. He will make a good station commander. The Knights like him. He's such a good listener and problem solver. He's a great guy. He would be my vote."

"Great choice," St Clair said. "So, it is agreed then?"

"But will it mean asking him to move away from his beloved Hull City football team, the Tigers?" Luther added.

"Let him stay there; he would miss them too much. I know he was born and bred in Hull. Let's not move him and his family from

209

where his heart is. Can we set up a new satellite station close by?" St Clair asked.

"We have the old farmhouse just outside Hull. We have the reserve station already in place under the barn there, so we'll just switch ops from Leicestershire to Hull."

The Templar satellite stations around the world were their on-the-ground eyes and ears. In each, a small band of men and women ran electronic surveillance and data capture operations. Now he would hand over the Eastern region to Tony.

"Will you go down to Hull tomorrow, to let him know the good news?" St Clair asked.

"I think I'll go tonight; the roads will be clear and I have a lot to do when I get there, if that's okay? Plus, I want to be ready in plenty of time for the flight to Rome, just in case there are delays at the airport given the time of year."

"When did you last see Tony?" St Clair asked.

"I saw him on the 11th November; we went to the London Cenotaph together, along with Rayvon. It was Tony's birthday so the three of us drank to our fallen Forces' heroes and celebrated Tony's birthday." Luther started chuckling at a memory. "There was a guy in the bar who was trying to sell one of those hover boards and Tony decided he should try it out. He got about five feet and then crashed into the pool table and has been limping around ever since, but no one is allowed to mention it. It was hilarious."

"I might send him one on his next birthday," John Edison said.

St Clair turned to Billy Jack. "Billy, you're going with Luther to help them with the facilities and our supplies. Can you also take charge of moving the satellite station from Leicestershire to Hull? Let's just mothball the one in Leicester for now but let's move the provisions. This will free Luther up to fully brief Tony on all the ops procedures he needs to know. As there are only temporary Knights in the Leicestershire station, they can now come back to the castle."

Luther's decision to drive down to Hull that night was a good one. The traffic was light, just a few gritters were out.

He called ahead from the car when he was about an hour out and spoke to Tony asking him if they could meet. Tony had just come off a reconnaissance mission in Southern Ireland with a three-man team and Luther wanted to give him the chance to square his kit away and get some rest, so he suggested they could meet in the morning.

"What time do you get in, Boss?" Tony asked him.

"ETA is about 11:30 p.m. Tony, you don't have to meet me tonight you—"

"I know Boss, but it will be good to see you and I am keen to brief you on the recce we just did. I'll let the Knights at the farm know to expect you."

Luther thought about it for a second or two. "Tony, do me a favour; don't tell them. Let's see if they're on their toes."

Tony smiled, "Roger that, Boss. We should keep it real." Keep it real was one of Tony's favourite expressions; however, Tony had an alternative plan on how to keep it real.

It was 11:45 p.m. They had travelled for twenty minutes down the winding B-road. Five hundred yards before the turning on the right to the farm, Luther switched off the vehicle's lights, slowed right down to a crawl and moved forward slowly.

He pulled up to a stop at the top of the dirt track that led down to the farm. The farm was four hundred yards away down the undulating track, worn by years of tractor use and cattle hooves. The galvanised gate to the track was open. Luther tutted: *sloppy*, he thought.

He flicked the interior light switch to off. It would not come on when the car door was opened. He gave the order, "Go, Billy." The passenger door opened, but the inside of the car remained in darkness. The passenger got out, kept low and quickly ran to the back of the car; he crouched behind it.

In almost complete darkness, Luther moved the car forward trying to manoeuvre around the potholes. In the distance stood the farmhouse and the adjacent barn. They looked like any other farmhouse and barn but with a little difference. Rotating teams consisting of three Knights occupied the farm every day of the year. The farm had a few chickens and two goats – all easy maintenance. It was enough for any casual passer-by to believe it was a small holding.

With a hundred yards to go, Luther cut the engine and freewheeled the car the rest of the way. In front of him was a dry-stone wall about five feet high; it went all the way around the perimeter of the house. The track stopped at the oak, ranch style double gates, which led into the courtyard of the farm. The gate was shut and padlocked; Luther knew where the key was.

The farmhouse was in darkness. There was no sound other than a watchful owl and the sound of a motorbike someway off in the distance, but it soon passed. The moon was high and in the clear December night, a million stars hung glittering.

Luther eased out of the car, silhouetted in the moonlight, and headed for a large black stone imbedded in the dry-stone wall, three feet from the gate. Behind it was the hiding place for the gate key. He bent down, removed the stone, reached in and retrieved the key.

He put the stone back into place and as he straightened, he felt the touch of cold steel on the back of his neck. A Katana sword was pressed against his skin.

"Got you, Boss," Tony said in a low voice. "You're slowing down." Tony Handley stood in camouflage trousers and jacket, his face streaked with cam-cream.

"You might want to look down there Tony, left side." Luther indicated to Tony's left side. Tony looked down and saw that Luther had his 9mm Beretta out of its waist holster and the barrel pointing at Tony's ribs.

"Getting old, Tony."

"Not quite Boss." Tony smiled with great satisfaction.

A figure, who had been hidden just four feet way, camouflaged, lying flat against the grass and not visible to a cursory look, emerged. His face was unrecognisable with heavy flashes of green cam-cream. He was holding a little snub nose P220 combat pistol, pointed at Luther.

"Hello, Boss," Rayvon said with a smile. Rayvon and Tony were the best of friends and had been for years. They both looked pleased with themselves. Rayvon was the bigger of the two, thick set and stocky.

Tony was wirier but faster on his feet and quick with his wit. "We got him," Tony said to Rayvon, with some joy. "After all these bloody years we finally got the boss."

They heard two clicks. Their smiles dropped; they knew the sound well. The doubled barrel shotgun was pointing straight at them and its holder just eight yards away. The passenger who had followed behind the car as Luther freewheeled down had remained out of sight.

"Hello, boys," Billy Jack said.

"I don't think we have got him, Tony," Rayvon said as he placed his gun on the ground and raised his hands. "You know your favourite sayings of never back down and don't take any nonsense? Just this once, do you mind if we back down and stop this nonsense? Besides, he looks like he can handle that thing and if he is who I think he is, he can definitely handle that thing."

"Knights, meet your Sergeant at Arms, Billy Jack, ex-para and *the* Regiment."

Tony put the Katana sword back into its scabbard behind his back. "A cup of tea, gents?"

As they walked away, Tony was limping slightly. "How's the hover boarding?" Luther asked laughing.

"Ended," Tony shot back.

"You'll go down in history, Tony," he told him.

"If not in history, Boss, then at least in a book. I've told Jane. Put me in a book one day, any kind of book, but put me in. She promised she would."

Time: Late
Place: Costa Blanca, Spain

Salah El-Din sat alone in his residence, as he often did, in his *casa de campo*. He felt safe in his seven-bedroom house in the Spanish region of Valencia on the *Costa Blanca.* His appearance and skin tone made him look like a local; because of his olive skin, he was often mistaken for a Spaniard. He blended in. He allowed himself to relax more there than anywhere. He was not known there and he ensured that he portrayed the lifestyle of a private businessman with a Spanish retreat, who liked to keep himself to himself. He kept two bodyguards with him at the house, three other bodyguards were housed in a small, rented house just next door.

He sipped his coffee, no milk, no sugar. The phone rested on a small olive wood table by his side.

He looked out of his window; it was dark. It was night time and late. His alarm system and twenty-three sensor lights had been checked an hour ago. They were all working. They were checked by his men four times per day.

As soon as morning came, he would call the Templars again. The Priest was scared on the beach when he had spoken to him. *That was good*, he mused. The Priest didn't know that he was in Spain, when he'd spoken to him. He didn't know that he'd had three men, contractors, watching the beach for days. When they spotted the Priest, they'd called him and he'd called the mobile phone Jonathan had just been given. He had a coms piece in his ear as his men relayed everything that they were seeing. Of course, Jonathan couldn't hear that communication. A half smile appeared on the criminal's face as he remembered how silent Jonathan had fallen when he told him what the dogs were doing with the seaweed. The Priest thought he was there, close by.

Four hours earlier, Salah El-Din had made the call to one of his men in Salalah, in the Sultanate of Oman. His man was waiting for the call.

When the Abaddons had tried to track him down in Salalah, although he was long gone, he had two of his men tail the men that were tailing Saeed Al Bateat, the young Yemeni intelligence officer. The cat and mouse game proved fruitful for him because they had been able to follow one of the men back to his house. He lived in the Yemeni city of Taizz. Salah El-Din knew that the Abaddon was still living there

214

because he'd had his men in the Yemen keep watch all this time. The Abaddon in Taizz was the key to getting his message to the Abaddons.

Outside, the stars lit up the dark Spanish sky. It was a typical damp, cold Spanish winter's evening. His central heating was working overtime to warm the seven-bedroom house; the house, like most Spanish houses, was not built for cold winters, only for hot summers.

The phone vibrated. He answered it.

"Yes?" he snapped. He was impatient: he'd been waiting.

His man on the other end of the phone told his boss that the message had been delivered to the man in Taizz.

"Tell me every step," he insisted.

The caller told his boss that the man in Taizz was in his house, and so was his large family. He said that he had told the man in the house to pass a message to whoever was in charge, to tell that man that Salah El-Din wanted to meet him. He relayed that to show his good faith, Salah El-Din had been leaving dead Christians for him, dead bishops, and now, Salah El-Din had a far greater prize for him: he would give him the Templars and wanted to talk about a trade with him. The caller said that he gave the man in the house the phone number he was supposed to and then he left.

Salah El-Din was pleased; his man had done well. He asked him if there was anything else and his man told him that the man in the house had a tattoo: three crescent moons on the underside of his right wrist. Salah El-Din told his man to go and rest; it was gone midnight in the Yemen.

Salah El-Din, his full name being Al-Malik al-Nasir al-Sultan Salah El-Din, was a man in his late fifties. He was tall with silver hair, sharp features and piercing black eyes. He was known to have killed more than forty people by his own hand and countless others on his direct orders. The man that had John Dukes, the ex-reporter, skinned alive and the man that had killed his own father, now retired to bed. He was satisfied that he would soon have the Abaddons in his pocket and then he would orchestrate their demise along with that of the Templars. They would destroy each other, put each other in the ground, and only he would be left. He would be left with the Ark. He slept soundly.

*

Just two miles away, two Abaddon acolytes watched. Four hours away in Madrid, Bo Bo Hak waited with seven Abaddon assassins. They had located his hideaway weeks ago after searching for him for months.

Thousands of miles away, the man in Taizz called a man in Morocco; that man was higher up the chain. The man in Morocco then called a man in Egypt. Five men were involved in passing on the message to Zivko Cesar Gowst: the Ghost, the elusive leader of the barbaric Abaddon *Alqatala,* the Abaddon assassins.

Zivko Cesar Gowst would sleep soundly with the thought that tomorrow would be Salah El-Din's last day. He had raised himself again; he had dared to reach out to them. Zivko had no interest in dealing with him; he would not tolerate him another day. Tomorrow he would send word.

Chapter 12

26th December Part I

Date: 26th December 2012, 6 a.m. UK time
Place: A remote castle in Scotland

St Clair was exhausted; it was 6 a.m. He'd asked Jonathan to meet him at 6:30 a.m. before he left for the airport to fly to Rome with Luther and Aldrich. He had also asked the Controller, Tiffany, now a Council member, to join them because it would be the first time she would see the prophecies.

He was on his way to one of the secure rooms underneath the castle. He was walking quietly; others were still asleep and he didn't want to disturb them. The mobile phone buzzed and it made him jump slightly. It was the mobile phone Jonathan had been given by Elaine on the beach. St Clair had it on him at all times, fully charged. He stopped in the corridor and answered the call.

"Ah, it's you?" Salah El-Din said surprised on recognising St Clair's voice. "We have not spoken since Cumbria. What is it now, four years? My leg still carries the scar from your knife. How is our friend, the Priest?"

"I was wondering when you would call," St Clair said, speaking quietly and ignoring his question about Jonathan.

"And so, here I am. Once an enemy and now, I come as a friend. Did the Priest give you my message?"

"He did."

"We have a common enemy, you and I. The solution is simple, no? We join forces and together we remove them."

St Clair knew he needed to try and find out about the fourth bishop and the stealing of the saint's head. It was the key to Salah El-Din's plan; it was the key that had thus far evaded them. "I see you have been leaving bodies about. I assume for our common enemy. Odd though."

"Odd? No, no, no; it is to draw them out, so we can destroy them. But I have a present for you, my peace offering. The head of the saint. I know you are looking for it in America; they are looking for it and I know you know I took it. I have it, yes. Of course. I will give it to you, my friend, to show you my good intentions."

Right then St Clair knew what the fourth bishop had to do with the series of deaths: nothing! New Jersey was all about the head of the saint and about them. But he didn't know why; he needed time to figure it out. "Let me think about it," he said. "Perhaps we can talk later today; maybe we can speak after breakfast."

"Breakfast, at 7:30 a.m.? Early for you English, no?" Salah El-Din laughed and then hung up.

St Clair looked at his watch. It was 6:30 a.m. *You're in Europe,* he thought. *Europe is one hour ahead.* He was replaying the call in his head. Salah El-Din had said: "I know you are looking for it in America, they are looking." *Damn it*, he thought. *You know the Indian and the Girl are there and I bet you know where. But what's your play?* He quickly made his way to the rooms below the castle.

Jonathan and Tiffany came into the room a short while after St Clair had got there. It was one of the secure rooms below the castle that contained many old parchments, scrolls, papers, charts, documents and codices. It was there where they kept the Cathar prophecies scroll, the scroll that contained ten ancient prophecies. The Cathars had hidden it at their stronghold at the Château de Montségur, in the Languedoc, France. However, they had managed to get it out in time before Montségur was destroyed and their Brothers burnt at the stake. They shared the scroll with the Templars, when the Templars helped to protect them.

The first prophecy foretold the first Seer: '*The daughter of the Maid of Pucelle shall have the gift to read the sacred words of God from within His Ark.*'

The second predicted the fall of another Seer centuries later, Zakariah's wife and Dominique's mother, Sophia: '*Beware, the slave warriors will take the Seer, a cherished one with Italian tongue; the Seer will be killed.*' The link with Sophia had escaped them because it had been wrongly translated. The prophecies were written in the ancient language of Aramaic, the language Jesus would have spoken. The Cathars translated them into French centuries ago, when they first discovered them. Then Templars translated them into English in the 14th century, when they fled to Scotland after the Templar persecutions and executions in France, in 1307. The prophecy, '*Beware, the slave warriors will take the Seer, a cherished one with Italian tongue; the Seer will be killed,*' was not what had been translated. The English translation read, '*Beware, the slave warriors will take the Seer, a friend speaking Latin; the Seer will die.*' The phrase 'a friend' was translated into English from the French version that read '*ami,*' which is the French masculine word for friend. However, when they finally worked out that the translations were not accurate, they had the Aramaic version checked by a world-leading expert. What that Aramaic version actually said was not '*ami,*' or 'friend', but 'cherished one.' So, they were thinking it referred to a male friend, who spoke Latin. What it should have read was a '*cherished one who spoke Italian*' as their mother tongue: Sophia! From that point on, St Clair made it his personal responsibility to check and double check the prophecies. Despite them now being correctly translated, they were still full of ambiguity.

The third prophecy involved Zakariah and Jonathan: '*A Knight will fall. A new Seer will come from the house of God and the fallen Knight will return.*'

The fourth prophecy was about Jonathan: '*He is the last of them. Keep the Seer alive; he is the last of them. He is the key to opening the Ark, but enemies are at your gate.'* St Clair had told Jonathan that he believed him to be the last of them; he was the Seer which the prophecy spoke about. It was around then that Jonathan started to understand. It was around then that he believed he finally knew what the Ark was for.

They were sitting at a small metal table in the middle of the room: Jonathan, Tiffany and St Clair. The temperature and air quality were all controlled to create the best conditions for the literary works to be preserved. St Clair had retrieved the Cathar prophecies' scroll from one of the sealed drawers and had placed it on the table in front of them. Jonathan had seen it many times before and was one of the few people, other than each of the Nine Worthies, allowed to study it – his place as the Seer affording him more access than most.

St Clair had told Jonathan that he wanted him to look at the fifth prophecy with him that morning, because there was something niggling him about it. Now they both looked at the fifth prophecy: *'In al-Andalus, the false one will crane its feathers but it brings only death.'*

"The problem is," St Clair began in a slightly frustrated tone, "this could have happened, or it could happen in the next one hundred years. We don't know if the false one was before, or is now, or will exist at some point in the future."

"So, when you talk about prophecy one, two, three and four, that's not the sequence by date of happening?" Tiffany asked.

"No, far from it," St Clair said. "That's my very point."

"So, why this prophecy? What is it about this one that has your interest?" Jonathan asked.

"Because it's the only one that—"

There was a knock at the door. The door swung open and Bertram fell in. He was out of breath and rather dishevelled.

"Miss Courtney asked me to come. I said I would be there in a minute and she said straight away, so I'm here, now." He gasped for more air. "We missed it, Mr St Clair, Sir, Mr Rose Jonathan, ah and Miss Daisy Picking." He took some quick breaths. "Sorry. We just never thought that, well, you wouldn't would you, he would never make such a silly mistake, what with all his shilly-shallies … it made us a little behindhand, you see?"

St Clair looked at Jonathan and Jonathan looked at St Clair, each checking if either did in fact see. The look on each other's faces confirmed that they didn't see.

"Bertram," Tiffany started gently, "I want you to take ten deep breaths then we can start again."

"Yes, Miss Daisy Picking. I understand; enhance my calm. More Adagio. You're such a cool dudet in a loose moodet." Bertram gasped again. "A cool d—"

"Bertram, breathe?"

After ten breaths, Bertram had finally slowed his breathing down and was able to speak without them fearing he would hyperventilate.

"I was atop just now to capture some gusts with the sketching and I was supine. I was blithe but then I was irritated because one of the aglets was missing."

"I got this," St Clair said to Jonathan and Tiffany. "So, you went to the top of the castle, and you were going to do some sketching of the wind, and you were lying on your back, face upwards. You were happy but then you noticed your aglet?"

"It's the end of a shoelace, the small plastic or metal thing," Tiffany said.

Jonathan looked at her. "Crosswords: sometimes it's a slow day in Islington."

They all looked down at Bertram's brown scuffed shoes, one of the small plastic ends had come off.

"Ah," St Clair said, "aglet. So, this irritated you and then?"

"Miss Courtney had asked me to put an electronic call tracer into the mobile phone Mr Rose Jonathan was given by Mr Saladin, and I did."

"Are you telling me you traced the call that he made to me this morning?" St Clair asked him.

"He called you?" Jonathan asked, startled, reaching for the change in his pocket.

"Yes, but right now I need Bertram to answer my question." He

221

turned towards Bertram. "Are you telling me you traced the call that he made to me this morning?"

"Yes, I traced the stinker's call. And the call came from—"

"Europe," St Clair interrupted him. He turned to Jonathan. "I knew he was in Europe because of something he said on the call." St Clair dared not ask Bertram but he needed to. "Do you know where in Europe?"

"Spain."

"Quick, the fifth prophecy," St Clair said turning to the scroll. "Al-Andalus is the old name for Spain, the name it would have been called when the scrolls were written."

"We should sally forth to the Costa Blanca, Mr St Clair, Sir, because that's where the call was made from."

"And do you know exactly whe—"

"Of course." Bertram stood there grinning like a Cheshire cat. "I am Cerebral. We got him Mr St Clair, Sir. We have his address." The man who looked twelve years old, but was twenty-five, dressed in a green tartan, tweed cloth suit, waistcoat, with a fob and scuffed brown shoes, with the end of a shoelace missing, an Oxford graduate, who had a 'first' in computer science, specialising in nanotechnology, artificial intelligence, blockchain, advanced electronics and gaming, Bertram Hubert Klymachak De'Ath, Cerebral, had just found Salah El-Din.

St Clair called Courtney and quickly briefed her. He then gave her instructions for six of their Knights in Spain to be ready to meet St Clair at Valencia airport later that day. He also told her that he needed two Knights to set up an observation post on the address Bertram had until St Clair and the other Knights arrived. St Clair asked Courtney to locate Marie-Claude and advise her she was mission 'active' for Spain, to book three plane tickets: one for him, one for Marie-Claude and one for Bertram. Bertram could hardly control himself. He so desperately wanted to speak but excitement wouldn't let him get his words out, just breath sounds.

"Bertram, we will need your drones," St Clair told him.

Well, that just about did it. "I remember my father's feet," he started.

"Bertram, go get the drones ready. We leave in an hour." And that was the end of Bertram's father's feet. Then St Clair told Jonathan to go and find Luther and catch their flight for Rome.

Under their rules, normally there was an age limit for mission 'active' Knights and St Clair was past the accepted norm. However, he would not risk more Knights with Salah El-Din, not unless he was there with them. Their lives were just as important as his own life, to him – more important.

As they were leaving the room, Tiffany went up to Bertram. "Can I walk back with you Bertram? You and I have not spent any time together. We don't really know each other."

"Yes, yes Miss Daisy Picking. I'm going to get my breakfast. Not too much mind. Indulge and you'll bulge; stuff and you'll puff. Just toast for me. Miss Daisy Picking, we've got him this time, haven't we?"

"Yes, Bertram, I do believe we just might have."

"Do you think he was always bad, Miss Daisy Picking, Mr Stinker Salah El-Din?"

Tiffany thought for a moment. "My adopted father, Harry Gannan, used to say, good people do good things even when nobody is around. Adam Smith called it the 'internal witness.' It's our consciousness and morals that keep us in check."

"So, bad people do bad things even when nobody is around."

"I'm afraid so, Bertram."

They were about to separate. Bertram was heading to the kitchen and Tiffany had a meeting with Courtney. She stopped and took Bertram's hand. "I've enjoyed our little chat, Bertram, and hope that we can speak again before I go back to Islington. I know you are coming down soon with Courtney to do the coms upgrade, so if we don't get a chance, I look forward to seeing you there."

"I am excited to be sallying forth to the Big Smoke, Miss Daisy Picking."

"Bertram," she said, "you know my name's not really Daisy Picking, don't you? It was a joke."

Bertram started laughing. "Yes, yes I know Miss Daisy Picking.

Heck chicory, I ride the ragged edge you know. I've howled at the moon with Mr Russian Klymachak, deceased, sung 'they came to snuff the rooster' with Miss Madison Davenport, deceased and chatted to Mrs Marie and Claude, alive, when the rain came."

Tiffany didn't know quite what to say. "Well, great! I'm glad we had this little chat and all is clear now. Bye for now, Bertram."

"Quite right Miss Daisy Picking. Let's go kick up the dust and see where our stumps land. Ha ha ha. Toodle-oo, see you in the Big Smoke."

Then, just as she turned a corner and was almost out of ear shot, he called, "And by the way, congratulations on your appoint-ment, Miss Tiffany Jane Clarke."

Place: Japan

They were both sad to see its demise. So many young hearts had gone through the old dojo; so many young street souls saved, first by Hinata Satō and then by Tanjkna, both honourable men; both exceptional fighters, both served as Master of the Blade in the Order of the Knights Templar.

They stood there, looking at the decay of a once well-known institution. Cameron Jack was convinced that going into the dojo was a mistake, even though he was with Tanjkna Sugata. Tanjkna had just told him that the person who owned the old dojo was the Yakuza boss of Katsushika district, the district they were in. Tanjkna had also told Cameron that he had arranged to meet the boss of the Katsushika district. And when Cameron asked who that was, Tanjkna had said that it was the man that had sacrificed his finger and taken Tanjkna's shame, so that he could leave the Yakuza and not be killed. He told Cameron that that man was not an evil man; in the beginning, he was just another eighteen-year-old street boy, hungry and with no future, trying to get by and look after his younger brother after their parents had been killed.

"Anything else I should know before we go in?" Cameron asked him.

"Yes," Tanjkna announced in that deadpan way of his, "the Yakuza boss of Katsushika district is my brother."

It was cold and dingy inside the neglected dojo. Pigeons fluttered high above; their entrances and egresses were a number of missing roof tiles that had also let in the rain over the years. It smelt damp and pungent with mould and pigeon droppings. All the internal doors had gone and anything that had been hung on the walls had long since been stolen or destroyed. Both men shook their heads as they entered, saddened by its demise and dereliction.

Five men stood side by side at the far wall. They were all dressed in black suits. It was a clichéd scene, like something from a comic book but that was their dress code. There was no mistaking their menace, its portent presence visual and tacit. No one spoke as Cameron and Tanjkna entered the dojo. Tanjkna was visibly nervous, but Cameron could now see that so too was one of the men who stood in the middle of the line of men. The others just stood there looking dangerous and edgy.

Tanjkna and Cameron stopped just six feet in front of the gangsters. Tanjkna bowed and the gangsters' boss bowed back. The resemblance between the two men was uncanny. One of the Yakuza gangsters walked forward. He approached Cameron first. Cameron tensed and prepared himself for combat.

"It is okay, Cameron-san," Tanjkna said, trying to reassure Cameron. "He is just checking us for weapons."

The gangster was young but looked mean. He had two sections of a finger missing.

"*Appu* – up, *Yasuke!*" – he used the Japanese name for an African slave in Japan in the old days. The insult rattled Cameron; he'd heard the term many times before. The man indicated towards Cameron's arms, "*Appu, ima* – up, now!"

"Cameron-san, remember he is ignorant," Tanjkna said.

The gangster frisked Cameron and then Tanjkna. It was obvious to Cameron that the Yakuza gangster knew Tanjkna was his boss's brother, but he also knew that Tanjkna had been a famous swordsman in Japan and therefore showed reverence to him. Tanjkna held many trophies and had been the Japanese Iaido champion for many years. This meant he held the record for the fastest draw of the Katana sword. Cameron could almost see the relief in the gangster's face when he frisked Tanjkna and discovered there was no Katana sword or a small Wakizashi sword. The gangster moved back to his line and nodded to his boss.

Tanjkna and his brother moved forward so that they were in front of each other. They had not seen each other in over forty years. They spoke in Japanese. Cameron's grasp of the language wasn't that good to follow every word they said because they were using a local dialect. He assumed it was from their hometown.

He made out that Tanjkna's brother told him that he had broken his vow not to return. Cameron knew that was the deal they had made a long time ago. But then, surprisingly he said he had missed his brother. His brother wasn't angry that he had broken his vow and had reached out to him. In fact, he was pleased he had because he had thought about Tanjkna many times over the years and now that the old bosses were dead, and he was now a boss, he was no longer bound by the vow he had taken: neither of them were.

The two men knelt down in front of each other. They were on their knees and the balls of their feet. One of the boss's men produced two Katana swords. He placed one in front of his boss and one in front of Tanjkna. Cameron went to move fearing the worst: a challenge to Tanjkna. Tanjkna felt Cameron's movement. He raised his hand and turned to Cameron. "It is okay, Cameron-san, these were our father's swords and my brother has kept them all this time. He has given me this sword." He pointed to the one in front of him. "When we were little, my father taught us how to clean the Samurai sword the right way. As children, we practised for hours on these swords with our father watching. Now we will clean his swords once again, as brothers."

The two brothers removed the cloth carrier that had covered the swords. They took the swords out in unison and held the swords, the bow of the sword facing upwards. As Samurai do, they both bowed to pay their respects to the swords. They then pulled the blades out of their sheaths and kept the cutting edge facing upwards.

Cameron watched his old Sensei.

"The *mekugi*," Tanjkna said. He held the slender six-inch tool, with an ornate, carved head and used it to push the holding pin through the *tsuka* – the handle and the blade and then placed the pin on the floor. With the holding pin out, he held his left hand at the bottom of the handle and with his right fist, tapped his left hand gently, which pulled the handle down and detached it from the blade. Next, he removed the *habaki* – the blade collar that encircled the base of the blade and he placed it on the ground.

"To support the *tsuba* – the guard, and to support the Katana in its *saya* – scabbard," Tanjkna said, imitating their fathers voice. They both smiled.

Tanjkna's brother barked an order, "*Uchiko!*" A fine powder wrapped up in a silk ball was given to each brother. They used a small stick to tap the silk ball and powder fell on the blade. Then they used tissue paper to wipe it off. Next, they applied *Choji* oil to stop the blades from rusting. Both men then reassembled their swords in unison.

They swapped swords and meticulously inspected each other's work. After a few nervous seconds, they both broke into big grins. They had not forgotten what their father had taught them.

Both men rose to their feet. Again, they bowed to each other. Then they spoke quietly together for some time. Cameron waited. The gangsters watched their boss for any movement that suggested he needed something. Quick to please, they all wanted to be first if he should require something.

Their conversation went on for fifteen minutes. Cameron heard Tanjkna explain to his brother about the Yakuza in Manchester, England and in Rome and that his friends were in danger. The brothers then moved away as Tanjkna's brother did not want his men to hear what he said. They were loyal; their severed finger sections proved it.

Again, Cameron waited until finally Tanjkna returned. "My brother said that the Yakuza in Great Brittan and in Rome were not his men. They belong to another boss from another district. He is a man he does not like and there have been many feuds between them, as there often are between the different Yakuza gangs. He said he would find out what he could. All we can do now is wait."

That night Cameron and Tanjkna stayed in a hotel close by and waited. They waited all the next day, the 25th of December, Christmas day, for news from Tanjkna's brother. By the end of that day, they still hadn't heard and so Cameron decided he would go to the US, as he felt he was no longer useful to anyone just hanging around a hotel in Tokyo.

The following morning, the 26th, he took a flight at 7 a.m. local Japanese time. It was a fourteen-hour flight to the East Coast of America, but because New Jersey was thirteen hours behind Japan, he took off at 7 a.m. and arrived in New Jersey at 8 a.m.

Time: 1 p.m. in Italy (1 p.m. in Spain, 6 a.m. on the East Coast of America, 12 noon in the UK)
Place: Rome, Italy

Luther, Jonathan and Aldrich arrived at Italy's largest airport, Leonardo da Vinci-Fiumicino Airport. It was eighteen miles from Rome. They had been told that a driver would pick them up and would be waiting for them in the arrivals lounge. He would be carrying a sign with the name 'Smithson' on it. Dámaso Nef had wanted to pick them up himself, but he was told that Cardinal Cristoforo Paradiso's office would arrange it and that Cardinal Paradiso would then meet with the outsiders first. Nef was not invited to that first meeting.

As advised, a driver was there to meet them. He was standing inside the arrival lounge with a board with the name 'Smithson' on it. The driver, a craggy-faced man with silver hair and a stern look about him, didn't offer to take any bags. They got a gruff *Buongiorno* – good morning, and that was it. For his age, the driver was remark-ably spritely on his feet, almost hectic as if he had no time, or patience to stay in one place too long because he was too busy. He wore a suit, which looked expensive and an overcoat, which also looked expensive. The overcoat collar was pulled up to keep out the Rome chill. He also wore a brown trilby hat and leather shoes – everything looked expensive.

They followed him at a pace as he made for the car park. After paying his ticket at the pay-station, he directed them to a red Lancia Montecarlo. They put the bags in the boot and all three of them got in the back – there were papers galore on the front passenger seat, along with a couple of empty water bottles and cigarette packets. The driver made no attempt to move any of it so that one of the guests could sit in the front and they would all be a little more comfortable.

He started the car. The driver crunched the gears, exhaled with a rasping sound through gritted teeth and set off. He pulled up to the barrier, inserted the paid ticket and then drove away.

Jonathan rarely took an instant dislike to anyone; it was not in his nature, but the driver made his way onto the list just as soon as he pulled on to the autostrade. Driving erratically, he tutted and cursed at every other motorist. The cantankerous driver wove in and out of traffic with free abandon and total disregard for his and his passengers safety. He also smoked – like a trooper. They had both back windows down and as they got into heavy traffic and city smog levels rose, compressed by winter mist, Jonathan and Luther thought they might die of petrol fumes and cigarette smoke before they made it to the Vatican. Aldrich watched them splutter a little and then he took out his favourite pipe from his pocket and lit it. The spluttering quickly turned to coughing.

On one occasion en route to the Vatican, the driver's trilby fell off as he waved one of his arms around in an animated gesture towards a lady in a small white Fiat. She was flustered at the sight of an old, mad man raving at her for something she didn't know she had done. His hat was only off for a few seconds before he placed it back on his head, but Jonathan spotted it straight away. He whispered to Luther that this was no civilian driver.

The driver kept asking them questions. With a cigarette hanging from his mouth, he would bark a question at them, raise his head and look at them through his rear-view mirror to see their reactions. When they failed to answer to his satisfaction, the crotchety old driver grew ever more irritated.

On numerous occasions, his feet slipped on the worn pedals causing him to slow down or unexpectantly pounce forward, forcing him to crunch the clutch plate or carry out an unintentional emergency stop – but none of it was his fault. The other drivers all got cursed at.

When they finally arrived at the Vatican, they pulled up outside a large, grand, historical building. Its facade was regal and extensively ornate; it seemed timeless, just like all the other buildings they saw around them. They found the architecture breath-taking. They were to find the relationship between religion and politics just as breath-taking, but for different reasons: a small group of powerful men, all vying for status in the curious, yet venerated, smallest independent state in the world, and the seat and spiritual leadership of nearly one and a half billion people.

When the car had come to a stop, they opened the car doors and a number of priests scurried around them. The snappy, bad-tempered driver seemed even more snappy and bad tempered now that they had arrived. He gave the car keys to one of the scurrying priests and the car was driven away. Their bad-tempered driver disappeared into a side door.

Two priests had already taken their small overnight bags and had also disappeared. Another priest beckoned for them to follow him inside the building. They followed him and were soon walking along resplendent corridors with stunning works of art and impressive plaster work on the high vaulted ceiling and decorated walls. It was impressive, clean and smelt of wax and polish.

The man they were following, a young Nigerian priest, was nervous around them but chatty; he seemed eager to please. On the way to wherever he was leading them, for they had not been told where they were going yet, they passed a number of people of differing stations within the Vatican's hierarchy – and lower. The priest noticed them looking.

"There are many of us here," he said, now walking beside them instead of out in front leading them, "from the nuns who iron in the sacristy ..." he saw Luther's look. "It is a room where we keep vestments. If you are not Catholic, perhaps you would know it as the vestry. We have many gardeners responsible for our splendid gardens, here at the pleasure of his Holiness the Pope and for the people. We have many people on the floristry team. We must not forget the floristry team because they do such a good job. The cleaners, renovators, curators, maintenance workers, they are called *sampietrini*. Builders, marble experts, electricians, plumbers, carpenters. Then we have the *sediari pontifico*, who used to be the Pope's chair bearers but now they are the hospitality team who take care of the rooms and access around the Apostolic Palace. We have many Keepers of Keys, mosaic artists, drivers, cooks and chefs, I'm sure I have left so many out."

Two old cardinals passed them. Once they had passed, the young priest started to tell them that the cardinals wear red because they were considered the closest advisers to the Pope and therefore should be ready to spill their blood for the church and Christ. Even his Holiness wore red, he told them, with his famous red slippers, with their gold braid and the cross in the middle. These represented the blood of Catholic martyrs. And during Advent and Lent, they wore purple, the colour that reflects sorrow and suffering. Aldrich was about to say something about the colour purple but Luther nudged him, scared of what might come out of his mouth.

After what seemed like an endless walk, they were finally shown into a small but comfortable room. It had two couches and a number of high back chairs covered in a floral design and a couple of bow-legged tables holding an array of vases, ash trays and objets d'art. The priest went to take their coats but only Aldrich gave his. Luther and Jonathan kept theirs on – they were not stopping. Another priest brought them some wine. A fourth glass was left, with red wine filled to the brim.

231

Outside the door there was a kerfuffle. The priest who had poured the wine scurried away quickly. Their driver walked into the room, bringing commotion with him. Jonathan, his dislike of the man festering because of his curt manner towards just about everyone in his line of peripheral vison, decided to burst the man's ruse. He stood to his feet and, as they had planned, set their own ruse in motion, which required a forthright Jonathan. Luther could be forthright when needed and Aldrich needed to be Aldrich, eccentric and forthright, as he was all the time.

"Cardinal Paradiso," Jonathan moved towards the cardinal-cum-driver. The cardinal was visibly irked that his ruse had failed.

"Ah," Jonathan said, "the indent on the hair, from years of wearing your *zucchetto,* your skullcap. Your trilby fell off in the car." Jonathan turned to Luther and Aldrich. "In the old days, when a priest took his vow of celibacy, a ring on their head was shaven. They wore skullcaps to cover that part of their heads, to help keep them warm."

Luther had told Aldrich they all needed to dominate the conversation once they were with Paradiso so that he and Jonathan could get away for their other meeting. Jonathan was playing his part well. Aldrich had yet to begin – but they knew Aldrich didn't need to do anything; he just needed to be himself!

"Well, then," Luther stood up. "Myself and Mr Bruce here," he turned to Jonathan, "I'm sorry, Cardinal, this is Mr Bruce and my name is Wayne, Mr Wayne. And this," he now turned to Aldrich, and that was Aldrich's cue, "is—"

"Is, Aldrich Manwin Tucker of Cambridge University, England, old fruit." Aldrich bellowed in his inimitable Aldrich way. "And these two, old fruit," he pointed to Luther and Jonathan, "Mr Wayne and Mr Bruce, wish to take a walk around first, to familiarise themselves with the area and get a feel for the place. However, I shall not be leaving you, no fear. I shall be staying right here with you. And as my good friend Herbert Clements always said, he was my dresser at Simpsons of Piccadilly you know, I always volunteer myself to do the talking because sometimes we need to have expert advice. So," he turned to Jonathan and Luther, "off you go old fruits, no need to blether on. Old Chris here and I have got this."

The cardinal protested angrily. "No, I do not think it will be all right for them to—"

"My dear Cardinal," Aldrich interrupted him, "they are not prisoners. Now, sit yourself down and let's take leisure to talk some! I see we have wine, and you know what they say, old boy, *vino veritas*, in the wine there is truth. Now, you must have so many questions I can answer for you, but first, I need to know, do you have a sword?"

Jonathan and Luther left. As they did so, they heard Cardinal Paradiso talking.

"I don't like your kind. Never did," he said in perfect English to Aldrich. "You come here thinking you—"

"My dear man," they heard the bellowing voice of Aldrich drowning him in bluster, "a fish rots from the head down. So, let's get to it shall we and you and I see if we can't find the dastardly fellow that tried to do away with your boss. Bugger me Brigadier, lets jump to it, old fruit."

The cardinal stood, his body stooping with age, his hands shaking slightly. He was one of a number of cardinals that resided in apartments on the Vatican perimeter. He was well known to the staff in the Vatican and not many ever volunteered to serve him. He was gruff and testy. He wasn't happy that other cardinals had felt the need to use outsiders. He wasn't happy the other two had left. He wasn't happy he was stuck with the pompous British man.

He had cutting sarcasm in abundance. When he was not in the Vatican and was outside its boundaries and was in civilian clothing, he drove a Porsche 911, 2.7 RS, 1973, which most people would think a quirky buy, but it was worth the well over a million dollars he'd paid for it. He regularly communicated with a man called Mackintosh about dodgy Bella Ross watches, had shares in Tottenham Hotspur and Milan football clubs. His poor housekeeper, at his country residence, Mara Di Venanzio, had suffered his bellicose nature for years. He drank heavily, watched his favourite film, 'Where Eagles Dare,' countless times and had a cellar full of unreturned videos, dating back from 1995 to 1999, from Blockbuster, Italy.

Since October 2011, Cardinal Cristoforo John Paradiso had been communicating, through an ex-lover, who was also an ex-priest and currently a convict, Father Michael, with a third party who had paid him handsomely for information. He had already secured 4.7 million Euros into his private bank account. He had supplied information about a ring. He had also supplied information about the whereabouts of Saint John's head. He had supplied information about the whereabouts of the last '*Gwrach Marwolaeth* Hag,' the last 'witch of death.' The Vatican had secret files on such people and he had access to such files.

The room phone rang. His Eminence answered it, curtly. "No. *Va Via* – go away." He placed the receiver down harder than he needed too. Then there was another reason for his agitation to rise several levels, a knock on the door. "*Si*," he barked. Aldrich was loving it and he played the non-existent gallery with much aplomb.

Luther and Jonathan took a local taxi to the address Nef had texted them and left their secret weapon, Aldrich, who was to keep Cardinal Paradiso busy for a few hours and so release them to meet Dámaso Nef. Nef had sent a message to Luther before he'd boarded the plane from the UK. It said that he would meet him outside the Vatican grounds so they could speak freely. He had texted the address. He also told Luther to be careful because the cardinals had many eyes and ears across Rome, not just in the Vatican.

Luther and Jonathan found Dámaso Nef at the café where he said he would be waiting. He was sitting outside, alone. It was cold but he wanted to make sure no one would overhear their discussion. He wore a broad cheery grin.

Luther and Jonathan liked him straight away. They greeted him and they shook hands. "I am Luther and this is Jonathan," Luther said, giving Nef their real names.

After they had greeted each other, Nef turned towards Jonathan and told him that another cardinal wanted to see him, alone. He asked them both if they were okay with this. Nef said it was a man called

Cardinal Gino Del Luca who wanted to see him. He also said that of all the cardinals, he trusted Gino Del Luca the most; many did. He told them that he was richly secular in nature and was extremely knowledgeable and well-schooled. Many looked to him for guidance and it was even said that he would make a great Pope. He didn't tell them what the cardinal's main role was within the Roman Catholic Church. He would leave that to Del Luca. Jonathan agreed to go and Nef gave him the address and a marked tourist map where the cardinal would be waiting. Jonathan started telling Luther that he would meet him back at the café, but Nef interrupted him and told him that Luther and Aldrich would join Jonathan and Cardinal Gino Del Luca in a short while.

Jonathan left the two men to talk and made his way to his next meeting point, following his tourist map.

Once they had settled, Nef turned to Luther. "The cardinals said my job was to find the assassin who had tried to kill our Pope. They said that I have to catch the assassin before they find out that they failed: his Holiness is alive and well. They are worried that they will try again but I have been talking to St Clair this morning, while waiting for you to arrive, and we agree that I must also find the traitor from within. St Clair has offered me your assistance."

"I know," Luther said, "I got his voicemail when I landed."

A waiter arrived, took their drinks order and then left. They were the only ones sitting outside – it was far too cold for locals and far too cold for tourists.

"It was an attempted poisoning," Nef began, "the attempt on the Pope's life. Like all the others. The poison was placed in his Holiness's food. We are waiting for the laboratory reports, but we are sure that's how it was going to be given to him. If we are right, it means that the assassin was close enough to the Pope to put poison into his food. That is the first thing that is troubling. How did they get so close?"

Luther searched and then found his coat pockets in which to bury his cold hands.

"The Pope had been off colour, just a light cold his doctor said.

So, as they do, they didn't want to alarm anyone, so they didn't tell anyone. He just stayed in his quarters in the papal apartments and food was sent to him there. Everyone was told he was working out of his quarters to catch up on some work after holding midnight Mass on Christmas Eve the night before.

"So, the food was prepared and sent to him. He didn't eat it. One of the nuns, working in the papal household, would normally have just removed it. She should have removed it and disposed of it. But that's where the assassination attempt of his Holiness turned into the murder of an innocent nun. She died within seconds of eating part of the vegetable pasta that was meant for the Pope. Her windpipe became excessively swollen and she experienced massive haemorrhaging in her abdomen. She bled from her nose, ears and eyes."

The waiter came back with their drinks. They started to sip their drinks straight away to add warmth to their cold bodies – it was 7 degrees celsius outside.

"Whoever got in," Nef continued, "knew the layout. His Holiness's apartments include ten large rooms, including a vestibule, an office for his secretary, his private study and his bedroom. There is a dining room and there are living quarters for him. There are quarters for the nuns, and separate accommodation for a number of Benedictine monks, who run the Prefecture of the Pontifical Household. The Pope's private chapel occupies the top storey on the east side of the *Cortile di Sisto V*. There is also a small medical surgery and equipment for most medical emergencies. It was no use to us because the nun was dead when she was found."

"As you don't advertise these things," Luther asked, "how many attempts have there been on Popes?"

"The last assassination attempt on a Pope was on the 13th May 1981, when Mehmet Ali Ağca attempted the assassination of Pope John Paul II in St Peter's Square, in the Vatican City. The Pope was shot and wounded four times and suffered severe blood loss. In the days and weeks that followed, the security services of the Vatican, the *Corpo della Gendarmeria dello Stato della Città del Vaticano* was on high alert. So were the *Guardia Svizzera Pontificia* – the Pontifical

Swiss Guards, the smallest army in the world. You will see them with their yellow, red and blue uniforms. They are in charge of protecting the Pope and the Apostolic castle.

"This last attempt was an act of betrayal, sedition or treachery. I think the killer must work at the Vatican. There are lots of non-clergy in the Vatican; most of the councils have permanent staff members from the lay population."

"We are not so sure it was a person from inside who carried out the attempt," Luther told him.

Nef looked at him. He wanted answers. "If this is what you and St Clair think, how would they know the *piano terra*, the layout as you call it?"

"It is what we think," Luther confirmed. "We believe the assassin is an outsider, but they did have inside help. However, the person inside would not have known what they were doing. It was a kind of hypnosis and one of the church's possessions was used to hypnotise that person."

"You mean the ring?" Nef said. "If not, why was it stolen."

"Yes, the ring," Luther confirmed.

"How did the assassin get the ring?" Nef asked him.

"We were hoping you could tell us. Who is it that your gut is telling you? Do you know that saying, a gut feeling?"

"I know that saying and my *stomac* – stomach, is saying Paradiso, Cardinal Paradiso. I think he is our *Sancti Furem* – Holy Thief. Two years ago, with the Vatican's anti-corruption authority, we suspected him of using church money for himself, but not just any money, he was suspected of using the alms money, *Denarii Sancti Petri*, the Alms of St Peter. This alms money is donations made directly to the Holy See. The Vatican Bank." He continued, "We suspected that he was more deeply involved in a controversial deal that was the subject of a financial investigation. We raided their offices, took away files and computers from clerks at the bank and from the office of the Congregation for the Causes of Saints. Cardinal Paradiso was heading the committee on the canonisation of saints, overseeing the steps of a declaration of heroic virtues and beatification. How crazy is that!

There were a number of others outside the church who were questioned, but in the end, very few were charged with the misappropriation of money, Vatican bank money. A few went to prison."

"Here?" Luther asked.

"No, not here. The Vatican City has no prison system. We only have a few holding cells for pre-trial detention. No, they are sent to Italian prisons and the Vatican is charged by the state for the cost of their incarceration.

"In his job, Cardinal Paradiso would have direct access to the Pope and access to funds. He also had access to the president of the Pontifical Commissions. The Pope is the ex-officio sovereign of Vatican City. He in turn delegates executive authority to the president, who is the ex-officio president of the governate and head of the government of the Vatican. But we couldn't prove it about Cardinal Paradiso. He is a very powerful man. He holds an important job in the Vatican's secretariat of state, a department of the curia, the administration of the Holy See. Through this his Holiness the Pope directs the Roman Catholic Church. The cardinal has many friends, mostly within the Congregation for the Doctrine of the Faith – *Congregtio pro Doctrina Fidei*. It's the oldest of the nine congregations seated in the palace of the Holy Office here in Rome. The main sponsor for his appointment to cardinal was the congressional leader, the prefect of the *Congregtio pro Doctrina Fidei*. He is well protected."

"It's a minefield," Luther said, shaking his head.

Nef didn't understand.

"It's full of traps."

"Too many traps. Many cardinals like *mediocrità* – mediocrity too much. They are afraid of change. They don't like, as you say, rocking the boat."

Nef's mobile phone pinged. He checked the message. It was from Cardinal Gino Del Luca. He told Luther that it was time to go.

Del Luca was waiting with Jonathan, and Aldrich was on his way. They needed to go.

*

Time: Earlier

Jonathan arrived at the address he was given. It was the Cathedral of St John Lateran, in the Piazza di San Giovanni in Laterano. He was awe struck at the building in front of him. A notice board explained that it was founded in the 4th century to honour John the Baptist and John the Evangelist. He already knew, as an ex-priest, that it was considered the Mother Church by the Catholic faithful. Now he was there, in front of it. It was another grand place; there had been numerous grand places along the way. Rome, he mused, was a place where religion and art mixed comfortably. He had never been to Rome before, though he had always wanted to. As a priest, it was the homeland, but he had never had the chance to visit. Now he was actually there, just not as he had imagined. He was absorbing everything he could; he marvelled at the grandeur of Rome, its greatness, its place in history. Despite the bitter chill and, of course, the reason he was there, he was loving Rome.

Jonathan stood outside the cathedral looking across at the other side of the street. He was pounding his feet on the well-trodden pavement trying to get the blood circulating again. He had no idea what Cardinal Del Luca looked like. Nef hadn't said and as far as he knew, the cardinal had no idea what he looked like: wrong!

"Beautiful, aren't they?" a man's voice behind him announced. "They are *Scala Santa,*" the voice continued. "The Sanctuary of the Holy Stairs, brought here in the 4th century. There are twenty-eight marble steps you know, but they are covered in wood because of the wear they have taken over the years. They say," the voice got a little closer, "they are the very steps that Jesus climbed on his way to his trial with Pontius Pilate." The history lesson showed no sign of stopping anytime soon. "They can only be climbed on your knees. Did you know that Martin Luther King climbed them? He heard a voice that said '*The just shall live by faith.*' I do hope so, don't you?"

Jonathan turned around. The voice belonged to a man with a shock of white hair on his head, neatly groomed – not a hair out of place. A traditional style. No facial hair. He had a round, well-proportioned face, a kind face, almost angelic. Jonathan placed him in his eighties. There was no hint of stress about his face, no hint of angst or consternation. Cardinal Gino Del Luca's eyes lit up every time he smiled. It was as if they smiled first, before his lips moved. At their corners, were the tell-tale lines of a happy face, smile lines. He was a neat man, a tidy man. He seemed a man who didn't need to wave his arms around in animated bluster to make a point, or use crude, crass words or his temper, unlike Cardinal Paradiso. He seemed like a man who's engaging presence would earn him the respect of many. His cassock – the long-sleeved buttoned garment worn as ordinary dress and under any liturgical garments – was neat, clean and pressed.

"Forgive me," the man said. He smiled and held out his hand. "I am Gino Del Luca."

Jonathan addressed him and shook his hand. "My name is Jonathan."

"Ah, not Mr Bruce, then?" Del Luca winked. "Oh, I have ears. Mr Bruce and Mr Wayne. Classic." He chuckled.

"It's a pleasure to meet you Cardinal Del Luca," he said, now slightly embarrassed at their schoolboy prank earlier on Cardinal Paradiso.

"Please, call me Father Gino. Everyone does," the old man said. "I could also call you Father, if you like?"

Jonathan wasn't sure if he heard right. He was slightly taken aback, but it didn't matter. Cardinal Gino Del Luca was back on his history lesson.

The old priest turned around and faced the building they had had their backs to. There were two large bronze doors. "Magnificent, aren't they?" Cardinal Del Luca said. He placed his hand on Jonathan's shoulder and Jonathan turned around. "Originally used at the senate house you know, the *Curia Julia*, in the Roman Forum before being brought here."

A passing tourist with his wife stopped and excused the

240

interruption. "Father," he said in a broad Texan drawl, "can you tell us where the Arch of Constantine is?"

The cardinal's face lit up. "A most splendid place to visit. The Arch of Constantine is just under a mile in that direction." He turned and pointed. "And the Basilica di San Pietro in Vincoli is about the same distance in that direction." He turned and pointed in another direction, his voice soft and accommodating. The Texan thanked him, took a picture of the cardinal and his wife standing together and then they left, striding out with purpose, as tourists tend to do when they are trying to cram in as many sights as the day and weather will permit.

"Shall we go into the cathedral?" Cardinal Del Luca said. "There is something I want you to see."

They climbed the stairs and entered the cathedral. They both made the sign of the cross across their bodies, as they bent on one knee.

The cathedral was the most grand, ornate place of worship Jonathan Rose had ever seen. He had seen pictures of the Cathedral of St John Lateran but he never imagined the scale would be so immense. The detailed frescoes, murals and friezes, arches, decorated ceilings and stunning columns stood like a colossal pantheon and at the far end of the cathedral was the most decorated, central arched tower he'd seen within any church.

They sat on the back row of rows and rows of chairs, thirty-five rows in all, and the same number on the opposite side. Some seats were taken; people had gathered in the Vatican over the Christmas period and as it was only the day after Christmas, some were still there. Mostly they were members of the general public but scattered about were nuns and priests sitting in silent prayer or contemplation. Others were walking about, admiring the statues and paintings, or just the regal splendour of the place.

Cardinal Gino Del Luca leaned over to Jonathan and said, "There are six papal tombs inside the archbasilica."

"Cardinal, why did you want to see me? With great respect to you, I am learning a lot about history but I don't think you brought me here to be my tour guide."

"Quite right," he said. He had looked several times towards the front. He did it again. "First, and please forgive me, I need to send a quick message." The cardinal wrote a brief message on his mobile phone and sent it. "There, that's done. Let's get down to it then!"

Over the course of the next thirty minutes, Jonathan slowly discovered that Cardinal Gino Del Luca was a well-travelled, worldly-wise man. He was extremely knowledgeable about the history of the church, but Jonathan also found out that Del Luca was more than he had first appeared to be.

"I have read the Interrogation Roll that is kept in the French National Archives," Del Luca began. "The record of the trial of the Templars by the French monarchy. They say it is the official record of the interrogations of most of the high-ranking Templars, after they were arrested in 1307. It might be a pack of lies," he continued, "invented by loyal scribes to the crown. However, the sixteen-mile-long scroll, handwritten on dozens of individual sheets of parchment and then all finely stitched together by hand, is a fine work of art."

Jonathan felt his nerves start. He reached for the change in his pocket; there were no coins – Luther had banned him from carrying any because it was a clear 'tell.'

"But of course, the scroll doesn't mention that King Philip IV of France, Philip the Fair, was heavily in debt. He had borrowed from many, including the Templars. He borrowed for all kinds of reasons, but I suspect that the wars with England and Aragon cost him the most.

"It seems the king came up with a plan to rid himself of some of his debt by ridding himself of his biggest creditor, the Templars. Now we get to the infamous October 13th, 1307, when most of the Templars were rounded up and thrown into prison. They were questioned and they were badly tortured. They were accused of many heinous crimes like depravity, heresy and even false worship. The Baphomet is mentioned in the Interrogation Roll; they say they washed the head of a beast, but some say it was the representation of John the Baptist, changed by the inquisition to support their charges.

"The goal of the interrogators was clearly to get all of the incarcerated Templars to confess. Many did, a lot didn't, and they died horrible deaths. Most of them were burnt alive. History would have us believe they were wiped out."

Jonathan twisted and turned on his seat. "Cardinal, I have no idea wh—"

"My dear young friend, you think we didn't know? Remember, before you speak, from your lips to God's ears, my son. As soon as we speak it goes from our lips straight to God's ears."

"Know what, exactly?" Jonathan asked him. "What is it that you think you know?"

"That they were not wiped out, of course. The original nine Knights, who were sent to the Holy Land to protect the Christian pilgrims, actually went for another reason, not the quest our history books teach, but a more secret one. Their quest was to search for and then rescue the lost Ark of the Covenant. It wasn't taken by the Babylonians, and neither was it in Axum, in Ethiopia; it was still in Jerusalem.

"When the Ark was found, we think it was then that the Templars, like the inner sanctum of the Holy of Holies, formed their own inner sanctum, an inner circle, a cabal, a council. And, its reason for being was to protect the Ark at all costs.

"We think in 1307, the cabal, sworn to protect their 'Charge,' escaped from France via the port of La Roche and disappeared from the eyes of the world. Actually, Father Jonathan Rose, we don't think this, we know this."

Two priests walked by Del Luca and bade him good day and he reciprocated, gracious in his manner.

The two men now sat quietly. Jonathan's head was spinning. He didn't understand how the cardinal could know that he had once been a priest; or know about their 'Charge?'

The cardinal was still watching the front, Jonathan couldn't see what had him so engrossed. More people walked by them.

"I'm not a priest anymore," Jonathan whispered.

"It's a distinction without a difference, Jonathan. You are still a man of God."

There were footsteps behind them, maybe two or three people Jonathan thought. He recognised one of the footsteps; the sound was familiar to him. Jonathan turned around and saw Luther, followed by Aldrich and Nef. Luther's cowboy boots always had their own distinctive sound. Jonathan was relieved.

"Ah, good; you got my text," Del Luca said to Nef. "Which one of you is Mr Bruce?" he asked them.

"I am" Luther replied.

"Splendid." He then turned to Aldrich. "So, you must be the British witch hunter?"

Aldrich moved forward. "Aldrich Manwin Tucker, at your service."

"I have heard of you, witch hunter." Del Luca slightly bowed in respect.

"And I of you, Cardinal Del Luca, over many years." Aldrich also bowed in respect to the famous cardinal.

The cardinal breathed in deeply and then he let it out as a sigh. "Tell me witch hunter, did you feel her presence?"

Aldrich nodded. "As soon as I walked in."

The cardinal turned towards the front of the cathedral. Off to one side, where he had been looking, and sitting alone and away from other people, was an old nun. "Then prepare yourself witch hunter for you and I have work to do this day." He pointed to the nun. "There," he said to the others, "there is the one you are looking for. There is your witch. There is the Hag."

Chapter 13

26th December Part II

Date: 26th December 2012
Time: 8 a.m. on the East Coast of America (3 p.m. in Italy and Spain, 2 p.m. in the UK)
Place: New Jersey, East Coast of America

Cameron had just hailed a cab and was sitting in the back heading out of the airport. It was freezing out, typical New Jersey December weather, but inside the cab it was warm. He gave the cabby the address: "Metro on the Inn, Brick, Ocean County, New Jersey. How long?" he asked.

"It's early, not much traffic right now. The snow ploughs and gritters have been out all night so, you're looking at about forty or fifty minutes if we don't get jammed up with any accidents," the driver replied.

He thanked the driver and then checked his messages. There was one from Tanjkna. He played it.

"Cameron-san, the Yakuza are in New Jersey. It was a good decision I think for you to go there. There are five or maybe six. Their boss has a cocaine deal with an Arab man called Saladin. He supplies them with drugs and the Yakuza boss sells them in Asia. Cameron-san, my brother told me that the Yakuza are there to kidnap someone." He then hung up.

"There's another hundred bucks in it for you if you get me to Brick faster," Cameron said to the driver, "and I'll cover any speeding fines." The driver put his foot down on the accelerator.

Cameron called St Clair. He did not route the call via Islington.

Place: Valencia, Spain
Time: 3 p.m. in Spain (3 p.m. in Italy, 8 a.m. on the East Coast of America, 2 p.m. in the UK)

St Clair had just arrived in Valencia with Marie-Claude and Bertram. He was checking through customs. His phone vibrated. He looked at the caller's ID on the screen; it was Cameron. He had not routed it through Islington, so St Clair knew it was urgent. He answered the call as he cleared customs. He heard Cameron's voice; he sounded anxious and worried.

"St Clair, I just got a message from Tanjkna Sugata. There are Yakuza in New Jersey. I think five or six of them. Their boss has a deal with a man they call Saladin. He supplies them with drugs and the Yakuza boss moves them throughout Asia. They've been doing business for nearly three years now. The Yakuza boss sent some of his men to New Jersey for the Arab, their task is to—"

"Kidnap a specific target," St Clair had just figured it out. "He's flipped it on us. He got us out in the open. He knew we would go looking for it, for the saint's head. The fourth present for Gowst is not the bishop or the head, it's us. It's now Wolf and Dominique. Where are you now?"

"I'm here, in the States. I'm in the back of a cab on my way to their hotel. It's a little after 8 a.m. local time. I'm forty minutes out from their location, so I should be there by 8:40 a.m." Cameron replied.

"I will call them now and warn them."

"Any news from Rome?" Cameron asked.

"No," said St Clair, "they must have their hands full. Get to Brick as soon as you can, Lionheart. They are going to need you."

*

246

Time: 3 p.m. in Italy (3 p.m. in Spain, 8 a.m. on the East Coast of America, 2 p.m. in the UK)
Place: Rome, Italy

It was Aldrich's plan. The others all agreed to it. Jonathan was slowly starting to admire Aldrich. He was beginning to find out that not everything he saw and thought about Aldrich was true. There was the mercurial and eccentric and then, seemingly, there was this other man, the witch hunter.

Jonathan asked them what he could do. He wasn't in Aldrich's plan; he was pleased about that but he knew he had to help.

"Pray for *annuit coeptis,* my young Corpse," Aldrich told him.

"Good idea," Luther said. "What is it?"

Aldrich was about to explain but Jonathan beat him to it. "It means we pray that God favours our undertaking today. He's borrowed it from one of the two mottos on the reverse side of the Great Seal of the United Sates. Mr Aldrich here borrowed it from the back of our one-dollar bill!"

The cardinal gave Jonathan a piece of paper. "Please also use this when the time comes. Read it and then keep reading it."

"When what time c—"

"She will whisper to you," Aldrich interrupted him. "You will not hear her in your ears; you will hear her in your head. You have to block her out at all costs. Just keep repeating what's written on the paper over and over again until she is dead, or you are dead." Aldrich laughed. "As we say in Welsh, it is her *sillafu,* her spell."

In Aldrich's plan, Jonathan was to stay at the back of the cathedral with Nef. They would be about a hundred yards away from where the Hag was sitting. Nef would cover her escape if she attempted to flee. Nef was armed. Jonathan felt slightly more secure but still, as there was no change in his pocket, he sat there with his left leg bouncing up and down on the ball of his foot like a ball attached to a wooden bat by a piece of elastic.

Aldrich saw he was nervous and leaned over to him. "Relax Jonathan, it's much worse than you think. It's like Jason and the

Argonauts in Homer's Odysseus, and the island of the sirens. The island was inhabited by evil creatures who would sing in an intoxicating whisper to enchant the sailors. Then they would kill them and send them to the underworld."

Jonathan's leg picked up pace.

Towards the front of the cathedral, ten priests appeared from a side door. They separated as soon as they were inside and started to speak to the people in the cathedral. Then, in ones and twos, people calmly started to leave.

"They are my people," Del Luca told them. "They are my students, priests who have shown more than a passing interest in my work. Now they work for me. They are asking the people to leave, telling them that the cathedral is closing for the day."

It didn't take long for the cathedral to empty. The old nun at the front had not moved. She had not looked around; there was no reason for her to.

Aldrich asked Del Luca to have the lights turned out. The cardinal indicated to one of the priests and the lights went out. Only seven lights remained on at the front, and one of the other priests went off to search for the switch to turn them off. Outside, the daylight was starting to edge towards the early winter dusk. Scudding clouds had unleashed a cascade of teeming rain outside and limited daylight now shone through the opaque and magnificent stained-glass windows.

"A Hag's eyesight is notoriously bad. We have about fifteen to twenty minutes," Aldrich said. "After that, we will also be at a disadvantage, so we will have to turn the lights back on."

Aldrich had just finished speaking when the old nun finally stood up and turned around. She looked old. She looked frail. Jonathan didn't believe that she was the same person who Aldrich had made such a thing about when he was talking about her back in Cambridge. Dangerous was one of the words Aldrich had used, but she looked far from dangerous in the cold cathedral – but that quickly changed.

As she turned around, she glowered. She grasped a pendant that she had around her neck. She held it with both hands: it was an upside down cross. She uttered an angry and scornful grunt. Then an eerie silence descended and shrouded the inside of the cathedral with an uneasy malaise. The witch looked around, her eyes everywhere, searching. She had angular features and a hawkish nose, a narrow mouth, hollow, grey eyes and deep sunken cheeks. She had a brooding nature about her. Her eyes darted about, absorbing every-thing. The last of the visitors had now left. The ten young priests stood no closer than twenty-five feet from her. At the back of the cathedral, she saw five men. She could not make out their features at that distance and in that light.

Del Luca moved off down the main aisle. He walked slowly and purposefully reciting psalm 23:4 in his head: *Yea, though I walk through the valley of the shadow of death, I will fear no evil: for thou art with me; thy rod and thy staff they comfort me.*

Aldrich moved swiftly with Luther by his side to the left and down one of the narrower aisles, each reciting their own words. The cardinal was the distraction; Aldrich and Luther were the strike team.

"You'll be fine," Luther told Jonathan before he left. "Just watch our six in case she makes a break for it and stay close to Nef." Jonathan nodded, his muscles knotting.

Now it was quiet inside the cathedral. The old nun stood there, waiting. She'd already seen where all of the priests were. Then she heard his light footsteps approaching. She turned around to see who it was.

"Ah, *exorcista* – exorcist," she rasped loudly, recognising him. "*L'esorcista del Papa.*" Her words echoed around the vaulted archways, central rectangular ceiling and fluted, powerful columns. A few of the other priests now started to close in on her; they didn't go unnoticed. Each was reciting their chosen words to protect themselves from her *sillafu*.

Jonathan heard her say "*L'esorcista del Papa*," as her words reverberated around the large, open space and he suddenly realised who Del Luca was. He was *the* Del Luca, *l'esorcista del Papa* – the exorcist of the Pope, chief exorcist and exorcist of Rome. Jonathan had heard of him; every priest had heard of him. He was famous within the clergy. He was the most experienced exorcist. Cardinal

Gino Del Luca was trained by the revered Father Russo, another famous Italian Catholic priest. Father Russo had performed thousands and thousands of exorcisms over a period of thirty years. Then the purger became the victim when an exorcism went drastically wrong. During the ceremony, it was said that he himself became possessed by a ferocious demon. The police said that Father Russo threw himself on spiked railings outside the *Cimitero Acattolico,* a cemetery also called the *Cimitero dei Protestanti –* cemetery of Protestants, where the poets Shelley and Keats were buried. It was his follower, Gino Del Luca, who found him. It was reported by his housekeeper that a few days before his suicide, Father Russo started talking to himself in words she did not understand and withdrew from everything and everyone. Nearly fifty years on, Del Luca was still exorcising demons from the otherwise damned. They called him *Diavolo assassin –* Devil Slayer.

Just then, the remaining lights went out. It was still light enough inside to see everything, but it was obvious that the witch was struggling with the lack of light, her eyelids half shut as she squinted to see.

"Your doing, exorcist?" she rasped mockingly at Del Luca.

"Faith sees better in the dark," he replied. All the time he was reciting the psalm 23:4 in his head: *Yea, though I walk through the valley of the shadow of death, I will fear no evil: for thou art with me; thy rod and thy staff they comfort me. Yea, though I walk through the valley of the shadow of death, I will fear no evil: for thou art with me; thy rod and thy staff they comfort me.*

"You quote Kierkegaard at me," she rasped back, edging towards the cardinal.

"You are a learned person, Hag."

She was about to say something, but she stopped. Her head darted around, first to the left then to the right. She smelt the air. "Is … is that you, witch hunter?" her voice raspy and scornful. "I smell your stench."

Aldrich moved closer from the left aisle. Luther moved stealthily to his right. Del Luca now moved closer to the witch and was only ten feet away from her. He was within striking distance: her striking distance.

At the back of the cathedral, Nef and Jonathan also moved closer and now they were only thirty feet or so away. Nef pulled his gun out of its shoulder holster and held it in front of him, its short stubby barrel trained on the witch. Jonathan's stomach churned: he was standing in the most holy cathedral in the Catholic world, in Rome, with a man he had only just met, who had his firearm drawn and pointed at a nun, with his finger on the trigger. It was then that Jonathan heard it, her *sillafu*. It was soft; enticing. It was like an angel singing, singing in his head. The sound was warm and comforting. He looked at Nef and saw the growing hollow stare of his eyes. He knew that Nef couldn't concentrate on anything else but the song because he felt it too, the pull was so powerful. The reason they were there started to fade. Jonathan looked at the witch and she was no longer a witch, she was an angel who was protecting him, engulfing him.

Two of the priests also moved in from the front, but they got too close. With her hand embracing the ring on her finger, she started directing the whispering song at them. One of the priests grabbed at his head; his cry of alarm emerged as a scream and it echoed. He picked up a large metal cross, ran to the other priest and buried its crossmember straight into the skull of the other priest. Del Luca shouted for them to pray in their heads to drown out the seductive yet deadly song of the Hag.

"In your heads, say the words in your heads; shout the words in your heads," he kept repeating it. "Don't say them out loud, not yet."

Just then the priest with the cross ran straight into a marble column, headfirst. His head split open. He rebounded. The light left his eyes and he fell dead. Another priest tried to lunge for her; she turned on him and directed her whispering towards him. He screamed, then turned and ran widely at a large, glass case housing religious relics, six feet tall and four feet wide. He ran straight through the plate glass screaming, lacerating his face and neck. He slumped in a kneeling

251

position and then he keeled over, his large wounds gushing with blood. Another priest ran to him. He knelt by his side. He held the dying priest's hand and started administering the last rights.

"Through this holy anointing may the Lord in His love and mercy help you with the grace of the Holy Spirit. May the Lord who frees you from sin save you and raise you up ..."

Del Luca looked back at Nef and Jonathan. "Now, now Jonathan," he called.

Jonathan looked down and opened the piece of paper Del Luca had given him. It was the prayer from an exorcism, it was the prayer of Saint Michael, Jonathan started to read it in his head, *Saint Michael the Archangel, defend us in battle. Be our protection against wickedness and snares of the devil; may God rebuke him, we humbly pray. And do though, O Prince of Heavy Hosts, by the power of God, thrust into hell Satan and evil spirits who wander through the world to ruin souls.*

Then Del Luca shouted, "Now out loud, Jonathan, shout it loud my brother priest!"

Jonathan raised his voice and spoke out loud, "*Adjure te, spiritus nequissime, per deum omnipottentem.* I adjure thee most evil spirit by almighty God." He looked at Nef. "Nef," he shouted at him, "what is the name of your wife and your daughter? Nef?" he shouted it at the top of his voice, "recite the names of your wife and daughter."

Aldrich had started his own incantation. He was shouting the words out loud, which no one understood. It was in an archaic Welsh language. The witch heard it; she understood it. It seemed to pierce her. She gave a shrill; it was a hideous sound.

She roared back at him. "Fuck you, witch hunter!" She pulled a knife from under her nun's robes.

"Now with me, Jonathan" Del Luca called to him. "Together, you and I, out loud." And both Jonathan and Del Luca started shouting out the words to the prayer of Saint Michael. "*Saint Michael the Archangel, defend us in battle. Be our protection against wickedness and snares of the devil; may God rebuke him, we humbly pray. And do though, O Prince of Heavy Hosts, by the power of God, thrust into hell Satan and evil spirits who wander through the world to ruin souls.*"

Now all of the other priests started to recite the prayer of Saint Michael out loud as well. Their words echoed around the great space and it lifted their syntax; it amplified and heightened their sound and the prayer boomed out.

The witch screamed, her face distorting in rage. She was visibly disoriented by the prayers. Aldrich's incantation continued but the sound of Saint Michael's prayer ringing out now stung her ears. She turned away from Aldrich and back towards Del Luca who had orchestrated the multiple reciting that wrecked her focus and pained her ears.

Aldrich edged closer. He was now almost within reach of her. Then, he saw his chance. He looked at Luther. "Now," he mouthed.

Luther picked up a chair and hurled it at the witch. She turned sharply and knocked the chair away before it hit her. Aldrich's plan was near its climax. Whilst she was distracted, Aldrich lunged at her by stepping onto one of the chairs two rows back and hurling himself at her. Her voice almost gurgling now, it was horrid and evil. Her eyelids narrowed further against the creeping dusk. She raised the knife above her shoulder so that she could strike at Aldrich's head as he landed. She pivoted, she reached to stab him, her twisted, muscle-stretching posture deadly. She cut him slightly as the knife caught the right side of his face, but the knife had fallen from her hand when Aldrich landed on her. Aldrich lay winded. She crawled over to him like a demonic banshee on all fours, shouting obscenities, lashing out with her nails and trying to bite his face. She craned her neck to see where the others were. Now with her left hand around Aldrich's throat, her right hand found the knife and was trying to drive its steel into his heart. Aldrich raised his voice; at full pitch his incantation visibly affected the witch. She screamed again and the soft, enchanting whispering had now changed. Del Luca, Jonathan, Luther, Nef and the other priests all heard it; they felt it. It was like radio waves in their heads at a thousand decibels and they all reached for their heads and doubled over in agony. With the madness now controlling her, her lips curled back in a mirthless and hideous grin, once again she rounded on Aldrich. Her witchcraft fuelled her demonic strength: she was much stronger than him and she was faster than him, as he knew she would be.

The others were now unable to help Aldrich, paralysed by the screech of the *Gwrach Marwolaeth* Hag. Only Aldrich's archaic Welsh incantation protected him from the same debilitating effect the others were experiencing of excruciating pain and immobilisation.

Her mouth was wide open, foam and froth spewed from her crazed lips.

Aldrich managed to raise himself up. Now, standing on his feet he faced her. She knew she had him; she had the witch hunter. She knew she was more powerful than he was and her screech held the others at bay. She would slay the witch hunter. Doubled up, the others looked on unable to do anything to help him.

She raised her knife and spewed out another barrage of obscenities and then, she brought the knife down.

Jonathan summoned every last bit of energy he had and asked his Lord God for help. His head felt like it was splitting apart but he managed to straighten and stand up straight. Remembering everything Dominique had taught him, he snatched the gun from Nef, turned and fired.

The witch recoiled as the bullet hit her in the neck; it didn't stop her but it gave Aldrich time. Aldrich Manwin Tucker, the eccentric professor from the University of Cambridge, Medieval Studies: Department of Supernatural, Occultism and History of Satanic Medieval Renaissance, reached inside his long jacket and withdrew a xiphos sword. It was a double-edged, one-handed straight sword used by the ancient Greeks and only eighteen inches long. As sharp as a razor. In one slicing upward movement, he cut the Hag from her waist to her shoulder. "*Byddwch yn wrach farw –* be dead witch!" he shouted in his native Welsh language. "*Byddwch yn wrach farw!*"

The Hag roared in pain. Her blood was a deep reddish-brown colour. There was no richness to it; it was a dull, pasty goo. Aldrich stood over her as she lay on the floor. Again, he recited in an archaic

Welsh language as the light left her eyes. The Hag was dead. The others felt the pressure in their heads leave immediately; the relief was almost euphoric.

Thirty minutes later, the bodies of the fallen priests had been taken away for a Catholic burial, which Cardinal Del Luca would perform. Under Aldrich's instructions, the body of the Hag was also taken away and would be incinerated within the hour. He had written out some words he asked Del Luca to recite at her burning. Before they took the body away, one of the priests removed the ring from her finger, the ring of King Solomon, the ring that allowed the Hag to amplify her vile malevolence. It had amplified her evil *sillafu* whispering that had killed so many over the last eight decades, slain four bishops and had just taken more souls.

The cathedral was now empty but for Cardinal Del Luca, Jonathan, Aldrich, Luther and Nef. The priests had gone to attend to all the arrangements. It was eerily quiet after the intensity of their fight with the last of the *Gwrach Marwolaeth* Hags. It was now time for them to go. Seats had been booked on the late flight out of Rome back to the UK. They started to make their way out of the cathedral.

Luther started smiling, which turned into a laugh. He stopped and turned to Aldrich. "There's just one thing I have to know, Aldrich. How on earth did you get hold of a sword?"

"Ha, you noticed that did you, Luther, old boy? You noticed I got one?" He looked at Jonathan and gave him a stern look. 'I got one,' he mouthed to Jonathan, his pipe alight and resting in his mouth. He carried on telling Luther his tale. "Old cod face Paradiso, he had someone show me their sword collection over there because, well I asked to see it, repeatedly. Because I was a pain in his arse, he could not wait to get rid of me once you two had left. So, he appointed one of his people, the jolly priest with an odd gait, to take me to the sword collection. Magnificent old fruit, truly magnificent."

"Yes, but how did you get it?"

"I stole it."

"You stole from the Vatican?"

"Yes." He laughed heartily and then he pulled the sword out from underneath his coat again and held it aloft. "'*And, gentlemen in England now a-bed, shall think themselves accursed they were not here, and hold their manhoods cheap whilst any speaks, that fought with us upon Saint Crispin's day. Hurrah and hurrah.*' Henry the Fifth; God love a royal." And then, almost as an afterthought, he said, "bugger me Brigadier, I'm not quite sure how we are going to get this through customs!"

Del Luca walked slightly ahead with Jonathan. Del Luca had made all their arrangements; Paradiso was still to learn what had happened.

"What about the ring?" Jonathan asked him.

"Oh, I wouldn't worry, Jonathan. We will hide it in a safe place and the cardinals do not need to know we have it back in our possession. I think it will be safer this way, don't you?"

Jonathan nodded.

"It is our loss, Jonathan. Losing you from the church," Del Luca lamented.

"Just how did you know I was a priest?" Jonathan asked.

"Same way I knew your name, same way I knew what Luther was, same way I know what you protect. You are not the only one with a secret my young friend." He smiled a reassuring smile. "You are not the only one with an order, a *senza volto* cabal, a faceless cabal." Del Luca's face lit up. Despite everything that had just happened, his shock of white hair still looked neatly groomed – not a hair out of place. Still his face showed no hint of stress. Still his eyes lit up every time he smiled. Jonathan could now see why he had such respect from his brethren. The Devil Slayer was a man of high integrity and faith.

They stood by the waiting car saying their goodbyes. Aldrich was first in the car. As soon as he sat down, he lit up his pipe again.

Luther shook hands with Nef. "St Clair sent me a message earlier from Spain. He told me that we are going to help you find your *Sancti Furem,* your Holy Thief, although, I think we all suspect who it is. I want you to know that we will be back in touch in the New Year."

Around the other side of the car, Del Luca and Jonathan stood saying their goodbyes. "We will talk soon, you and I. There is much for us to discuss," Del Luca told him. Then he gave him a small wooden cross. "To keep you safe my son." Jonathan took it and thanked him.

As they pulled way, Jonathan looked at the small wooden cross Del Luca had just given him. Faintly engraved on the cross was a crown of thorns and in the middle of the crown of thorns, a small rose.

Time: 8 a.m. on the East Coast of America (3 p.m. in Italy and Spain, 2 p.m. in the UK)
Place: New Jersey, East Coast of America

Dagmar Grey woke up with a thumping headache, she groaned slightly. Daniel Hightower woke up with a thumping headache, he too groaned slightly. After talking for a few hours in the café last night, they had gone on to a bar. It was far enough away from his car, which they believed was still being watched; it was dark enough inside for them to blend in and loud enough with thirsty patrons for them not to be overheard.

They had talked until two in the morning and both had told their life stories – almost, because she still hadn't told him about the skull. What they quickly realised was that whilst geographically they were from very different places, their lives were very similar: drink, drugs and violence having played their parts in each of their lives. Both were unhappy and looking for something to lift them out of the crappy lives they had.

After drinking until 2 a.m., Daniel had suggested that they book another hotel; they could not risk that either of their hotels were being watched. He suggested a single room; she could have the bed and he would take the floor – there was no couch. By 3:30 a.m. they'd had sex twice and fell into a deep sleep, exhausted. Nobody slept on the floor.

Now the sun was up. He hadn't pulled the curtains shut and it was shining directly in her face. She was bursting to go for a pee, she didn't want to get out of bed first. She was naked and her clothes were over on

257

the other side of the room, where she had stripped, with his help.

He also laid there a while bursting to go for a pee but, after a short while, rose and sauntered off to the bathroom, buck naked.

"You need to pee," he called to her from the bathroom. The toilet flushed. "I was thinking we could go get breakfast or something." He carried on talking as he walked back into the bedroom. "Does that work for you?" He pulled back the covers. He looked down at her. "Let's grab breakfast a little later." He jumped back into bed.

"Wait, wait, wait," she told him, "I have to pee first. A woman can't, you know, if they have to pee, it would … Never mind wait there! Don't move!" She ran to the bathroom. Then she ran back into the bedroom.

It was after 8 a.m. and they had finally left each other alone long enough to get dressed. They both knew there was something pretty special going on between them. She wondered if being petrified for your life gave you a higher sex drive; she felt she'd known him all her life. But she was also eager to find out if the two people he had followed could help her get out of the unhealthy predicament she was in. It was the only play she had left. They decided they would try and find a discreet way round to the back of the hotel and go inside to see if they could find the two people. It was snowing outside; they dressed and left the hotel.

It was to be their last day. Dominique and John Wolf hadn't found out anything of any value to the Order or Nef. The local police were still working on the death of the bishop, but they were getting nowhere. They were not working on the theft from the church because they didn't know about it; they didn't know that the skull of one of the most famous and revered saints in history had been stolen, because no one had told them, or were ever going to tell them.

Dominique and Wolf were happy they were leaving. The guy in the car, the guy that had watched them at the church and followed them back to their hotel, hadn't done anything. He had sat in his rental car for a long time just watching the hotel. However, now he had disappeared. The car was still there but he was not. Although they now knew who he was, it had been a miserable waste of time for them and they hoped St Clair had other leads.

They had packed and had already checked out. Bill Meeks was flying in with two Knights and was meeting them at the hotel. They would debrief him; he would take their weapons and then he and the two Knights would carry out the final mop up once they had left, just in case anything came up later that day.

Accompanied by Meeks, they were going to make one stop before catching their respective flights. They were going to see Father Angelo Fugero one more time, but they didn't hold out much hope that he had anything new to say. However, it was a good opportunity to introduce Meeks as the new contact should anything new turn up.

The receptionist, Sally-May Bernstein, had long given up any thoughts of taking the good-looking Indian home to meet her mother and instead she had turned her attentions to a salesman with a generous waist line and a cheery enough disposition. She checked Dominique and Wolf out; they paid for their rooms and added breakfast for that morning – the hot food smells were too much for Wolf and he insisted they eat breakfast. Sally-May wished them well with a "Y'all come back real soon, ya hear."

Breakfast was a buffet style breakfast. The help-yourself food counter was full of freshly cooked bacon, eggs, biscuits, gravy, mushrooms and several other tempting treats.

They were at the food counter; she was getting fruit and black coffee, Wolf was getting hash browns and bacon, plus biscuits, gravy and coffee. She'd left her mobile phone on the table. With no one answering, St Clair's message went to voice mail and she missed the alert ping.

They chose a table where they could sit, as always, with their backs to a wall so they had a clear line of vison.

Dagmar and Daniel found a small service road that led to the back of the hotel. It was lined with bushes and so gave them an element of cover from anyone keeping watch. They thought they had got away with it. They hadn't; they were seen.

The Yakuza gang had guessed that was the hotel where the two people were staying but could not be a hundred per cent sure. So, the Yakuza boss had people watching the parked car and people watching the front and the back of the hotel. They had no idea what the two new people looked like, the two who had gone to the church, but they believed they were their kidnap mark. They needed to find the man Crowthorp's female burglar had called Flapper; he could identify the two in the hotel. So, they waited and watched.

The Yakuza at the back of the hotel called his boss – his boss was stationed inside the hotel where it was warm. He told his boss that the British man he had with him, Crowthorp, had just identified Dagmar Grey and the man called Flapper; they were going into the hotel via the back. His boss told him to stay where he was. The boss then called the other Yakuza who had been watching the parked car and told them to get to the hotel straight away.

Daniel and Dagmar found an unlocked door at the back of the hotel, which was clearly used by smokers because the door was unlocked and the area covered in cigarette butts. The two quickly moved through the service corridor, which was full of used plates and glasses on trays, next to piles of bed linen waiting to be laundered. They opened another door, which led them into the main reception area. Sally-May didn't notice them; she was too busy gushing at the salesman and laughing at his well-rehearsed jokes.

They smelt the biscuits and bacon. "Might as well wait in there and watch for them there," Daniel said, indicating the open plan eating area. "They have to go past there to go in and out. It's open, so we will see everything."

Dagmar agreed. They moved into the eating area; it was small, around ten yards by ten yards, it seated twelve people at a push. There were a few more tables in the main foyer where the reception desk stood. The breakfast counter looked inviting and the cooking smells were enticing. They made for the food.

The Yakuza boss watched them. He knew what Daniel looked like, thanks to the information Dagmar had given Crowthorp. He knew what Dagmar looked like, because he had seen her in Crowthorp's room. He pulled the newspaper up to cover more of his face and waited for his men to arrive.

Wolf saw them first. He recognised the man; he was the man who had been watching them at the church, the man who had followed them back to their hotel. He was the man St Clair had told them was Jamal's grandson, after they had sent pictures they had managed to take with their mobile phones whilst he was sat watching from his car. "Our 2 p.m.," Wolf whispered to Dominique, whilst holding a mug of coffee to his lips to cover his mouth.

Dagmar and Daniel were just five feet away now. Dominique looked up and at that very moment Dagmar looked at their table.

"Dagmar?" Dominique exclaimed.

"Dominique?" Dagmar said with incredulity.

Daniel moved to Dagmar's side and Dominique instantly saw there was something physical between them. "Hello Mr Hightower," Dominique said to him. Daniel was bemused and confused because these were the people he had been watching.

"Well, as you all seem to be old friends, that just leaves me then," Wolf said. He stood up, towering and held out his hand. "I am John Wolf; I am the Indian," he said quietly so he could not be overheard by anyone else.

"Fuck me," Daniel said.

Dominique and Dagmar hugged. Daniel waited. He looked at Wolf's biscuits and gravy.

"Go ahead," Wolf said, indicating towards the breakfast

counter, "they might take a while to get back to us."

Daniel went over and filled his plate with biscuits and gravy and then did the same for Dagmar.

He sat back down; they were still reminiscing, but Daniel was beginning to feel pretty bad because he had been spying on them; he had to say something. He interrupted Dominique and started to tell her and Wolf that he had been watching them. Wolf stopped him and explained that they already knew; they had known at the church, had driven slowly to allow him to follow them to the hotel, where they could keep an eye on him. They had taken pictures of him watching from his car. Finally, Wolf told him that they had sent those pictures off to Jordan, via some friends of theirs and, his grandfather Jamal had confirmed the man in the picture was his grandson and explained why he was there.

"Stroooth!" Daniel said, his Australian accent slightly thicker now his mind was racing seeking answers. "Just who are you people?"

"Yeah," Dagmar said, turning to Dominique. "Just who are you people; you never really did tell me four years ago."

They had been talking for about ten minutes. Dagmar was explaining how she had met Daniel and that she too had been watching the church. She didn't finish the story because she tracked back to the beginning and told them about her first meeting with Crowthorp and his blackmail over her brother's life, Tony's life. She told them about each of the robberies she had committed for Crowthorp. Now she was back full circle and starting to tell them about leaving the UK for the US but had not begun to tell them why. She noticed the Indian and Dominique were no longer listening.

"Are you feeling what I'm feeling?" Wolf asked Dominique.

"Yup," Dominique replied, opening her coat slightly in readiness.

"Who the hell is watching us?" Wolf whispered.

An Asian man started to walk towards them. He looked mean. He had another man with him.

Sally-May screamed. She had never seen a Samurai sword

before, not one in real life; now there was one at her neck. The salesman stood terrified next to her. Dominique noticed that the telephone cable at the reception desk had been cut and both Sally-May and the salesmen's mobile phones were on the floor, smashed.

Another man came in dragging the valet by his collar. He pushed the petrified young man over to where Sally-May and the salesman were standing. The man then went back and positioned himself by the hotel doors in case anyone came in.

A family of three and two older people, a few tables along, also had their mobile phones smashed. There was another man watching them; his Katana sword pointed at them. They heard a door being banged shut, then another man appeared. They figured he had just disabled the lifts and barred the fire escape stairway door, because that's what they would have done.

All the men were dressed the same, all in black suits, all gangster looking. They looked like bad extras out of a *Pulp Fiction* film. Dominique reached inside her coat for the gun nestled in her shoulder holster and Wolf let his right arm dangle by his side so he could clasp his hand around his fourteen-inch bone-handled knife, which was holstered in its sheath on his side. His other hand curled round his six round Beretta M9 semi-automatic handgun.

The mean-looking Asian man approached their table; he pointed to his prisoners. His men held their swords closer to the prisoners' throats and they began crying. Both Dominique and Wolf stopped reaching for their weapons and dropped their hands. One of the old people, the husband of the women, made a grab for the captor and his sword, but his agility was faster in his memory than in reality. The captor moved to the side slightly, pushed his hip forward, and at the same time he arced his sword over his right shoulder and down, onto the left shoulder and neck of the old man. He was cut through and fell to the floor like a rag doll. His wife screamed, loudly and the captor hit her on the head, hard, with the *tsuka,* the handle of the sword. She fell to the floor, unconscious.

Dagmar was petrified. She recognised the Asian man in front of them. It was the same man who had gone to Crowthorp's room and had taken him outside and told him to get rid of her. She looked at Daniel and saw that he was scared too; he knew violence but not like this. He looked as lost as she felt.

The mean-looking Asian man looked and acted like the boss. He pulled up a chair and sat down with them. Close up he was hideous looking, with a bulky frame and a squat face, scarred and lined through frowning. His eyes were empty of anything other than rage. His English was clipped and harsh. He looked at the people in front of him. He opened his jacket slightly and revealed a gun. They knew he was just letting them know it was not all swords. The man who had walked over with his boss now frisked them. He took all their weapons and their mobile phones and placed them on a chair close by. He then stood by the chair.

"If you give me trouble, I will kill all these people, and then I will kill you, you, and you," the boss said as he pointed to Wolf, Dominique and Daniel. Then he turned to Dagmar, "and you, I will leave for my men to have fun with." The man protecting the weapons looked down at Dagmar and gave a dispassionate smirk and then pursed his lips. She felt his look crawl all over her skin.

On the floor by the reception desk, Sally-May was still sobbing. The salesman kept telling her to be quiet, that she'd make it worse.

"I'm going to die. I'm going to die," she sobbed.

"Jeez, ya' think!" he finally shouted at her. "I'll do it myself if you don't stop sobbing."

It was snowing by the time Cameron got to Brick, in Ocean County, New Jersey. He paid the cabby, including the extra one hundred he had promised him, then another one hundred to cover the speeding fine he would get for setting off a speed camera by the last turnpike. He drew the collar of his long black coat up around his neck. He could already see from the window that the reception area was full of Yakuza. They were all looking in one direction, so he knew where their boss was and he suspected that's where he would find the Templars.

Cameron approached the hotel's double automatic doors. He took in a deep breath and then slowed everything down in his mind. He

264

took away all his thoughts other than to understand what he saw in front of him. Where each Yakuza stood, who looked like they would react first, who might move better and what fixed elements he could use to his advantage.

Then he approached. The sensor went off and the hotel's double doors swooshed opened. The swoosh startled some of the men inside. Cameron stood in the doorway, keeping the doors open, letting in the cold – he wanted the distraction; he wanted to create unease. The smell of freshly cooked biscuits, gravy and bacon drifted out into the cold, frosty New Jersey air. In front of him and just inside, was one of the Yakuza. Ahead and slightly to the left, three people lay on the floor, Sally-May Bernstein, the salesman, and the valet. Another Yakuza watched them. A quick check confirmed the phone line had been cut to the reception telephone unit.

Two, he told himself.

Just past the reception desk were five more people; two were on the floor. They were old and he didn't know if they were dead. They were being held by two more Yakuza.

Four.

Then he looked to his right and saw Dominique and the Indian, John Wolf, sitting at a table. At the table were two people he knew were civilians from the looks on their faces. There was also a mean-looking Japanese man sitting at the table with them.

Five.

And, finally another Yakuza was standing just a few feet away from Wolf and Dominique. He was standing next to a chair that had their weapons: her Heckler Koch.40, a pump-action 12-gauge shotgun, Wolf's Beretta, his knife and their phones were all piled up on a chair.

Six. Damn. Tricky, he thought.

He knew the power and strength of the Indian. He was a true-blooded Shawnee Indian, tall and lean with solid broad shoulders, and chiselled, weathered features. He was a fighter. He also knew the skill of Dominique. Whilst she was a small petite woman – attractive with short mousy brown hair – she was also a 7th Dan in Karate and a skilled shooter, not to be messed with.

He scanned the room and quickly worked out who he would pick the fight with first. The Yakuza guarding the main door was younger than the others. His body language suggested he was quick to reach ice cold rage, given the slightest prompting. He was also the closest to Cameron.

Cameron moved further into the reception area and the automatic doors closed behind him. The cold left outside. Now it was deadly quiet after the rush and tug of the wind and only the whimpering of Sally-May broke the silence.

Cameron bowed slightly to the Yakuza. "*Shinshi* – gentlemen," he said, never taking his eyes off them. Then he turned to the young Yakuza. Cameron gave a half smile and said "*Gakusei* – pupil." The insult was there for all to hear. Now he'd left the young Yakuza no way out. As predicted, he went for his Katana. He was not slow, but Cameron was faster; he was lightning fast. Cameron grabbed the man's hand with a jujutsu hold and with his other hand, he withdrew the Katana sword himself. Now the Lion-heart was ready.

Armed, he said to himself. *Time to go to work.*

The disarmed Yakuza looked startled. He wanted to run but he had been indoctrinated by *Bushido*, the Samurai's code of honour, as had Cameron. He also knew his boss was watching and so were the others. He was going nowhere. The young Yakuza pulled out his second sword, his Wakizashi, used when a Samurai is fighting close to his opponent, or for the ritual of *seppuku*, suicide. The young Yakuza prayed it was not going to be a sign of his death: he viewed Cameron through a belligerent, scowling glare.

Cameron saw that part of his little finger was missing. "The problem with that," he started, looking down at it, "is that particular little finger," he indicated on his own left hand, "on that particular hand, controls a lot of the more complex Katana moves. The deadlier ones." Cameron's tone was calm, almost conversational. He said it in English. He didn't know if the young Yakuza understood him, but the creeping concern in his dull eyes began to show: he was realising that he was in trouble. He was beginning to realise he was up against a more superior swordsman.

"This will not be Kendo: we will not be fighting with sticks," Cameron told him. "This is Kenjutsu and I am a pupil of Hinata Satō-san's and Tanjkna Sugata-san's Kenjutsu dojo. Unlike Kendo, this has all the nasty killing stuff left in." He knew the mention of both Hinata Satō and Tanjkna Sugata would put the fear of God into the young Yakuza, because everyone who ever held a Katana sword in Japan had heard of them.

All eyes were on Cameron. He looked towards Wolf and Dominique and smiled. "*Ubi positus est, ut omnis –* where one stands, so stand us all," he said. Dominique and Wolf nodded: they confirmed they were ready.

"Remember, Dagmar," Dominique leaned over to her, "remember four years ago, in your house, when you asked Jonathan and myself who we were. Do you remember what Jonathan told you?" Dagmar nodded. "Well, he is one of them." She gave Dagmar a comforting smile and whispered, "Be ready."

The Lionheart breathed deep and purposefully. He shifted his weight, first on to his left leg, and then to the right, almost in a rocking motion, backwards and forwards.

The Yakuza guarding the weapons pushed his thumb against the small round guard that separated the handle of his sword from the blade. He pushed it upwards and his Katana clicked as it broke from its scabbard ready to be drawn. Dominique watched him; she heard the click. She gave Wolf the sign – she would take him.

Wolf's eyes moved past her; she followed them. On the wall was a fire alarm. She knew his play. Next, he looked at the Yakuza boss, who had turned around and was watching Cameron and his young Yakuza, eager to see blood. Wolf tilted his head slightly towards him. She knew he would go for the fire alarm first; that would bring confusion and then the fire department and the police. Secondly, he would take out the Yakuza boss after the fire alarm. Wolf was a big man. He had about five feet to get to the fire alarm and then seven feet back to the Yakuza boss. She knew he was agile and fast. He could make it. They were set.

Cameron raised the sword in front of him and said *"Odorimashou* – let's dance!"

Then all hell broke loose.

Instead of striking with the sword high in front of him and striking downwards, as would be traditional, Cameron moved his weight quickly to his left leg, pushed his leg out and to the left, almost semi-crab like. Crouching low and the sword three feet off the ground, he brought it round in a wide arcing motion towards the legs of the Yakuza. The Yakuza was ready for the high strike. He was out of position to defend against Cameron's low sweeping move and woefully out matched anyway. Because he'd had one leg slightly ahead of the other, in a bow stance, the razor-sharp blade sliced directly through his right calf, all the way through to the bone. He screamed. Sally-May screamed. The salesman screamed.

As Dominique leapt from her chair, Wolf lunged for the alarm on the wall. His fingers straight and rigid broke the glass and hit the button. The interior siren alarm was deafening. At the same time, Dominique brought her leg high and over, in a roundhouse movement and snapped her kick hard, right across the side of the face of the Yakuza guarding their weapons.

Dagmar and Daniel had not been party to their plans and they dived for the floor in blind panic.

The Yakuza boss was faster than he looked. He was already reaching inside his coat for his weapon and was drawing it.

The man guarding the weapons shook his dazed head. He staggered. He turned as his assailant was about to round on him again with his sword out now. He went to bring it down, hard, but Dominique crossed her wrists and blocked the handle from coming down. She then moved her right hand down slightly, turned it inwards, almost half looping back on itself. She grabbed his wrist vice-like and twisted hard, forcing his left hand upwards. He dropped the sword and yelped. With her other hand, she grabbed the closest weapon; it was Wolf's knife. She threw it to him. Wolf caught it, turned and was now face-to-face with the Yakuza boss.

The Yakuza boss had Wolf because his hand was already on his gun; his bulky frame was square on to Wolf – he could not miss. A smirk came across his squat face, the rage in his eyes alight. But, he took his hand off his gun. He pulled out a Wakizashi from its scabbard. It was smaller than most Wakizashi; it was almost bayonet-like. Brought up on *Bushido* and fighting, the Yakuza always tried to prove their power and dominance. Besides, he had enough men with him, should he falter.

Daniel was breathing heavily. He was holding onto Dagmar, trying to shield her. "Jeeezus," Daniel exclaimed. "Look at that knife compared to that bloke's bloody big one."

Wolf reached down. He grabbed Dagmar. "Get out!" he yelled. He looked at Daniel, "Get her out now!"

Dagmar and Daniel started to run, instinctively the same way they had come in, through the back of the hotel. Daniel turned around and looked back at Wolf as Wolf leapt at the Yakuza boss. "That Wolf's got bloody balls of steel. I bet you they click when he runs."

"Well, let's not hang around to find out, shall we?" Dagmar grabbed Daniel's hand and they ran for the door.

Cameron was now with the Yakuza guarding Sally-May. The other two Yakuza had joined him, letting Dagmar and Daniel escape because they knew who was waiting at the back of the hotel.

Sally-May and the salesman, along with the valet, scurried along the floor and straight for the office. Inside, Sally-May locked the door and wept uncontrollably. In shock, the salesman put his arms around her and wept uncontrollably. The valet put his arms around them both and wept uncontrollably.

The three Yakuza all had their swords poised in front of them, all holding them with two handed grips. They would deal with Cameron first, then take care of their captives; they were going nowhere locked in an office.

Cameron was skilled. He could wield a sword with one hand, but he could also strike with either hand. This gave him greater dexterity. He stood in front of them. Then, he attacked. His stance was solid, his movements flowing and his fight tactics superb. Step, twist, step and step, thrust, pivot, breathe, concentrate; step, step, headshot, twist and then, wrist, back up and head shot, down, just as the two old masters had taught him, and as he now taught the younger Knights in the Order. The Knights Templar Master of the Blade pierced and struck blow after blow; he lunged and arced. He wove in and around the three assailants like an orchestrated ballet. There was no rush to his attacking style, just a flow. They tried to overwhelm the man who they had scoffed at when he had first walked through the door, the man who looked like he had the blood of two races flowing through his veins.

Cameron was breathtakingly fast and graceful. Sometimes he held his sword down, sometimes aloft at a 45-degree angle to the left, and sometimes to the right. And, sometimes he held his sword out pointing down in one hand; then he would suddenly start to rotate it. They had not seen sword mastery so up close and personal like this before. The elegant dance intensified and the Yakuza started to make mistakes. They were lashing, slicing, cutting, carving and slashing. They were out of breath; bullying and extortion were more their staple daily exercise. Cameron trained six hours a day, every day.

They tried gashing, hacking and flaying but every time they thought they had him, he made a slight sidestep or a twist of the body and their blows found nothing but empty space and every time they struck and missed, they exerted a little more effort. The wasted energy was mounting up. They started running on empty, getting in each other's way. The clattering of steel on steel, the grunts, the groans: it seemed to have been going on for an hour to the Yakuza, but they had only been fighting for a few minutes. The adrenalin that had swept through their bodies was now sapping away their energy and replacing it with lactic acid that made their limbs feel like lead.

Blow by blow, cut by cut, they tried to fight back the lone swordsman. His momentum, force, propulsion, speed, his twisting, spinning and spanning had them beat, and they knew it. The first of them to die felt Cameron's blade enter his lower abdomen and move upwards into his ribcage. He fell with nearly eighteen inches of steel inside him. Cameron left the sword imbedded in his victim and picked up his victim's sword.

The second one died soon after the first one, but he had got in the way of the other Yakuza's thrust at Cameron's head and took the blow himself. It penetrated his skull and he was instantly dead.

Cameron heard the first of the responder's sirens from outside, then another; they were getting closer. He looked across to the other Templars. Wolf was retrieving his knife from the Yakuza boss's chest and Dominique had just snapped the other Yakuza's neck by twisting his head sharply. They all knew it was time to go.

Cameron turned on the remaining Yakuza and rotated his sword one-handed about to bring it down across the Yakuza's torso when he heard a gunshot. The swordsman dropped to the floor; his sword followed with a clatter. Cameron looked up and saw Dominique; there was smoke still coming out of the barrel of her gun. She shrugged her shoulders. "Quicker, I thought?" she smiled.

Daniel and Dagmar had run through the service corridor and then outside where the cold air hit them. They both nearly slipped; they'd forgotten in the mayhem that it was snowing outside. They stopped abruptly. They stopped directly in front of Timothy Crowthorp and one of the Japanese gangsters.

Crowthorp couldn't believe his luck. He'd lost the girl and lost the skull, but now she was back and she represented both his retribution and his salvation all in one go. He raised his handgun. "You fucking bitch," he shouted, his voice wavering with the cold – they had been out there a long time. Dagmar still had Daniel's hand in hers. "How sweet," Crowthorp said sarcastically, "Flapper and the thief. I should have known you were in this together." He turned to the Yakuza, "Kill him; I want her alive. I want her because she has the—"

A thin red beam appeared on the Yakuza's forehead, then one appeared on Crowthorp's chest, exactly where his heart was. Bill Meeks moved out from the shadows. He'd arrived just a few minutes before with two armed Knights. He'd seen the fighting from the window at the front. He made for the back with the Knights to cover the Templar's retreat if they needed it, or to stop anyone making an escape that way. As he turned the corner, he saw Crowthorp holding a young man and woman at gun point. He recognised Crowthorp from the internal report St Clair had circulated four years ago. He was fifteen feet away.

"Drop your weapons," he called. As an FBI agent, he'd made the same call over a hundred times, but he knew from experience, very few people actually ever put down their weapons. Meeks held a gun in one hand and was holding the other hand up, at head height, palm open. He looked at the girl and the man with her. "Tell me who you are!" he demanded.

"Dagmar, Dagmar Grey and this is—"

"Daniel Hightower," Daniel interrupted.

"Jamal's grandson," Meeks said. "Daniel, do we need these two?" he looked at Crowthorp and the Yakuza.

"No fucking way," Daniel shouted back.

Bill Meeks closed his hand into a fist. Two shots rang out. Two bullets followed the red laser lights and the last Yakuza and the crooked barrister, Timothy Crowthorp, were dead.

The door burst open. The red laser lights now switched to the doorway. Then Dominique, Wolf and Cameron came running out. Bill Meeks held his palm open quickly and then called, "Stand down! Stand down!"

Time: Later

They were all sitting in the lounge of a downtown hotel bar, some twenty or so miles from the scene of the mayhem and dead bodies, bodies with the sign of the cross written in blood on their foreheads. Sally-May, the salesman, the valet and the other captives had all agreed not give away their descriptions. They also agreed what they would say: they would use the descriptions of the cast of the Magnificent Seven. Dominique, Wolf, Cameron, Daniel and Dagmar were all given a character from the seven. And, the captives relayed that exact story of whatever each of them had done, really done during the ordeal.

Dominique was tall and bold and smoked a long, thin cigar!

Meeks and the two Knights had gone back inside and retrieved the CCTV tapes. Meeks would destroy them later. Now there was no record of what had taken place, just bodies of Japanese gangsters and one brave old man.

Dagmar and Daniel were beginning to relax a little now. Outside, Meek's two Knights kept watch. Daniel was on his third whisky; Dagmar Grey was on her third whisky. They were sitting close to each other, very close.

The group had been talking for some time when Dominique brought up the subject of the saint's head. Daniel started to tell them how devastated his grandfather was going to be and his grandfather's people, when Dagmar reached for her backpack. She opened it and showed everyone what was inside.

"Give him this from me," she said and then smiled.

Daniel was now the one with a grin on his face. He looked at Dagmar: it was a questioning look.

"No, no, no. I didn't kill the bishop. Good God no! But, yes; I stole it. Please give it to your grandfather."

"How ...?" He stopped short and thought for a moment, "... why don't you give it to him yourself. Come with me!"

"Love to," she said. Then as an afterthought she said, "but how in the hell are we going to get this through customs?"

"Oh, leave that to us," Dominique said. "And by the way, Dagmar, we made a call a few minutes ago. First thing tomorrow, your brother Tony will be moved to an open-air prison. He'll be safe from now on."

"Just who are you lady?" she asked smiling, because those were the very words she had used four years ago.

"Well," Dominique started laughing, "if I recall right, you called me Miss Selfridges back then, but Jonathan told you that we are Knights, Dagmar, Knights in shining armour."

"I don't know about that, but you are certainly the good guys, eh Daniel?"

And all Daniel could say was "Fuck me! what a day!"

Time: 3 p.m. in Spain (3 p.m. in Italy, 8 a.m. on the East Coast of America, 2 p.m. in the UK)
Place: Valencia, Spain

They cleared Spanish customs without a hitch. As usual for the Templars, they travelled on false passports. Masquerading as drone enthusiasts and carrying authentic UK flyer IDs and operator IDs, their equipment was passed through security: Bertram's stealth sky-eyes, eyes in the sky.

Six Knights were waiting in a parked vehicle outside. They drove a black Mercedes transit van with dark, tinted windows that made it impossible to see inside. The six Knights had come armed and had brought along weapons for their visitors. Marie-Claude, as a trained sniper and one of the best shots in the Order, got the 7.62 calibre sniper rifle. St Clair took a semi-automatic and a small handgun which he slipped into his coat pocket. Most Knights carried a Katana sword; the Templars favoured weapon, which they concealed in a back-body webbing under their long coats, that held their lightweight titanium *saya* – scabbard and Katana sword. The group all looked pretty much the same, with long black leather coats and a quickness about their step. Bertram was not armed. He was not passed as a mission 'active' Knight. Bertram would not physically be in any combat situation.

The black Mercedes pulled away out of *Aeropuerto de Valencia* – Valencia airport, and onto the A3. Shortly after, it turned off onto the AP7, which would take them all the way down to Gandia. Then they would take a right and head into the country on the CV60 for approximately twenty minutes.

The Spanish Knights felt the pressure of having their Grand Master there with them. For some, it was the first time they had met the legendary Payne St Clair and they all wanted to do well for him on the mission. They were also pleased to meet Marie-Claude: news of her heroics in the extraction battle in Romania had quickly spread throughout the Order. In total contrast, they were somewhat bemused meeting Bertram. His white teeth flashed at them from his deep brown skin and his curly, unkempt hair flopped about. His black square glasses kept slipping off his nose every two seconds and under his long, black leather coat, was a green tartan, tweed cloth suit, complete with waistcoat and a fob. He introduced himself as soon as he got into the Mercedes and shook everyone's hands, enthusiastically.

"Bertram Hubert Klymachak De'Ath, and a jolly pleasure to meet you all. Hola."

The Spanish Knights smiled; then one of them turned to the others and said, "*Maldita sea, pensé que los españoles teníamos nombres largos*" – damn, I thought we had long names.

"I brought the stealth sky-eyes," Bertram told them. "I'll show them to you if you like. I'll be right there in a minute right now just."

"*Necesitamos volver a nuestras clases de inglés*, – we need to go back to our English classes," one of the Knights commented to the others.

"I'm a bit loosey goosey," Bertram said apologising for taking so long and still fumbling with one of the latches on one of the cases that held a drone. "It's my first mission and I'm … Now, Bertram, enhance your calm," he said to himself sternly and out loud.

"*Arreglaré las clases tan pronto como regresemos* – I'll arrange the classes as soon as we get back," another Knight said.

"You just wait until you see them," Bertram continued. "I call them stealth sky-eyes, or se for short." He laughed heartily. "Do you get it, 'se' like to see?" Miss Marie and Claude, did you get my joke?"

"You do know that I am one person, don't you Bertram?" Marie-Claude asked him.

"Yes, Miss Marie and Claude."

St Clair was chuckling in the front.

*

Al-Malik al-Nasir al-Sultan Salah El-Din, the man known as Salah El-Din, or sometimes Saladin, had hidden away in his *casa de campo*, in the Spanish region of Valencia on the Costa Blanca, for four years. The seven-bedroom house he bought through an offshore company offered him a semblance of peace he hardly ever felt, because there he could relax slightly. He felt like he had been running all his life; running away from one attempt on his life to another. He was a criminal; he always had been, but he was of the more dangerous variety because he had no conscience, no moral values. He'd ordered people's deaths and he'd ordered people to be skinned alive, including the man Jonathan went to see back in Washington DC, John Dukes, when Jonathan's life irreversibly changed.

Salah El-Din was not known in the small village of Zoran, twenty minutes' drive away from the coastal road and into the interior. It was a mountainous region, full of large, jagged grey and bleached Mediterranean mountains that looked so high that their tops seemed to scrape the clouds. Each range was imposing and omnipresent, guarding the hundred and fifty miles of the White Coast. There the criminal portrayed the lifestyle of a private businessman with a Spanish retreat. He kept two bodyguards with him at the house at all times and three other bodyguards were housed in a small rented house just next door. They were all trained assassins, all with exceptional fighting skills, but thugs, killers and extortionists all the same. They were all Yakuza.

The Templars pulled up just a mile from the house. They'd followed a narrow *camino* – small road, for a few miles, traversing a number of drainage ditches via unsteady looking bridges. They hadn't seen any people for the last three miles, just munching goats, ambling donkeys and a few stray dogs running amok in the *campo*. They mobilised quickly. Four of the Knights joined the other Knights who had been keeping watch on the house. They formed a kill-zone perimeter around the house. Their guns were trained and ready.

Bertram opened one of the rigid plastic cases; inside was a drone. On the inside of the case, the label read 'Unmanned Aerial vehicle. Aviation. Non-Military.'

"Ha," Bertram exclaimed to everyone excitedly, as he pulled a small, six-inch nano drone helicopter from one of the rigid, black plastic cases. "Navigates automatically via pre-planned GPS weigh points. I have written versatile flight planning software, with a range of just over a mile. But today, I need to fly it." He strapped a small electronic console with a screen and joystick to a strap and then put it around his neck. "Old school," he said, his face lighting up. "Could use touch screen but there's nothing like a joystick.

"This little beast operates day and night and under adverse weather conditions," he said pointing to his drone. The pride resonated in his voice. "Carbon fibre and titanium fuselage. Reconnaissance from the air, it has thermal imaging capability. Let's see what 'se' can see." He laughed again at his own joke. The others crowded around the screen of the console to see what the drone was seeing.

The drone was practically silent. It was fast and over the target house in a short space of time. Adeptly, Bertram flew the drone, hovering then lowering, hovering and lowering further, until finally it was at window height. He took the drone around the perimeter of the house.

"Strange," he said, "nothing on the thermal imaging but look." They all saw three bodies in the grounds of the house and they saw blood. None of the bodies were moving. "They are not registering on the thermal imaging, so, either they are mannequins, frozen or dead."

One of the Spanish Knights asked what Bertram had said about the bodies. "Que – what?"

"*Saltamontes, Congelado, o maniquíes,*" the other Spanish Knight told him.

"We will have to go in," St Clair announced. "Bertram can you cover us from the air?" Bertram's face lit up; it was the first time the Templars had deployed drones. He could hardly contain himself. After bringing the first drone back safely, he opened the second black plastic case and took out a mini drone helicopter. This one was two feet long. He held it in his hands like the crown jewels.

"Payload and endurance. Can be deployed for sea or land based tactical intelligence. Can be used for search and rescue or to carry a payload. It also fires rounds. Today it will give you advance air cover. It has nearly sixty rounds on board."

St Clair, Marie-Claude, Bertram and the remaining two Spanish Knights made ready. St Clair informed the other Knights what they were doing. He turned to Bertram, "When you are ready Bertram, you give the command."

"Me?" Bertram gushed.

"Yes, Bertram. Give the command to move out: Templars go green!"

"Yes, Mister St Clair, Sir. Templar hombres, stir your stumps, time to buckle up and bounce."

With St Clair trying to hide his mirth, they set off with Bertram's drone ten yards ahead of them and hovering in an attacking position twelve feet above them. They walked slowly through barren olive trees, then into a citrus patch. At all times, they were in V formation with St Clair at the front and Bertram at the back. They passed two of the Knights on the perimeter. They were in a prone position, rifles locked and loaded and their rifle butts firmly in their shoulders ready to fire.

As they'd seen from the first drone's surveillance, the metal electric gates were open. All was deathly quiet in the whitewashed house, with its terracotta-tiled roof. Just a few feet into the house's grounds, and lying on the block-bricked driveway, a body lay sprawled on the floor. It was pretty messed up because it had several puncture holes from bullets, but it also had multiple cuts. It had been hacked but Marie-Claude checked for a pulse anyway. She shook her head. He was dead. Then she moved his coat collar and revealed a tattoo. They saw the end of a dragon's tail in the distinctive twist. The deceased's little finger had been chopped off. St Clair knew, thanks to the Lionheart and Tanjkna Sugata, that the Yakuza gang he belonged to was the Nagal tsume – long claw. Two more bodies lay dead around the house: they too had been hacked, they too were Yakuza. One of the Spanish Knights asked why this had been done to them and Marie-Claude answered him.

"We have seen this before. In Romania. This is the work of Bo Bo Hak!"

The main door lay open. They checked around the back and that door was closed and locked. There was no other way in. All of the windows had *rejas* – vertical ornate metal bars, attached to them.

St Clair went in first, the drone ahead of him, just four feet ahead, covering his advance. Marie-Claude came next, then the two Spanish Knights. On the brown tiled floor, they found two more bodies lying in pools of blood. All of the bodies were Yakuza and all of the bodies had been severely hacked and mutilated. Around the bodies were Katana swords; around the bodies their handguns and spent shells were scattered all over the floor. There was no sign the intruders had sustained any casualties, unless their dead had been removed.

The drone moved forwards into a large room off to the right. A very low hum from the drone's electric engine was the only noise. Then the drone crashed into a wall – Bertram had stopped flying the drone.

"Bertram, speak to me?" St Clair called out.

There was a short delay then Bertram spoke. He stuttered. "It's … Mr St Clair, Sir …"

St Clair called to Marie-Claude and the Knights. "Cover me, I'm going in." His gun held in two hands, his arms outstretched, he eased around the door frame just a few inches and then darted back waiting for the gun shot. None came. He nodded to Marie-Claude. Then he ran in, followed by his Knights.

A naked man was strung up by ropes, his arms outstretched, his head fallen forward. St Clair reached up and lifted the head. He was Middle Eastern looking, in his mid to late fifties, tall with silver hair and a sharp featured face. The man they knew as Salah El-Din hung dead. His piercing black eyes were now lifeless and yet they still seemed to hold the horror of his death, with his face contorted as he'd roared and screamed with the pain. Upon his forehead there were three small streaks of dried blood.

"Someone's bloody fingers," Marie-Claude asked, "perhaps as they grabbed his head?"

"No," said St Clair. "Look how they curl; they are three crescent moons. They were left for us."

Marie-Claude asked him what it meant.

"It's a message for us. They wanted us to know it was them. They are telling us we're next."

St Clair looked at the tortured remains of the criminal they had chased for over four years. It was the same fate that his own Knight, Tarik Tahir, had suffered in Romania. Salah El-Din's back had been cut along the length of his spine, from top to bottom. Another cut went across his shoulders and a third across his waistline. Each cut was deep and all the way through to the bone. His flesh and sinew had then been peeled back. His ribcage had been detached from his spine and opened out. His lungs had also been pulled out from the back.

A young Knight threw up – most felt sick by the horror. Salah El-Din had been bloodeagled. The man the Colombians called *magico,* the magician, had just run out of luck.

"Take note, Knights," St Clair told them, "always stay ahead of your mistakes or they will come to find you. His found him today. It seems they knew where he was and all his intrusion counter-measures and the bodyguards could not stop the Abaddons. I guess he misjudged them, badly."

As Payne St Clair looked at the bloody body hanging there, he finally understood the fifth prophecy. 'In *al-Andalus*, the false one will crane its feathers, but it brings only death.' He shook his head, "In Spain the false one, Salah El-Din, because he believed he was the great Saladin of the Crusades, will crane its feathers, bloodeagled, but it brings only death." He sighed, "And indeed it did."

St Clair's mobile phone vibrated and it made him jump. It was a message from Luther, which read: 'Hag dead, mission complete, all Knights safe and coming home.' The sick feeling, he always felt when there were Knights out on missions, began to subside slightly. Minutes later, another message came through. This time it was from Dominique: 'Yakuza dead. The saint is heading home to Jordan with Jamal's grandson and, Dagmar Grey! Will explain later. All Knights safe and coming home.'

Now St Clair really felt relieved. He sent a message to both Luther and Dominique: 'Salah El-Din dead; sanction completed. All Knights safe and coming home.' Then he sent Dominique an additional message: 'By the way, you've moved house. Jonathan will explain.'

Chapter 14

The Start of Something New
That Always Comes at The End

THE END, PART I: JORDAN

Date: 27th December 2012
Place: Jordan

His grandfather stood motionless, his eyes closed, arms outstretched, palms upwards and his head ever so slightly tilted back, just as John the Baptist had done over two thousand years ago. He breathed deep and inhaled the smell of the river. It stretched out before him, the *Nahr Al Sharieat* – the river Jordan. It flowed from the sides of Mount Hermon, between Syria and Lebanon and on to the Sea of Galilee. He could feel the river's motion through the ground where he stood. Its waters raced and swirled; in other parts it meandered steadily along the riverbank. He stood on the riverbank close to a sandbank, where the water would be shallow. It was a place called *Al-Maghtas*.

He found two pieces of wood. He lashed one as a cross-member and drove the other into the ground. Then he removed the white stove cloth that had hung around his neck and placed it over the wood, the same as Daniel's pendant, the one his grandfather had given him just five days ago.

Back then, when Daniel had last stood on the riverbank, he had thought his grandfather crazy to send him all the way to America to find something that he knew very little about and with a set of skills that would not match the job he had been given. He remembered their meeting:

"Why are you asking me to do this, Grandfather. I have no idea what I'm doing. This is crazy."

"We thought, my grandson, that you would be able to handle trouble and, you would be good at sneaking around." The old man smiled, thinking his explanation was a good explanation.

"Sneaking around, what in Christ—" he stopped himself. "What in bugger's sake do you mean, sneak around. Sneak around what? Where? Why sneaking around?"

His grandfather started to walk towards a line of taxis that were lined up a few hundred yards away, waiting for tourists to finish taking pictures with their cameras and video cameras.

"Joseph will tell you everything when you get there. Now, you need to get one of these taxis and go straight to the airport. You don't have much time."

"You're not coming, Grandfather?"

"Who me? No, no, not me. It is far too dangerous for me and I'm not a good sneaker."

Daniel watched his grandfather; his demeanour was reverent. Dagmar moved closer to Daniel.

"He looks so happy, your grandad. You did this, Daniel. You brought this happiness into your grandfather's life. You should be proud." She put her arm around him.

"No, we did," he said and he leaned over and kissed her. "We did, my gorgeous Dagmar Grey."

Just then his grandfather stopped what he was doing and straightened up. He looked towards Daniel and Dagmar; then he narrowed his eyes and looked past them. He held his hand above his eyes to shade them from the sun. A big grin appeared on his face. He waved. Daniel and Dagmar turned around to see what he was looking at. Along the riverbank a group of twenty or so people, young and old alike, men, women and children, were all walking together in a group, all wearing white. They were singing and laughing. They waved back to Daniel's grandfather. Then beyond them another group and beyond them, yet another. Daniel turned towards his grandfather for answers.

"They are our people, my grandson. They are the Mandaeans of Jordan. They have come to be baptised in the presence of our beloved saint, Saint John."

About ninety people had come to be with Jamal, the holy man from Iraq, and to be with their saint for the first time ever, John the Baptist.

Now they were all there: over ninety devout Mandaeans, a man from Australia and a thief from Manchester, England, a relic hunter who had given the relic back.

His grandfather started to walk into the river by the shallow sandbank; others followed him. Jamal stopped and turned to his grandson. "Do you remember, my grandson, what I said to you when we were here last? I said when you are finished, promise me you will come back to see me. You asked me where I would be and I said I would be right here, my grandson, I would be right here by the river. You suggested we meet at a hotel where we would be more comfortable and I said, 'But how can I baptise you my grandson, if we are at the hotel and not here by *his* river.' Do you remember?"

"I remember, Grandfather."

"Are you ready then, my grandson?" Jamal asked. He held out his hand.

Daniel looked at Dagmar. She leaned into him and whispered, "This is not one of those celibacy ceremonies is it?"

Daniel laughed. "No, it is not."

"Then, go for it! You go get wet with your grandad." She kissed him on the cheek.

Daniel walked into the water and he felt at peace for the first time he could remember. His grandfather put his hand on his shoulder. He looked at Dagmar. "What did she say?"

"She asked me if we could still have sex."

His grandfather gave a hearty laugh. "Ah, smart girl! I think

283

you two are, what do they call it? An item?"

"I think you are right, Grandfather. She has even given me my first demand. She will not change her name to Hightower."

"I cannot blame the girl, my grandson. What kind of a name is that anyway?"

"Grandfather, really! Your last name is Faka!"

"Pinch your nose, my grandson," the old man said. "It's going to get a little wet."

THE END, PART II: SCOTLAND

Date: 27th December 2012
Place: A remote Scottish glen

Jonathan and Dominique had been in their new home, Ceó *Gleann* – Glen Mist, less than a day. Jonathan had arrived from Italy late the night before, on the 26th and Dominique had arrived from New Jersey just a few hours ago. St Clair and Zakariah were their first visitors. Zakariah wanted to see his daughter and St Clair wanted to talk with Jonathan.

Whilst they left Dominique and Zakariah in the warmth of the cottage, Jonathan and St Clair took the dogs, Simba and Cleo, for a walk. It was windy and rain clouds gathered in darkening skies that threatened a storm.

Simba and Cleo soon ran off, Ridgeback ears flapping in the wind like windsocks. They chased in the vain hope of catching a Scottish grouse that had been disturbed by their presence.

"I hear you did well in Rome," St Clair began as they both leaned into the wind.

"I think Luther, Cardinal Del Luca and Aldrich did well," Jonathan replied.

"No, I heard you did well." Then he chuckled as he thought of Aldrich. "He's an enigma isn't he, Aldrich? You just never know what he's going to do next, but he does make me laugh."

Jonathan stopped. "Do you think we really should give him a sword? I mean af—"

St Clair laughed again. "Jonathan," he interrupted, "he has a sword. He has at least five Katanas that we have sent him over the years."

Jonathan shook his head and he too started laughing at the absurdity and the crazy brain of Professor Aldrich Manwin Tucker.

The grouse had got away but the dogs were not ready to give up the chase just yet and lay crouched, watching as the bird settled a few hundred yards away. The bird took flight again and the lion hunters were back on the hunt.

St Clair and Jonathan looked to the horizon. They could see the storm making its way towards them. A crack of thunder announced what they could already see.

"I was thinking about Salah El-Din," Jonathan said. "His death, that horrible death and the word that came to mind was 'Perdition.' I looked it up: it means 'a state of eternal punishment and damnation into which a sinful and unrepentant person passes after death.'" He sighed ruefully. "How many people do you think would still be alive today, if we'd have got him in Cumbria four years ago?"

"You shouldn't look back like that, Jonathan. Back is not the direction you are going in, so there is no need to look that way. The future is where you need to look because the future is where we need to be. So now, just think how many more people would have died in the future, if he had not been killed. I know we didn't get him, but he was 'got,' and that's all that matters. Another one who can no longer kill, maim and extort the unprotected."

"I guess," Jonathan said, a little unconvinced.

They walked on some more. Scudding clouds whirled around in aerial combat, buffeted by the violent tug of the wind. A grey curtain of rain was heading their way fast from the east. The dogs, Cleo and Simba, smelt it and were making their way back to Jonathan and St Clair.

"I like the saying by Mark Twain," St Clair broke the silence whilst giving Cleo and Simba some fuss as they arrived breathless. "He said that the two most important days in your life are the day you are born and the day you find out why."

"And have you found out why, Payne?" Jonathan asked him.

"I did," he said, "a long time ago." He smiled and narrowed his eyes from the lash of the wind. "But don't ask me about it, Priest. Maybe another day. I am interested in your answer."

"Me? I think we both know the answer to that, thanks to you. I now know exactly why." Then he paused and he turned to St Clair. "Do you want to tell me what you've really brought me all the way out here to tell me?"

St Clair smiled. He liked Jonathan; he liked his company. He had a soft spot for the ex-priest and ex-schoolteacher from Washington DC. He liked his values and his self-effacing nature. "Ah, Priest: how far you have come. You are right, there is something I want to tell you."

Jonathan's hands were already in his pockets because they were cold in the battering wind, but there were no coins for him to help calm his nerves.

"I think I have identified the sixth prophecy. The cross, the cross Del Luca gave you. Do you remember what was on it?"

"I do."

"The sixth prophecy says: '*The flower of the martyrs and the plaited crown shall join to battle 'El S'hhi te Abyann' for the way back.*' The red rose is sometimes the sign of the martyrs because red signifies the blood they have shed. And a plaited crown—"

"Matthew," Jonathan interrupted. "'*And when they plaited a crown of thorns, they put it upon his head ... And they bowed the knee and mocked him, saying Hail, King of the Jews.*' But 'battle with whom' and 'back where'?" Jonathan asked him.

"We don't know what '*El S'hhi te Abyann*' means, it has never been translated; we have no idea what language it is.

"Could it be talking about *the* battle?" Jonathan asked. "You know the one I am talking about?"

St Clair shook his head. "I don't know but if it is, th—"

"Then it's time?" Jonathan said nervously.

"Then it's time, Seer."

THE END, PART III: EGYPT

Date: 1955
Place: Cairo, Egypt

In 1955, a young twenty-two-year-old man arrived in Cairo, Egypt. He had intended to stay for a week with his mother's family and then journey down through Africa by train and road to start his mining career.

He was a rich man: he was a very rich man, thanks to his father's dealings with the Nazis and their stolen gold and trading on the black market and on people's despair, war-driven poverty and starvation.

The young man visited with his mother's family for just two days in Cairo. Then he wired a telex to his lawyers back in his home country of Serbia and told them to transfer all of his money to his mother's family: it was several millions. He gave them the bank account details where they should transfer the money. Only a second cousin in the family had a bank account; the others were all too poor and so they had no need of bank accounts. The money was transferred. The second cousin was called Samir Fancy. Then the young man, Zivko Cesar Gowst, disappeared.

In 1957, nearly two years later, he re-emerged. A man answering his description presented himself at the Argeen border crossing on Lake Nubia. His passport was stamped and he was recorded as leaving Egypt and crossing into Sudan. He was remembered because of two reasons: one was because of the way he dressed and travelled. He was dressed in black, in handmade tailored suits, finely cut and stitched by Egyptian tailors. And secondly, because he travelled with two companions, both were Egyptian and both wore traditional Egyptian garments. They did not speak to the other passengers. They wore hard, stern looks. They never left Zivko's side and always watched everyone else. They looked menacing. They always sat either side of Zivko; he was never alone.

No one knew what had happened to Zivko Cesar Gowst during

those two years, the man who killed priests, a Russian itinerant and his own father back in Serbia, the man who would eventually kill the Templar André Sabath and countless others by draining them of their blood.

Date: 27th December 2012
Place: Cairo

It used to be a mosque. In downtown Cairo, there were many mosques, all roughly the same. However, people stopped going to this one a long time ago. Local people knew the reason and even the local authorities left it alone. It was poorly built because there was always a lack of building materials for the poor; they had to take what they could get, which wasn't much. A lot of mud and straw, mixed with Arab sweat and blood had built the mosque. But it had ceased being a mosque in 1955, when a young twenty-two-year-old man arrived in Cairo, Egypt. Two days after his arrival, a man called Samir Fancy took him to the mosque for the first time. He stayed there for two years.

Now the mosque was his. He led his flock. He owned them and they were loyal to him; his barbaric zealots.

In the back of the building a barred, rusting door led to stairs hewn from the rock that led down to underground passages and a series of rooms. There was only artificial light down there. A string of bare lightbulbs hung limply from the ceiling, giving off little light and flickering as the overworked generator struggled to maintain enough power to penetrate the dark and feed his hell-machines.

The sound of sick people moaning joined the gloom. At times screams could be heard coming from the rooms. There was an overpowering stench: it came from a concoction of aloe vera, llama milk, bees' honey and antiseptic components, like chlorhexidine gluconate, hexachlorophene, boric acid, Lugol's iodine and formal-dehyde. It was an oppressive stench from the location where Zivko's skin was being treated three times a day. It was a distinctive, overpowering, ghastly stench that resembled the smell of a mortuary.

Zivko had been treated with the lotion in Romania when the Templars found his germ-free plastic isolation room in the mining town. Now, however, he had no such isolation room. His treatment was administered in the rank and filthy conditions below ground.

In small, cramped rooms, his captives lay rotting; they were all dying. Their bodies starved of their good blood were topped up with toxic blood, his blood, to keep them alive. With the bad blood attacking their nervous systems, their bodies were slowly destroying themselves, but allowing enough time for him to take all their healthy blood.

His blood was highly compromised and toxic, as he strived to purify it over the years using all sorts of experimental applications, poisons and diluents that had been pumped into his body. His body had not fared well from the experiments, but as they had been going on for some seventy years, there was some tolerance, although not for the poor souls who received his blood. Like all the captives which Zivko and his doctors had bled, injected and experimented on, their organs were failing and their bodies shutting down. And, because of that, Zivko's doctors kept them in comas for ten days at a time. Then they brought them out of their comas for three days. Then they induced the coma again, because that way they could manage the organ functions better.

For years, Zivko followed his unhinged pursuit to purify his blood and reverse his albinism. His poor, wretched captives lay with two tubes in their right arms, leading to large, white transfusion machines. The constant hum of the hell-machines served as an endless reminder of what was taking place there.

It was very late on the night of the 27th of December. His bodyguard had just returned from the Costa Blanca, Spain, with the men he had taken to assassinate the Arab imposter, Salah El-Din.

Zivko was alone in one of the rooms, lying on an ill-constructed wooden bed, his body covered in the lotion. The stench was unbearable but his bodyguard, the African Bo Bo Hak, had long since stopped noticing it.

The African bowed in front of Zivko. "You heard we were

successful?"

Zivko gave a grunt.

"We bled him. We opened his back. We left the mark for them to find."

Zivko, the man they called the Ghost, ripped the tubes from his arms and growled. His pink eyes peered into the gloom at the African. "But I want the *Alkahin* – Priest. I want the Seer before it's too late, for only the Seer can destroy us now! Only the Seer can stop *him*."

THE END

Book I ~ ARK
Reviews

5.0 out of 5 stars
Ark: A Templar thriller series. Book 1
Thoroughly enjoyable book. A fast paced read, fabulous character introduction and build up. Can't wait to read the other books. *Reviewed in the UK*

5.0 out of 5 stars
Fab read
Excellent read from page to page with a great twist at the end. He's Looking forward to the next one! Absolutely loved it! *Reviewed in the UK*

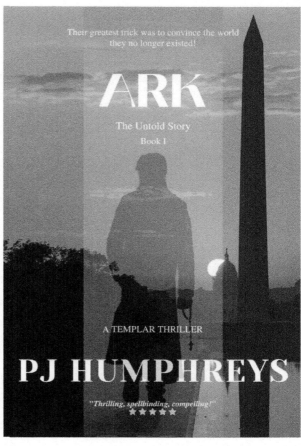

5.0 out of 5 stars
Fantastic read
A great storyline and frantic pace, in a world of chaos and instability it's what we would all wish for. I would highly recommend this book. *Reviewed in the UK*

5.0 out of 5 stars
Excellent yarn!
Really well paced and involving story, good mix of fact and fiction which keeps the interest level high throughout a very engaging tale. *Reviewed in the Italy*

5.0 out of 5 stars
Gripping read front to back from a truly visionary author
Reviewed in the United States
I loved this book. Like other reviewers I finished it in a matter of days and am excited to pick up the next installment in the series- which is already out! So exciting. Amazing first book to what I imagine will be an amazing series of novels. *Reviewed in the United States*

Book II ~ PROPHECY
Reviews

5.0 out of 5 stars
Excellent read. Couldn't put it down.
So fast paced that my heart was racing. The story is so interactive that you feel like you are in the story with the characters. Can't wait to read the next book. *Reviewed in the UK*

5.0 out of 5 stars
Excellent Read!!!!
Great follow on from Ark Return of the Templars. Keeps you on your toes and edge of seat. A lot of thought and research went in to this I believe, to create realistic feel. Hard to put down. *Reviewed in the UK*

5.0 out of 5 stars
Leaves You Wanting More
Really enjoyed reading this, it is a great follow up to book one - Ark.
Loved the characters and the plot. Can't wait for the next one. *Reviewed in Australia*

5.0 out of 5 stars
Tremendous
Once again gripping and not able to put the book down. These characters are fascinating and the information on the templars is leaving me wanting more x *Reviewed in the UK*

5.0 out of 5 stars
Excellent read. Totally engrossing.
The second book about the Knights Templars of today. As like the first book I just couldn't put it down. Totally lost myself in it. The characters came to life with each word. Brilliant read but be warned once you start reading it everything around you disappears and time stands still. Roll on book three. *Reviewed in the UK*

Book IV

PARADOX
Spring 2023

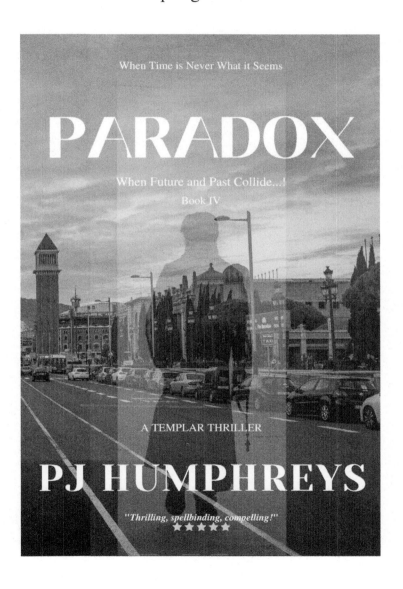

Printed in Great Britain
by Amazon

38060913R00179